Bleeding Hearts . . .

"Well written."
——*The Capital (WI) Times*

"Engrossing . . . Albert's characterization is strong—China delights."
——*Publishers Weekly*

Dead Man's Bones . . .

"China's warmth and sensitivity . . . will endear her to readers, while her investigative skills make her a leader among female sleuths."
——*Publishers Weekly*

A Dilly of a Death . . .

"More than just a whodunit . . . Readers will relish this more-sweet-than-sour adventure."
——*Booklist*

Indigo Dying . . .

"Albert's skill in weaving everything together into a multilayered whole makes the reading smooth, interesting, and enjoyable."
——*San Antonio Express-News*

Bloodroot . . .

"Albert has created captivating new characters and a setting dripping with atmosphere."
——*Publishers Weekly*

Mistletoe Man . . .

"Breezy . . . The characters are an appealing bunch."
——*Chicago Tribune*

More Praise for the China Bayles Mysteries

"[China Bayles is] such a joy . . . An instant friend."
——Carolyn G. Hart

"Engrossing."
——*The Times-Picayune*

SUSAN
WITTIG ALBERT

CAT'S CLAW

BERKLEY PRIME CRIME, NEW YORK

THE BERKLEY PUBLISHING GROUP
Published by the Penguin Group
Penguin Group (USA) Inc.
375 Hudson Street, New York, New York 10014, USA

USA / Canada / UK / Ireland / Australia / New Zealand / India / South Africa / China

Penguin Books Ltd., Registered Offices: 80 Strand, London WC2R 0RL, England
For more information about the Penguin Group, visit penguin.com.

CAT'S CLAW

A Berkley Prime Crime Book / published by arrangement with the author

Berkley Prime Crime Books are published by The Berkley Publishing Group.
BERKLEY® PRIME CRIME and the PRIME CRIME logo are trademarks of Penguin Group
(USA) Inc.

For information, address: The Berkley Publishing Group,
a division of Penguin Group (USA) Inc.,
375 Hudson Street, New York, New York 10014.

ISBN: 978-0-425-25202-4

PUBLISHING HISTORY
Berkley Prime Crime hardcover edition / March 2012
Berkley Prime Crime mass-market edition / April 2013

PRINTED IN THE UNITED STATES OF AMERICA

10 9 8 7 6 5 4 3 2 1

Cover illustration copyrigh © by Joe Burleson.
Cover photography copyright © by Anest/Shutterstock.
Cover design by Judith Lagerman.
Interior text design by Tiffany Estreicher.

ALWAYS LEARNING   **PEARSON**

For Bill, always and ever
partner, lover, husband, best friend

A Note to the Reader

When I began the China Bayles mysteries in 1992, I chose to write in China's voice, in a story-telling mode in which the tale is told by one person, from a single first-person point of view. Over the intervening years (*Cat's Claw* is the twentieth book in the series), I've found that this choice has sometimes limited the kind of stories I can tell. China Bayles is observant (by nature and because of her legal training), she knows a great deal about a great many things, and she's always glad to tell us what she knows and what she thinks. But like the rest of us, China views events through a screen of her personal experience and preconceptions, so the story slants strongly toward her likes and dislikes (which readers occasionally confuse with my own). Her stories are necessarily about *her*.

As the series has gone on, however, other interesting characters have emerged, together with tantalizing fragments of their stories. And while I like China Bayles very much, I've often found that some of these other stories are every bit as interesting as hers. In *Wormwood,* for instance, part of the mystery is set in 1912 and the characters who lived in the Shaker village during that year tell their part of the story, with the help of journal entries, letters, and newpaper clippings. In *Holly Blues,* Mike Mc-Quaid tells a story that goes back to the time before he met China, when he was married to Sally, Brian's mother. Now, in *Cat's Claw,* Sheila Dawson takes center stage, and we get a glimpse into the life of Pecan Springs' female police chief, who not only has a crime to clear and a criminal to bring to justice, but political, professional, and personal conflicts to resolve.

But this is still China's series and there will always be plenty of herbs in each of the books: culinary suggestions, craft ideas, history and lore, as well as medicinal information. I probably don't need to remind you that *Cat's Claw* offers fictional entertainment, not a prescription for what ails you. But I'll say it anyway: before you attempt to treat yourself with any herb that China (or another friend) might happen to mention, do your own due diligence, consult the appropriate professionals, and use common sense. Plant medicine is not one-size-fits-all.

As usual, I need to thank the writers whose books and articles supplied information for this book. In particular, I would like to mention Connie Fletcher's *Breaking and Entering: Women Cops Break the Code of Silence to Tell Their Stories from the Inside,* and *Breaking the Brass Ceiling: Women Police Chiefs and Their Path to the Top,* by Dorothy Moses Schulz. Both of these books provided valuable insights into the career challenges of women police officers and helped to shape the character of Sheila Dawson and some of the dynamics in the Pecan Springs Police Department. I am also grateful to Rhonda Esakov for her recommendations about police weapons and firepower: Rhonda, you helped to fill in some serious gaps in my knowledge base!

Thank you, too, to the herbalists and researchers who have compiled the various books and monographs I always rely on for the botanical background for this series, and to China's many friends around the country who have shared recipes, craft ideas, and gardening information with me. I want especially to thank the International Herb Association for the Book Award they have bestowed on this series, and to Alice Le Duc for sharing her thoughtful and extensive botanical wisdom. I am also grateful to Martha Meacham, winner of a "cameo character" raffle for the benefit of the Story Circle Network. Martha agreed to appear in this book as a volunteer coordinator of the K-9 Search and Rescue Unit for the Pecan Springs Police Department—a job for which she is very well suited!

And of course, to Bill Albert, ever and always, dearest friend.

Susan Wittig Albert
Bertram, Texas

Prologue

Four members of the Texas Star Quilting Club, armed with needles, thread, thimbles, and scissors, were seated on either side of the wooden quilting frame set up in Ethel Wauer's dining room at 1113 Pecan Street. As usual, the ladies were discussing their friends and neighbors—in this case, Dana and Larry Kirk, who lived two doors west, at 1117 Pecan. Or rather, Larry lived there. Dana had moved out.

"Well, I for one am sorry to hear that they're getting a divorce," Ethel said. The eldest of the group, she had celebrated her eighty-first birthday the month before and wasn't above claiming the prerogatives of age. She poked her needle through the Double Wedding Ring quilt, which was one of her favorite patterns. Of course, the club could have paid Mrs. Moore, two streets over, to quilt the pieced top on her long-arm sewing machine, which would make short work of it. But while the Texas Stars didn't agree on everything (on much of anything, as a matter of fact), they agreed that there wouldn't be any fun in turning the job over to a one-armed mechanical wizard. So they stretched the quilt top and batting and lining over Ethel's frame and spent several hours each week quilting it by hand.

Luckily, they were all expert stitchers. That is, none of them put in big, sloppy stitches that had to be surreptitiously taken out after the offending stitcher had gone home. Ethel herself was proud of the fact that she could still see to stitch and that her quilting stitches were every bit as tiny and neat as Hazel Schulz's, whose eyes were younger by twenty-five-plus years but not nearly as good as hers. The fact that Ethel wore two hearing aids didn't slow down her stitching in the slightest.

"The divorce wasn't much of a surprise, though," she added astutely. "Not after Mrs. Kirk went and got herself a boyfriend."

Jane Jessup peered at her over the tops of her tortoise-shell reading glasses. "I knew she'd moved out, but I had no idea she has a *boyfriend*. Who is he?" Jane, who was younger than Ethel by five years and three days, lived at 1115 Pecan, between Ethel and the Kirks, and had a big vegetable garden in her backyard, where she grew most of the food she put on her vegetarian table. Of all the Texas Stars, Jane had the greenest thumb—and the bluest hair, arranged in springy curls over her ears. She got it done every Wednesday at Bobby Rae's House of Beauty, just off the square in downtown Pecan Springs.

"His name is Glen Vance. He's her boss at the library." Ethel leaned across the quilt, her blue eyes sparkling. There was nothing Ethel liked better than a bit of extra-juicy gossip. "But it mustn't go outside this room, girls. It's extremely hush-hush. I wouldn't know it myself, except that my niece's daughter-in-law works at the library. Mr. Vance and Dana Kirk are plannin' to get married as soon as she gets her divorce." Because she was hard of hearing, Ethel spoke very loudly—loud enough to be heard on the front sidewalk, if anybody was out there listening. So much for hush-hush.

Mildred Ewell sighed. "Well, poor Mr. Kirk is all I've got to say." Mildred, who was on the pudgy side, lived at 1114 Pecan, across the street from Ethel and Jane. She was five years younger than Jane and ten years younger than Ethel, but she was already having trouble with her ankles. "He is such a nice young man, so handsome. And always has a smile." Mildred frowned down at the fat white poodle that trotted into the room with Mr. Wauer's well-chewed leather slipper in his mouth. (The slipper had outlived its owner by at least ten years.) "Ethel, I wish you'd put that wretched little dog in the kitchen. You know he doesn't like me. He has never liked me."

As if to prove Mildred's point, the poodle dropped the slipper, planted his feet, and growled at her.

Ethel sighed. "I really hate to shut Oodles in the kitchen, Mildred. It makes him feel left out. He loves to be part of the party." She leaned over, crooning at the dog. "Don't you, my precious little boy?"

"Poodles have a long memory, Mildred," Hazel Schulz remarked. Hazel lived on the other side of the Kirks, at 1119. Of the four Stars gathered around the frame, she was the youngest, at fifty-five. "He remembers when you swatted him on the rear with a newspaper that time you caught him pooping in your iris bed." She picked up a pair of scissors to clip a thread. "He's had it in for you ever since."

"That's right, Mildred," Ethel agreed. "If you'd be nice to Oodles, he'd be nice to you."

"That dog doesn't have a nice bone in his body," Mildred said fiercely, as Oodles' growls escalated to a barrage of high-pitched, teeth-bared yaps. "He is a menace to the neighborhood."

"Do something, Ethel," Jane pleaded. "We can't hear ourselves think with all that noise."

With a put-upon sigh, Ethel got up. "Come on, Oodles. You can take your slipper out to play on the front porch." She unhooked her cane from the back of her chair and started for the door. The dog picked up the slipper and followed her out, casting a baleful glance back over his shoulder at Mildred.

"Peace at last," Mildred muttered under her breath. She wiped her perspiring upper lip with a lace-trimmed hanky. "I despise that dog."

Jane pushed her tortoiseshell reading glasses up on her nose. "It's too bad about the Kirks," she said thoughtfully, going back to the subject. "Mr. Kirk is really very nice. My grandson's laptop computer got sick with a virus and he came over and disinfected it."

"How much did you have to pay him?" Hazel asked. "I hear it costs a lot to get those silly things fumigated, or whatever it is they do to kill the bugs. And even then you can't be sure they're all dead." She paused. "Something like bedbugs, I guess."

"I offered to pay," Jane replied, "but he wouldn't take it. I know he owns that computer shop and I would've been glad to give him a little something for his time." She pushed her glasses up on her nose and bent over her stitching. "But he said he was just being neighborly."

"Well, Larry Kirk may be nice and neighborly, but he's got a woman friend, too," Ethel said, coming back into the room. She hung her cane over the back of her chair and sat down at the frame. To Mildred, she added. "I hope you're satisfied, Mildred. Oodles hates being out there by himself. He's barking at Mr. Kennedy down the street. He's out there trimming his hedge."

Jane sighed. "That poor hedge. Mr. Kennedy trims it within an inch of its life. Looks like a square green box."

"It's better than being in here, barking at us," Mildred said, plying her needle firmly. "Really, Ethel, I don't know how you can stand to live with that constant yap-yap-yap. Such an irritating noise."

"It's easy." Ethel smiled. "I just turn down my hearing aids."

Hazel picked up her scissors and stared at Ethel. "Larry Kirk has a woman friend? Ethel, I don't believe it! At least, not in the way you mean. He is such a fine, upstanding young man."

"What way *do* you mean, Ethel?" Jane asked, arching her silvery eyebrows. "Is he *sleeping* with her?"

Ethel shrugged. "Maybe he is, maybe he isn't. Whoever this woman is, she always seems to pick the wrong times to drop in. After Mr. Kirk has gone to his shop, I mean. I've seen her." For emphasis, she tapped her thimble sharply against her scissors, once, twice. "Two different times."

Keeping track of the comings and goings of her neighbors was Ethel's favorite hobby—next to quilting, that is. A few of the residents of Pecan Street resented her insistent, intrusive nosiness and wished she would stop. But Ruby Wilcox, who lived next door on the east at 1111, pointed out that Mrs. Wauer was a useful adjunct to the Neighborhood Watch (especially since Oodles the Poodle was on guard as well), and most agreed that Ethel was a nuisance, but well-meaning. And harmless.

Hazel Schulz was not one of them. "You have been snooping again, Ethel," she said reproachfully. "That's not very nice, you know. People have a right to their privacy."

Ethel frowned. "Well, I have to wash my dishes, don't I? And the window over my kitchen sink looks out onto the alley, doesn't it? I can glance right out my window and see her, sneakin' down the alley and goin' through the Kirks' back gate. In fact, I'd have to shut my eyes to *keep* from seeing her, Hazel, in spite of the fact that she obviously doesn't want to be seen, which is why she's goin' down the alley in the first place." She sniffed. "And I don't know about you, but when I see a black-haired lady walkin' in her high heels down the alley, I take notice."

Jane took her thimble off. "Now that you mention it, I've seen her, too, Ethel," she said thoughtfully. She wiped her fingers on a tissue and put her thimble back on. "Long black hair, straight, stylish, early forties?"

"That's the one," Ethel said, nodding. "A little too much makeup for my taste. And not a happy look on her face."

"I didn't see her in the alley," Jane said. "But I did see her getting into her car the other day—one of those little foreign cars, Hyundai or something like that. She was parked down at the end of the block, in front of the Mc-Nallys'. I asked Mrs. McNally who she was, but she didn't know. She did say, though, that she'd seen her parked out there a couple of times. Just sitting in the car, like she was waiting for somebody." Her pause was meaningful. "Now that you've told us about her going into Mr. Kirk's backyard, I'm wondering if she was maybe waiting for him to come home."

"These young people," Mildred said with a sigh. "Always getting up to monkey business."

Ethel cackled. "It's not like you ever did that in *your* younger years, is it, Mildred?"

"Not hardly," Mildred retorted in an injured tone. "At least, not *that*. We might've gone out behind the barn for some neckin', but that's as far as it went." She tilted her head and a remembering smile ghosted across her lips. "Mostly, anyway."

"I wonder if the Kirks will sell their house," Hazel said. She squinted at her needle, trying to rethread it. "You know, that garage of theirs is two feet over on our side of the property line. Sam has been having fits about it for years. Sometimes he gets so mad, he could just chew bullets." She stopped squinting and handed her needle and thread to Jane. "I can't see to thread this dratted needle, Jane. Will you?"

"Yes, Hazel, we all know about Sam and the property line and the Kirks' garage," Mildred said crisply. "And we all wonder why you and Sam don't just sell them that piddling little strip."

Hazel rolled her eyes. "Oh, you know Sam. What's his is his and he won't give up one single inch of it."

"Except that the Kirks' garage has taken two whole feet instead of one single inch, and has for years and years," Ethel put in. "So let's not talk about it again, shall we?"

"Anyway, now that the Kirks are getting divorced, they'll probably sell the house," Hazel said, taking her threaded needle from Jane and going back to her sewing. "And Sam can blow his cork at whoever buys it next."

"Maybe Ruby's sister will buy it," Mildred said. "You know, she finally left that husband of hers up in Dallas— they've had trouble for years and years—and she's staying with Ruby. I heard she was looking for her own place. The Kirks' house would be perfect for her, just three doors down from Ruby."

Ruby Wilcox was also a Texas Star, but since she worked during the day (she owned Pecan Springs' only New Age shop, the Crystal Cave, and was the part owner of Thyme for Tea), she could only come to night meetings.

"Or maybe Chief Dawson and her sheriff husband will buy it," Jane suggested. "You know they're renting Aubrey Drew's mother's house, across the alley from me, on Hickory Street. But Aubrey might want that house back, and of course it would be better for us if the chief and the sheriff would stay in the neighborhood. The Kirks' place would be perfect." She smiled archly at Hazel. "Except for poor Sam, who couldn't get too mad at *them*, even if their garage does lap over the property line by two feet."

"Chief Dawson." Ethel snorted. "For the life of me, I can't think why these modern women don't use their right names. Their *married* names. Why couldn't she be Chief Blackwell? She's married to the sheriff, isn't she?"

"He's not sheriff any longer," Mildred pointed out. "I don't understand why he quit. There's been a Sheriff Blackwell in Adams County for as long as I can remember." She shook her head sadly. "I'm sure his daddy would be disappointed, if he were still alive."

"I don't suppose he gave up his guns just because he quit

being sheriff," Jane pointed out. "I heard he's working as a private investigator, like on TV. Anyway, if anybody tries any funny stuff in this neighborhood, it's good to have them right here to protect us. When the bad guys see the chief's car parked in the driveway, they know they need to go somewhere else."

Hazel smiled wistfully. "I just think it's so romantic, don't you? Two law enforcement officers, falling in love and getting married. And Chief Dawson—why, she's *beautiful*. If you ask me, she could have had a career in modeling. I wonder why she decided to be a cop instead. Doesn't make any sense to me."

"Wonder if their kids will grow up to be police like their mommy and daddy," Ethel remarked.

"I don't think a chief of police should *have* any kids," Mildred said, and bit off her thread. "She wouldn't find time to raise them right. And what would happen to the children if she got herself killed?"

"Well, I personally don't think a woman has any business being the chief of police," Ethel asserted. "Or a policeman, either. It's not natural." She shuddered. "What if she meets some big huge man in a dark alley somewhere? Why, he could *rape* her and she wouldn't be strong enough to stop him!"

"She's got a gun, doesn't she?" Mildred asked tartly. "She'd just shoot his you-know-whats off. *I* would, if some man tried to put a finger on me."

"It's policewoman, Ethel," Jane said. "She's not a police*man*, she's a police*woman*."

"It's police *officer*," Hazel said. "I read that somewhere. They don't want to be called policemen or policewomen. Officer is what they want to be called."

"Well, I think the chief and the sheriff should definitely buy the Kirks' house when it goes on the market," Jane said. "I personally would feel very safe with them living next door—with or without children." She pushed back her chair and stood up. "It was my turn to bring the refreshments today, girls. I baked some curry and cardamom cookies from a recipe I got from China Bayles, over at Thyme for Seasons."

"That's Thyme *and* Seasons," Mildred amended.

"Whatever," Jane said, with a wave of her hand. "China made them for one of our craft workshops last month, and everybody raved, so I thought I'd give them a try. Oh, and there's coffee, of course. Are you ready?"

The Texas Stars put down their needles and nodded. They might not agree on everything, but they could achieve a strong consensus where cardamom cookies and coffee were concerned.

Chapter One

Some herbs have hooks, designed to clutch and hold on to anyone or anything that comes near. One of the most interesting is cat's claw acacia (*Acacia greggii*, also called devil's claw and wait-a-minute bush), which grows on alkaline soils in semiarid grasslands and chaparral from Central Texas westward into California and south into Mexico. It is a perennial shrub or small tree that produces numerous slender, spreading branches studded with stout, quarter-inch, recurved thorns. In spring, creamy-yellow flowers (much loved by bees and butterflies) bloom in two-inch spikes, producing gray-brown beans that may be as much as five inches long.

Cat's claw has been used by Native Americans as food, medicine, and fiber. But it is always the thorns that attract attention. They are sharp, strong, and clawlike, holding fast and refusing to let go. Writing about it in *Arizona Flora*, naturalists Thomas H. Kearney and Robert H. Peebles remark that the cat's claw acacia is probably the most hated plant in the region, "the sharp, strong prickles tearing the clothes and lacerating the flesh."

China Bayles
"Herbs That Hold Fast"
Pecan Springs Enterprise

Ruby Wilcox climbed onto the stool beside my cash register and propped her elbow on the counter. "I've been thinking, China."

"About what?" I asked absently, only half-listening.

I was online, on my laptop, wrapping up a reply email to the guy who manages the Thyme and Seasons website for me. I'd just finished telling him (in answer to his question) that he didn't need a lawyer to deal with a stalker. If he knew the person's identity, he could simply go to the Adams County courthouse and file a temporary ex parte restraining order. Four pieces of paperwork and a short hearing and he was done. The next time he spotted the stalker, he could pick up the phone and the cops would be on the case. On the other hand, if he didn't know who the stalker was and he was seriously worried about the situation, he should go straight to the police. They used to dismiss stalking as a nuisance rather than a serious crime. Now, they take it more seriously. At least, that's what they say. I haven't had to test their claim.

"About our business," Ruby answered. "I've just finished going over our books, China. I don't want to be smug about it, but the bottom line for October looks really good, especially when you consider that the economy's not that great right now." Ruby traced out a dollar sign on the counter with the tip of a purple-painted fingernail decorated with silvery glitter. "We need to keep up the momentum. So I've been thinking about some of the things we can do to gear up for the holidays."

I hit "send" and the email zipped off into cyberspace. I felt guilty because I was several days late in replying to Larry. My inbox was too full again (I really have to do something about this state of affairs) and I hadn't noticed his email until just now. The situation worried me and I hoped he would do what I was suggesting. Maybe I was overreacting. But when it comes to stalking, experience has taught me that it pays to be a worrywart.

I turned my attention to Ruby. "The holidays? Oh, puh-leese, Ruby. Give us a break, can't you?" I puffed out an exaggerated sigh. "I'm glad that you're glad about the October bottom line. But let's take a little time off before we start thinking about Christmas, okay? Relax for a few days. Catch our breaths."

Our shop Siamese jumped up on the counter, stepped delicately past my laptop, and rubbed his head against Ruby's arm, rumbling his deep-throated purr. Khat isn't a demonstrative creature, but he's especially fond of Ruby, who gave him his name. His first owner had the bad luck to die under unpleasant circumstances, so he came to me. At the time, he was called Pudding, which neither he nor I thought even remotely appropriate. I called him Cat, or The Cat. (As far as he is concerned, he is entirely singular. No other cats are fit to enter his imperial presence.) But Ruby objected that this wasn't nearly distinctive enough for such a regal being. She is a great fan of Koko, the talented Siamese cat–sleuth of the Cat Who mysteries, and has always wanted a cat who could tell time, talk to ghosts, and had fourteen tales. Which is how Pudding became Cat and Cat became Khat K'o Kung.

"Catch our breaths?" Ruby stroked Khat's charcoal ears. He purred even louder. "Well, sure, we could do that—it might be nice. But it's also good to be ahead of the pitch."

I frowned. "Pitch? What pitch?"

"In a manner of speaking." She leaned forward, her eyes glinting. "Listen, China, I got this great idea last night while Ramona and I were eating supper."

Ramona is Ruby's sister, younger by about three years. She's not as tall as Ruby (who is six feet and impressive in sandals, six-plus and stunning in heels) and she doesn't have Ruby's outrageous sense of style. But she has the same frizzy red hair and freckles and shares Ruby's weird interests: the tarot, the I Ching, and the Ouija board. Ramona was working in a Dallas advertising firm, but she received a large cash settlement when she and her doctor husband divorced. To get a new start, she quit her job and moved to Pecan Springs, where she's staying with Ruby while she figures out what she wants to do with the rest of her life. I'm sympathetic (I've been there and done that myself), but I am not Ramona's greatest fan. In my opinion, she takes advantage of Ruby's generosity. This time, she's been at her sister's house for three weeks and she hasn't contributed a penny toward expenses—even though the settlement left her with plenty of pennies.

Ruby was leaning forward with an eager look. "So here's my idea, China. How about if we—"

"Stop!" I logged off the computer. "Don't you think we've had enough on our plates for the past couple of months? And our November calendar is already full. Let's not add any new events."

"But, China, I wasn't talking about adding events. I was talking about promoting—"

"But nothing, Ruby," I said firmly, and closed my laptop. "Let's just *don't*, okay?"

Khat sat down, curling his charcoal tail around his charcoal paws, regarding us thoughtfully, his blue eyes flicking from one to the other. He likes to hear us argue. He thinks it's a game, like tennis or badminton. He keeps score.

Ruby wasn't finished. "But really, China—this won't take a lot of effort." She fluffed her carroty red hair with her fingers. "And it's got a huge payoff. Potentially, that is, with just a little extra work. I don't know why I didn't think of it before now. And of course Ramona will be glad to contribute her—"

"No!" I put the laptop on the shelf under the counter. "Enough already, Ruby! I am not taking on any new projects. Meanwhile, it's five o'clock. I am shutting up shop and then I am going home." I waved her away. "Good-bye, Ruby. Scat."

With an exaggerated sigh, Ruby unfolded her six-foot-plus self from the stool where she had been perched. She was wearing a gauzy raglan-sleeved top, brown and black with orange stripes, over an orange turtleneck and black leggings. She looked like a Monarch butterfly about to take flight—a disappointed Monarch. But she waggled her fingers to show that she didn't harbor a grudge and disappeared through the connecting door that links our shops, Thyme and Seasons Herbs (mine) and the Crystal Cave (hers). Then she stuck her head back through and delivered a parting shot.

"Someday, China Bayles, you'll come to me on your hands and knees and say you're sorry. You just wait and see—you'll grovel."

Khat gave a commanding meow, directing me to grovel right now.

"I'm already sorry," I muttered sarcastically. Khat flicked his tail twice, reprimanding me. Then he jumped down from the counter and went to take sides with Ruby. As far as he was concerned, she'd won that round.

It was Monday, and our shops were closed, which of course hadn't meant that we'd taken the day off. Ruby had spent the day cleaning and dusting and restocking shelves, and I had come in to work in the garden and do some reordering and bookkeeping. Now, I finished up my chores and started putting things away. But by the time I was ready to leave, I was feeling thoroughly ashamed of myself. Ruby and I have been best friends for well over a decade and business partners for most of that time. In all those years, I have rarely known her to have a bad idea. Some of them may have been a little . . . well, flaky. But even those mostly turned out okay in the end.

After all, our tearoom—Thyme for Tea—had proved to be an outstanding idea, hadn't it? Ruby had thought it up.

And our catering service, Party Thyme, which handles a lot of the weddings and parties and other big events in town? Ruby's idea.

And Ruby had been the one who suggested joining forces with Cass Wilde, who runs her Thymely Gourmet meals-to-go service out of our tearoom kitchen and handles the tea room lunches and the Party Thyme food—an inspired idea, since Cass is an inspired cook.

There you have it. Thyme and Seasons, the Crystal Cave, Thyme for Tea, Party Thyme, the Thymely Gourmet. Five profit centers under one roof, three of them Ruby's bright ideas. Of course, they're not all hugely profitable every month. But enough of them are profitable enough to keep the bottom line from bleeding an ugly red all over our account books. And in lean times like these, with the Pecan Springs business community struggling to keep its collective head above water, showing a profit every month is something to brag about, even if we do have to work our fingers to the bone to make it happen.

I held out my hands and looked at them. They were a mess, as usual. Unless you wear gloves, which I usually don't, the Hill Country's caliche soil will dry your skin and collect under your nails. But my fingers weren't exactly worked to the bone. I was exaggerating.

Still, it had been an exceptionally busy few weeks. For one thing, October is always a whirlwind where families with kids are concerned, with school and extracurricular activities and Halloween. And our family is no different. Brian, my husband's son, is a senior in high school and getting ready to choose a college. Caitlin, our adopted daughter, has just turned twelve and is practicing for another violin recital. (The adoption is a long story. I won't go into it now.)

October had been busy for my husband, too. McQuaid teaches part-time in the Criminal Justice Department at Central Texas State University and invests the rest of his working hours in his business: McQuaid, Blackwell, and Associates, Private Investigators. "Blackwell" is Blackie Blackwell, former Adams County sheriff and McQuaid's new partner. (Long story there, too.) Since Blackie joined the firm in August, the caseload has tripled. McQuaid says that having a former sheriff as a partner is very good for business.

And of course, autumn is busy in the shops and the tearoom. In addition to the day-in, day-out activities (lunches, teas, and other special events), Ruby and I offer a crafting series that runs every Saturday afternoon until Thanksgiving. There's the Pecan Springs Farmers Market, open Saturday mornings through the end of October—a great market that brings foodies and locavores (people who are trying to shop and eat locally) from Austin to the north and San Antonio to the south. We have a booth there, which is fun but a lot of work, even when Caitlin and Brian and Ruby's daughter Amy pitch in to help. And then there's the task of keeping the herb gardens around the shop looking halfway decent as the summer heat dwindles and the long Texas autumn begins. That's mostly handled by a group of volunteers, bless 'em. But somebody has to supervise, and since Ruby doesn't know a weed from a wonderberry, that somebody is me.

And then there was the wedding.

Ah, yes, the wedding. That was what really kept us busy in late summer and early fall. It took place on a September Sunday in the garden, primped to perfection and looking its prettiest. I worried about the weather, because when McQuaid and I were married (also in September, several years ago), Hurricane Josephine nearly swamped us. But the day was bright and decently cool and the outdoor wedding was gorgeous. The reception was held in our tearoom and catered by Party Thyme, with a Texas-style buffet and table centerpieces of orange and yellow marigolds, purple gayfeather, sprigs of garden herbs, and colorful squash, as well as take-home favors: herbs in tiny terracotta pots, each herb labeled with the name of the plant and Sheila's and Blackie's names and wedding date. We had to hire six extra helpers and servers, and even then, we were stretched. But it was worth it, just to see Sheila Dawson and Blackie Blackwell finally become husband and wife. Or police chief and husband, as *Enterprise* editor and local wit Hark Hibler put it.

"I never thought they'd actually pull it off," McQuaid remarked, after the bride and groom had driven away for a short honeymoon at an undisclosed location, and the rest of the hundred-plus guests had wolfed down the last chipotle meatball, nibbled the last piece of wedding cake, and drunk the last champagne toast. The cleanup crew would be working for several more hours, but McQuaid and I were getting ready to call it a day.

"Sheila looked absolutely stunning, didn't she?" Ruby said, tossing a dustpan full of birdseed (a good substitute for rice) onto the grass.

She did. Sheila Dawson is beautiful at any time, any place, no matter what she is wearing: jeans and sandals, a chic suit with pearls and heels, or her trim blue cop uniform with a duty belt loaded with guns and gadgets. (I've always said that you have to wonder at somebody who looks like a homecoming queen and thinks like the regional director of the FBI.) Since she and Blackie had decided on "ranch attire" for their wedding, the bride was dressed in a sheer, off-shoulder, ivory blouse, western denim skirt, and cowgirl boots, with a wreath of rosemary and white rosebuds on her shining blond hair and a bouquet of lavender and white roses in her hand. She might have put Blackie off while they got their respective careers sorted out, but anybody with eyes could tell that she believed that "yes" was the right thing to say at last, after several long years of "yes," then "no," then "maybe." She was radiant.

"You gotta admit that Blackie looked pretty good, too,"

McQuaid said with a grin. "Especially for a guy who lost his job in a coin toss." McQuaid had been the groom's best man. He and Blackie had worn open-collared white shirts, dark jackets, jeans, and cowboy boots. They looked like ranch hands who were cleaned up for Sunday church.

"Well, yes," I said. "But you have to remember that he lost a job and won a wife."

McQuaid is right, though. Throughout the ceremony, Blackie wore the stunned, disbelieving expression of a man who'd just learned that he'd won a ten-million-dollar Super Jackpot in the Texas lottery, instead of the regretful look of a man who had given up a job he enjoyed. He and Sheila had long agreed that two law enforcement careers in one family were a train wreck, so marriage hadn't seemed in the cards. But when they decided (after several false starts) that they really wanted to get married, they couldn't decide which one of them should quit.

If I'd been guessing, I would have said that Sheila (known to her friends as Smart Cookie) would be the one to hand in her badge. She has worked like the devil to break the brass ceiling, but while she doesn't talk much about what goes down in her cop shop, it's an open secret around town that PSPD is not a congenial place for women. If she weren't as stubborn and tough as she is—we sometimes call her Tough Cookie—she probably would have called it quits already. What's more, the Blackwells count three generations of Adams County sheriffs in the family, and Blackie loved his job. He was good at it, too. The best sheriff that Adams County ever had, according to some.

Either way, each of them had a lot to give up. They had reached a serious impasse: a Mexican standoff, as it were. They wanted to get married, but neither Blackie nor Sheila was ready to quit. So a few months ago, after another frustrating evening of weighing pros and cons, they gave up trying to make a logical choice and decided to toss for it. Heads he'd keep his job as sheriff and she'd give up hers as

Pecan Springs' police chief. Tails she'd keep her job and he wouldn't run for a third term.

The coin came up tails, and Blackie bowed out of the next election. But the toss is a close-held secret, known only to a few friends. As far as the rest of the world is concerned, Blackie had simply decided that he'd been in the sheriff's office long enough. He was leaving to join McQuaid at McQuaid and Blackwell. Now, a couple of months after the fact, he is a licensed private investigator. He seems to like the job.

McQuaid cocked his head, regarding me, his lips pursed. "You look pretty great, too, China." There was an admiring glint in his eyes.

I had been the bride's attendant. Sheila and I picked out a blouse exactly like hers, except it was a steel blue color that went with my denim skirt. I wore my red cowgirl boots and carried a bouquet of red roses, with lavender, mint, and rosemary. Justice of the Peace Maude Porterfield conducted the ceremony, and in the spirit of the occasion, wore a white cowboy hat, white pants and cowboy boots, and her best Dale Evans shirt. Judge Porterfield has been a JP in Pecan Springs for nearly fifty years and still leads a busy and colorful life, holding traffic court, issuing warrants, signing death certificates, and marrying people. She says she much prefers to marry people. It doesn't leave a bad taste in her mouth, like death certificates.

As long as they stay together, that is. Maude regards the ones who don't make it as her own personal failures. "I guess I didn't put enough emphasis on 'until death do you part,'" she says sourly, whenever she hears about the latest divorce. "Sad to say, but some are in it just for the good times. Married folks, they gotta be like that cat's claw acacia I've got growin' in my yard. Gotta grab hard and hold on tight when the going gets rough. Only way to get through the bad times. Grab hard, hold on, and ride. No matter what."

But even though Maude gave "until death do you part" her very best shot, it may not be enough. Sheila's and Blackie's careers in law enforcement have created a great many conflicts between them over the past few years, and after a couple of broken engagements, I'm afraid to be too optimistic. Or maybe I'm just realistic. I'm married to an ex-cop, and I understand why McQuaid's first marriage ended in divorce. So did Blackie's, and while I don't know all the details, I'm guessing that it happened for pretty much the same reasons. I'm sure that he and Sheila will give it all they can, and I hope it works. Their friends and well-wishers gave them a great sendoff, and we all wish them the best. The rest is up to them.

I picked up my shoulder bag and paused for a moment before I switched off the lights, liking what I saw. Thyme and Seasons, the Crystal Cave, and the tearoom are housed in an old two-story building that is constructed of blocks of Texas limestone. The shops and the tearoom have stone walls, deep-set casement windows, and the original wooden floors. My shop is small and very full, but I like it that way—there's an intimacy about it that's lacking in larger, more open shops, seems to me, and the rustic space suits the down-to-earthiness of my wares. The ceiling-high shelves along the back wall display dozens of jars and bottles of dried herbs, salves, and tinctures. A corner rack holds herb, gardening, and cookery books, as well as copies of my own *China Bayles' Book of Days*. There's a display of essential oils, diffusers, and other aromatherapy supplies on an old wooden table—everything you need to create and enjoy herbal fragrances. Along another wall are herbal items from local crafters: jellies, vinegars, seasoning blends, and soaps. There are baskets of dried herbs in the corners, bundles of dried plants hang from overhead beams, and raffia-tied braids of red peppers and garlic are displayed on the stone walls. The air is rich with the sweet-spicy scents of patchouli, nutmeg, cinnamon, and sandalwood—

fragrances that remind me of a lingering autumn. I won't start putting up the holiday items for another week or two. I absolutely hate going to malls and seeing the Christmas stuff up before Halloween. This is *my* shop, and I don't rush the season.

People sometimes ask if I miss my former profession—I was a practicing criminal attorney—or long for the excitements and entertainments of Houston, where I used to live. But I don't have to hem and haw and fumble for an answer. I love it here. I'm doing something that feels right and healthy for me, for my customers, and for the planet. I don't know what the future holds—nobody does. But I intend to do this for as long as I can.

I reached for the switch to turn off the lights. But before I could flick it, the door to the Crystal Cave popped open and Ruby stood there, her cell phone in her hand, her eyes round, her face white.

"It's Ramona!" she gasped. "She's just— She—"

"Uh-oh," I said, under my breath. Ramona is a little ditzy. She collects weird accidents, like the time the car ahead of her on the freeway threw a hubcap through her windshield, or the afternoon she was sailing with a friend on a lake near Dallas and a big fish jumped into the boat and bit her toe. Aloud, I said, "What's happened to Ramona now?"

Ruby gulped. "She . . . she's found a body."

"A dead one?" I was startled. Even for Ramona, finding a body is not something that happens every day. "Where?"

Ruby gave me a look that said, *Yes, dead, you dummy.* Into the phone, she asked, "Where?" After a moment's listening, she said to me, "Three doors down from my house. In the kitchen. There's a . . . a gun."

I could've asked why Ramona was wandering through the neighborhood kitchens, but I didn't. Urgently, I said, "Tell her not to touch a thing. Tell her to call nine-one-one, then go around front and stand on the curb until the cops get there."

Ruby repeated my message. Ramona must not have processed it, so Ruby repeated it again before she closed the phone, biting her lip.

"She says she's already done all that, and there are cops on the scene. I've got to go over there, China. Will you go with me?"

"No," I said automatically. "I'm sorry. I've got to go home and cook supper for—"

And then I remembered. Brian's school baseball team was playing at Seguin this afternoon, and McQuaid had picked Caitlin up after school to go and watch the game. Afterward, they planned to have supper with Mom and Dad McQuaid, who live in Seguin. I would have joined them after I closed the shop, but McQuaid hadn't had a chance to spend an evening with the kids lately.

Ruby was looking at me plaintively. "Please?" she whispered tremulously. "I don't want to do this by myself. Ramona is— Well, you know."

I knew. But hubcaps and toe-biting fish are one thing. Dead bodies are something else altogether.

"Okay," I said, deciding. "Let's go."

Chapter Two

"That about does it for now, I guess," Deputy Chief Clint Hardin said in his slow drawl, getting out of the chair on the opposite side of the chief's desk. Hardin was six-two with burly shoulders, craggy face, unflinching dark eyes. Impressive in his dark blue uniform. A cop's cop. Looking up at him, Sheila thought with a tug of irritation that he never missed a chance to use his height and size to make a point with the women on the force, including (or maybe especially) his boss.

He picked up the file from the desk. "If we get anything actionable on the blackmail, I'll let you know, Chief. But you can look for an arrest on the trespass and burglary charges in another—" He looked down at his watch. "Fifteen, twenty minutes. You'll get the word when it happens."

"Good job, Captain," Sheila said, although she knew that the arrest was more Bartlett's work than Hardin's. The deputy chief had a reputation for taking credit for his subordinates' work when it was good and giving them hell when it wasn't. Not a positive character trait, in her opinion. But Clint Hardin had spent the better part of his nearly twenty-year career developing and perfecting it and wasn't likely to change.

She rolled back the black leather desk chair and stood up. The massive chair had belonged to the former chief, Bubba Harris, and was much too large for her—another of the things about the Pecan Springs Police Department that didn't fit but were hard to change. It was the chief's chair. She was stuck with it.

"Pass that word along to Bartlett," she added, "and put a note in his file. This one is dicey, considering who's involved. Bartlett handled it well—this part of it, anyway."

The commendation would go through channels, of course, but Sheila would take a minute to speak to Jack Bartlett herself. He was in charge of PSPD's four-person detective unit. Young, newly promoted, and ambitious, he'd go by his gut when Hardin would've gone by the book. On the surface, the case had seemed minor, a random break-in at a local computer firm, Kirk's Computer Sales and Service—one of a string of several break-ins at other small businesses. But as things turned out, it wasn't the size of the crime that was important; it was the status of the criminal whose shadowy image had been caught on video. A prominent citizen who was going to be mightily embarrassed when his arrest became public later today.

But desperate people did desperate things, and George Timms—who was about to find himself printed, mugged, and booked for criminal trespass and destruction of property—must have been very desperate. According to his attorney, Charlie Lipman, Timms was being blackmailed. He had broken into the business in an attempt to retrieve the incriminating evidence, then removed some of the shop's items to cover up his purpose and make it look like a burglary. Lipman hadn't yet said what the evidence was or who the blackmailer was, and that part of the investigation was still pending. The attorney was no doubt holding the information back as leverage for the plea deal he was expecting to work with the DA, who just happened to be a friend of Timms, and he wouldn't want the police to have it until he was good and ready. Sheila knew and respected Lipman, who was the best—and the busiest—lawyer in Pecan Springs. But he could also be damned frustrating. They'd get the information when he was done dealing with the district attorney and not a minute before.

But from Sheila's point of view, getting this far with this particular case was not an insignificant victory. City council member Ben Graves had been making a crusade out of the unsolved minor burglaries. He had made up a three-by-four-foot chart and posted it prominently at every council meeting. It wasn't that Graves cared for seeing justice done—if he did, he would stop opposing nearly every budget request she made for upgrades to police personnel and equipment. All he cared about was making himself look like a guardian of community safety and making her look as incompetent as possible, in the hope that Pecan Springs' first female police chief would give up and turn in her resignation. She would be more than happy to rub his nose in the outcome of Bartlett's investigation, especially since George Timms was a former business associate of Graves and a golfing buddy of the mayor's. Timms owned the Chevy dealership, as well as several rental properties around town and some prime Hill Country real estate—which made him a very odd burglar, indeed.

And while Clint Hardin had been a thorn in her side ever since she'd been appointed chief, Sheila had to admit—grudgingly—that he had done a good job on this particular investigation. He'd given the detective unit the backup it needed and kept a tight lid on possible leaks after it became apparent that this wasn't your ordinary, everyday break-in. That was crucial, considering who their suspect was and who his friends were. Hark Hibler had a nose for police news, especially when he thought there might be scandal in high places. The *Enterprise* would break this story big, once Hibler got his hands on it.

But Bartlett had done his job, Hardin had played the

investigation close, Hibler hadn't gotten even a whiff of anything rotten in Denmark, and the arrest would come as a shocking surprise. Not to Timms, of course. Bartlett had negotiated the man's surrender with Charlie Lipman last night. And as soon as the arrest and booking were complete, Sheila would give Ben Graves a call.

"I thought you might appreciate a heads-up on this one, Mr. Graves," she would say smoothly, sweetly, and maliciously. Then she would add, "Although I'm not sure it's what you want to hear."

Hardin cleared his throat assertively. "Don't know if you saw the duty roster, Chief. I'm due to take the next ten days for vacation. Brother-in-law and I have rented a boat at Rockport. We're supposed to leave this afternoon. Of course, when I put in for the time off, I didn't know we'd be so shorthanded. If you want me to hang around—" He eyed her.

"Negative," Sheila said firmly. Yes, she had seen the duty roster, and yes, they were even more short-staffed than usual, between court appearances, vacations, and a couple of guys out sick. But Hardin had the time coming. They'd manage.

"The Timms case is in the bucket," she added. "So go, Clint. Get yourself some trophy redfish."

"Yes, ma'am." Hardin said it with a slight touch of insubordination, as he always did. Not heavy enough to call for anything like a reprimand or even an informal reproof, but noticeable. And definitely irritating. He headed for the door, adding over his shoulder, "I'll remind Bartlett that he's reporting directly to you while I'm gone."

The door clicked shut behind Hardin, and Sheila sank back into the oversize chair, pushing out a long, weary breath. He had been one of the candidates for the chief's job when she was appointed, and he never let her forget it. She ought to be glad that he was out of her hair for a few days. It was one less conflict to manage, although their relationship was such a perpetual source of conflict that it more or less faded into the background and only came up when one of them felt like butting heads. She ought to be looking forward to the gotcha conversation with Graves, too. Opportunities like that were few and far between.

But right now, Sheila couldn't whip up a lot of enthusiasm about anything. She had been up since before five for her morning run with Rambo, her drug-sniffing Rottweiler who worked the day shift in the K-9 Unit—nights, too, when he was called out. She was at the desk at six thirty, uniform sharply creased, tie neatly tied, duty belt fastened around her waist. She always came in before seven to get an early start on the stack of paperwork. Didn't count for much, though, because there'd be an even bigger stack the next day.

The paperwork was all part of the job—just not the job that all those TV cop shows portrayed. She had never seen a single episode that showed the chief sitting behind a desk pushing papers, or logged onto a computer displaying the latest report. Unfortunately, the shows made everybody think that policing was a nonstop game of cops and robbers, every car chase ending up with three bad guys on the ground in an ankle-deep pool of blood, a detective standing over them with a smoking 40-caliber Smith & Wesson. But it wasn't. At least, not her end of it. Her end of it was forms, memos, notices, and reports, more of them all the time. If she didn't stay on top of things, she'd be overwhelmed.

And like it or not, the chief's desk was the last stop for all that paperwork. Even though she might prefer to be out on an investigation—interviewing, following leads, connecting the dots—this was her job now. Bottom line, it was up to her to create a supportive environment in which every police officer could do his or her work. It was *her* job to get them the resources and tools and training they needed to do *their* jobs safely and effectively. It was the job she had wanted and fought every day to keep—although there were plenty of days when she'd a heckuva lot rather be out on patrol or doing an investigation instead of sitting in this oversize, ill-fitting chair.

Which was ironic, wasn't it? After hours and hours of discussion, she and Blackie had tossed a coin to see which one of them would stay, which of them would go. Heads she'd quit, tails he would. She sighed. The way she was feeling about the job at this moment, she wished she'd called it heads.

Today had been a typical desk day—a day like most of the others. Before she'd started on the morning's stack of papers, she'd turned on the computer, pulled up the monthly incident stats, and scanned the columns. 9-1-1 calls were up about 12 percent for the year, which just about tracked Pecan Springs' population growth. Traffic stops and accident reports, down slightly. Burglaries up from the previous month. DWIs up. Possession, drug dealing, both up—a trend that wasn't going to change. Homicides, zip for the month (but November was still young), eight for the year, all either domestic or drug-related and all cleared within a week, which was a pretty good record. Cases cleared, by percentage, down a little but still acceptable. (Down a lot from when Bubba Harris was chief, but he had pumped the stats in order to make the department look good.) All in all, a decent report for a small town on a busy Interstate corridor between Dallas and the Mexican border.

She glanced at the large laminated map of Pecan Springs on her office wall, where pushpins marked the recent burglaries, noting that most had occurred within a twelve-block area. She printed out the computer report and circled some numbers to comment on at the briefing with her department heads, then went on to yesterday's incident report, the personnel report, and the budget. She was still trying to squeeze out the money for another couple of computers for Records, so they could clear out the data-entry backlog, and three more dash cams for patrol cars. She'd like to have computers in the patrol cars, too, but the dash cams were more important. Video was an unbiased record of what happened. It told the truth and helped build public trust in the police. Good cops wanted dash cams.

Paperwork caught up (temporarily), phone messages and emails answered, it had been time for the morning briefing with Hardin and the other department heads. Then she had gone over to the city building for the weekly council meeting, where she had been on the hot seat until just before noon, patiently answering questions about her budget request and looking Ben Graves and Mildred Wilbur straight in the eye when their questions were dumber (or more deliberately malicious) than usual.

The meeting had dragged on, making her late for lunch with Blackie, who was on his way to El Paso on a missing-child case that he and Mike McQuaid were working on. She was glad to see how eager he was to find the little boy whose photo he had shown her. His eagerness took a little of the edge off her guilt for winning that coin toss, but not quite enough. If she'd called heads, Blackie would be doing the job he loved, and she could have resigned and taken the next available detective slot. She hated to admit how tempting that sounded.

After lunch, Blackie had left for the airport and she headed back to the office for a meeting with Lieutenant Jim Sumner, who was also their media officer, about staffing turnovers in the Support Services Division, which employed mostly civilians. After that, an update meeting with Mark Quintana, of Internal Affairs, and Chuck Canady, the Operations Division sergeant in charge of the two night units. The subject: Quintana's investigation into the arrest of one of Canady's officers.

It was serious heartburn. The previous Friday, Harry Blake, a veteran with an outstanding record and nearly twenty years at PSPD, was arrested by deputies in neighboring Travis County and charged with making a terroristic threat. Blake had gone to his ex-wife's house and gotten into a shouting match with her current boyfriend. The officer would plead it out to disturbing the peace, likely. In the grand scheme of things, not a biggie—at least Blake hadn't drawn his weapon. Even so, it was an embarrassment to the department. Ben Graves would bring it up in city council. Hark Hibler would get an editorial out of it.

And there were staffing consequences. Blake had been put on a desk while IA conducted a review, which meant that the night patrol unit was now short two officers, since one was already out on medical leave. Sheila had been fairly successful in beefing up the force to the point where they could cover court appearances and vacations, but illnesses and family emergencies were a different matter. Overtime was eating up the budget.

So yesterday, she and Canady had gone over the duty roster, juggled assignments, and come up with a solution of sorts. It involved shifting an officer from Jeraldine Clarke's day patrol unit to Canady's night unit, and moving a rookie officer, Rita Kidder, from her training stint in Records to the day unit, where Clarke would be her field training officer. Nobody in the unit was eager to FTO a woman—and Sheila had already heard (gossip traveled at warp speed in Pecan Springs) that the officers' wives were even less eager for their husbands to ride with Rita, who was young, bright, and shapely, although her shape was not quite so evident when she was in uniform. Women had been policing since 1910 and patrolling with the boys since the 1972 Equal Employment Opportunity Act required state and local governments to adopt the 1964 Title VII rules. You'd think the old macho attitudes would have come unglued by now, wouldn't you? Maybe that was true in big-city departments. But not in small-town Texas, where the more things changed, the more they stayed the same.

Sitting behind her desk now, Sheila smiled faintly, remembering her own FTO in the Dallas PD some fifteen years before. The two of them worked out of the West Dallas station, which wasn't a picnic in anybody's book. Orlando had been a burly twelve-year veteran with hands like hams and a fighter's nose, ugly as sin. They hadn't been in the squad car for more than ten seconds before he turned to her, stuck out his chin, and growled, "I'm gonna tell you this just once, Dawson, so you listen hard. I don't like it that you're riding with me, but I got no choice, I'm stuck with you for the next four weeks. So this is the way it goes down. I get in a fight, I wanna see your nose bloody. I get shot up, you better take a bullet. You aim to be a cop, you act like a cop, not like a damn girl. You got that?"

She'd got it, knowing that it wasn't just that she was a woman and slender, but that she was also blond and pretty. Being attractive, sexy, even, was something she had always viewed as an asset, like a fast-acting brain, the reflexes of an athlete, and good upper body strength. But she found out on her first day at the Police Academy that *pretty* definitely wasn't an asset in police work. It gave her brother cadets ("brother"—that was a laugh) another reason not to take her seriously, and her sister cadets, the few there were, something to envy. By the time she graduated, she would have traded her looks for dark, stringy hair, sallow skin, and another three inches and twenty pounds.

That first night on patrol with Orlando had been ordinary, even boring. Nothing happened until they got a 10-10, code for a fight in progress. It was in a dark, dirty bar and had already turned into a pretty decent brawl when they arrived. By the time she and Orlando got the three drunk ringleaders cuffed, the pair of officers who had been called in as backup were standing there with their mouths gaping. Orlando had a bloody nose and a bite on one hand. But Sheila hadn't been black belt in karate for nothing. She was unscathed, even though she'd taken down the two biggest guys by herself. And she only had to do it once. From then on, the word was out. "Dawson gets the job done, whatever it takes," they said. "She does what she has to. She hustles."

She wasn't one of the guys—Sheila knew she never would be *that*. She would always be an outsider, a woman in the biggest boys' club in America, and like the other rookie women, the target of a barrage of immature, frat-boy hazing stunts involving dead rats, used sanitary napkins, and porn photos. Sheila wasn't privy to everything that went on in the locker rooms at PSPD, but she suspected that Kidder and the three other women on the force were probably getting the same treatment. Or maybe not. The harassment was likely to be more subtle these days, after the civil suit that had cost the city a bundle, forced Bubba Harris into retirement, and resulted in her being hired away from her post as chief of security at CTSU to take charge of a department that was in serious trouble.

Anyway, over the years she'd been in police work, Sheila had learned to give as good as she got, and while she saw plenty of discrimination, she stopped feeling that she was being singled out. Orlando had become her mentor and her friend, as well as her partner. They'd made detective together, and for a couple of years in Homicide, they'd been partners, been a team. She had learned from him, and he had a lot to teach. She'd gotten bloody for him and when she was shot in a stakeout, he'd taken a bullet, too. For a while, their working relationship seemed to offer the promise of something more personal. But then Dan Reid had come along and pulled Sheila into his irresistible orbit. And a few months later, Orlando found the right woman.

But neither he nor Sheila had forgotten their time together. He had gone on to be chief of police in a rural Oklahoma town, and she was here in Pecan Springs. They traded Christmas cards, and he'd sent a note when she got the job as chief. "Don't forget what you're there for, Dawson," he had written, in his sprawling script. "You've got a job to do, and it ain't just the paperwork. Do whatever you can to keep yourself from getting stuck behind the desk. You hear me? Just *do* it."

Stuck behind the desk, Sheila thought uncomfortably. Well, she wasn't totally stuck. There were other things in her life. Her glance went to the silver-framed photograph on the corner of the gray metal desk. She and Blackie, looking relaxed and happy in the easy, everyday outfits they'd decided on for their wedding—nothing like what her mother thought they should wear. If her mom had had her way, Blackie would have been trussed up in a tux and Sheila would have been on display in a white satin wedding dress with a six-foot train and her grandmother's wedding veil, a couple of acres of floating tulle capped with a pearl tiara.

"Now that you're past thirty-five, you'll likely only be married once, dear," her mother had said, with only a hint of her usual snarkiness. "It should be an occasion to remember. You'll let me pick out your dress, won't you, sweets? Pretty please?"

Well, she was nearly forty and old enough to plan her own wedding, thank you very much. It had been memorable without her grandmother's wedding veil and the kind of dress her mother would choose. Memorable because officers from both their departments had been there. Memorable because Maude Porterfield had come down so hard on the words "'Til death do you part" that a titter ran through the audience. Memorable for the wonderful food and the warmth and affection of their friends, and for the idyllic three-day honeymoon they'd managed to steal at Blackie's fishing cabin on Canyon Lake. They'd taken a couple of other short trips together, of course—once, they'd even flown to Cozumel for a weekend. But they'd never been able to hang out all morning in bed together, swatting at mosquitoes while the sun climbed high over the live oak trees. Or fish for their breakfast together, and eat fresh-caught bass with fried eggs and ketchup-soaked hash browns and then tumble back into bed for as long as they liked, without a single peep from their pagers. Bliss. Sheer bliss. But both Sheila and Blackie were realists. They knew that bliss never lasts forever, which maybe just made it sweeter.

Sheila reached for another stack of papers, scrawled her name at the bottom (she'd gotten very good at that), then glanced at her watch. Nearly five o'clock. By this time, Blackie was landing in El Paso, which left her on her own for the evening. She looked around the office, seeing that everything was in place. She disliked personal clutter, so there was nothing but books, cop magazines, and stacks of computer printouts on the gray metal bookshelves; the map of Pecan Springs and the surrounding county on the wall; the computer and a plastic philodendron on the desk. No plants to water, no doodads to dust, only the minimum number of framed certificates and diplomas on the wall. It didn't look like a woman's office at all. Sheila had learned a long time ago that the officers in her command were more comfortable that way. Policing was a man's world, and she had gotten into the habit of hiding her femininity as much as she could. It wasn't always easy, because there was no changing her light voice or the way she looked, although the unisex uniform and clunky duty boots helped. She was glad she hadn't gotten into law enforcement back in the days when policewomen were required to dress like airline attendants in tight skirts, three-inch heels, perky bow ties, and little caps—all designed to emphasize their femaleness.

Impatiently, she swept the rest of the papers into her briefcase and snapped it shut. If Timms' surrender had taken place as scheduled, she hadn't gotten the word. But she didn't have to hang around here and wait. Bartlett would call her cell phone when it happened. She was picking up her briefcase when the phone rang on the desk. She reached for it, expecting to hear about the arrest.

It wasn't Bartlett. It was the dispatch supervisor, Mary Lou Parker, with a 10-87, a dead body report that had just come in on a 9-1-1 call. White male, apparent gun suicide, according to the patrol sergeant who was first at the scene. Detective Bartlett had been notified and was on his way.

The call from Dispatch was routine. Sheila had asked to be immediately notified on all 10-87s, but unless there was a special reason for her to be there, she didn't usually go to the scene. That was Hardin's job. She looked at her watch again, thinking that he had probably already left for Rockport.

"Is Deputy Chief Hardin still around?" she asked, just in case.

"He's ten-seven," Dispatch replied, "about fifteen minutes ago. Want me to ask him to come back, ma'am?"

"Negative." No need to call Hardin back—he'd earned his time off. "Where's this ten-eighty-seven, Mary Lou? I'll take it."

Dispatch read off the address. When Sheila heard it, she was startled. She jotted it down, although she didn't have to. She knew exactly where it was.

"Let Detective Bartlett know I'm ten-seventy-six," she said.

A 10-76 was the code for officer in route. The address was on Pecan, Ruby Wilcox's street, and the 10-87 was three doors down from Ruby's, at 1117 Pecan—and directly across the alley from the house where Sheila and Blackie had been living since they got married.

It seemed that one of her neighbors had killed himself.

Chapter Three

❀ Pecan Springs was a small town, and nothing was very far away from anywhere else. Sheila could have been at the location on Pecan in five minutes, maybe less, if she'd put on both the lights and the siren. But there wasn't any hurry on a suicide. She'd give Bartlett plenty of time to do his preliminary work. She'd just drop in and take a quick look, then head home—conveniently, right across the alley.

Sheila stopped at the small outbuilding where the K-9 Search and Rescue Unit was housed, and where Rambo, her Rottweiler, spent his day with a kennel mate, a white German shepherd named Opal that belonged to the SAR coordinator, Martha Meacham. The unit was new and still under development, but Martha—a tall, big-boned woman with silvery hair, a ready smile, and a cheerful expression—was committed to expanding it and getting the volunteer handlers and their dogs certified for air scent and cadaver search, trailing, and water search and rescue. Rambo had already proved his worth as a drug-sniffer, but there were plenty of other jobs to do. Martha was in charge of finding the dogs and handlers who could do them.

The project was something that Sheila had been eager to support, and when Martha had come to her with the idea of creating a volunteer unit, she hadn't hesitated. Finding the funding was difficult—the city council wasn't sold on the idea of using volunteers, and Ben Graves had wanted to know what would happen if one of those dogs *attacked* somebody. Could the citizen sue the city? What if one of the volunteers got hurt? And who was going to pay for all that training? The citizens of Pecan Springs couldn't be expected to pick up the tab, surely.

Graves didn't need to worry. The volunteers—most of them with experience in outdoor survival, navigation, and rescue work—were so dedicated that they had paid for their own specialized training and even raised the money to buy communications equipment. Their efforts were rewarded when they were called out to search for a four-year-old girl who had wandered away from her family's campsite in a nearby state park. In fact, it was Martha and Opal who had found the child, earning the parents' undying gratitude, not to mention some very good publicity for the program.

Now, Rambo jumped joyfully into the passenger seat of the chief's black Chevy Impala, leaned over the console, and gave Sheila's cheek two slurpy kisses. Then he settled onto his haunches and fastened his gaze on the street ahead, to make sure that she drove home the usual way. That was his job—one of them, anyway. True to his Rottweiler nature, Rambo had a very strong sense of responsibility, and Sheila had learned that it was wise not to try to dissuade him from whatever assignments he might decide to undertake. Stubborn was his middle name.

Rambo was also big and tough-looking and there had been a time when Sheila had been afraid of him, just as she had been half afraid of the big, hard man who once owned him. That was Dan Reid, who worked undercover narcotics for the Dallas PD's Organized Crime Division while Sheila was an investigator with the department. She hadn't seen him for over a year, until, under the name Colin Fowler, he had shown up in Pecan Springs and opened a shop on the town square. The next thing she knew, he was romancing Ruby, one of her two best friends.

The situation got complicated in a hurry. Sheila felt she ought to warn Ruby about Dan's freelance love-'em-and-leave-'em habits, which she understood all too well from their own intimate, intense, and brief love affair. But she suspected that Dan was in Pecan Springs on some sort of official undercover assignment, and she didn't feel she could explain to Ruby how she had known him or reveal his real identity.

Then, just as she was deciding that she had to come clean, she didn't have to, because Dan had been murdered. It had taken some doing, but Sheila (with some help from China) had caught his killer and snagged the shipment of drugs that he'd been tracking. Ruby inherited the proceeds from Dan's sizeable insurance policy and a hefty hazardous-duty payment. And Sheila inherited Dan's Rottweiler, who turned out to be a well-mannered, well-trained drug-sniffing dog. In the long run, she thought, it was all for the best. Rambo liked to boss her around but he was far more devoted and loyal and uncritical than Dan Reid had ever been. And she always knew where he was when she needed him.

As Sheila pulled out of the parking lot behind the police station, the radio on her dash crackled into life. It was Bartlett, saying that he'd reached the Pecan Street address and was setting up the scene. She turned right on Crockett and a couple of blocks later, stopped in front of Cavette's Market, a small family-owned shop with wooden bins and wicker baskets of locally grown fruits and veggies lined up under the sidewalk awning. She rolled down the windows a couple of inches and left Rambo to guard the Impala (not that anybody would be stupid enough to mess with a police car with a Rottweiler in the front seat) and went into the store. She usually made it a point to stop in one or two shops every day. It was good community relations—another part of her job. The more face time she could put in with the community, the more trust was created. And trust was a valuable commodity.

"Hello, Chief." Young Mr. Cavette—nearly seventy and bald as an onion—put a hand on his back as he straightened up from a basket of acorn squash he was putting out on the produce counter. His father, old Mr. Cavette, who was perched behind the old-fashioned cash register, had recently celebrated his ninetieth birthday. Junior, in his forties and the youngest Mr. Cavette, made deliveries on his red motorbike. Sheila always had the feeling that the shop and all three of its owners ought to be registered as historical landmarks.

"Hello, Mr. Cavette," Sheila said, picking up a wire basket. "How's it going today?"

"'Bout as good as expected when you get to my age," old Mr. Cavette wheezed from his stool. "But it's allus good when you can get up and get your pants on in the mornin'."

Young Mr. Cavette raised both scrawny eyebrows. "Met that new gal o' yours this morning, Chief. Real nice, she is."

"New gal?" Sheila picked up a bottle of wine and scanned the label. Texas wine, local winery. "Oh, you must mean Officer Kidder. Stopped in to say hello, did she?"

Taking the rookies around to meet the local merchants had been Sergeant Clarke's idea. Sheila liked and supported it. The drop-in visits looked spontaneous and casual, but they served two purposes: introducing the merchants to the new officer and giving the rookie a look into the stores and shops. From her own street experience, Sheila knew that prior knowledge came in handy when an officer had to respond to a burglar alarm on a dark, rainy night. Most of the alarms were false. It was the one that wasn't that could get you killed. PSPD had not lost an officer in her time as chief. She wanted to keep it that way.

"Kidder." Young Mr. Cavette pursed his lips deliberately. "That's the one. Nice smile. A real looker, too. But if you don't mind me sayin' so, Chief, she's just a little thing. I gotta wonder how she's gonna handle a drunk cowboy in a dark alley."

Sheila chuckled wryly. Every woman cop got the dark-alley question, over and over again, in a dozen different forms. How would she deal with a rabid gorilla, a seven-foot seaman, a three-hundred-pound sumo wrestler, all of them drunk or high on crack? There was no point in getting your hackles up. It was just something that every civilian (and some male cops, as well) had to ask. She had developed a stock answer.

"I pity the drunk cowboy," she said with a laugh. "Officer Kidder has some pretty convincing take-down moves." For good measure, she added, "She was first in her class in Defensive Tactics at the academy. We're glad to have her on the force." To the wine in her basket, she added a package of fresh ravioli and a jar of tomato sauce and the makings for a spinach salad—tonight's supper for herself. For Rambo, she picked up a pound of beef liver and a package of dog treats. Old Mr. Cavette checked her out and she paid the bill.

"Y'all give us a call if you need anything," she called as she headed for the door.

"Hope we won't have to," young Mr. Cavette said. "But if we do, be sure and send that young'un. I'd like to see some of them moves."

Back in the Impala, still chuckling, Sheila looked at the clock on the dash. It was five thirty and by now, Bartlett had secured the scene and begun his investigation. She opened the package and gave Rambo a treat, then started the car. Driving slowly, she headed north up Guadalupe, through the hills just to the east of the CTSU campus, above the river.

Pecan Springs was located on the long-inactive Balcones Fault, where eons ago, a series of earthquakes had produced a palisade of limestone cliffs with springs of clear, cold water at their feet. To the west of the palisade rose the rugged Texas Hill Country, famous for its upland string of spring- and rain-fed lakes cupped like blue gems in the rolling limestone-and-cedar hills. To the east, on the other side of I-35 and stretching all the way to the Gulf coast, lay the flat, well-watered lands of the Blackland Prairie: fertile farmland once upon a time, littered now with dozens of sprawling real-estate tracts and shopping malls.

The town had been settled in the late 1840s by German colonists, about the same time as New Braunfels and Fredericksburg. It lay halfway between Austin and San Antonio. As far as Sheila was concerned, this meant that they got the spillover of the crime—mostly drug related—that lapped like a dirty wave along the I-35 corridor, as well as up from the border and north as far as Dallas. But a town didn't have to be centrally located these days to feel the current of drug crime. It was everywhere, all the time. And that wasn't just a cop's paranoia talking. It was a fact.

But this neighborhood had the look and feel of a safe and pleasant enclave, with genteel Victorian houses aging gracefully under arching live oak trees in large, well-kept yards bright with blooming crepe myrtle and roses. On the interstate to the east, the rush-hour traffic was as slow as molasses in January, road rage tempers hot as July firecrackers. But here, there were more people than cars on the street and everybody moved slowly: young moms pushing baby strollers on the sidewalk; a pair of girls walking arm-in-arm down the street; older people rocking on their porches, digging in their flower beds, deadheading their roses. One old gray-haired guy even paused, leaned on his rake, and waved cheerfully at the chief's car as it cruised up the street.

Sheila waved back, thinking what a pretty neighborhood this was. A genuinely residential neighborhood, too, where many folks actually lived full-time in their houses and where "neighborhood watch" meant what it said: neighbors looking out for neighbors, not just for themselves. It wasn't the kind of place where the residents left for work at dawn and smash-and-grab burglars pulled up in their vans, kicked in the back doors, and hauled out the loot, secure in the knowledge that there was nobody at home to see them.

Not the kind of neighborhood where people killed themselves.

Except.

Except that Sheila saw the daily crime reports, and knew that the usual human passions—anger, hate, fear, greed, lust, jealousy, despair—lurked behind many of the well-kept gardens and cheerful wreaths and attractive facades. She knew that a fraud victim lived in the two-story house on the right, the one with the serious roof damage. A scam artist had agreed to repair the roof and made off with the owner's thirty-five-hundred-dollar "deposit." A couple of blocks away, an eighty-year-old woman had become the victim of repeated elder abuse: her abuser was her daughter, who lived with her. The old woman was now in a nursing home and the daughter was in prison. That pretty gray house on the corner, the one with the late-blooming roses in front and the autumn wreath on the door? The wife had reported two domestic violence incidents in one week there, and the husband was under a restraining order. And just a block down and a block over, in an upscale house with a pool in the backyard: an attempted teen suicide—a girl who had been bullied at school. Luckily, the mother had come home from work early. She'd found her daughter before it was too late. A pretty neighborhood, yes, if you only looked at the facades.

Sheila made a left onto Pecan, suddenly conscious that she envied Detective Jack Bartlett. Of course, there probably wasn't much involved in this investigation, since it was a suicide. But if there were, she would love to join him, maybe even team up with him. It would be a pleasure to get out from behind the damned desk and do some serious fieldwork, instead of simply tending to the endless crop of memos and reports. And with the sudden envy came the recollection of the heady, almost joyful rush she always felt when she knew she had righted a wrong, when she apprehended someone who had broken the law. When she brought to justice a man or woman who had inflicted pain on a weaker, less powerful, more vulnerable person.

Brought to justice. For her, the phrase had never been empty, not just one of those things you tossed off without thinking what it meant. Those three words had always held a profound significance, always made her feel that what she was doing wasn't an ordinary job. It was *important.* She was helping to preserve order in an otherwise disorderly and chaotic world. She was enforcing the laws that bound people together, that preserved their rights and upheld their obligations—although the law was never as simple and clear-cut out there in the world as it seemed in the criminal code.

And on top of all that, there was the pleasure of collecting odd bits of seemingly unrelated information, assembling and reassembling the pieces like a complicated jigsaw puzzle, until finally you could see the whole picture come together, you could say, *Yes! Yes, that's it! That's the answer!* to the only and obvious conclusion.

Sheila's hands tightened on the steering wheel and she took a deep breath. What was stopping her from teaming up with Bartlett on this one? Nothing really, was there? And with Hardin off fishing in the Gulf for the duration, this might be the only chance she'd have. Why not go for it?

Then she made herself loosen her grip. Not a good idea. Since this was likely a suicide, the investigation would be limited. Anyway, it was Bartlett's investigation. It was her job to make him look good, not steal the limelight or intrude on his turf, the way Hardin often did.

No. She would put in a brief appearance, take a quick look at the scene (mostly to remind herself of what real, on-the-ground fieldwork was all about), and then let Bartlett get on with his work while she went home and had her supper. But first, she needed to get Rambo settled. So instead of stopping at the scene, she made a right at the next cross street, a left onto Hickory, and another left into her driveway.

The house where she and Blackie were currently living was an older two-bedroom, two-bath rental that Ruby Wilcox had found for them on Hickory Street, on the other side of the alley and a couple of doors down from Ruby's house on Pecan. It had a large yard with a dog run and shelter for Rambo, which was what had decided the matter as far as Sheila was concerned. She had loved her little, low-upkeep frame house on the west side of town, but it was too small for two people and a big dog, so she'd put it on the market and (luckily) had sold it within a couple of weeks. Blackie had a big house with a barn and thirty-five acres, and Sheila would have loved to live there. But it was a half-hour drive from town, and her job meant being on call twenty-four-seven. So he had rented the house to a CTSU faculty member and kept the barn and pastures for his horses. The two of them spent time out there when they had it to spend. Sheila was learning to ride, and Rambo loved having plenty of open space to run.

Sheila let Rambo into the fenced backyard to take care of his business while she went into the kitchen to get his dog food, then put him in his run with his dinner, which he happily attacked. She briefly debated whether to walk across the alley to the crime scene but decided it would be better to use the chief's car. It would let the neighbors know that PSPD was on the job—another helpful bit of community relations.

She drove back around the block onto Pecan, checked the street number for 1117, then pulled in to the curb behind two black-and-whites; a paramedic vehicle, lights flashing; and a white van with *Adams County Crime Scene Team* on the side. She regarded the vehicles with raised-eyebrow interest. Bartlett must have found a reason to call out the county crime-scene unit, which was under the authority of the sheriff and shared by PSPD and the smaller municipalities in the county.

On the other side of the street, she saw Maude Porterfield's Ford F-150 pickup truck. Adams County operated under the Inquest Law, an old segment of the Texas Code of Criminal Procedure that conferred on justices of the peace the responsibility of determining the cause of death in cases of accident, homicide, or suicide, or where a death occurred under suspicious circumstances. Larger counties were required to operate under the newer medical-examiners law, which—as Judge Porterfield jocularly put it—took the JPs out of the cause-of-death business. Sheila had the feeling that Maude secretly liked being in the cause-of-death business. It kept her abreast of what was going on in Pecan Springs.

Neighbors were gathered in two or three self-conscious knots on either side of the street, trying not to look too curious as they watched the official comings and goings at the two-story frame house. Whatever had happened here, it was obviously a neighborhood event—one that people would be talking about for quite a while. Sheila took another look. She didn't see Hark Hibler's car or anybody from the *Enterprise*. And Pecan Springs was forty-five minutes from both Austin and San Antonio. The TV stations didn't send a camera unless there was a major disaster. A suicide didn't qualify.

Sheila was opening the car door when she thought of something else. Unsnapping her briefcase, she took out a small red notebook and a pen. She glanced at her watch, opened the notebook to a fresh page and noted the address, the date, and the time. She didn't stop to ask herself why she was doing this.

As she got out of the car, a commotion rippled through

the onlookers. "Hey, it's the chief!" a man in the nearest group said. In his sixties, with thinning hair, he wore a pink-and-green Hawaiian print shirt and red flip-flops. His beer belly bulged out like a beach ball over green polyester pants. He raised his voice. "Hey, Chief, what's going on back there? What's the scoop?"

"I just got here," Sheila replied in a friendly tone. Community relations, she reminded herself. It was good for citizens to see their police officers at work. "I haven't checked with Detective Bartlett yet. He's in charge." She went over to the group and put out her hand. "What have you heard, sir?"

Green Trousers grasped her hand briefly. His was sweating. "Just that somebody's dead in the kitchen." He swiped his hand across his shirt front and pointed across the street. "Mr. Kirk, is what I heard."

"Lawrence Kirk," an older woman said excitedly. "He's really nice—came over and fixed my grandson's computer when it got this really terrible infection. I live right next door." She pointed, her tight blue curls bobbing importantly over her ears. "I was pickin' the last of my spaghetti squash in the backyard when Ruby Wilcox's sister went in the kitchen and found him. Really, you'd have thought somebody shot *her*. Run out of the door and fell right down the steps."

Ruby Wilcox's sister? Ramona Donahue? That was a surprise. Sheila was about to speak, but Green Trousers beat her to it.

"Hate to think stuff like this can happen in our neighborhood," he said.

"What're you talkin' about, Joe?" another woman demanded. "This kinda stuff happens everywhere. Why, somebody lifted my mother's wristwatch right out of the drawer beside her bed. In the nursing home!" She slanted a look at Sheila and added accusingly, "Cops never did find out who did it."

"I'm sorry, ma'am," Sheila said. She wanted to add, *Tell your mother not to put her valuables where somebody on the staff can be tempted*. But she only said, in a regretful tone, "We do the best we can, but we can't clear every theft."

"Betcha *CSI* would've solved it," the woman muttered.

"We don't have a *CSI* budget," Sheila replied smoothly. It was another one of her practiced phrases. "You might speak to the city council about that." She turned to the next-door neighbor. "Mr. Kirk fixed your grandson's computer?" she asked. "Is he by any chance the owner of Kirk's Computer Sales and Service?"

"That's him," the woman said. "But he wouldn't take any money when I offered to pay. Said he was just being a good neighbor, which I appreciated. A very nice young man." She pulled down her mouth. "So sad."

The green-trousered man was clearly turning something over in his mind. "O'course, people do go a little crazy sometimes." He squinted at Sheila and lowered his voice. "Don't mean to tell tales outta school, Chief, but you might oughtta have a little heart-to-heart with Sam Schulz, at 1119." He pointed to the house just west of the Kirks'. "He's bore a grudge against Mr. Kirk ever since him and his wife moved in there. About the property line, you know."

"The property line?" Sheila asked. She took out her notebook. Kirk's Computer Sales and Service was the business that George Timms had broken into. A coincidence—or something else?

"That's Schulz with no *t*," Green Trousers said, pleased to see that she was writing in her notebook. "It's the line between their places, y'see. The Kirks' garage is two feet over on Sam's property. Happened by accident, back, oh, forty, fifty years ago, when John Jenson built the place. Kirk wanted to buy two feet on that side to make it right, but ol' Schulzie, he won't sell. Stubborn as all git-out."

"Thank you," Sheila said, writing down *Kirk's Com-*

puter Sales and Service. She added *Garage, Schulz, property line dispute.* "And your name, sir?" She'd pass it along to Bartlett.

"Al Peters," the man said, and gave her his address and phone number. He jerked his thumb at the woman who wanted *CSI* to investigate the theft of her mother's watch. "I live next door to Mrs. Howard here. At 1118 Pecan."

"And yours, ma'am?" she asked the blue-haired neighbor.

"Jane Jessup. I'm at 1115. But Mr. Schulz didn't have anything to do with it, Chief. Ruby Wilcox's sister told me Mr. Kirk definitely killed himself. With a gun." She shook her head in utter disbelief, tears welling up in her eyes. "Such a nice man. Clever, too. Why would he go and do something awful like that? I just don't understand it."

"Maybe it had to do with the divorce, Jane," another woman said, dropping her voice. She was pudgy, with thick ankles. She was wearing an apron, as if she had been interrupted in the middle of cooking supper.

Jane Jessup's eyes got big. "You don't suppose he killed himself over *that*?" she asked. "Oh, that would be terrible!"

"Divorce?" Sheila said.

"The Kirks," the woman with thick ankles replied. "I just found out about it myself, yesterday morning at our quilting club. Texas Stars. That's our name. After the pattern, you know." She scowled. "Seems the wife has a boyfriend." The scowl deepend. "The monkey business these young people get up to."

"Mildred," Jane said in a warning tone. "It's not good to gossip."

"Your name?" Sheila asked the woman who had mentioned the divorce, and wrote *Divorce, wife's boyfriend.*

"Mildred Ewell. I'm 1114."

Sheila wrote it down. "Thank you, Ms. Ewell. And Ms. Jessup, too. If we need any additional information, we'll get in touch."

"That's *Mrs.* Ewell," the woman said sharply. To Jane,

she added, "If anything gets my dander up, Jane, it's this *Ms.* business. Sounds like bees buzzin'."

A couple of kids had come along and were peering into one of the patrol units. The girl looked up and her eyes widened. "Hey, you're the chief! I saw you on TV the other night." Her companion wolf-whistled, low, then blushed bright red and ducked his head.

Sheila put her notebook and pen into her shirt pocket. "It's okay," she said to the whistler. "I'll take that as a compliment." She lifted her hand to the group, adding, "Thank you all very much. One of our officers will probably be talking with you. If you think of anything else, please mention it." She was sure Bartlett would assign an officer to conduct a neighborhood canvass, given the identity of the dead man.

"Don't forget what I said about ol' Schulzie," Green Trousers cautioned. "I'd hate to see that fella get away with murder."

Jane Jessup gasped. "Murder! You don't mean that, Al!"

"You damn betcha I do," Green Trousers said grimly.

Sheila turned away to cross the street. Crime scenes were chaotic. The first person on the scene, even trained first responders, sometimes got the facts wrong. She had seen cases where the dead man turned out to be a dead woman. A gunshot death might be reported as an accident or suicide, but investigation proved it to be a homicide. A crime scene—and a suicide scene was a crime scene—was always a work in progress, and the investigators were constantly revising, building new theories as new information came in.

So was Kirk's death a suicide or something else? Was there a connection between what happened here and the break-in at his business? In spite of herself, she could feel the excitement that always ran like an electrical current through the first phases of any investigation, could feel the adrenaline surging, the questions—already, a great many

questions—pushing, nudging, shoving, demanding answers. She checked her watch. By now, George Timms
should have showed up at the station to surrender and be
booked, but she still hadn't gotten the word. Why the delay?
What was going on here?

"Chief Dawson! Hi!"

Sheila looked up. Ruby Wilcox was standing in front of
the yellow plastic police tape strung across the driveway.
She was wearing one of her outrageous outfits, some sort
of gauzy striped top that made her look like a butterfly with
wilted wings. China Bayles was with her, dressed in her
familiar working clothes: a green Thyme and Seasons
T-shirt, jeans, sandals.

And Ruby's sister, Ramona Donahue, the woman who—
according to the next-door neighbor—had discovered
Kirk's body. Sheila had met Ramona the week before at a
picnic that she and Blackie had attended in Ruby's backyard. She had Ruby's frizzy red hair and freckles, although
the resemblance ended there. She was short and as round as
a dumpling, where Ruby was tall and string-bean slender.
She was wearing a white short-sleeved blouse with a silky
purple scarf and gray pants. But one knee of her pants was
shredded, her face was tear-stained and blotchy, and she
was gulping back sobs.

"Everybody okay?" Sheila asked, glancing at Ramona
but directing her question to China. "What happened here,
China?"

China, a former criminal attorney, was the logical one
to ask. Not that Sheila had any love for defense lawyers—
cops didn't, generally speaking. The justice system was
adversarial, with law enforcement on one side, defense lawyers on the other, and a big empty field in between where
the facts were always in dispute, like a soccer ball kicked
back and forth by two competing teams. China Bayles,
however, was not your average defense lawyer. She was
smart and observant and quick-witted, but she was also

sympathetic to cops. She was married to one—a former cop, anyway—and she understood how they worked. Sheila knew that she'd get a more organized story from China than Ramona.

China answered the question tersely. "This is the Kirks' house. Larry Kirk and his wife Dana. Ramona found Larry dead in the kitchen, about an hour ago. Gunshot wound. She phoned the shop. Ruby and I told her to call nine-one-one and wait here until somebody came."

"I see." Sheila glanced at Ramona. "Hello, Ramona. Has somebody taken your statement yet?"

"Yes," Ruby answered for her sister. She lifted her butterfly arms and let them fall with a whoosh. "China and I were right here when she did it. Took the statement, I mean."

"It was a policewoman," Ramona said. "Sergeant Clarke."

"A police officer," Ruby corrected her. "They're not called policewomen these days."

"Whatever," Ramona said testily. "She wrote everything down, just the way I said it. I'm supposed to go to the station to sign the statement tomorrow." She whimpered. "My knee hurts. I fell down the back steps."

"I'm sorry," Sheila said. "Would you like one of the medics to take a look at it?"

Ramona shook her head. "It'll be all right," she muttered. "But thanks."

"Tell her how you happened to find the body," Ruby said, nudging her sister.

Ramona sucked in a deep breath. "I . . . I was on my way to an appointment. I stopped to return a dish that Larry left at Ruby's house the night of the picnic. I was thinking I'd just put it on the back steps, where he would see it when he got home from work. But then I noticed the kitchen door standing open, so I decided I'd just go in and put the dish on the counter. That's when I saw him. On the kitchen floor.

I never imagined—" She closed her eyes and swallowed whatever she was about to say.

Sheila understood and sympathized. People saw death in the movies and on television all the time, but that was remote, staged, unreal. Up close, death—easy death or violent death, accident, suicide, homicide—was something else altogether. It was final, absolute, unconditional. Nobody, not even the most experienced cop, could be completely blasé about it.

"Did you notice anything else?" she asked. "A gun, a note? Did you touch anything?"

"There's a gun in his hand." Ramona opened her eyes. "There's blood and beer all over the floor. I think he'd been sitting at the table. The chair had fallen over. There's a laptop on the table. If there was a note, I didn't see it—but I didn't look. I touched the door knob, I guess, to push the door open wider." With another little whimper, she retreated to the comfort of her sister's shoulder. "I just don't understand how a person could do that to himself."

"Thanks, Ramona," Sheila said. "We appreciate your help. You'll be around if we have any more questions?"

"Yes," Ramona said, her voice muffled. "I'm staying with Ruby for a while longer."

"For another week," Ruby put in. "Maybe two." She added, "Ramona has started looking for her own apartment. And a business opportunity." She smoothed her sister's hair. "It's taking longer than she thought to get over . . . well, things. But she'll be back on her feet in no time."

"I'm sure she will," Sheila said, although she thought a week or two was optimistic. Ramona looked like a whipped puppy, and Ruby was a comforting, reliable refuge. Too comfortable, maybe. "Thanks again." She lifted the yellow plastic tape to duck under it.

"Chief, wait, please." China took several steps forward, then spoke in a lower voice. "There's something you should know, Sheila. Larry Kirk installed some inventory software for me about a year ago. He also helped me remodel the Thyme and Seasons website so people could order on-line. I liked working with him, and we got to be email buddies, sort of. I know him—knew him—pretty well."

Sheila wasn't surprised by this. Pecan Springs was a small town, and China had been in business here for eight or nine years. She knew a lot of people—customers, fellow merchants and businesspeople, members of the gardening community. It was understandable that she should know the dead man.

Sheila gave China a closer look. "There's something else?" she asked, knowing that there was.

"Yeah." China looked down. "Last Friday, Larry emailed me that he was being hassled. *Stalked* was the word he used. He didn't go into detail, but I got the idea that this was something that had been going on for a while. He wanted to know what his options were, legally. I told him that if he knew the stalker, he should go to the courthouse and file a restraining order. If he didn't, and if he felt seriously harassed, he should go to the police." She looked up, and Sheila saw a grimace of pain and guilt cross her face. "I really feel bad about this, Sheila. His email got buried in my inbox. I didn't answer it until today. Until just a little while ago, in fact." Her voice dropped. "By that time, he was probably dead."

A stalker. Sheila felt that jolt again, that electricity. Something going on here, something important. She took out her notebook and pen. "Did he identify the stalker? Describe the stalking? Give you any details?"

China shook her head. "It was pretty bare-bones. No name, no where-when-how, just the bottom line. I can get you a copy of the exchange. You'll probably also find it in his email, with my answer." She paused, then sighed. "Something else you might want to know, Chief. Larry and his wife Dana are—were—in the process of getting a divorce. It's been messy."

"Ah." The divorce again. Sheila was making notes. "Messy how?"

"Judging from what Larry told me over the past couple of months, there were both property and personal issues. He seemed pretty much okay about it, though. He didn't like what was happening, but he was dealing with it." She put her head to one side, studying Sheila, anticipating the next question. "I doubt if the stalking and the divorce are related—Dana doesn't strike me as the vindictive type. And Larry didn't seem overwhelmingly distraught. Certainly not suicidal. Just irritated about the divorce."

"You said there were both property *and* personal issues," Sheila prompted.

"He was thinking he might have to sell part of the business, since it was Dana's money that originally capitalized it. He was hoping to find somebody who would buy out her interest and give him an option to buy it back when he could scramble the money together." She nodded toward the house. "And there's this place, as well. He and Dana bought it five or six years ago, at the top of the market. She wants her share. He was concerned that the way things are these days, it might be hard to sell for what they've got in it."

There was always a painful story behind every divorce, especially when property issues were involved. There could be some hard feelings that China hadn't picked up on. Maybe Dana Kirk—or her lawyer—had hired a private investigator to dig up some dirt that would give her more leverage in the property settlement. Maybe the PI was the stalker Kirk had spotted.

"The two of them were still living together?" Sheila asked.

"I don't think so," China replied. "I don't know where she's living. Larry said he was trying to work it out with her—the property thing, I mean. I got the idea that Dana wanted out of the marriage more than he did. Larry hinted a couple of times that she was involved with somebody else."

"Did he say who?" Sheila asked.

China shook her head. "I don't know the story, but Ruby and Dana are friends. I'm sure Ruby knows. I'll find out for you."

Sheila paused, then asked, "Did Kirk say anything to you about the break-in at his place of business? It happened a few days ago."

"He didn't mention it to me. But McQuaid read about it in the *Enterprise* and told me about it." China raised an eyebrow. "Has there been an arrest?" She didn't ask, *Do you think the break-in is somehow related to Kirk's death?* But Sheila knew she was thinking it.

"We're expecting an arrest this afternoon." Sheila glanced at her watch. "Actually, any minute now."

"Oh, yeah? Who?"

Sheila didn't answer. Instead, she asked, "Did Kirk work at home?"

China glanced at her, understanding. "At home, at his shop, both. The company does computer repairs, installations, and so on. Larry had several guys working for him."

Sheila nodded. The names of Kirk's employees were in Bartlett's report on the break-in investigation. If it became relevant, she'd have another look.

China stepped back. "I saw Detective Bartlett while I was waiting here with Ramona, but I didn't volunteer any of this information. Didn't want to distract him. I figured he was going to be busy, especially after he brought in the county crime-scene unit." She paused, her eyebrow raised again, and Sheila knew that she understood the significance of that. "But if you guys have questions, I'm available." She pushed her hands into the pockets of her jeans, tilting her head and smiling a little. "How come I haven't seen Deputy Chief Hardin?"

"Hardin's gone fishing," Sheila replied, mirroring China's

smile. Once, she had broken her own rule—never talk shop with friends—and complained bitterly to China about Hardin's attitude. She took a breath. "I'm on this investigation with Bartlett."

There. She'd said it.

"Glad to hear that, Sheila." China nodded approvingly. "It'll do you good to be away from the desk for a day or two. Get out in the field—get a load of the stuff your officers have to put up with every day from us ungrateful civilians." She flashed Sheila a crooked grin. "Bubba Harris did that, you know. Not often enough, but sometimes. People liked it when they saw him doing something other than administrative stuff."

Sheila heard what China was telling her. She pocketed her notebook. "Thanks again, China. I appreciate it. We'll be in touch."

She ducked under the yellow tape and went up the drive toward the garage. She was almost there when her cell phone offered its cheerful digital chirp. She flipped it open, expecting Dispatch with the notification of Timms' surrender and arrest.

But it wasn't Mary Lou. The caller's soft, good-old-boy drawl was colored with irritation. "Charlie Lipman, here, Chief. I want to know where he is."

"Where who is?" Sheila asked warily. Timms was a no-show?

"Aw, come on, Chief. Don't play that game with me. If you've booked my client in my absence—although that was *not* the process we agreed to—I want to talk to him." His voice became hard. "*Now.*"

"If it's George Timms you're looking for, counselor, I don't know a thing about him. I understood from Deputy Chief Hardin that he was supposed to surrender—" She glanced at her watch and was surprised to see how late it was. "More than an hour ago. Have you tried his home?"

Lipman grunted. "His home, his cell phone, his business, the golf club, his party place in the Hill Country. If your guys have him, cough him up, damn it. I don't want him talkin' to y'all unless I'm in the room. And no media. Got that? Timms is not your average—"

"Mr. Lipman," Sheila broke in sharply. "Your client is overdue for surrender, booking, and arraignment. We do not have him. Since you can't produce him—since you can't even locate him—we'll be glad to help you out. I'm putting out an APB."

Lipman softened his tone. "Now, now, let's not be hasty, Chief. As I said, we don't want any media. You folks put out that bulletin, Hark Hibler'll jump on it faster'n a rooster on a big ol' juicy grasshopper. Let's jes' downplay this for a few more hours. He's bound to turn up." Charlie Lipman was bidialectal. He talked Texan when he was hanging out at Bean's Bar and Grill, presenting a case to a Texas jury, or trying to appear harmless. Otherwise, he employed the vocabulary of a Harvard law professor and the standard English of a network news reporter.

"Nothing doing, counselor," Sheila said firmly. "You hear from your client, you let me know, pronto. And that means *me*, personally." She paused and added emphatically, "You got that?"

"Got it," Lipman growled, and hesitated. "Maybe something else goin' on, huh? Related to Timms' case? If so, I need to know."

"I'm not at liberty to say," Sheila replied.

There was a brief silence while Lipman considered this. "Yeah. Well, what's happened to Hardin? He's not returnin' my calls. Where is he?"

"Gone fishing," Sheila replied shortly, and broke the connection. She called Dispatch and ordered the APB on Timms' vehicles.

She stood for a moment, thinking. At this point, all they had was the first report of a suicide. There was no way to know whether this incident was in any way related to Timms' alleged break-in at Kirk's place of business the previous week or to the stalker Kirk had mentioned to China. But Sheila had long ago stopped believing in coincidences, and she wanted to see Timms in custody as soon as possible.

Was there a connection?

What was it?

Chapter Four

Uncaria tomentosa is another hold-fast herb with the folk name of cat's claw, or Uña de gato. This woody vine is native to the Amazon rain forest and other tropical areas of South and Central America. Like a cat, it uses its sharp, hooked-shaped horns to cling to the trees it climbs, often more than twenty feet.

For over two thousand years, the Ashaninka rain forest people of Peru have used the inner bark of the stems and roots of this hold-fast herb as an immune enhancer, a contraceptive and abortifacient, as well as a treatment for a wide variety of diseases: gastric ulcers, diarrhea, gonorrhea, arthritis and rheumatism, intestinal disorders, diabetes, and cancer.

China Bayles
"Herbs That Hold Fast"
Pecan Springs Enterprise

Still thinking about Larry Kirk's death, I watched Sheila walk away, then turned back to Ruby and Ramona. Ramona was wiping her eyes and sniffling. Ruby was rubbing Ramona's back and murmuring sisterly words.

"Look," I said. "This has been pretty rough for everybody." It was the understatement of the week. I took a deep breath. "Ruby, how about if we go to your house and have a cup of tea?"

Ramona brightened. "Or supper? I made corn chowder with sausage. Plenty for all of us. And we could have a salad."

Ruby gave her sister a hug and dropped her arm, her gauzy sleeve fluttering. "There are peaches, too, so there's shortcake for dessert." She glanced at me. "McQuaid and the kids are spending the evening in Seguin, aren't they? You'll join us, China?"

"Thanks," I said gratefully. "I'd like that."

To tell the truth, I didn't want to be by myself just now. Larry Kirk had been a friend—and a reliable helper. He was a jack-of-all-computer-trades. He had repaired my ailing printer, added more memory to my computer, and taken over my faltering website, making it not only attractive, but functional. And no matter how busy he was with his business, he always found time to update the shop's website and answer my questions without making me feel like a totally incompetent person with a brain the size of a BB. I was going to miss him. A lot, damn it. And I couldn't help feeling responsible. Maybe the stalking had nothing to do with what had happened. But maybe it had. If I'd answered his email earlier—

I shoved my hands into the pockets of my jeans. "I can't believe he's dead," I said, mostly to myself. We started to walk down the driveway to the street. "What a horrible thing."

"Ghastly," Ramona said. She wrinkled her nose. "The kitchen reeked of beer. There was beer all over the floor. I guess he knocked it off the table when he . . . when he shot himself."

I cleared my throat. "How do you know that's what happened? That he shot himself, I mean."

She turned to stare at me. "Well, because of the gun. It was right there in his hand."

In his hand? I thought. If he had fallen from the chair, knocking the chair over, wouldn't the fall have dislodged the gun? "Where was he shot?" I asked. "In the head, the chest?"

Ramona pressed her lips together. "There was a round hole above his temple. And a lot of blood." She shuddered. "Do we have to talk about it, China? It's too horrible."

We reached the sidewalk and turned toward Ruby's. Suddenly, a cute, athletic blonde broke away from the nearest clump of neighbors and dashed toward us, a journalist's steno pad in one hand. It was Jessica Nelson, a reporter for the *Enterprise*. Last spring, as an intern, Jessica had scored a big story when she foiled her own abduction and helped to solve a murder, gaining national notoriety as the Seven Iron Slugger. Now, she's finishing grad school and working part-time at the newspaper. I wasn't surprised to see her here. She shows up whenever anybody whispers the words *breaking news*.

"China!" Jessica exclaimed. "And Ruby! So great to see you again!" She put out her hand to Ramona. "Hi. I'm Jessica Nelson. I write for the local newspaper. You're Ramona Donahue?"

Ramona nodded wordlessly.

"I understand that you discovered Mr. Kirk's body." Jessica flipped her steno pad to a new page. "Can you tell me about it?" She glanced down at the shredded knee of Ramona's pants. "Gosh, I hope you're not hurt. I heard that you fell down the back steps."

"That's right." Confronted by the possibility of media attention, Ramona forgot that she hadn't wanted to talk about it. "What would you like to know?"

"Stop." I put up my hand. "Jessica, you know better. Ms. Donahue isn't talking to you until Chief Dawson says she can."

"Aw, come on, China," Jessica wheedled. "Mr. Hibler

says we're going with a front-page story on this. All I want is a little human interest. I'm not asking for state secrets."

Ramona frowned at me. "Really, China, I don't see why you're being so mean. It's not—"

"I'm being mean in order to keep Jessica out of Sheila Dawson's doghouse. She can have all the human interest she wants, *after* the police release." I smiled at Jessica. "Check back tomorrow, Jess. And in the meantime, check with the chief."

Jessica sighed. "You're a hard woman, China Bayles."

"You think I'm hard?" I chuckled wryly. "Try crossing Sheila Dawson."

"Actually, I've already got quite a few nice little bits," Jessica said defiantly. "I talked to the next-door neighbor who was picking her squash when Ms. Donahue discovered the body. That's human interest, don't you think? She said she was going to make a casserole for her nephew, who was coming over for supper." She flipped a page. "I also talked to the old lady who heard the gunshot. That's what she thought it was, anyway."

"A gunshot?" I asked sharply. This was news to me. "Who? When?"

Jessica peered at her notes. "Mrs. Wauer," she said. "Ethel W-a-u-e-r. A sweet little old thing. She says she heard it just before two o'clock." She began to read. "'I was giving Oodles a bath—I have to wear my raincoat because he shakes water all over me, and of course then I have to mop the floor. The bathroom window was open because when Oodles is wet, he doesn't always smell real sweet, which was how come I happened to hear it.'" She frowned. "I guess I should have asked Mrs. Wauer about Oodles."

"He's a miniature white poodle," Ruby volunteered. "I know, because Ethel Wauer lives next door to me. Between me and the squash lady."

"Oh, really?" Jessica was scribbling. "So it's you, Mrs.

Wauer and Oodles, Mrs. Jessup and her squash, and the Kirks, in that order. Right?" Ruby nodded and Jessica paused, looking back at her notes. "Mrs. Wauer said she thought at first that the noise was a car backfiring or maybe a door slamming, so she didn't think anything of it. But Oodles began to bark like crazy and—"

"Oodles barks like crazy at everything," Ruby said. "Oodles barks at cars, skateboards, airplanes, lawnmowers, and the garbage truck. I'm sure there are people on this block who wish somebody would shoot *him*. That's off the record, Jessica," she added hastily.

"Oh, pooh," Jessica pouted. "But I'll leave it out if you insist, Ruby." She turned back to Ramona. "Now then, Ms. Donahue. How did you happen to go to the Kirks' house this afternoon?"

I intervened. "That's enough, Jessica. Why don't you give Ms. Donahue your card? She can call you when this conversation is appropriate."

"China, you are such a spoilsport." With a disappointed sigh, Jessica took out a card and handed it over.

"Thank you, Ms. Nelson." Ramona flipped an icy look in my direction. "I'll be glad to talk to you whenever. You can bring a photographer, too." She touched her hair. "Just be sure to give me a little notice."

"Thanks, Ms. Donahue," Jessica said with a grin. "I really appreciate it." She turned to me. "China—"

"And that information about Mrs. Wauer and the gunshot—you need to be sure it gets to the police before it gets to the front page of the *Enterprise*. There might be nothing to it, or it might help establish the time of death. Okay?"

"Okay." Jessica raised her hand in a wave, turned, and jogged off in pursuit of more human interest.

The little knots of onlookers had begun to disperse as the neighbors found better things to do than hang around gawking at a flock of police and emergency vehicles that didn't seem to be going anywhere. Ramona, Ruby, and I began to walk back toward Ruby's house.

Ruby was musing over the information Jessica had given us. "Mrs. Wauer says she heard the gunshot at two o'clock. Ramona, what were you doing at two? Did you hear it?"

Ramona shook her head. "I was having a nap," she said guiltily. "I had an appointment to talk to somebody about a business opportunity, but I thought I'd lie down first. Just for a few minutes—but I fell asleep. When I finally woke up, I had to hurry and get dressed, so I wouldn't be late. And then I went to the Kirks' to take back the dish and then—"

Ruby looked at me over Ramona's head and rolled her eyes.

"And to think that while I was napping," Ramona went on in a dramatic voice, "poor Mr. Kirk was—" She stopped, shivering. "What if I had walked in on him just as he was deciding to do it? Maybe I could have stopped him. Maybe—"

"Hush, Ramona," Ruby said. "You didn't and you couldn't, so don't go making out that you're responsible. Larry Kirk was a grown-up. He was going to do whatever he was going to do."

Ruby wasn't talking to me, but I was listening, and I appreciated her advice. She was right. Even if I had answered Larry's email when I got it, likely the outcome would have been the same—which didn't make me feel any better, of course.

Ruby turned to me. "I couldn't help overhearing. It sounds like Sheila is planning to take this case herself. That's a little unusual, isn't it, China?"

"Clint Hardin went fishing," I replied, "so she's stepping in for him." I meant what I said to Sheila about getting out from behind the desk. She has done a lot for the police department since she became chief, but she has a tendency to stay in the office, almost as if she's hiding out. That's just my opinion, of course, but McQuaid shares it, I know. He'd mentioned to me that Sheila should get out on the street more often.

"That police chief," Ramona remarked thoughtfully. "She is certainly a beautiful woman. And young."

"Sheila isn't as young as she looks," I replied. "She's nearly forty."

Ruby linked her arm into her sister's. "Didn't you meet her at the picnic last week, Ramona?"

"I did. Met that hunky husband of hers, too. The one who used to be a sheriff." Curiously, she looked from Ruby to me. "How did you guys get to know her?"

"Well, let's see," I said. "Ruby and I first met Smart Cookie when she—"

"Smart Cookie?" Ramona interrupted, surprised.

"That's what China and I call her," Ruby replied. "But don't say it where her officers can hear. They wouldn't understand."

"We met her when she was the chief of the security service at CTSU," I went on. "Before that, she was deputy chief of security at the University of Texas campus in Arlington."

"No kidding." Ramona sounded impressed. "Chief of security."

"And before Arlington," I added, "she was a detective with the Dallas Police Department. She moved into campus security after she got shot for the second time. Can't say I blame her."

"Eek," Ramona said faintly. "You mean, really shot? Like, with a gun?"

We were approaching Mrs. Wauer's house. Oodles was out on the front porch, bouncing up and down behind the folding baby gate that keeps him from running out and biting passing pedestrians on the ankle. He was yapping at the top of his lungs, telling us exactly what he was going to do if we had the nerve to come within reach of his killer teeth and claws.

"Really shot," I replied, "with a gun. She doesn't like to talk about it, but I know that she almost died. She's had a long career in law enforcement—although it hasn't been an easy one. There are more women in policing than there used to be, but it's still a man's world. A woman has to be plenty tough to move into a command position in a para-military organization dominated by men, especially in a small town like Pecan Springs. A small *Texas* town."

"Doesn't sound like you're a big fan of the police," Ramona remarked wryly.

"China used to be a defense attorney," Ruby said with a laugh. "Defense attorneys hate cops."

"Defense attorneys don't hate cops," I protested, as we turned up the walk to Ruby's front porch. "They're fine with the police when the cops do what they're supposed to do, obey the law, and behave themselves. Which they don't always do, you know. There are plenty of examples of cops acting *outside* the law."

Like most other residences in the neighborhood, Ruby's two-story frame house sits in the middle of a large, shady yard. But while the other houses are traditional Victorians—which is to say that they look like dowdy old ladies on their way to a friend's funeral—Ruby's Painted Lady is nothing short of dazzling. Ruby has radically rejuvenated the old house by painting the siding, shutters, porches, and gingerbread trim with wonderfully wild color combinations: spring green, smoke gray, fuschia, and plum. The wicker furniture on the front porch is daffodil yellow, the cushions are covered in a bright red-and-green tropical print, and green-painted buckets of red geraniums march up the steps. Ruby says she knows why her house makes its next-door neighbors uncomfortable. "It's as if your grandmother painted her nails passion purple," she says, "put on fire-engine-red lipstick and mauve eye shadow, and went out dancing with a man half her age. The other houses are all jealous."

"I guess that's what I don't understand," Ramona said thoughtfully. "Chief Dawson really *is* an exception, isn't she? I mean, this is Texas, which has to have more macho males per square mile than anywhere else in the world. And she could be a fashion model. How in the world did she ever get the job?"

"Right time, right place," I replied, as Ruby opened the door and we followed her inside.

"I want to hear about it," Ramona said, heading for the stairs. "But first I have to get out of these pants. They're ruined. Excuse me."

Ruby and I went down the hall toward the kitchen. When she moved in, the house was in terrible shape, outside and in. It took months to restore the golden oak woodwork and floors. And then, being Ruby, she papered the walls in bright orange, yellow, even red, electrified with black-and-white stripes and checks and zigzags and polkadots, like a Mary Englebreit painting. *Bam. Pow. Kazaam.*

But for all this sizzling color and pattern, it's still a comfortable house, with Ruby's quilts and weavings hung on the walls, baskets and sculpture and bowls and books arranged on the shelves, with a star map painted on the dark blue living room ceiling. And the kitchen—well, a couple of years ago, Ruby grasped the decorating possibilities inherent in watermelons. She put up red-and-white striped kitchen wallpaper, added a watermelon border, and painted the table red and the four chairs green and red, with little black seeds painted on the seats. A watermelon rug, watermelon place mats, and red and green dishes. It's a picnic.

Ramona came back downstairs in jeans and a white sleeveless top and the three of us collaborated on supper.

Ruby sliced peaches for shortcake, I made a simple salad with greens from Ruby's garden, and Ramona took the lid off the slow cooker to stir the soup. While we worked, Ruby and I filled Ramona in on Sheila's back story. Actually, I was glad to be able to talk about this and get my mind off Larry's situation, which loomed like a somber cloud at the back of my mind.

"It began with a bad situation in the police department," I said, "which at the time was all male. A woman named Dolly Patterson applied for an opening as a patrol officer. She had completed three years of college, graduated from the police academy, and had four years' street patrol experience in El Paso, with excellent evaluations from her field officers. Bubba Harris—he was the chief at the time— passed her over in favor of a guy with no college, no academy, and no experience, who just happened to be the nephew of the city attorney. Ms. Patterson filed a discrimination suit and won, as anybody with a lick of sense could have predicted. Especially the city attorney."

Ramona put the lid back on the slow cooker. "But I still don't see what that has to do with—"

"At the time," Ruby said as she sliced peaches, "Sheila was serving as chief of security on the campus. She had been there only a couple of years, but during that time, she completely reorganized and upgraded the department. She started a training program, purchased new equipment, hired more people—including women and blacks—and earned a couple of national law enforcement awards."

"Do you have any fresh dill, Ruby?" I asked. "It would be nice for the salad."

"There's dill and basil in pots outside the door," Ruby said. She paused, frowning. "Do we want hot bread? I can open a can of refrigerated crescent rolls and spread them with parsley butter before I roll them up. That would be quick."

"Sounds perfect," I said. "Chives with the parsley, too, maybe? And you could grate some cheese into the butter, as well."

"Make it Parmesan," Ramona put in. "There's some in the fridge. And add a squirt of lemon."

"Parsley, chives, Parmesan, a squirt of lemon," Ruby said, counting on her fingers. "And butter."

"Go for it, Ruby," I said.

"No, you go, Ramona," Ruby instructed, getting out the can of crescent rolls and turning on the oven to preheat it. "You can bring in the herbs while I lay out the rolls. And don't forget the dill and basil for the salad."

A few moments later, Ramona was back in the kitchen with snips of herbs. "So this miracle worker—Chief Dawson, that is—earned a couple of national awards for her work at the university," she said. "Then what?"

I took up the story. "Dolly Patterson's discrimination lawsuit resulted in a U.S. Department of Justice consent decree mandating that the department hire women, Hispanics, and African Americans." I grinned. "The decree came down about the time Smart Cookie was making headlines at CTSU."

"Ah," Ramona said, in a knowing tone.

"You got it, Ramona," Ruby put in, as she mixed the herbs and cheese into the butter. "The time was ripe for a change."

"Very ripe." I began tearing basil leaves into the salad. "As it happened, the federal mandate coincided with the election of a pair of women activists to the Pecan Springs city council. They decided that now was the time to turn the department into something that wouldn't be a permanent legal and social liability and would stop costing mucho dinero in discrimination settlements. They persuaded the council—with a little help from the new city attorney—that it was time to look for another chief. Bubba Harris resigned, and McQuaid filled in as acting chief for a while. Six months or so, maybe."

"Some of the council wanted Mike McQuaid to stay on as chief." Ruby slid me a glance. "But China wouldn't let him."

"I couldn't have stopped him if he'd really wanted to do it," I replied. "McQuaid hates politics, and the chief's job is super political. It's a desk job and he hates that, too."

Ramona frowned. "I've never understood why you call your husband by his last name, China. It seems a little, well, strange."

"He wasn't always my husband," I said. "He was a homicide detective when I met him, and I was a defense attorney. We started off as McQuaid and Bayles. He's still McQuaid, far as I'm concerned."

"Anyway," Ruby put in, "when McQuaid pulled out, he left the field open to Sheila."

"There were several others in the running," I said, setting the salad bowl on the table with a pair of salad tongs. "A female sheriff from one of the Valley counties, if I remember right, and another woman who was chief in a little West Texas town. There was a guy from Beaumont, and Clint Hardin, from inside the department. Sheila wasn't even going to apply—she was starting to get serious about Blackie, who at the time was the Adams County sheriff."

Ruby had finished buttering the dough triangles and was now rolling them up, wide end first, placing them on a baking sheet. "But Blackie kept encouraging her," she said "And when the search committee compared years of training and experience, awards, recognitions, that kind of thing, it was clear that Sheila was the top candidate."

"Her biggest competition," I added, "came from Clint Hardin. He was Bubba Harris' handpicked favorite. And of course, he had the support of the police department. To a man."

"To a man." Ramona repeated with a chuckle. "I'll bet."

"Which is still a problem," Ruby picked up the baking

sheet. "Anyway, the council hired Sheila. They told her to clean up the personnel problems and pull the department out of the nineteenth century. Make it modern and professional."

"Or rather, *some* members of the council did," I corrected her. "It was a five-four vote—not exactly what you'd call an overwhelming mandate. Sheila would be the first to tell you that it hasn't been easy. There's been opposition from inside the department and from the council—as well as the usual community anger that's directed at the chief whenever the police get out of line, which they do, from time to time." I leaned against the counter. "Sheila isn't crazy about the paperwork and she hates politics as much as McQuaid does. To tell the truth, I was hugely surprised when she kept her job as chief and Blackie quit his as sheriff. I fully expected it to go the other way."

Ramona shook her head. "It's not a job I'd want," she said thoughtfully. "Why does she do it?"

"Because she believes in justice and in the law," I said. "And she wants the law to be fair. To everybody. Not just people with money and influence."

"And because she's a tough cookie," Ruby added, putting the rolls into the oven.

"So that's the story," Ramona said quietly. "Amazing."

Ruby laughed. "That's just the first chapter. Stay tuned for further developments." She checked the oven temperature and set the timer. "It'll be about ten minutes. Who's ready for wine?"

We poured glasses of chilled white wine and adjourned to the back porch. "Well, Ramona?" Ruby asked, as we settled into our chairs. "Are you going to tell us what kind of business opportunity you intended to check out today? Before you went over to the Kirks'."

I sighed, thinking of Larry. He'd been a friend, a good and thoughtful person. I would miss him.

Ramona propped her sneakers on the porch railing. "I

wasn't going to tell you until I knew something for sure. But I've been talking to your neighbor about maybe going into business with her."

"Our neighbor!" Ruby exclaimed, both gingery eyebrows going up. "Constance, maybe?" Constance Letterman owns the Craft Emporium, at the corner of Crockett and Guadalupe. "Or—"

"Molly McGregor, at the Hobbit House." Ramona looked from one of us to the other. "What do you think of the idea?"

There was an awkward pause. Finally, I said, "Molly is a terrific gal, Ramona. And she's done wonders with that children's bookstore. The concept is good, and the location is—well, it's right next door to us, so I think it's just about perfect. But do you really think—"

"That independent bookstores are going to survive—especially specialty bookstores?" Ramona finished my question. "I know the situation's scary, China. Between ebooks and online etailers and the big chains, local shops are having a hard time everywhere. But one of my accounts at the advertising agency in Dallas was an independent bookstore, and the owner and I got to be good friends. I could believe in what she was doing, because she believed in it, too." She made a face. "Which is more than I could say for most of my other accounts. So yes, I'd love to invest in the Hobbit House, if I can. If Molly wants me."

I looked at Ruby's sister with a new respect, feeling that there might be more to her than I had given her credit for.

Ruby sat forward in her chair, excited. "Gosh, Ramona, I think it's a wonderful idea. And your advertising and marketing experience would be a real asset to Molly."

"You could be right," Ramona said. "Anyway, I've stopped at the Hobbit House several times, just looking around. Yesterday, I mentioned my idea to Molly. She's interested, so we're getting together to talk about it." She made a face. "Or rather, we planned to get together. After I found . . . well, you know. I had to cancel."

That sobered us. Ruby sighed. I stared into my wine-glass, thinking of the emails that Larry and I had exchanged last week, planning another upgrade for the website. I loved his enthusiasm and appreciated his expertise. He was always upbeat and optimistic. If I were betting, I'd bet that he was *not* the kind of person who would do himself in.

"Dana is going to take this very hard," Ruby said sadly. "I feel so sorry for her."

"For *her*?" I asked acidly. "Hey. Larry is the one who's dead. Why aren't you feeling sorry for him? Now that he's gone, her life will definitely be less complicated. She won't have to go through a divorce." That might be a cruel thing to say, but it was true.

"Didn't you tell me that Dana is involved with some-body else?" Ramona asked Ruby, frowning.

"Yes. Which is why it'll be much harder than it would have been otherwise," Ruby said.

Ramona shook her head. "I don't understand."

I didn't, either. It seemed to me that it would be easier.

"Sure you do," Ruby said. "It's guilt. If you very badly wanted somebody to go away and he ended up killing him-self, wouldn't you wallow in guilt?"

"Maybe," Ramona said doubtfully. "Unless the some-body was my ex. Nothing that jerk could do would ever make *me* feel guilty." She paused, tilting her head curi-ously. "Who's Dana's boyfriend?"

"He's not just her boyfriend." Ruby studied her wine. "I don't know if I should tell you, though. Dana didn't swear me to secrecy, but—"

"Of course you should tell us," Ramona said indignantly. "We can keep a secret. Can't we, China?"

"Well, I guess," Ruby said. "As long as you don't go spreading it around. He's her boss. The library director."

I blinked. "Glen Vance? Mr. Straight himself? You're

kidding!" I couldn't believe that Dana Kirk had left Larry for Glen Vance, who (in my book) is a pompous and self-important guy who ends up being smarmy when he thinks he's being nice. What in the world did she see in *him*?

Ruby frowned in my direction. "The way Dana tells it, China, 'Straight' is not his real personality. Underneath that dignified appearance, Mr. Vance is a tiger."

"A tiger," I said disbelievingly, and sat back again, shaking my head. So it was sex, huh? I would never have guessed.

"How long has Dana been doing this . . . this tiger thing with her boss?" Ramona wanted to know. "Is he married?"

"About six months," Ruby said. "And no, he's a widower. His wife died two years ago. When she and Larry separated, Dana moved in with a friend, who has an apartment in Mr. Vance's complex."

"How convenient for both tigers," I said dryly.

Ruby opened both eyes wide. "What on earth are you suggesting, China? You can't possibly imagine that Dana Kirk and Mr. Vance would—"

My cell phone tinkled its digitized rendition of the opening bars of "Mamas, Don't Let Your Babies Grow Up to Be Cowboys." I fished it out of my jeans pocket and flipped it open. It was Jessica Nelson.

I waved to Ruby and Ramona. "Gotta take this one, guys." Wineglass in one hand, phone in the other, I walked to the end of the porch so I wouldn't interrupt the conversation. A ruby-throated hummingbird hung in the air beside a feeder, its wings a blur, the sunlight sparking its iridescent feathers. A honeysuckle vine wrapped itself around the pillar, its tendrils clinging fast to the wood, its sweet scent filling the air. "What's up, Jessie?"

There was no preamble. "China, do you have any idea what kind of connection there might be between Larry Kirk and George Timms?"

"Kirk and . . . George Timms?" I was taken aback. If she

had asked me about a connection between Larry Kirk and Glen Vance, I could've come up with something right off the top of my head. Her name would have been Dana. But Kirk and *Timms*? What was this about?

I leaned against the porch pillar. The hummer, startled, flew a dozen feet away and hovered, watching me reproachfully. I moved to the other pillar and the hummer returned to his supper. "I know George Timms, of course," I said warily, mindful that I was talking to a reporter. "Everybody does. But what in the world makes you think—"

"I didn't want to mention this when you were with your friends," Jessica said, "but I got a phone tip this afternoon. George Timms is about to be arrested for breaking into Kirk's computer shop. And now Kirk is dead." She let that hang for a moment, then added, "I thought maybe you'd have some idea what the link is."

"Arrested?" I stood up straight, astonished. I hadn't gotten any further than her second sentence. "George Timms?" Sheila had said they were expecting an arrest in the burglary case that afternoon, so that much seemed to fit. But *George Timms*? Jessica must have heard it wrong or—

"That's crazy, Jessica! Why the hell would somebody like George Timms break into a geek shop?"

"Because he was being blackmailed."

"Blackmailed!" I lowered my voice and looked over my shoulder to be sure that Ruby and Ramona hadn't heard me. "Who told you that?"

There was a moment's silence. "Well, I didn't get it right from the horse's mouth, if that's what you're asking. I've been trying to get in touch with Timms' lawyer—Charlie Lipman—for verification. No luck yet. But my source is very close to the action, and she says—" Jessica stopped, conscious that she had unintentionally let something slip. Her information had come from a woman, and I had an idea who. Charlie Lipman's secretary. I knew that he'd had to warn her once before about spilling secrets outside the office.

"Believe me, China," Jessica added. "This is going to happen. Timms' surrender has already been arranged." She was trying to stay cool, but I could hear the suppressed excitement in her voice. "This is going to be a big story. Front page."

I know Jessica well enough to know that she wouldn't be talking to me like this unless she was absolutely convinced that she had her facts straight. But I still couldn't get my mind around the idea that George Timms—a stalwart citizen who was active in the Chamber of Commerce and a member of the local Fight Crime in Our Community group (political friends and supporters of our do-gooding district attorney, Howie Masterson, who is farther to the right than Archie Bunker)—would break into Larry Kirk's computer shop.

Of course, Timms isn't exactly a one-sided character. He is an influential and well-heeled member of the community, yes. But he also has a reputation as a maverick with a short fuse and an interest in young women. He's in his forties, blond, good-looking, well built, twice divorced, and something of a playboy. According to the local gossip, he occasionally veers to the wild side.

Of course, you can't believe everything you hear: gossip is one of the worst small-town vices, and in this case, I imagine there's some envy in the mix. But there's an abundance of rumors floating around, mostly about parties at a place Timms owns in the Hill Country. And it didn't take much imagination to make a connection between those rumored parties and the alleged blackmail. But how that might be connected to a break-in at a computer shop, I hadn't a clue.

"We're off the record, China," Jessica went on. "You knew Kirk, and you've served on community projects with Timms. Can you come up with *any* possible connection—no matter how remote between this burglary and Kirk's . . . suicide?"

I heard the skepticism in her last word, but I wasn't going to encourage her by responding to it. No, I didn't think Larry killed himself. But, I wasn't going to admit it—not to a reporter. If Jessica was going in that direction, she was going without me.

"Sometimes coincidences really *are* coincidences," I said in a cautionary tone. "And anyway, just because somebody is arrested, it doesn't automatically make him guilty. Cops have been known to make mistakes. They're not infallible." But a mistake was not likely in this case, I thought. The police wouldn't risk miscalculating where a prominent citizen like George Timms was concerned.

"I didn't say he was guilty," Jessica retorted. "I just said he's being arrested."

I knew. But I also knew that once the story of Timms' arrest appeared in the papers, the community, serving as judge and jury, would render a verdict of guilty. I changed the subject. "Have you told the police what Mrs. Wauer said about that gunshot?" The officer who canvassed the neighbors would no doubt pick up the information, but that could be tomorrow. Sheila could use it this evening, when she was trying to fix the time of death.

"Not yet. Guess I'd better do that soon, huh?"

"Not soon, *now*, as in the minute we hang up."

"If you insist," she said, and clicked off.

"Right." I closed my phone, then stood there, sorting out what needed to be done. This called for action.

I scrolled through my cell phone directory to Charlie Lipman's office number. Charlie is not only the best lawyer in Pecan Springs and a frequent client of McQuaid, Blackwell, and Associates, but my long-time personal friend and fellow member of the Texas bar. I wasn't surprised to hear that he was Timms' lawyer. He had represented Timms in a property dispute a few months before. McQuaid had been the investigator on the case, which involved the boundaries of a piece of very nice Hill Country land not far from where we live. Charlie needed to be told that Jessica Nelson, intrepid girl reporter, had learned about Timms' arrest. He wasn't going to like it, but he needed to know.

But there was something even more important. While it might not be exactly kosher for me to spill the beans about Larry Kirk's death, I felt obliged to tell Charlie about that, too. It wasn't a state secret—the *Enterprise* knew about it, the whole neighborhood knew about it, and half the people in town would know about it before they went to bed. There was no reason Timms' lawyer shouldn't know and every reason he should, since his client was about to be arrested for burgling the dead man's business.

The office was closed for the day, but Charlie likes to be close to the action. If he was still around, he might pick up. He did—on the first ring.

"Lipman here." He was not at his most congenial.

"It's China, Charlie. Listen, I wouldn't be bothering you after hours, but I just got a call from a reporter at the *Enterprise* and I thought you ought to know about it. Somebody tipped her that George Timms is about to be arrested for breaking into Larry Kirk's Computer Sales and Service a few days ago."

"Aw, *hell*," Charlie growled. "How do they get stuff like that?"

"Yeah," I said sympathetically. "The free press is a damn nuisance, isn't it? So don't be surprised if there's a reporter and a cameraman lining up outside the door when your client surrenders." I paused, giving him a chance to put in a word or two of denial. He didn't, so I went on. "There's something else you should know, if you don't already, Charlie. Larry Kirk is dead."

"Dead?" An audible gasp, then a roar. "*How? When?*"

"Gunshot wound to the head. This afternoon. Ruby Wilcox's sister found him in his kitchen. The first uniform on the scene called it in as a suicide. But I knew the guy personally and I have my doubts. I'm sure the police are keeping other possibilities in mind."

"Aw, jeez!" Charlie said. I flinched at the ringing smack of a hand slapping the desk, hard. "I am flat not *believin'* this!"

"I know," I said sadly. "I can't quite get my mind around it, either. Kirk was one of the good guys, in my book, anyway." I paused, and then decided to trade on our friendship. "I also had a hard time believing that George Timms would break into Kirk's business, but I guess that's true, huh?" I lowered my voice. "Just between us, why did he do it, Charlie? He needed to get his computer back, maybe? Something on it he'd forgotten about? Or maybe a little under-the-counter extortion?"

Now that the surprise was wearing off, I was starting to conjure possibilities, and blackmail wasn't out of the question. Most people keep private documents on their computers and some people probably spend a fair amount of time visiting questionable websites. Child porn sites, for example, where they download photographs. But they don't think about these ugly things when the computer crashes or it picks up a virus or some kind of malware and they take it in for repair. Maybe there was something on Timms' computer—websites, photos, documents—that he desperately needed to hide. Maybe somebody had discovered whatever it was and was demanding something in return for not spilling his dirty little secret to the public at large.

"Absolutely not," Charlie hooted. "And you know better than to ask that question, China."

Now I knew for certain. It was blackmail—or, more precisely, felony extortion. Which raised the question: was it Kirk who was blackmailing Timms? That didn't fit with my experience of Larry Kirk, but extortionists don't necessarily look like criminals. Extortion is a white-collar crime, and often a crime of opportunity. An otherwise decent guy, in temporary need of some cash (to meet his wife's divorce demands, for instance), inadvertently stumbles onto something criminal on a customer's computer. So this decent guy feels justified in shaking down the customer for whatever he can get, threatening to expose him if he doesn't fork over. In Timms' case, the threat alone might have been enough to push him into breaking into the place in order to get his computer back—although if he'd given the matter some thought, he might have figured out that the extortionist could easily make a copy of the incriminating material. Or maybe they struck a deal, but the extortionist upped the ante, which pushed Charlie's client into—

"And for your information," Charlie growled, "I am no longer representing George Timms. The man was due in my office at two thirty this afternoon, and the surrender was scheduled for two hours later. He didn't show up here. Didn't show at the station, either. Dawson has called in an APB." His voice hardened. "Timms probably threw one of his famous parties last night and blew off his appointments today. Life is too short, China. Timms can find himself another attorney."

A *no-show*? "Uh-oh," I said. My skin was prickling. "Kirk's dead, your client is nowhere—sounds like trouble to me." Of course, Charlie didn't need me to tell him this. And he was right. I knew better than to ask him what he knew about the blackmail. That was privileged. And attorney-client privilege extends beyond the termination of the attorney-client relationship.

"My *former* client," Charlie reminded me. He made a low sound in his throat. "Timms may be one of Pecan Springs' stalwarts, but the guy is a first-class jackass."

"And Kirk is dead," I said again, more emphatically. "Are you making the same connections I'm making, Charlie? What if Timms—" I swallowed. "What if he decided it would be expeditious to simply kill the extortionist? What if—"

I stopped. I was way out of line here. And anyway, what I was thinking didn't make any sense. The cops had the goods on Timms—enough to arrest him, anyway. With charges already pending against him, it would have been stupid to go after Kirk. Unless, of course, Timms was so angry that he was past making sense of anything. That happens sometimes—more often than we might like to think. Many of the defendants I'd represented had done whatever they did in what's called the "heat of passion"—more like a lightning storm of passion, if you ask me.

"I don't want to hear any more what-ifs," Charlie said bleakly. "Officially, I don't give a damn. I am done with Timms. I am off his case. Period. Paragraph. End of story." The receiver went down, hard.

I stared at my cell phone for a moment. I could imagine that Timms might have done one or two things that he shouldn't, and that his bad judgment might have opened him to an extortion attempt. But it was still hard for me to believe that he had actually burgled a business. And as for killing Larry Kirk, that was even harder to believe. But somebody had broken into the computer shop. Larry thought somebody was stalking him. And now Larry was dead.

But this was getting me nowhere, and there was something else I needed to do. I punched in Sheila's cell number. I knew she'd still be at the scene, and she wouldn't be thrilled by an interruption. By now, she undoubtedly knew that Timms was a no-show. But she probably wasn't aware that Jessica Nelson knew that Timms was going to be charged in the break-in case. The arrest—when it finally happened—would take place in the glare of the media spotlight. Or as much spotlight as can be mustered in a small town like Pecan Springs.

Chief Dawson wouldn't be any happier about this than Charlie had been. But she ought to be prepared to meet the press.

Chapter Five

When Sheila went through the gate into the Kirk backyard, Officer Kidder stepped out in front of her. "I need your name on the scene log-in sheet, Chief Dawson." The rookie extended a clipboard.

"Thank you, Officer." Sheila wrote her name, badge number, and the time, and ran her finger down the names on the list—Sergeant Clarke and Officer Kidder, detectives Bartlett and Matheson, Judge Porterfield, the two-man county crime-scene unit, Dana Kirk, herself. The scene log-in sheet was one of the first things Sheila had instituted when she took over the chief's job. Officers weren't supposed to leave anything at the crime scene, especially contaminants such as footprints, fingerprints, and DNA. But it happened. People dropped hairs, they sneezed, they touched stair rails and doorknobs. What they left behind could wreck an otherwise solid case. It was important to know who had been on the scene in the event there were questions later. And there almost always were. In an investigation, nothing was simple or straightforward.

"Thanks, Chief," Kidder said, and took back the clipboard.

Sheila regarded her. The rookie barely made regulation

height, but she was trim and athletic, with deep-set gray eyes and a pleasant smile—a looker, young Mr. Cavette had called her. "You and Sergeant Clarke were the first to arrive?"

Kidder nodded. "We were on the east side of the campus when Dispatch gave us the ten-eighty-seven. The woman who called it in—Ramona Donahue, from down the street—was standing on the curb. The body is in the kitchen, on the floor. A male, gun in his right hand. Sergeant Clarke had me tape off the scene while she took Donahue's statement. Detective Bartlett got here, gave it a look, and called out the county unit. They've started processing the scene." She looked down at the log. "The others on-scene are on the list."

"Thanks." It was a concise summary. Sheila glanced around. She'd seen everyone except— "Detective Matheson? Is he inside?"

"Negative. He just went out to the street to work the neighbors, ma'am."

"Good." They'd probably need someone else for the canvass, too, although that could wait until Judge Porterfield ruled. If this turned out to be a clear case of suicide, neighborhood interviews might not be necessary.

"Hey!" The woman was heavyset, borderline obese. She was reaching over the gate, fumbling with the lock. "I'm Dana Kirk's friend. We work together at the library. I need to talk to her. Let me in."

Sheila nodded at Kidder, who stepped forward. She was brisk but polite. "Sorry, ma'am. You can't come in here. And you're not supposed to cross that crime-scene tape out front, on the driveway. So turn around and go back. Now, please."

"But you don't understand!" the woman protested frantically, pushing against the gate. "I'm Dana's friend! Donna Givens. She'll want me with her. She'll need me to—"

Kidder interrupted sharply. "Do you have any information pertinent to what's happened here this afternoon, Ms. Givens? Anything the investigators need to know to do their work?"

The woman hesitated, her face a study in indecision. "No, I—" She swallowed. "No, not really. I just want to—"

"Then I'll have to ask you to leave." Kidder's voice softened. "But if you have a business card, I'll be glad to let Mrs. Kirk know you stopped by. I'm sure she'll appreciate your concern."

Admitting defeat, the woman fished in her handbag and pulled out a card. "Tell her I'm available whenever," she said urgently, and handed it to Kidder. "And tell her that Mr. Vance would like her to phone just as soon as she can. He's worried about—" She stopped, flushing. "Thank you, Officer. I appreciate it." She turned and went back down the drive.

"Good job, Kidder," Sheila said. Empathy was a powerful tool. Not all cops understood how to use it. She held out her hand. "I'll be talking to Mrs. Kirk, so I'll deliver the card. And it might be a good idea for you to station yourself at the tape line."

Kidder nodded, gave her the card, and went through the gate. Sheila glanced around, looking for Detective Bartlett, and spotted him on the narrow wooden deck at the back of the house, talking to Maude Porterfield. A guy in a white jumpsuit with ADAMS COUNTY CRIME SCENE UNIT in red letters on the back stood by the back door, waiting to go in. He was wearing a plastic cap, mask, gloves, and booties and carried a forensic case. In the backyard (fenced with a six-foot privacy fence), two white-uniformed med techs stood with their arms folded beside an empty gurney with a body bag on it. On a small concrete patio beside an ornamental pool thick with green pond lilies, a dark-haired woman in a skirt and sweater and low heels was huddled in a white plastic lawn chair. Sergeant Clarke crouched beside her. The woman was weeping, big, gulping sobs. The widow, no doubt.

Sheila regarded her. Maybe a little too histrionic for a woman who was seeking a divorce from a man who now lay dead on the kitchen floor? But you never knew about people. She caught the sergeant's eye and motioned to her. Clarke got up and came over.

"Evenin', Chief. Want me to go out and help Detective Matheson with the canvass?" Jeraldine Clarke was a short, muscular woman with boy-cut ginger-colored hair who went by the name of Jerry. She had grown up on a ranch where her favorite sports were calf-roping and bull-riding. Clarke said she liked it when somebody was stupid enough to resist arrest. Gave her an excuse to practice her skills.

"This is Detective Bartlett's investigation," Sheila replied. "He'll let you know what he wants." She ignored the look of surprise that crossed Clarke's face. It was natural for an officer to think that when the chief showed up, she was there to kick butt or claim the case. "Kidder's first body, was it?"

Clarke nodded. "She's gonna be okay, ma'am. A little bit of a flinch, didn't want to look, but after that she was fine."

"Good." Sheila knew from her own experience that the first dead body wasn't necessarily the hardest—that was likely still to come. But it sounded like Kidder was off to a strong start. She nodded in the direction of the weeping woman. "Did somebody call Mrs. Kirk or did she just show up?"

"Don't believe notifications have started yet, ma'am," Clarke said diffidently. Sheila nodded. People expected the police to get on the phone immediately when a family member was found dead. But it was a rare death where a please-notify list was taped beside the phone. Bartlett would be going through the victim's wallet and scrolling through his smart phone.

Clarke went on: "Mrs. Kirk said she'd just got off work at the library. She came over to talk to her husband about some personal business. Detective Bartlett asked her to ID the victim, which she did. I was just kinda keepin' her comp'ny while she's waitin' for him to interview her." She nodded in the direction of the house. "He's been in there with the judge and the crime-scene photographer."

Sheila nodded. First the JP, for a ruling. Then the photographer, for videos, digital stills, and Polaroids. After that, the forensic specialist would get to work. "It was called in as a suicide, I understand," she said.

"Yep." Clarke squinted at her. "I made sure he was dead, did a quick search of the house to be sure there were no other victims or shooters, and secured the scene. The gun's in his hand," she added. "Looks like suicide."

"Oh, yeah?" Sheila frowned slightly. The recoil of the weapon on firing or the act of falling could have (perhaps should have) dislodged the gun and sent it flying. But where guns were concerned, anything could happen and often did. "Thanks, Clarke."

Sheila looked up to see Maude Porterfield limping across the yard toward her, leaning on her cane. The old judge's arthritis had been bothering her for a while. Getting around was difficult—which had nothing to do with her eyesight or judgment, of course. The judge was as sharp as ever.

"I'm finished in there, Chief Dawson," she said in her cracked voice. "Got my grandkids comin' for supper and we're cookin' up a big pot of chili and a pan of cornbread." She looked around. "Where's Captain Hardin?"

"On his way to Rockport. He's got some vacation time coming."

Judge Porterfield snorted. "Gone fishin, huh? Then it's all yours, Chief. This one might be interestin'."

Interesting? Sheila raised an eyebrow but said only, "Have you ruled yet?"

"Leavin' it open for now," the judge replied. "Body's on the floor. Gunshot wound to the head, right temple." She lifted her blue eyes to Sheila's. "Thirty-two automatic—Llama—in his hand. *In* his hand," she repeated. "Wallet on the table, two fifties and a couple of credit cards. Didn't see a note."

Sheila considered the implications of this. There weren't too many Llamas around—the gun was Spanish and hadn't been manufactured since the fifties. It wasn't big and didn't have a lot of recoil, so maybe he could have held on to it. The wallet and credit cards would seem to rule out robbery. And no suicide note. "Powder burns?"

"Not so's I noticed right off. I'll wait for the autopsy report before I rule. Let me know if you turn up a note somewhere." Judge Porterfield pursed her lips. "Messy in there, Chief. A small space to work in. Not easy to tell exactly what happened, just lookin' at things." She added, "I'll start the paperwork in the mornin'. Gotta feed those grandkids tonight."

"You bet," Sheila said with a smile. "Can't let the kids go hungry. We'll get back to you if we uncover anything. You have a nice evening, Judge."

"You, too," the judge said. She paused and looked Sheila straight in the eye. "And remember what I told you and that ex-sheriff of yours. 'Til death do you part."

"We'll give it our best shot," Sheila said, with immense gravity.

"See that you do," the judge snapped. "You young folks got to learn to take your vows serious. Won't work 'less you do."

As the judge left, Sheila turned to see Jack Bartlett watching her with a quizzical look on his face. She lifted her hand.

"Detective Bartlett, may I have a word?" They stepped over to the side of the garage. Sheila cleared her throat. "Captain Hardin is taking a few days' vacation."

"He told me, Chief," Bartlett said. "Also told me to report direct to you while he was gone."

The young detective was taller than Sheila, with crisp dark hair, olive skin, a slender build. Not much over thirty, too craggy to be handsome, but with a reputation as a ladies' man just the same. And a hard drinker. Sheila had heard a couple of stories about his good-time style, although tales of that kind had a way of snowballing as they rolled around the department. He had come from the San Antonio PD a couple of years back, bright, ambitious, self-confident, with an air of danger about him and tales of a temper with a dangerously low flashpoint. He was dressed in plainclothes today—pressed jeans, dark shirt, and dark tie, tan corduroy jacket, and cowboy boots.

He gestured toward the house. "We don't get many like this one. Looks like suicide. My guess, it's a homicide."

"No note anywhere?"

"No, although I haven't checked the laptop." He paused. "Think we should let Captain Hardin know? He might want to postpone his trip. Hell, for a homicide, he'd probably even turn around and come back."

"The captain has the time coming to him," Sheila said. "Anyway, I'd like to assist on this investigation, Jack. Not because you couldn't handle it alone or with Matheson, but because I want to get out from behind the desk for a while. Put in some time in the field." She paused. She could tell him that she'd had it up to here with politics and paperwork, but complaining to the troops was probably not a good idea. "Do you have any problems with that?"

"Problems?" Bartlett gave her a calculating, narrow-eyed look, then relaxed into a crooked grin. "Hey, I'm happy to hand it over, Chief. It'll be a pleasure to work with you."

She knew Bartlett just well enough to guess that he meant what he said, and she was glad. But she shook her head. "I'm not taking this case, Detective Bartlett. I said 'assist.' This one is yours. You call the shots."

He frowned, shifting uncomfortably. "That isn't necessary, Chief Dawson. I'll be glad to backstop you, same way I'd backstop Captain Hardin." He added, matter-of-factly and without judgment, "Case like this, he'd take the lead for sure."

Take the lead and take the credit, Sheila thought, out in front of the team that did the work. "Do I have to pull rank?" she asked. "Look, Detective. I want to get my head out of the office for a while. Do some footwork, talk to people, take notes, do some serious police work." She shrugged. "Not that what goes on in the office isn't serious. But . . . well, you know. Anyway, you're taking the lead. It's your show. I'm here to assist."

He studied her with a wary mistrust, as if he were trying to figure out her real motives. "Yes, ma'am. I hear you. But Captain Hardin isn't going to like—"

"Noted," she said briskly. "And for the duration, can the 'ma'am.' It's Sheila when we're together. Okay?"

He hesitated, guarded, cautious. "Roger that." He looked around, then added, testing the word, "Sheila."

"You got it, Jack." She straightened. "Judge Porterfield said she didn't notice any powder burns. What did you see?"

"I did a close visual before the county team got here. Looked for stippling but didn't see it. I did spot a thirty-two cartridge casing on the floor." He frowned. "I'm thinking that we should have the autopsy done locally, rather than sending it to the Travis ME's office. We'll get the report back faster." Adams County autopsies could be done either at the county hospital or sent to the Travis County Medical Examiner's Office, which served a forty-two-county region in Central Texas. There, the out-of-county corpses got in line behind the local traffic, which could mean a delay of several days.

"Works for me." Sheila glanced over her shoulder, in the direction of the weeping woman. "Have you talked to the wife? Widow," she corrected herself. "Mrs. Kirk."

"You want to handle that?" Bartlett was diffident, and Sheila knew why. Next-of-kin conversations were always tough. He didn't want her to think he was dumping something unpleasant on her plate. "The county photographer will finish up pretty quick and the forensic tech is ready to get started. I'd like to keep an eye on the scene. And I haven't walked the house yet. There might be a note somewhere." He gave her a testing look. "Of course, if you'd rather take over inside, I'll do the interview."

"I'll have a look when you're finished." Sheila took out her notebook, thinking ahead. The scene was important, but so was the wife. The Department of Justice had recently reported that, in spousal murders, women represented 41 percent of the killers. If this turned into a homicide, Dana Kirk was automatically a suspect. And if she had killed her husband, her defense—when the case came to trial—might be spousal abuse. That was what made this first interview so critical. It would tell them something about both the victim and the woman he left behind, who could benefit from his death. The *how* and *when* were easy—forensics would tell them that. *Why* was another matter. And *who,* if this turned out to be homicide.

"Anything special you want me to check out with Mrs. Kirk?" she asked.

"Find out what guns her husband owned." Bartlett glanced at his watch, frowning. "You know who this guy is, right, Chief?" She saw his jaw go red. "Uh, Sheila," he said, in a lower voice.

She nodded. "The owner of the computer shop that George Timms broke into."

"Yeah." He shifted his weight. "I'm wondering about Timms' arrest. He was supposed to be booked over an hour ago, and both of us should have been notified. I'd better see what—" He reached for the radio clipped to his belt.

She put out a hand. "Don't bother, Jack. Timms is a no-show. Charlie Lipman called my cell phone a few minutes ago, looking for him." She grinned wryly. "You know Lipman. He was hoping we had his client so he could accuse us of holding him incommunicado."

"I'll bet," Bartlett muttered. "I can hear him now." He looked back at the house again. "Hey, maybe we should—"

"I called in the APB right after I got off the phone with Lipman," she said, reading his intention. "I saw your interim report on the break-in. After his surrender, Timms is supposed to come clean about that blackmail business—his so-called motivation for the burglary. Did you get any sense from Lipman of what that's about?"

"Nope. In fact, I got the idea that Lipman himself didn't have the full story, although you never know with that guy."

"Did you uncover any sign of a personal connection between Timms and Kirk?" Sheila asked. "Anything—" She hesitated. "Anything suggesting that maybe Kirk was helping himself to a little blackmail on the side?" *Was,* she thought. Past tense. "Might not be too hard, if he had Timms' computer in the shop for repair or cleanup and happened to notice something incriminating on it." *Happened to notice, or went looking on purpose.* Maybe it was part of an ongoing racket, and Timms wasn't the only victim.

Bartlett shook his head. "I didn't pick up any personal connection. It looked like Timms got out of Kirk's shop without finding what he was after. Kirk himself wasn't involved, so far as I knew, anyway. But this—" He jerked his head toward the house. "This is something else. And I don't like coincidences."

"Here's another thing," Sheila said. "I just ran into China Bayles, out there on the drive. She's a friend of the woman who stumbled onto the body. She told me that Kirk had emailed her about a stalker—his word. China is a former criminal attorney and one of Kirk's computer clients. He was looking for some inside advice on how to deal with the situation, maybe thinking he needed a lawyer."

"A stalker, huh?" Bartlett's head jerked up, his eyes

bright, alert. "Interesting. Wonder what that means, exactly. Male, female?"

"Kirk didn't give her any details. I'll get her to forward his email. And it's likely on his computer."

"Yeah." Bartlett pursed his lips. "I wonder if the widow knows anything. Maybe Kirk mentioned the stalker to her."

"The Kirks were getting a divorce, I understand." In response to his questioning look, she said, "Got that from a neighbor out front, and also from Bayles, who said the divorce was quote 'messy,' unquote. And wives sometimes hire private detectives to find out what their husbands are up to. Could be our stalker right there." Sheila opened her notebook. "I'll check back with you when I'm finished with Mrs. Kirk."

"Yeah," Bartlett said. He looked at her. "Thanks, Sheila," he said, testing again. It sounded awkward and he straightened his shoulders. "Thank you, Sheila," he said more firmly.

Sheila smiled. "No problem, Jack."

DANA Kirk was as soft and round and sweetly attractive as a stuffed doll, her makeup muted, her brown hair tumbling in soft curls around her flushed and tear-stained face. Her voice was soft, too, and so choked that Sheila had to ask her more than once to speak up. Sitting down in a chair across from her, Sheila expressed condolences on the loss of her husband, then took notes as the story spilled out in rapid, breathy fragments, between gulps and swallowed sobs. Sheila kept her talking as much as possible. Tears could be a distraction. Or an act.

Dana had been at the Pecan Springs Library all day. She worked in the office there eight-to-five, five days a week, which sometimes but not always included Saturdays, in which case she took a different day off. Lots of people could vouch for her being there today, with only bathroom breaks and an hour for a late lunch between one and one forty-five, which she had eaten with—hesitation, a quick breath—a friend, at the diner on Nueces, about six blocks away. Asked the name of the friend, she hesitated again, then said, with eyes cast down, "Actually, my boss. Mr. Vance."

She had worked at the library for six years, before that, for Jackie Harmon at Harmon Insurance, in Pecan Springs. Then she and Kirk had married and she'd gone to work at the library. They'd lived in an apartment first, then they bought this house. No, they'd never had any children. (A pause to wipe her eyes with a tissue and blow her nose.) Not even a dog or a cat. She'd wanted at least that, but Larry was allergic.

No, she wasn't living here now. Yes, she and her husband had been separated for a couple of months, since (a pause to think about it) last April, which now that she thought about it, was more like (a pause to count on her fingers) six months. Had there been any spousal abuse? No, of course not (the answer delivered emphatically). When asked to reflect and be sure of that answer, she repeated it, watching Sheila make a note. No, no abuse. Larry was a kind person—thoughtless, too busy, but basically kind. Yes, she had filed for divorce. The name of her lawyer? Angela Binder. Had she and Binder hired a private investigator to work on the case? Eyes widening, she said no, no, of course not. She had no reason to hire an investigator, and anyway, she didn't have any extra money until Larry could sell the business.

So if she wasn't living here, Sheila asked, where was she staying? With a friend, Donna Givens, until she and Larry could work out some financial details. That's the reason she was here this afternoon. She had called and left a message, telling Larry that they needed to talk about money. And now— Well, she couldn't (more tears and a sob), she just couldn't, she would *never* be able to understand why Larry would do something like this. He was so level-headed, so self-contained, so—

And anyway, he hated guns. She didn't know he *had* a gun. In fact, she herself had suggested that they get a gun last year, when the house down the street was broken into, but he refused. He put his foot down. He wouldn't let her have one, either, which was ridiculous, since—

Sheila stopped writing. "Your husband hated guns?"

Dana Kirk squeezed her brown eyes shut, then opened them. "Yes, and that's why this is really so weird. I mean, it was a big thing with him, huge. He was an anti-gun activist. Last year when those college students were trying to change the concealed-carry law to let them bring their guns on campus? He thought it was the stupidest thing he'd ever heard of, letting kids carry guns to class. He even went up to Austin to join the protest at the capital." She brushed her hair out of her eyes. "So if he was going to . . . kill himself, I would have thought he'd do it a different way. Lock himself in the garage with the car running, maybe, or take some pills. I would never have thought he'd—" She closed her eyes and clenched her hands. "But if he didn't do it, I don't see how in the world . . ."

Sheila cleared her throat. "Do you know if he was having problems with anyone? At the shop, maybe? A client, a customer, somebody who works for him?"

She shook her head. "If he did, I didn't know anything about it. Somebody at the shop would know if there's been any trouble."

"Can you give me the names of the employees?" Sheila flipped a page.

"There are three, I think." She frowned, concentrating. "No, four. Henry, Jason, Richie, and Dennis. I don't know their last names. Henry is the only employee, though. He's the assistant manager or something—he's in charge when Larry isn't around. The rest are contract people, techs. They only work when there's a job. From what I hear, things have been pretty slow lately." She made a face. "That's what Larry said, anyway. But he might have been saying that so I would settle for less money."

Sheila let that go by, at least for the moment. "What about debts?" she asked. "Personal? Business? Did he owe money to anybody?"

"I think he was still paying off some student loans. The mortgage on this house, car payments, credit cards. The usual, I guess." She firmed her shoulders. "And me. He owed money to me."

It was the opening Sheila had been waiting for. "I understand that you have an investment interest in your husband's business. Had you worked out the settlement details?"

A brief flare of anger flashed in the woman's eyes. "How did you—?" Then she sighed. "Small towns. I hate small towns. Everybody knows everything about everybody's affairs." She colored prettily and corrected herself. "Everybody's *business*, I mean. Yes. My father died just before Larry and I got married, and I inherited some money from his estate. I wanted to buy stocks, but Larry talked me into investing it in his computer business instead. Larry's really good with computers. And patient with people who don't understand the technology."

She sighed and her shoulders slumped. "But no, we hadn't worked out the settlement yet. He was trying to figure out how I could get my investment back without his having to sell the business. And of course, there's this house. It's underwater, as they say. It won't appraise for what we paid for it. He was going to have to sell—" She stopped and took a breath.

"Sounds difficult," Sheila said sympathetically. "Not just the house but the business, too—I'm sure that lots of couples would be fighting about it, tooth and nail. There weren't any hard feelings?" She paused, then gave Dana Kirk a direct look. "Especially about your other relationship?"

"My . . . relationship?" The woman tried to hold the glance, but her eyes slid away.

"Yes. I understand that you've been involved with another man for some time and that this was why you were seeking a divorce." Sheila looked down at her notebook, flipped a page, then looked up again. She waited, letting the silence build for the space of a couple of breaths. "I'm sorry. Did I misunderstand? I can always check back with the person who—"

Mrs. Kirk gave a resigned sigh. "No, you didn't misunderstand. Yes, I am involved with . . . someone. But it doesn't have anything to do with what Larry did today." She pressed her lips together. "I am not going to say anything more about it. Really. You don't have any right to—"

Sheila spoke softly. "Mrs. Kirk. We're not sure yet what happened here today. Until we are, we will be investigating everyone and everything that is related to your husband. We will be talking with his business associates, the neighbors, you, the person you're involved with—"

"No!" she cried, sitting straight up, a dull color flooding her doll-like cheeks. "That's not right! He has nothing to do with Larry's suicide! He—"

"Mrs. Kirk, I am sorry to be blunt. We are keeping everything open. *Everything.*" She turned to a fresh page in her notebook. "Now, perhaps you can help by giving me the names of people we need to notify of Mr. Kirk's death. Just the names, relationships, and cities right now—we'll likely be able to fill in the contact information from what we find in the house. True?"

Mrs. Kirk nodded. "Yes," she said, barely audible. "Well, there's his phone. You can look there. And he keeps a red leather address book in the top drawer of the desk in the living room. That's where it used to be, anyway. His mom's address is there. Her name is Jenny. Jenny Kirk. She lives in San Antonio. His father is dead. His sisters—"

Sheila noted down the names, then close friends, then

neighbors that Kirk might have been especially friendly with. Apparently, he had been a collegial guy, for the list was a long one, although (in his wife's version, anyway) it was exclusively male. When Dana Kirk ran out of names, Sheila said, "What about women he was dating?"

"Dating?" Dana's eyes grew round. "I don't think he— I'm sure he wouldn't—"

"What? No casual dates? No girlfriends? He didn't say something like, 'Hey, Dana, what's sauce for the goose is sauce for the gander. I'm seeing so-and-so'?"

She laced her fingers together tightly. "If he was seeing someone, he didn't tell me. And I didn't spy on him. If he wanted to date, that was his business. Although if he didn't have time for his wife, I doubt he'd have time for a girlfriend." A little shrug, a little too casual. "I guess you could ask the guys at the shop. They'd probably know."

"Okay, then," Sheila said, and went back to a subject she'd opened earlier. "Help me with the other side. Enemies. People who didn't like him. People he didn't like. People he'd quarreled with. Clients, customers, guys at the shop."

Dana pulled her eyebrows together. "Enemies? Gosh, I don't know. Larry's such an easygoing guy. He gets . . . he got along with just about everybody." She swallowed. "We had a little trouble with Sam Schulz, the neighbor over there." She nodded toward the house on the west. "After we bought this place, it turned out that the survey markers were wrong and our garage is two feet over the property line. That's been a problem. But otherwise—"

"No long-term feuds? Did he ever mention being concerned that somebody might be stalking him?"

Mrs. Kirk shook her head. "No feuds, other than Mr. Schulz. And . . . *stalking*?" Her eyes widened. "Is that what you said?"

"Stalking, following, somebody hanging around. Did he mention anything like that?"

"Absolutely not." She frowned again. "I don't see what you— He killed himself, didn't he? I mean, I saw the gun in his hand, in there, in the kitchen." She shivered. "So why are you asking—"

"How about former employers? Where did your husband work before he opened his own business?"

Dana sighed. "Both of us were working for Harmon. He installed this big software package, set up the new accounting system, and put up a website, too. Ms. Harmon was really impressed. Larry blew her away. In fact, they were . . ." She broke off, smiling crookedly.

"Were what?" Sheila asked.

She looked down at her hands. "Oh, friends, I guess. I don't know."

"More than friends?"

"Maybe. But then we started going out together. He blew me away, too, you know, with all that energy. He was working his way through school—a master's in computer science—and doing freelance stuff, too. Harmon wasn't the only place he worked. He'd take jobs whenever they came along. I thought it was great that he could manage everything. His classes, consulting, all that stuff." She flexed her fingers and Sheila noticed that she wasn't wearing any rings. "But I guess it should have told me something."

"Told you what?"

She hesitated, then looked up, holding the look almost defiantly. "That there wasn't room in his life for anything or anyone else but work." She took a deep breath. "If there had been, I never would've . . ." She ran out of steam, puffing out her breath. "Oh, never mind. Just never mind."

Sheila understood. When you loved your work, it was hard to find time for other things. For people, even the ones who mattered to you. She changed directions. "I need the names of the people you work with, who can verify your whereabouts today."

"But *why?* I don't understand—"

"I'm sorry, Mrs. Kirk. It's necessary."

This list was shorter. On it was Donna Givens' name, the woman that Dana Kirk was currently staying with.

"That reminds me." Sheila took out the card. "Ms. Givens wanted you to know that she was here. I'm sorry we couldn't let her in."

Mrs. Kirk took the card. "Donna is so sweet. She's been an angel through—" She waved her hand vaguely. "Through everything."

Sheila nodded. "Oh, and she also wanted me to tell you that Mr. Vance would like you to call as soon as you can."

"Oh, really?" Mrs. Kirk's breath quickened. "I— Uh, thank you."

"Vance." Sheila read the rising flush on the woman's cheeks. She looked down at the list. "You seem to have left his name out. He's the man you've been seeing?"

Mrs. Kirk shook her head, chewed her lip, and looked away. Sheila waited. Finally, she said, "Yes. He's— Yes."

"Thank you. Vance." Sheila made a point of scribbling it down. "First name?"

"Glen. He's . . . the director of the library. My . . . boss."

Sheila remembered the man. Ingratiating, she thought, too quick with the flattery. The sort of man an affection-starved woman might be attracted to, when her husband was working nights and weekends.

"You won't have to . . . to talk to him, will you?" Mrs. Kirk asked. "It would just upset— I mean, Glen isn't involved in any way."

"You said you returned from lunch with Mr. Vance at one forty-five," Sheila said crisply. "Did he return to the library at that time?"

"No. He . . . he had some errands to run. I don't know what time he got back." Her mouth twisted and she put out her hand in a pleading gesture. "Please. *Please* don't bother him about this. It has nothing to do with him. It would be just awful."

"I understand the situation, Mrs. Kirk," Sheila said, and tucked her notebook and pen into her shirt pocket without acknowledging the woman's plea. She stood up. "Thank you—you've been very helpful. You can go now. Before you do, though, I'm going to ask one of our officers to take your fingerprints."

"My . . . fingerprints?" Dana Kirk asked, alarmed. "But I don't understand. Why—"

"It's just one of the things we do," Sheila said with a reassuring smile. "It's part of our process of elimination. It'll just take a minute."

"Well, I guess, if it's necessary." Dana Kirk got up. She smoothed her skirt and then her hair, glancing toward the house. "I was planning to pick up a few things today. Linens, mostly. From upstairs. Can I— May I go in and get them now?"

Sheila shook her head. "The house is off-limits for the time being, maybe as long as a couple of days. We'll let you know when you can have access." She took out a card with her work number on it, added her cell number, and handed it to the woman. "I'd like you to call me if you think of anything I should know—or if something happens that's in any way related to your husband's death."

Mrs. Kirk's fingers closed around the card. She looked toward the house, her eyes filling with tears. "I suppose . . . I suppose it's my house now, isn't it?" She sounded disbelieving, but there was also a note of something like relief in her voice. Sheila wasn't surprised. The marriage was over, and without all the bother and expense of a divorce.

"You'll have to ask your lawyer about that," she said. "Do you know if your husband left a will?" If this became a homicide investigation, they would need a copy.

"Yes. We both have—had wills. I don't think he changed his after we separated. Which means . . ." Her voice trailed off.

Which means, Sheila thought, that the widow was now

the owner of the house where her husband had died. And likely the business, as well. She wondered what kind of difference this was going to make in Dana Kirk's life, and whether that difference might have been enough to tempt her.

"Insurance policies?" Sheila asked.

Mrs. Kirk frowned. "Yes," she said reluctantly.

"How much?"

"Two hundred fifty thousand." As if in explanation, she added, "I was working for an insurance agent when we got married." Her tone was defensive. "Ms. Harmon wrote the policies for us. There's one on my life, too. The same amount."

Sheila made a note. It sounded like the insurance had been in force long enough for the suicide exclusion to be lifted. "You're the beneficiary of your husband's policy?"

Her "I am" was barely audible. Mrs. Kirk was putting two and two together, and realizing that she was about to come into a substantial sum of money. She might also be realizing that a quarter of a million dollars, plus the house and the business, might look to the police like a lot of incentive. It was. People killed for much less.

Chapter Six

Sheila stood at the open kitchen door, looking at the crime scene. Orlando always said that when you were investigating homicides, you had to remember that you'd never get to know the victims personally. They were dead. You were never going to *know* them the way they were when they were alive. So you had to get to know them in reverse. Backward, he'd say. From the way they lived and worked, from the people they knew, from what they left behind. That would never be enough, but it was all you were going to have. So you had to get what you needed backward, then work it forward, detail by detail, putting the picture together until you knew the victim as well as if he'd been your next-door neighbor, your friend.

She had gotten a pair of latex gloves from the med techs who stood behind her, waiting to pick up the body as soon as she was finished with her preliminary walk-through. The county team—photographer and forensics specialist—had wrapped up their work, packed their gear, and departed, leaving a stack of a dozen Polaroids on the kitchen table. The videos and digitals would be emailed tomorrow. The forensic report would be sent as soon as the lab work was complete.

The county crime-scene unit was only a year old, and the protocols were still being worked out. Before it was in place, PSPD had gotten by with whatever the detectives could handle on their own, or they'd brought the Travis County Medical Examiner's Office into the case via a telephone consultation, which was never completely satisfactory by anybody's reckoning. For Sheila, the county alternative had been a viable alternative, at least as long as Blackie was the county sheriff. They had worked comfortably together without having to spell out who was responsible for what or worry about whether they were trespassing on the other's turf. The new sheriff, Curt Chambers, had been Blackie's chosen successor and was elected with Blackie's endorsement and support. But he didn't have Blackie's experience or confidence. Maybe he'd grow into the job, but for now, he was a by-the-book guy who seemed to need everything in triplicate. Sheila wasn't sure just how that situation was going to work out.

She gloved up and began her survey, working methodically from right to left around the small room. The door behind her, the white-painted knob smudged with dark fingerprint powder, open, so the cloying smell of blood and beer was probably less overpowering than it had been when Ruby Wilcox's sister stumbled onto the body. The side-by-side fridge-freezer, a grocery list stuck to it with a teakettle magnet. The kitchen range with an egg-crusted skillet on one burner, a half-empty can of pork and beans beside it, a spoon stuck in the can, a fly on the end of the spoon. A bulletin board on the wall displaying a calendar with a flock of pasted-on yellow sticky notes. On the floor directly beneath it, a dark chalked circle with an arrow pointing to nothing—to the empty spot where Bartlett had spotted the cartridge casing.

Another door opened onto a hallway and then onto what looked like a dining room, where she could see Jack Bartlett, his back to her, using his small digital camera to photograph a table filled with what looked like computer components. Then a space of empty wall with a wall phone, also smudged with dark powder. A kitchen counter with a microwave. The remains of a Chinese meal—a white take-out container beside a smaller empty box, a spill of cooked white rice, one wooden chopstick, a broken fortune cookie. The usual cupboards over and under the counter, doors hanging open, draped with dish towels. A dead geranium on the windowsill over the sink. The sink piled high with dirty dishes, several days' worth, Sheila guessed. In the corner, a kitchen trashcan overflowing with cans, beer bottles, and plastic boxes that had once held cookies or pastry, now just crumbs. The kitchen of a guy who was eating alone and wasn't watching his diet.

In the center of the room, a round wooden table. Laptop on the table, beside the laptop, a wallet. A wooden chair on its side on the floor. A puddle of blood and spilled beer. Kirk was lying on his back on the floor next to the chair, head slightly turned to the left. The entry wound at the right temple was small, round, neat. No visible powder marks. No visible exit wound. He was unshaven, his brown hair a little long on the back of his neck and over his ears. He was dressed in a blue T-shirt with the name of his business across the front, jeans, no belt, Birkenstocks on bare, hairy feet. His fingertips were smudged with ink, so she knew he had been printed. He wore a digital wristwatch, nothing fancy, and no wedding ring. Larry Kirk looked the way dead people usually looked. Terribly human, frighteningly frail, terrifyingly vulnerable. Sheila was struck again by the irrefutable fact that a life was gone and with it decades of lived experience, successes, failures, celebrations, regrets. She remembered something else Orlando used to say: "Somebody's gotta stick up for the dead, Dawson. They can't do it—it's gotta be you. You're all they got."

She knelt beside the body for the space of a dozen breaths, looking, taking in as much as she could, letting herself feel the familiar sickening clench in her stomach, the sense of absolute finality that swept over her like a dark, chilly wave. No more laughter, no more love, no joy, no fear of the past or hope for the future. Just . . . nothing. Nothing but what was left to her and her partner: the task of seeking justice. *Don't forget what you're there for, Dawson,* Orlando had written to her. Barricaded behind the paperwork, bulwarked behind the desk, it was too easy to forget. But here in this room, she remembered. This was what she was here for. To stick up for the dead.

After a few moments, she took a deep breath, got to her feet, and turned to the Polaroids on the table. The gun was already gone. So was the .32-millimeter cartridge casing, the beer bottle—all three items bagged by the tech and carried away to the lab, where they'd be printed. But the Polaroids, shot from several angles, showed what the forensic tech had taken.

One photo showed the Llama loosely gripped in the victim's right hand, his fingers lightly curled around the crosshatched wooden grip.

Another photo, this one of the cartridge head-stamp, showed it to be an R-P 32 auto. The indentation in the primer was slightly off-center. The casing would be run through NIBIN, the National Integrated Ballistic Information Network, a database imaging system that compared images of bullet cartridge cases, shell casings, and bullets. If the gun had been used in a previous crime and the casings entered in NIBIN, they'd get a match.

Sheila looked at the photo of the man and the gun. She never liked to leapfrog over the evidence, but she had already seen and heard enough to feel pretty certain that Larry Kirk had not shot himself. They'd know a great deal more after the autopsy and the results of the testing on the hands and the entry wound. What was puzzling her right now, though, was the sound of the shooting. A .32 automatic wasn't as loud as, say, a .357 Magnum, but it still produced a sharp report that, in this quiet neighborhood, somebody should have heard. Maybe Matheson would pick up something while he was canvassing—something to pinpoint the time of death more definitely than the autopsy surgeon was likely to do.

Sheila put down the photographs. There were a couple of other things she needed to check out before the med techs came in to remove the body. She went to the fridge and looked closely at the grocery list, noticing that the usual items—bread, beer, sausage, hot dogs, pizza—were penciled in a crabbed, backward-slanting script. She turned to the calendar. It was topped by a large full-color photo of the Alamo, the months in fold-down pages below. The photo page was studded with five yellow sticky notes. They all said about the same thing, in the same backslant: *Saw JH* or sometimes just *JH* and the date. The first one was October 21, the last was the previous day, the intervals between were two or three days. Two were written with a pen, three with a pencil. She copied the text and the dates and surveyed the calendar, flipping up the pages for October and September and pulling down the page for December. There were a few other penciled notes—dentist, Mom's birthday, climbing club meeting—but nothing else of consequence.

She frowned. The cryptic *Saw JH*. "Saw" could mean one of several things. Kirk (assuming that he wrote the notes) could have seen a doctor. Or he could have spent the evening or had lunch with somebody, a woman, maybe, a date. Or he could have noticed JH, as in seeing him—or her—on the street, outside his house. Stalking him.

She was turning to the laptop when her cell phone chirped. She flipped it open. China Bayles.

"What's up, China?" she asked.

"Brace yourself, Chief," China said. "I just got a call from Jessica Nelson, at the *Enterprise*. Somebody tipped her that George Timms is about to be arrested for breaking

into Larry Kirk's computing business. Jessica is planning
to break the story, and she wanted my opinion as to whether
there was any connection between Timms and Kirk."

"Aw, crap," Sheila muttered.

"Yeah." China sighed. "My sentiment exactly." She
paused. "Has the arrest happened yet?"

"No," Sheila said shortly. Then she remembered that
China had given her the lead on the stalking and helped her
get information from Dana Kirk that would otherwise have
been slow in coming. China was plugged into the Pecan
Springs newswire—the gossip channel that was on and
open pretty much twenty-four-seven. She softened her tone.

"Timms was a no-show, China. We've got an APB out
on him. Lipman is livid, naturally. Accused us of holding
his client incommunicado."

"Yeah, I'll bet he did," China said dryly. She was silent
for a moment. "I hope I'm not jumping to conclusions, but
I keep wondering if there's a connection between Timms
and Kirk."

"Yeah," Sheila said. "I wonder, too. Thanks for the tip
on Nelson."

She folded the phone and turned to the laptop that was
open on the table. The computer was still on but the screen
was blank, the monitor asleep. The keyboard hadn't been
dusted for prints. *Why not?* she wondered. *Just overlooked?*
She used the tip of her pen to wake the computer. After a
few seconds, the screen came to life and displayed Kirk's
email program, the last thing he had been viewing before
he died. The most recent was from a client asking about a
project, and had arrived about two hours before. The one
above it was from China Bayles. Both were unread.

She glanced through China's message quickly and the
original message from Kirk embedded within it. Then she
used her pen to scroll upward through the inbox. Most of
the emails appeared to be business-related, from clients or
employees, with a scattering of casual notes from guys in a

rock-climbing club. None from women, and none that looked ominous or suspicious, at least at a glance. And if there was anything from someone with the initials *JH*, she didn't immediately see it.

She opened the "sent" folder and immediately spotted it. An email to Dana Kirk, from her husband. It was time-stamped at 2:04 p.m. It read like a suicide note.

> *Dana—I'm sorry. You can stop worrying about me. I'm tired and I just can't go through with the divorce. It's all yours, the house, the business, everything. Have a good life. Love, Larry*

Sheila read it again, frowning, then copied the sentences into her notebook. Was this what it sounded like? Or was it something else?

She used her pen to scroll up to the next message, which had been sent at 1:42.

> *Colin, your printer will be ready tomorrow. Stop by the shop about 2 to pick it up. No charge—it's under warranty. Glad I could help.—Larry*

The skin prickled on the back of her neck. This message didn't sound to her like it came from the same guy who— some twenty minutes later —wrote what purported to be a suicide note and then blew his brains out. She looked briefly at the other five emails that had been sent that day from this computer. They were all business-related, in the same tone as the email to Colin. One of them mentioned a lunch the following week.

She brought up the final message again, then raised her voice. "Hey, Jack. You got a second?"

Bartlett came back into the kitchen, pocketing a small tape recorder that he'd been using to take scene notes. "Yeah. Found something?"

She pointed to the computer. He bent over and read the message, then straightened, glancing at her. "What do you think?"

"Look at this one, too," she said, and brought up the earlier message. "Written twenty minutes earlier."

"Huh." Bartlett grunted. "Doesn't match, if you ask me." He glanced down at the keyboard. "Looks like the tech didn't dust this. In too much of a hurry, maybe. I'll get an evidence bag. Let's take the laptop to the station and get Butch to print it."

Butch Bedford was PSPD's in-house fingerprint technician, a young black officer who had recently finished a two-week training course in print analysis run by the Texas Department of Public Safety. When Sheila took the chief's job, the department's fingerprint work had been sent to Austin, a turnaround of four or five days, sometimes a week—just not fast enough. Then Blackie beefed up the county's forensic capabilities and Sheila sent the print work there, which was faster, at least in the beginning. Now, with more work to do, even the county lab was frequently backlogged, which could mean a couple days' wait.

And then Bedford had come along, a new hire with four years of college and a major in forensic science from Sam Houston State. He had already completed a basic course in fingerprint analysis as part of his major, but she sent him off for further training and purchased some minimal equipment—not enough to do the job the way it should be done, but enough to get a preliminary report done quickly, when they needed it. The confirmation analysis, if necessary, could be done at the county lab or in Austin, where there was better equipment.

Bartlett glanced around. "If you're finished in here, the med techs can take the body. I've let Dr. Morse know that we're sending her an autopsy. She said she'd get on it as soon as she could."

The techs bagged Kirk's hands and head and then removed the body. Sheila and Bartlett watched, paying attention. Sometimes things turned up when the victim was being moved and readied for transport. But there was nothing this time. Bartlett bagged the computer, Sheila picked up the Polaroids, and they went outside, where Jack lit a cigarette, inhaling deeply. Sheila had given up smoking when she left Dallas Homicide, but she inhaled the second-hand smoke with more than a little longing. A cigarette would taste good right now.

"The widow give you anything useful?" Bartlett asked.

"A couple of things. Kirk hated guns—wouldn't have one in the house. In fact, he was an anti-gun activist. Campaigned against the campus concealed carry."

"Good for him," Bartlett grunted. He eyed her, as if he were testing. "This ain't no suicide, at least that's my feeling. How much do you want to bet?"

"Not one red cent," Sheila said. She opened her notebook and began to scan her notes. "Okay, here we go. Kirk had lots of friends, no enemies, according to Mrs. Kirk. She doesn't know anything about a stalker, doesn't want her boyfriend bothered, etcetera. She was at work all day, at the library—except for an hour when she was supposedly having lunch at the Nueces Street Diner. With her boyfriend. From one to two. Oh, and there's insurance. Two hundred fifty thou. Plus she gets the house —*and* the business."

Bartlett whistled. "That's enough motive."

"Agreed." Sheila hesitated, thinking about the woman she had interviewed. "But she's a softie. Motive, yes, but no starch. Not saying she didn't kill him or that she doesn't know who did. But if she's involved, she's a damn good actress." She cocked her head, listening. There was a flare of lightning in the dark sky to the north, and in the distance, thunder rumbled. She thought of the email to Dana Kirk, time-stamped at 2:04.

"Any idea of the time of death?"

Bartlett blew a stream of blue smoke from his nostrils.

Instead of answering, he said, "I just got a call from that kid reporter at the *Enterprise*. Jessica Nelson."

"That one," Sheila said darkly. "She got a tip on Timms' arrest, according to China Bayles. When we finally book the guy, she'll no doubt be there. With a camera."

Bartlett chuckled. "Yeah, that one. But she did pick up on something, Sheila. She was looking for human interest and talked to a neighbor two doors east, a Mrs. Wauer. The woman says she might've heard a gunshot around two o'clock. She remembers thinking it was a backfire. And Matheson located a guy across the street and a couple of houses down, who claimed to have heard the same thing, about the same time. He told Mattie he thought it was the garbage truck."

"Garbage truck," Sheila said thoughtfully, and thought again of the email. Somebody sent it at 2:04—if not Kirk, then the killer.

"The garbage guys are pretty noisy," Bartlett was saying. "That's what the neighbor said, anyway. They like to bang the cans around, make as much racket as possible, hoping to wake up the taxpayers." He pulled on his cigarette. "Nothing else—at least so far. No one saw a suspicious vehicle, or anybody leaving the scene on foot. I'll have Mattie follow up with the Wauer woman."

Sheila made a note. "I wonder if that garbage truck always shows up at the same time."

Bartlett pursed his lips. "Let's check that out. You're thinking that maybe—"

"Right. If this is a homicide, and if the shooter knew the neighborhood well enough to know what day and time the garbage truck picks up, it would be an easy thing to time the job for when the truck was on the street. I'll give the garbage company a call, find out who was on today's route. Maybe the garbage guys saw something."

Bartlett was frowning. "I was thinking how this would've gone down. No sign of a struggle, nothing out of place except for the chair and the beer on the floor. Seems to me that it had to be somebody Kirk knew—somebody who could come in, maybe talk a little, then step forward, pull a gun, and fire when he wasn't expecting it. When he was still seated at the table."

"And if Dana Kirk didn't write that email to herself, it had to be written by somebody who knew about the divorce," Sheila said. "Who knew the wife's name and email address or knew that it was in the address book on Kirk's computer." She glanced at Bartlett. "So what's next?"

Bartlett gave her that slanted grin of his, and she thought again of his reputation as a dangerous man. "You're really gonna do this, aren't you?" he asked. "Let me have the lead."

"Yep," Sheila said, straight-faced. "Really gonna do it." She liked this guy. Orlando would have liked this guy.

"Okay." He was brisk. "Okay, here's what we do next. We take the computer for printing. We get a search warrant for the business, then we go to the shop, have a look around. Pull the names of the employees, talk to them, see what they know about this stalker Kirk mentioned."

"Timms' computer," Sheila put in. "Where is it?"

"In the evidence locker at the station. Timms didn't find it when he broke into the shop. Somebody had stuck it in one of the file cabinets."

"Might be a good idea to ask Annetta Blount to take a look at the data files on Timms' machine," Sheila said. Blount was one of the detectives who worked under Bartlett, specializing in fraud and financial crime. She had taken a couple of courses in forensic computing at the academy. "See if she can find whatever it was Timms didn't want anybody to see. That is, if there is such a thing, which we don't know."

"Yeah. I'll put her on it." Bartlett glanced at his watch. "After I leave here, I'll stop by the station, leave Kirk's laptop, and punch up the warrant request. I'll get the warrant signed and meet you at the computer shop—say, maybe forty minutes." He paused, thinking. "Hey. We haven't cleared the break-in yet. We might not need a new warrant."

"Uh-uh. We're both thinking homicide, Jack. New case. May be connected to the break-in, but maybe not. Let's do it by the book, so we don't get any crap from anybody when we go to trial."

"Especially crap from the chief." Bartlett grinned.

This time, Sheila returned the grin. "Right. I'll phone the judge and let her know you're bringing the warrant." She paused. "Okay if I take the Polaroids? I didn't get a chance to look at them."

"Yeah, sure."

There was another clap of thunder, closer. Sheila looked up. The sky was gray and dark. "Maybe we ought to get something to eat before we do the shop. You think?"

Bartlett put out his cigarette and bagged the butt. "Sounds good. There's a fast-food joint across the street from the computer shop. Meet you there."

Chapter Seven

If you have ever tangled with the greenbrier vine [*Smilax bona-nox*, aka catbrier, blaspheme-vine], you can appreciate its common names. The thorns cling like the claws of a cat and have induced more than one blasphemous response from this explorer.

Edible and Useful Plants of
Texas and the Southwest
by Delena Tull

The name *bona-nox* means "good night" in Latin. Why did Linnaeus give [the catbrier] this unusual name? Perhaps *bona-nox* was a curse in Latin—the species certainly causes lots of cursing by field biologists when they get stuck by its prickles!

Charles Wilson Cook

McQuaid and the kids and I live off Limekiln Road, twelve miles outside Pecan Springs, at the western edge of the developed part of the Hill Country. A couple of miles east of us, back toward town, a gated community of half-million-dollar homes is under construction behind an outpost palisade, the houses thrusting into the sky like medieval stone castles. To the west, the wilderness begins: rocky, thin-soiled uplands thickly blanketed with nearly impenetrable brakes of cedar, elbow bush, and catbrier; grassy clearings studded with spiny prickly pear; and swaths of open valleys braided with clear creeks. That's what you can see, and it's beautiful. But there's more that you can't, and it's beautiful, too. Underground, the folded hills are honeycombed with labyrinthine limestone caves, carved by eons of seeping, dripping, trickling water.

This wilderness is home to whitetail deer and armadillos, rangy coyotes and feral pigs, wild turkeys, turkey vultures, the endangered golden-cheeked warblers, and—in the underground caves and the open night skies—the Mexican free-tail bats. For over a century, cattle ranchers scrabbled a hard living from these hills and valleys. That era has come to an end, for in the past decade, factory-farmed cattle have swamped the market. Range-fed cattle are no longer profitable. Now, few people have the know-how and the stamina it takes to live off the land.

It was warm for early November, and it had been looking like rain all afternoon, a thunderstorm to the north offering a brief, glittering show of lightning. It had been full dark when I left Ruby's house, and the rain was just beginning to fall. I was heading home down Limekiln Road, not far from the turnoff to our house, when I caught a quick movement out of the corner of my eye. Before I knew what was happening, a ghostly apparition sprinted out of the thick underbrush and across the road at the moving edge of my headlights. A mountain lion—a splendid wild cat, lithe and lean, its tail more than half the length of its body, its gray fur glistening like liquid silver in the rain.

I jammed on the brakes, clenching the steering wheel, my heart pounding. This was the first big cat I had ever seen, and I couldn't help wishing he had stopped so I could get a better look. Of course, I was safely in the car—I'm sure I would have felt differently if I'd been on foot. But the sight was a reminder that I live at the edge of the wild lands, and this glimpse of real wildness left me as breath-less as if I'd been within reach of those razor-sharp claws.

I took a deep breath and drove on, still enthralled by the magic of what I had seen. But it was frightening, too, and as I made the left turn off the highway and onto our narrow gravel lane, I was glad to be coming home.

We live in a large two-story Victorian, painted white with green shutters, a porch on three sides, a turret in the front corner. It was built in the interval between the world wars, when Central Texas State was still a teachers' college and Pecan Springs was still a very small town. When our house was new, there were no near neighbors and the land all around was largely unsettled.

Our closest neighbors are the Banners, who have a ma-roon mailbox shaped like a Texas A&M football helmet bearing the words BANNERS FOR AGGIES! in large gold let-ters. Tom and Sylvia are both employed in Pecan Springs, Tom at the university, Sylvia at Ranchers State Bank. In addition to their town jobs, they share the work of a big vegetable garden, Tom maintains a small peach orchard, and Sylvia tends a flock of ten Gulf Coast native sheep, brought to Texas in the late 1500s by the Spanish and bred over the centuries for their fine wool. The best thing about the breed, Sylvia says, is their tolerance for our Texas heat and humidity. She is a talented spinner and weaver and dyes her own fiber from plants she grows or gathers: gold-enrod, madder, burdock, clematis, coreopsis, and yarrow—even bark from the osage orange trees and the cochineal bugs she picks off the prickly pear. She's raised her sheep from lambs and loves them as if they were her children.

I parked my Toyota on the gravel area beside the fence and ducked through the drizzle to the porch. The house was dark, which meant that McQuaid and the kids weren't yet back from Seguin. However, our elderly basset—Howard Cosell—was on guard as usual, stationed just inside the kitchen door to make sure that his house was not invaded by burglars, skunks, rats, or other unapproved intruders from the wilderness beyond the stone fence. (I'm sure he would also do his best to defend against mountain lions.) Howard was irritated because his dinner was three hours late, and he told me about it in no uncertain tones. If you've ever had an aggravated basset lecture you about his delayed dinner, you know what I'm talking about.

Pumpkin, Caitie's orange tabby cat, isn't as vocal as Howard, but he let me know that he wasn't at all happy with the way his household was being managed. This scruffy, battle-scarred, down-at-the-heels character showed up on our doorstep earlier this year, having already deployed eight of his nine lives in search of a forever home. The fellow immediately clawed his way into Caitie's soft heart. She adopted him without hesitation—never mind that what I had in mind when she asked for a kitty had been something on the order of a cute, cuddly kitten.

"He's like me when I came to live here," she said. "He doesn't have any family. He doesn't have a home. He's lonesome. He needs somebody to take care of him. He needs *me*." And since this guy had been around the block a time or two and knew an outstanding opportunity when he saw it, he unpacked his bags, powered up his purr, and took up residence on Caitie's pillow.

The gang showed up as I finished feeding the animals and was brewing myself a cup of tea. Brian thudded into the kitchen, whirled me around twice, announced that he had won the game with a bases-loaded single in the ninth, and then did a celebratory dance around the kitchen table, followed by another bone-crushing hug.

Brian came permanently into my life when he was just ten, and now I have to bend over to give him a hug. Not quite seventeen, he's two-plus inches taller than I am and outweighs me by twenty-plus pounds. His craggy face is still unformed, but he has McQuaid's dark hair and steel-blue eyes. He also has his dad's interest in sports, although (happily, in my opinion) he doesn't care much about football. I was delighted when he joined the baseball team. Baseball (again, in my opinion) is a civilized sport, a game of skill and timing. And the players do not try to kill one another. .

"You *rock*," I said, gasping for air, and then pointed out that it was now past nine o'clock and that he'd better rock on upstairs and do his homework.

McQuaid came in, kissed me briefly, reported that Brian had been named the game's most valuable player, grabbed two ponchos, and went out to help Caitie shut up the chicken coop. Her chickens—three red hens and three white hens—are the dearest loves of her life, next to Pumpkin and the violin my mother gave her. (The rest of us bring up the rear.) Using money that she earned helping me at the shop, Caitie bought the chickens in early summer. She decided to get teenaged pullets rather than baby chicks because she wanted to launch her egg business as soon as possible. Her "girls," as she calls them, live in the chicken palace that McQuaid constructed.

And I do mean *palace*. The sizeable chicken yard is fenced and covered with wire netting in order to foil enterprising skunks, raccoons, and Pumpkin. The coop has a main floor and a chicken ladder to the loft and the three nest boxes. Caitie requested a box for each girl (with her name on it), but we pointed out that all six girls would not be laying eggs at exactly the same moment and that they ought to be willing to share the nests. So far, though, we haven't seen any evidence of sharing. We haven't seen any eggs yet, either. Until—

"It's an egg!" Caitie cried ecstatically, bursting through the kitchen door, her poncho wet with rain. "Somebody laid an egg, Mom! A real egg! And in a nest, too!"

"An egg?" I asked, in an incredulous tone. "I don't believe it! Come on, Caitie—you're foolin'. A really truly egg? In a *nest*?"

"Really truly! The very first one!" She opened her hand and we looked down at the small egg cupped in her palm. It was a little bigger than a golf ball. "Isn't it *awe*some?" she whispered. Her tone was as hushed as if we were admiring the Hope Diamond.

"I have never seen a more beautiful beginner's egg in my life," I said truthfully. "Who laid it? Was it a red hen or a white hen?"

"I don't know," she said, stroking it with her fingers. "It's *brown*, Mom. Why is it brown? I don't have any brown chickens."

I know next to nothing about the egg production habits of chickens, but I remembered reading some information that had come with the birds. "The Rhode Island Reds are supposed to lay brown eggs. The other chickens are Leghorns. Their eggs are white. The chicken that laid this egg must have been a Red."

She looked confused. "Well, okay." She carefully put the egg in a saucer in the middle of the kitchen table. "I'm going to get my camera and take its picture. And then I'm going to cook it and *eat* it."

"Or maybe save it for breakfast?" I suggested. "You had supper with Grandma and Grandpa McQuaid, and I know how Grandma loves to cook. Bet you had cake for dessert, didn't you? You're probably full right up to here." I put my hand on the top of her head. She giggled, that sweet little-girl giggle that never fails to pull at my heart.

Caitlin—the daughter of my half brother, Miles—has just turned twelve. She's small for her age and slender, with pixie-cut dark hair and dark, waiflike eyes. Sad eyes, with good reason. She's still waking from a string of horrible nightmares that must have seemed unending in her short life: her mother's drowning, her father's murder, her aunt's death from cancer—more awfulness than any child ought to endure. McQuaid and I have adopted her and are trying to help her build as normal a life as possible. And a few months ago, we were rewarded when she said she wanted to call us Mom and Dad.

"I'm guess I'm sorta pretending," she admitted. "I know I'll never have my own mom and dad back. But I'd like it if you'd be Mom and Dad, if that's okay with you."

It was okay with us, and the three of us shared a hug to seal the bargain. I'm not a sentimental person by nature, but I don't mind saying that I had tears in my eyes. I had put off marriage because I valued my independence and wanted to be free of binding, entangling commitments. For a time, I'd had a law career, and then I had the shop, and in both circumstances, I cherished my freedom and autonomy. I had never planned to have children, and even after McQuaid and I moved in together and I became Brian's mom, I didn't consider myself a genuinely domesticated person.

Now, a husband, two kids, a dog, a house cat and a shop cat, innumerable lizards, snakes, and spiders (all Brian's), and six chickens later, I'm still getting used to it. But it's hard to think back to a time when McQuaid and Brian and I weren't a family, fitting together like pieces of a puzzle, sharing everything that came along. And now there's another piece, a sweet and fragile little girl, and much more to share.

Mom and Dad?

Yes, it was okay. It was definitely okay.

"I'll get my camera," Caitie said now, and scampered up the stairs. When she first visited our house with her father, she had been enchanted by the round room in the turret—the Magic Tower, she called it. When she disappeared from the family picnic that afternoon, I found her asleep on the window seat there, my tattered childhood copy of *The Secret Garden* on the floor beside her. So when she came to live with us, the Magic Tower became hers.

She chose two shades of pink for the walls and ceiling and she's hung her drawings of fairies and filled the shelves with the books and stuffed animals she brought from the life she shared with her parents. She spends a lot of time there, playing her violin and reading and looking out the window.

And one memorable afternoon, she put all six of her girls in a bushel basket and carried them up to her room. Judging from the clucking, I'd say that they enjoyed themselves.

Chapter Eight

🌸 The Chipotle Chicken was across Blanco Street from Kirk's Computer Sales and Service, not far from the CTSU campus. From their table at the front window, Sheila and Jack Bartlett could see the shop, which occupied the middle unit in a small strip mall. All three stores in the mall were closed and dark, although the all-night Washateria on the corner of Blanco and Bur Oak was brightly lit and busy—students, mostly.

Sheila and Bartlett didn't talk much during the meal, both preoccupied with their thoughts. By the time they finished, the misty rain had turned into a drizzle. They left their cars in the Chipotle Chicken lot and walked across the street, where Bartlett used Larry Kirk's key to let them in the front door. From his investigation into the earlier break-in, Bartlett knew his way around the shop and swiftly deactivated the alarm unit before it could go off, using the code he'd written in his notebook.

"Good move, Jack," Sheila said. Burglar alarms were a big-dollar headache for the department. Ninety-eight percent of the alarm calls that the police had to answer were triggered by accident or operator error, but each one still had to be checked out by patrol officers.

"Figured that code might come in handy," Bartlett said with a grin, and flicked on the lights at the front of the store.

The shop was longer than it was wide, with a glass display window across the front. Along both sides of the room were floor-to-ceiling shelves of computers, monitors, keyboards, printers, modems, carrying cases, and accessories— a large inventory, Sheila thought, representing a sizeable investment. A sales counter with a cash register was located about midway to the back of the shops. Above the counter was a sign:

COMPUTER SALES AND REPAIR
HOME AND OFFICE NETWORKING
SPYWARE REMOVAL/VIRUS PROTECTION
AUTOMATED REMOTE BACKUPS
FULL SERVICE TUNE-UPS STARTING AT $99

Behind the counter was a work area with several file cabinets and two desks, each with a computer and a couple of chairs. Along a partition wall near the back of the area was a workbench, a couple of tall stools, and racks and shelves of computers and parts.

As they went through the darkened work area, Sheila said, "Tell me about Timms' break-in."

"He came in the back way," Bartlett said, and opened the door next to the workbench. It led into a storage area that was stacked with empty boxes and assorted computer equipment. In the concrete block wall at the back was another door. Bartlett turned on a light, disarmed the alarm, and pushed the door open. Outside was an empty, asphalted parking area, rain puddles glittering in the blue glare of a mercury vapor lamp at the far end of the strip mall, near the Washateria.

"Timms didn't set off the alarm back here?" Sheila asked, looking at the keypad beside the back door.

"Beginner's luck," Bartlett said. "Apparently, the last guy out that night—the assistant manager, a kid named Palmer—failed to set the alarm. This door is pretty flimsy, and Timms came equipped with a crowbar. Probably took him all of three minutes to pop that lock. If the alarm had been on, our guys would've caught him in the building." He grinned wryly. "If they got here quick enough, that is."

The door repair was an amateur job, Sheila saw. The lock plate had been replaced but not the splintered section of the jamb.

Bartlett gestured around the storage room. "We don't know how long he was in this area or how much searching he did back here. The video camera picked him up near the register, where there was enough light from the street to capture an image of him pushing a few things around, scattering papers, and so on, to make it look like vandals had broken into the place. When Kirk came in the next morning and saw what had happened, he reported it and began an inventory. Nothing turned up missing—not even Timms' computer. It's the shop's practice to put the smaller units that come in for repair into one of the file cabinets, out of sight. This one was a notebook computer."

"Did Kirk recognize Timms from the surveillance camera?" Sheila asked, as they walked back into the work area.

"It was the assistant manager who tagged Timms. That was the next afternoon, after he looked at the video. He told Matheson—he was the one who handled the initial investigation—and Mattie bumped it up to me." He grinned slightly. "Seein' as how it was George Timms on that tape, Mattie knew right away that he didn't want any part of it."

Sheila chuckled, imagining how Detective Matheson must have felt when he understood that what he was investigating as a minor break-in by a couple of teenagers was the work of a major player in the Pecan Springs business community.

"I let Captain Hardin know what was going down,"

Bartlett went on. "We immediately seized Timms' computer and the surveillance tape and moved to charge him. His lawyer came forward with the surrender offer and mentioned extortion—nothing specific, just the mention. Said we'd get the full story later."

"You didn't look at the computer yourself, to see what might be on it?"

Bartlett shook his head. "Didn't seem important—not then, anyway. The only thing big about the deal was Timms. Anyway, I figured we'd have a look at the computer when it became clear what kind of blackmail charge Timms was going to make."

Sheila folded her arms and propped one hip against a desk. The lights at the front of the shop dimly lit the area behind the counter. "Who worked on that computer here in the shop?"

"That's the interesting thing. Nobody worked on it—at least, that's what they all claimed. Palmer checked it in just before five on Thursday and left it for the next available tech. The guys who work here sometimes come in after the shop is closed to catch up on a job. But none of them—that would be Henry, Dennis, Richie, and Kirk himself—would admit to coming in on Thursday night, or taking it out of the file cabinet on Friday."

"What about Jason?" Sheila asked.

"Jason?" Bartlett asked, frowning. He reached into his pocket and took out his notebook. "I only know about three guys. Richie Potts, Dennis Martin, Henry Palmer. Four, counting Kirk. I spoke to all of them. None of them owned up to having a look at Timms' computer."

"Dana Kirk mentioned a contract employee named Jason. She didn't know his last name. Maybe he's not working here any longer. But we might want to check him out, see if he's still got a key."

"Yeah." Bartlett took out a pen, clicked it, and made a note. "Anyway, Timms brought his computer in late Thursday afternoon. The break-in happened on Friday night. He was identified on Saturday. The surrender deal was made on Sunday, for today."

"So if there was a blackmail threat, presumably Timms received it sometime on Friday. Which is why he came back for his computer on Friday night."

Bartlett shrugged. "Possible. Or it's possible that he's blowing smoke with the blackmail allegation, which we haven't nailed down yet. Maybe he simply thought of something naughty that he left on the machine and wanted to get it back before anybody saw it."

"If that's the case, why didn't he just walk into the shop and ask for it?" Sheila asked. "I'll have a talk with Charlie Lipman," she added. "Maybe he knows more than he's telling us right now." She pushed out her lips. "Prints on Timms' machine?"

Bartlett frowned. "Not sure it was printed when we took it in. And I don't think Mattie printed the guys who work here, either." He shook his head ruefully. "I'll get Butch to dust and print the computer. Didn't seem important at the time. But now—" He pocketed his notebook.

"Yeah. Now is a different story," Sheila said, straightening. "Kirk's dead and Timms has disappeared."

Bartlett cocked his head. "Got a theory or three?"

Sheila smiled. It was a question Orlando had taught her to ask. How many theories can you spin, kid? The trick was to sketch all the possible explanations that might fit the facts, one, two, three, however many she could think of, no matter how far-out they seemed. Then leave every one of them on the table until more pieces of evidence became available, eliminating some, making others seem more plausible.

"A few," Sheila replied. "The most obvious one is suicide—why, we don't know. Money, maybe, or the divorce, or his wife sleeping around. There's the suicide note. But we'd have to understand why he'd write back-to-back emails, one all business and future-oriented, the other announcing that he was ending it. And one way or another, the suicide email rules out accident." She paused. "A second theory. A robbery gone bad. But there was money in the wallet on the table—*and* the suicide email, both of which cancel that one out."

Bartlett nodded. "Agree. Okay, here's a third. Kirk himself finds something juicy on Timms' computer and demands money to keep his mouth shut. Timms kills Kirk to keep him quiet and then gets the hell out of Dodge. Seems the likeliest, to me—at least so far. It explains Timms' absence."

"Or one of Kirk's employees was blackmailing Timms," Sheila said thoughtfully. "And maybe putting the bite on other customers as well. It might've been some kind of long-term racket, small scale, so people paid up and kept their mouths shut. Maybe Kirk found out what was going on and confronted the employee."

"Makes sense." Bartlett pointed a finger and pulled an imaginary trigger. "*Bang.* Employee shoots the boss and attempts to make it look like a suicide. The employee is likely to know the wife's name, and where to find her in Kirk's email address book, which would account for the fake suicide note. And in this scenario," he added, "Timms isn't involved in the shooting. He decided to blow off the surrender for his own reasons."

"Yeah," Sheila said quietly. "And then there's the wife and her boyfriend, Glen Vance. She says that she was back at the library by one forty-five—which we can check out—but that he had errands to run. She doesn't know what time he got back. Vance could have dropped her off, then driven over to Kirk's and shot him."

Bartlett nodded. "Vance could easily have written the email, both to reinforce the appearance of suicide and to exonerate his girlfriend. Classic piece of misdirection."

"And that stalker that Kirk emailed China Bayles about,"

Sheila said. "Did you happen to notice the five yellow sticky notes on the calendar? *Saw JH?* I wonder if the notes refer to the stalker."

"Yeah, I saw them," Bartlett replied. "It's certainly possible." He began ticking off the possibilities on his fingers. "So far, what we've got is shot by robber, which we don't like, and shot by self, which we doubt but it's still a maybe. Shot by Timms, which seems likely. Then, shot by blackmailing employee, shot by wife's boyfriend, and shot by stalker with or without the initials *JH*. That's six—five if you count out robbery. Anything else off the top of your head?"

"Could be none of the above," Sheila said, liking Bartlett's succinct summing up. "Something else, maybe. Something we haven't picked up on yet." Orlando had always reminded her of the importance of keeping an open mind. The evidence might seem to point them in one direction when the truth lay somewhere else entirely, somewhere they hadn't looked yet. She turned at the sound of the front door opening and closing and a high-pitched male voice.

"Who's there?" the voice called. "Hey, Larry, is that you? Who's back there?"

"Police," Bartlett stepped around the cash register counter as the rest of the store lights came on. "Hello, Henry," he said. "Chief Dawson, this is the shop's assistant manager. Henry Palmer. Henry, Chief Dawson."

The young man was tall and gangly, with narrow plastic-rimmed glasses and dark hair parted on one side and plastered to his head like shiny patent-leather. He wore a neon-striped bicycler's vest, wet from the drizzle, and had a white helmet under one arm. He had pushed a bicycle through the front door and leaned it against one of the displays.

"Have we had another break-in, Detective?" He blinked at Sheila. "The chief of police? Why are you—"

"We have a warrant," Bartlett said, and took it out for Palmer to see.

Sheila spoke. "What are you doing here after hours, Mr. Palmer?"

Palmer put the helmet down. "Well, Larry and me, we really don't keep hours. We just come in whenever—" The young man swallowed, his Adam's apple jumping in his skinny neck. "You know, like whenever there's work." Shrugging out of his bicycling vest, he pointed toward the bench at the back of the work area. "I started a job this afternoon. Pulling data off a hard drive that was in a house fire. Thought I'd come in for a couple of hours tonight and see if I could get it done." His glance darted between Sheila and Bartlett. "Don't tell me there was another break-in? I made sure to set the alarm this time."

Bartlett glanced at Sheila and she gave him an imperceptible nod. "No break-in." His voice was gruff, his expression grave. "We're very sorry to be the bearers of bad news, Mr. Palmer. Lawrence Kirk is dead."

"Dead?" Palmer put out a hand as if to steady himself, hit a monitor on the desk beside him, and had to grab it to keep it from tumbling onto the floor. "Omigod! Dead? Oh, no! What was it? A bike accident? I keep telling Larry that he needs to wear some sort of reflective gear when he's riding that bicycle after dark, especially when it's rainy. Leg bands, a jacket, something. But does he listen?" His voice rose. "No, of course he doesn't. He never listens! Larry always knows better than anybody else."

"It wasn't a bicycle accident," Bartlett said. "He was shot."

"Shot?" Palmer gasped. "You're— No!"

Sheila watched the young man closely. His eyes were round, huge, and he was suddenly pale, struggling to make sense of what he had just heard. Some people are good actors. They can mime shock, surprise, astonishment. But not this guy. Clearly, the news was a stunning blow.

She waited a moment to let him catch his breath, then asked quietly, "You and Mr. Kirk were close?"

"He's my cousin," Palmer said in a weak voice. He sank down in the nearest desk chair and put his head in his hands. "We grew up together." He pulled in his breath, despairing. "What am I going to tell Aunt Jenny?"

Bartlett lifted an eyebrow, letting Sheila know that this relationship was news to him.

"I'm sorry, Mr. Palmer," she said quietly. "I'm sure this must be a shock to you. Did you see your cousin today? Did he come to work?"

"I saw him this morning." Palmer's voice was muffled. "He was here until just before noon, then he went home. He usually works there after lunch, and comes back here before closing time. When he didn't show up, I figured—" He wiped his nose with the back of his hand. "I just figured that he'd gotten involved with what he was doing and wasn't watching the clock. That's Larry. I mean, he's like that. He . . . he gets involved and loses track of time."

"Were you here in the shop by yourself this afternoon?" Bartlett asked.

"No. Richie was here for a couple of hours. Then Dennis came in. And some guy looking for work." He frowned. "I called Larry to ask whether he wanted the guy to fill out an application, but he didn't pick up. Didn't call back, either."

"You were never alone here?" Bartlett pressed.

Palmer shook his head. "No. Why are you—" He stopped suddenly, connecting with what Bartlett was asking. "He was . . . shot? Is that what you said?"

"Yes," Sheila said. "Do you know if he owned a gun?" The alternating rhythm of their questions—Bartlett's and hers—felt good. They were in sync, which was something of a surprise, since this was the first time they'd worked together. Usually it took a while to develop the kind of back-and-forth cadence that made for effective questioning. She couldn't imagine developing the same kind of rhythm with Hardin.

"A *gun*?" Palmer jerked his attention away from Bartlett

to look at her, incredulous. "You gotta be joking. Of course Larry didn't own a gun. He hated guns. He—" He looked from one to the other of them. "Wait a minute. Where was he shot? I mean, where was he when—"

"In his kitchen," Bartlett said.

"Oh, jeez," Palmer whimpered, and started to cry. "You mean, somebody—" He choked. "Somebody *killed* him?"

"We don't know exactly how it happened, Mr. Palmer," Sheila said, softening her tone. "It could have been suicide. The shooting is still under investigation."

But Palmer only caught the first part. "Suicide?" he exclaimed, turning on her. "Hey, no *way!* Not Larry, Chief. You just get that out of your mind, right now. The guy had everything going for him. He'd never—"

Bartlett interrupted. "He seemed okay to you when he left here before noon?"

"Absolutely okay," Palmer said. "One hundred percent okay. But that means—" He stopped. "What about robbery? Did you think about that?"

"We're considering all possibilities," Sheila said. "Can you think of anyone who might want to kill him?"

"Kill him?" Palmer repeated incredulously. "But who would want to do that? Larry was the nicest guy. Everybody thought so, except maybe his wife." He wiped his eyes and his voice took on a bitter edge. "Dana was getting a divorce. It wasn't a good situation. But she's not the type to . . ." His voice trailed away.

"There was bad blood?" Bartlett asked. "They fought?"

"Fight?" Palmer was cautious. "Not exactly, at least, not so much. She just . . . well, she found somebody she liked better. She didn't want to be married to Larry."

"And Kirk was upset?"

"Well, sure. He was pretty pissed at her. Wouldn't you be?" Palmer waved his hand impatiently. "I mean, first, she goes out and gets mixed up with this other guy. Then she starts asking Larry for the money she put into this place."

He sighed. "But the only way he could get her what she was asking was to find a business partner, which isn't easy in this kind of economy. And then there was that house. I'd've helped Larry if I could, but what she thought her share was worth was way beyond me. I couldn't come up with that kind of money."

Sheila changed the direction of the questioning. "Did Mr. Kirk ever mention that he was being followed? Did he ever suggest that someone might be stalking him?"

"Stalking him?" Palmer sounded surprised. "No. He didn't mention anything like that, although—" He stopped, frowning. "He'd heard from a woman he used to know, though. She was sort of a pest, I guess. He said he wished she'd stop hanging around and go away and leave him alone."

"A former girlfriend?" Sheila asked. She took out her notebook. "Did he say who she was?"

"No. Larry wasn't the type to talk about stuff like that. I didn't get the idea that she was ever a girlfriend. Just somebody he knew from someplace he used to work. The insurance agency, I think he said." He shook his head dismally. "Listen, I really would like to go back to the bench and finish up that hard drive. The customer wants it first thing tomorrow. And work kind of makes me feel better, you know?"

Bartlett glanced at Sheila and they traded mute signals. "I'm afraid that won't be possible, Mr. Palmer," he said. "At least, not tonight. You can open for business tomorrow at the usual time, but we'll take the business files and employee records with us." He gestured to the laptop on the sales counter next to the cash register. "And the shop computer. This is it?"

Sheila knew that finding anything related to Kirk's death was a long shot, but they had to take a look. There might be something in the emails that had come to the shop, or in one of the other documents.

"That's it." Palmer bit his lip. "I guess that won't be a problem. But what about the customers? And the guys who work here? Should I tell them about Larry? *What* should I tell them?" His voice rose. "And what's going to happen to the business?"

"You might want to put a notice on the door, letting people know that the owner is deceased," Sheila replied.

"Yeah," Palmer said. "Maybe I won't open up until ten or eleven. There's going to be a lot to sort out."

"And as far as the business is concerned," Bartlett put in, "you may need to consult with Mrs. Kirk."

"Oh, hell," Palmer groaned. "That's all I need. Dana doesn't know diddlysquat, but she'll want to take the shop over and run it. She always did, you know—want to run it, I mean. And now it's hers, I suppose." Distractedly, he ran his hands through his hair. "Damn. Damn, damn, *damn*."

"How many people have a key to the shop?" Bartlett asked. "You? The other employees?"

"Yeah, I do, of course. And Dennis Martin and Richie Potts, sure. But they're not employees. That is, they're contract guys. They come in when there's work. When we call them to do a job. Larry or me, I mean." He waved toward the Rolodex on the counter. "They're both in the Rolodex. There's a card up front with their phone numbers and email addresses."

Bartlett's cell phone gave three digital notes and he flipped it open, checking the caller ID. "Yeah, Mattie," he said, and turned away to talk.

Sheila flicked through the Rolodex, finding the card. "And Jason?" she asked. "Is he here, too?"

He blinked at her. "Jason Hatch, you mean? Yeah, I guess. But we haven't called him for a while."

"Why?"

"Dunno." He cleared his throat. "Larry just said to stop using him unless it was a have-to case. Unless we got really busy and couldn't handle the load otherwise."

"So Mr. Hatch hasn't been in the shop recently," Sheila said. "Since how long ago?"

"Oh, maybe a couple of months. August, maybe." He shrugged. "Couldn't tell you exactly."

Sheila made a note and repeated her earlier question. "Do you know why Mr. Kirk didn't want to employ him?"

His glance slid away. "Uh-uh. Larry just said to put him at the bottom of the list and ask before I called Jay to come in."

She persisted. "Would any of the other guys know why?"

Palmer's lip twitched nervously. "I doubt it. I wouldn't think so."

Jason Hatch. Sheila jotted down the name, noticing the initials. *JH.* "Does Mr. Hatch live in Pecan Springs?"

"Yeah, in a trailer park on the other side of I-35. At least, he did. The address is probably in the Rolodex." He paused and added, more sharply, "I don't know what you're getting at with all these questions about Hatch. But you'll find some other names in the Rolodex, too. Guys who have worked here at one time or another since the place opened. Hatch isn't the only one."

"Does Mr. Hatch still have a key to the shop?" she asked, and made a note to check the employee records for others who might have had keys.

"Of course not," Palmer said defensively. "I mean, why would he? He doesn't work here anymore." He reached into his pocket and produced a ring with several keys. "If you're looking for keys, here's mine. The front door and back door are marked. The little brass one is the cash register. There are some file cabinet keys on there, but we don't lock the drawers."

Bartlett closed his phone and stepped back to the counter to look over the keys. "Thanks," he said, returning the ring to Palmer. "We have Mr. Kirk's keys, so you can keep these. First thing tomorrow," he added, "please come to the station so we can print you. Okay?"

"Fingerprint *me*?" Palmer frowned. "But I don't see—How is this connected to—"

"Just take our word for it," Sheila said. "We need your prints, Mr. Palmer. In fact, we'll be printing everyone who's worked in this shop."

Palmer's shoulders sagged. "Yeah," he said. "Yeah, sure. Whatever you need."

Bartlett added, gently, "And about Mr. Kirk's mother—we've already started the notification process, and she's been contacted. You can get in touch with her whenever you like. I'm sure she'd appreciate hearing from you."

"Thanks," Palmer said glumly. "Yeah, right. I'll call her when I get home."

Sheila thumbed the Rolodex and found the card with the names of the contract people on it, written in the same backslanted hand that she had seen on the grocery list and the calendar notes in Kirk's kitchen. As she looked at it, something clicked. She turned to Palmer.

"Larry Kirk," she said. "Right-hander? Left-hander?"

"Larry?" Palmer chuckled sadly. "Southpaw, his whole life. Except when one of his teachers—maybe first, second grade—tried to get him to change. 'Course he couldn't. Aunt Jenny finally had to tell the teacher to lay off."

Sheila read the quick look Bartlett gave her, but neither of them said anything. At their request, Palmer pulled a half-dozen manila file folders from the cabinets—employee records and job tickets—and put them into a box. Most of it, he said, was also on the computer. Bartlett filled out an evidence sheet, and Palmer signed for the records and the laptop. Then he pushed his bicycle out the front door and locked it behind him.

"Wow," Bartlett said admiringly, walking around the bike. "A Madone. Lance Armstrong's bike."

"You bet," Palmer said, fastening his helmet. "Lance won seven Tour de France titles on a Madone. You know bikes?"

"A little," Bartlett said. "This looks like a sweet ride."

"Nothing better, in my opinion. It's a 6.9 Pro, Dura Ace equipped, 7850 carbon laminate wheels. Top-end Bontrager components throughout. Only fourteen pounds. Can't beat it for racing, especially on hills. Good for commuting, too."

"Yeah," Bartlett said. He grinned. "Bet it came with a sweet price tag."

"A little over ten grand," Palmer said, "by the time I customized it."

Bartlett chuckled. "Guess I'd better start saving my pennies, huh?"

"If you're serious about bikes, you can't do better than a Madone," Palmer said, and rode off into the rainy dark.

A few minutes later, the evidence stowed in Bartlett's black-and-white, Sheila and Bartlett stood together under the awning in front of Chipotle Chicken, the red and green neon rooster in the window coloring the darkness around them. The rain was coming down a little harder now, and the air was turning chilly. It was more like November than it had been that afternoon, Sheila thought. The weather was fickle this time of year.

Bartlett flicked a lighter to his cigarette. "So he was a southpaw," he said quietly, leaning one shoulder against the brick wall. Water sluiced off the awning, the streetlights turning the puddles to silver. "Looks like our shooter didn't know Kirk very well, after all."

"Either didn't know or forgot," Sheila said. "It's not the kind of thing you'd automatically think about, if you were trying to make a homicide look like a suicide." There would have been lots of stress in the situation. Apprehension, fear of discovery, perhaps even regret. The killer might have known the victim intimately and have forgotten that one simple detail.

"Either way, we can scratch self-inflicted, as far as I'm concerned," Bartlett added. He blew out a stream of smoke. "Never heard of a left-hander shooting himself with his right hand. I suppose it can be done, but it doesn't seem likely."

"Which leaves us with four. Theories, that is, discounting robbery and suicide." Sheila thought of Kirk on the floor in his kitchen, still and vulnerable, alone in the indignity of death. Talking about him like this—as if he were part of some scientific equation to be solved—left a bad taste in her mouth. She knew they couldn't afford to get emotionally invested. That was how you missed things. But you also had to retain your personal connection with the victim, your sense of the fragility of life and the awful finality of death.

"Yeah." Bartlett pushed himself away from the wall. "Timms, an employee, the wife and/or her lover, the stalker. Or none of the above. We don't have Timms yet, and you've already talked to the wife. The lover can wait until tomorrow, but I'm thinking that we need to connect with Potts, Hatch, and Martin. Arrange to get them printed, find out what they know." He looked sideways at her. "Want to work on this together or separately? Tonight or tomorrow?"

Sheila glanced at her watch. It was after eight and she'd been on the job for fourteen hours. Now that she thought of it, she realized how tired she was. She also knew that Bartlett was giving the boss an out, if she chose to take it. She didn't.

"We need to get this done. It'll be faster if we split up tonight, compare notes tomorrow. I'll take Potts. And Jason Hatch. He was in the Rolodex, too." Now that she thought about it, it was Hatch she really wanted to see. "How about letting Matheson get a preliminary statement from the lover—Glen Vance? He could do that first thing in the morning."

"Okay," Bartlett said. "I'll take Dennis Martin. Tomorrow, we can get started on the files and get Annetta started on the shop computer. If we're lucky, we'll have something from the county forensics guys by noon. And by that

time, somebody will have picked Timms up and we
can wring a confession out of him. My money's on that
sonovabitch."

Sheila considered. "That bike of Palmer's—a pretty
pricy item, isn't it?"

"Yeah," Bartlett replied. "Ten grand plus, custom. Not
something you'd think an assistant manager could afford.
By the way, that phone call—it was Matheson, reporting on
his neighborhood canvass. He didn't pick up anything more
than what we've already heard. A couple of the people were
gone, though, so he'll be going back tomorrow to pick
them up."

"I'd like to go back to the scene in the morning, too,"
Sheila said. "You've got the key?"

Bartlett got an evidence bag from his squad car, took out
the key, and gave it to her, along with an evidence receipt
card. He grinned as she filled it out and signed it. "We do
things by the book on this case," he said pointedly, and they
both laughed.

"Where are you headed?" Sheila asked, as she put the
key in her shoulder bag.

"To see Martin," Bartlett replied. "Then I'm going back
to the station to open the homicide book." The homicide
book was the case file that the lead detective compiled for
every murder investigation. It typically included crime-
scene photographs and sketches, autopsy and forensic reports, transcripts of witness interviews, and investigators'
notes, documenting the investigation from the time the
murder was reported through the arrest of a suspect. After
the arrest, a copy went to the prosecutor in the DA's office,
where it became an essential part of the criminal case as it
went to court.

"While you're at the station," Sheila said, "you might
put a note on Jim Sumner's desk." Sumner was the department's Public Information Officer. "We know that the *Enterprise* is already onto this investigation."

"How much information do you want released?" Bartlett asked, frowning a little.

Sheila thought he seemed uncertain and realized that this was probably something that Hardin would have handled if he had been managing the case—especially if TV was involved. Hardin liked his moment of fame in front of the camera.

"For now, let's go with the usual bare-bones stuff," she said. "Who, where. Fuzzy on the when and how. Investigation continuing, etcetera. Nothing about the shop break-in, no mention of Timms." She paused. "Especially nothing about Timms. We need to keep the lid on that as long as we can."

"I'll do it," Bartlett said. "Briefing at oh-nine-hundred? Matheson and Blount can join us. By that time, I'll have put together a plan for the day's work."

"Sounds good to me," Sheila agreed.

Bartlett dropped his cigarette, stepped on it, and slid her a sideways glance. "Thank you, Chief," he said.

"Sheila," she said. "And thanks? What for?"

"No, *Chief*," he replied. "Thank you for giving me the lead on this case. Means a helluva lot to me. More than you know."

Sheila thought of Hardin and his habit of taking credit and understood what Bartlett was saying.

"You're welcome, Detective," she said.

Chapter Nine

If you're interested in wild foraging, try a spring nibble of the succulent tips of catbrier, aka greenbriar, *Smilax bona-nox*. (You'll want to stay clear of the thorny claws of this clutching vine.) Euell Gibbons, in *Stalking the Healthful Herbs*, claims that a jelly can be made from the catbrier root. Delena Tull, writing in *Edible and Useful Plants of Texas and the Southwest*, reports that she had no success with Gibbon's catbrier jelly but found that the root material produced an attractive red-brown dye. The tropical *Smilax regelii* was used to treat a variety of ailments, including syphilis. Also known as sarsaparilla, it was an ingredient in old-fashioned root beers. Obviously, a plant of many talents.

China Bayles
"Herbs That Hold Fast"
Pecan Springs Enterprise

Caitlin was still upstairs. I was finishing my tea and studying the new egg on the table (are first eggs always so *small*?) when the phone rang. I got to my feet to answer it, but McQuaid came in at that moment, shrugging out of the yellow poncho and brushing the rain out of his dark hair with one hand. Since he was nearer, he picked up.

"Hey, Tom," he said. "What's up, fella?" *Banner*, he mouthed to me. Our neighbor up the lane.

Whatever was up, there must have been a lot of it, for the conversation went on for several minutes. It was mostly Tom talking, though, with McQuaid listening, occasionally saying things like, "You actually *shot* him?" and "How many did you lose?" and "*That* big?" (in a surprised tone). Then, "You're going to report it to Parks and Wildlife?" Finally, he said, "Thanks for letting us know, Tom. We'll keep our eyes peeled, but she's probably long gone by now." He hung up the phone, went to the fridge, and took out a bottle of Saint Arnold root beer.

"What was all that?" I asked worriedly. "Who did Tom shoot? Who's long gone?"

"Not who," he said, opening the freezer and getting out a carton of vanilla ice cream. "What. A mountain lion." He carried the ice cream to the counter and found a large mug. "There were two. They panicked Sylvia's sheep, but Tom got out there with his gun before they killed any."

"He shot a *mountain lion*?" I asked, thinking immediately of the lithe and lovely wild animal I had seen crossing the road.

"Yeah. Six-foot male, measured nose to tail. The female got away. She's probably long gone, but he wanted to warn us to keep tabs on our animals." He turned to me, holding up the root beer. "I'm making a float. Want one?"

"That would be nice," I said. Root beer floats are a special treat at our house, and Saint Arnold is a favorite, brewed in a Houston microbrewery and sold (among other places) at the Pecan Springs Farmers Market. But I was still thinking of what I had seen.

"I may have seen that mountain lion tonight," I said. "Crossing Limekiln Road, heading north. A beautiful animal, silvery, pale—almost like a ghost. I'm glad to hear that Sylvia didn't lose any sheep. She loves those creatures."

"Tom said the male had a four-inch open gash on his head," McQuaid said, scooping ice cream into two mugs. "Not a bullet wound—almost like he'd been hit with an implement, a spade or something." He popped the cap on the bottle and poured fizzy root beer over the ice cream. He added a couple of spoons and brought the mugs to the table.

"Thanks," I said, picking up my spoon. "Is there a season on mountain lions?"

He shook his head. "Nope. They're not considered a game animal. No bounty, either, although the ranchers around here probably wish there were. It might encourage hunting." He picked up the egg and frowned at it. "I didn't know eggs came this small, China. If they're all the size of golf balls, we'll need a dozen for a decent breakfast."

"That one's just practice," I said. "They'll get bigger. I hope." Still thinking about that mountain lion, I put my spoon down, went to the door, and called Howard Cosell, who had gone out to take care of his evening business. He always goes all the way to the end of the stone fence, where the woods threaten to spill over into our yard. He trotted back without complaint, although I'm sure that if he'd suspected that a mountain lion was lurking out there in the rainy dark, he would have insisted on staying out to patrol the perimeter. But Howard is a well-fed basset and would be a tasty snack for a hungry mountain lion. I wasn't taking any chances.

"Do you think the chickens will be okay?" I asked worriedly, closing the door behind Howard.

"I hope you're not suggesting that Caitie take them upstairs for the night," McQuaid said with a chuckle.

"I'm not, and she won't—not after she had to clean up after them the last time. Lesson learned. Chickens live in the chicken house."

He nodded. "Anyway, I'm sure they'll be fine. A lion isn't going to waste his time on a few chickens. *Her* time," he amended. "She's probably out looking for a deer, since

Tom drove her away from the sheep. And anyway, if she's the one you saw crossing Limekiln, she's already miles from here. She and the male that Tom killed were hunting together, I guess. Both the male and female are solitary, except when they're breeding."

We shared a moment of silence. I was glad that Sylvia's sheep were safe and hoping that the cat I'd seen had found an unwary deer for dinner, out there in the rainy darkness. Mountain lions have been making a comeback in the past couple of decades, with reported sightings and kills—most of them roadkills, like my near miss—in Adams County and the counties around us. Hill Country ranchers have been selling out to developers in record numbers, which means that more and more people are moving into prime lion habitat. The Banners' sheep weren't the first livestock to be attacked, and they wouldn't be the last. It was a sharp reminder that the boundaries between our human-built world and the natural world are not fixed, that humans don't control nature (even though we might like to think we do), and that wild cats are not as tame and well-behaved as the domesticated cats that share our homes and backyards.

"Mom," Caitlin called from the top of the stairs. Her tone was plaintive. "I can't find my camera. I've looked everywhere. Do you know where it is?"

I grinned at McQuaid on my way out of the room. "Better put that egg down. If it gets broken, your daughter will never let you hear the end of it." Over my shoulder, I added, "Don't go away. I have something important to tell you. And keep your mitts off my root beer float."

Caitlin was with me when I came back to the kitchen, after we found her camera behind the books on her dresser. She took several photos of McQuaid admiring the miniature egg on the palm of his hand, then fixed a root beer float for herself and one for Brian and carried them both upstairs. She was going to email the photographs to her grandmothers—McQuaid's mother in Seguin and my mother, who lives on a ranch near Kerrville. She hoped they would be her first customers, although McQuaid pointed out that it might be a while before the girls produced eating-size eggs.

"Something bigger than a marble," he said, and laughingly pretended to be injured by the girl-size shoulder punch that Caitie threw at him.

When she was gone, McQuaid picked up our empty mugs, rinsed them off in the sink, and sat down at the table again. "So what did you want to tell me?"

It took a little while to relate what I knew about Larry Kirk's death and George Timms' disappearance before his scheduled arrest.

As the tale unfolded, McQuaid regarded me with increasing disbelief. He just misses being handsome—his nose was broken in a football game and there's a jagged scar across his forehead—but he's ruggedly good-looking, with slate blue eyes and dark hair that falls across his forehead and dark eyebrows that pull together when he's puzzled. Now, his brows were firmly knitted together, and when I was finished, he gave a low, incredulous whistle.

"George Timms?" he asked, shaking his head. "Sheila had better be dead sure she's got the right man, or the department will be facing a suit for false arrest. Timms is a litigious sonuvagun." He sighed. "And I would never have figured Larry Kirk for the kind of man who would *shoot* himself. I read his letter to the editor in the *Enterprise* a while back, arguing against concealed-carry on college campuses. I got the impression he was anti-gun in a big way."

"I guess I'm not surprised to hear that," I said. "Of course, you never know what's going on inside people's heads, but Larry didn't strike me as the suicide type, either. I didn't see any sign of self-pity, depression, sadness—the kind of feelings somebody might have if they were thinking of suicide." I paused. "As far as Timms is concerned, Charlie Lipman confirmed that Timms was due to surrender on

the charge. It apparently has something to do with extortion.
Timms' computer was in the shop for repair. Maybe there
was an incriminating file or two on it."

"Hmm. Yeah, well, that could be a pretty powerful motive, depending on what was in the file. Photos of Timms
with a naked beauty or two? That could be embarrassing.
But Charlie will be able to leverage it into a plea deal, especially if nothing else was taken. Name the extortionist
and—"

"Charlie's not going to leverage anything," I put in.
"He's off the case. Apparently, he and Timms weren't getting along before this, and when Timms didn't show, he
decided to call it quits."

"I guess I'm not surprised," McQuaid said thoughtfully.
"They weren't all that friendly when Charlie was representing him on that land deal. In fact, their relationship turned
pretty frosty by the time everything was all over. Timms
doesn't like to lose, especially when it comes to property."
Howard Cosell came over and leaned against McQuaid's
leg. He reached down to gently tug on the dog's long ears.
"Hey, Howard—see any mountain lions out there, old
buddy?" He looked up at me. "You know, the piece of land
Timms was suing over isn't far from here."

"I guess I knew that—but I don't know exactly where. I
never knew the details of the lawsuit, either. At the time
you were working on the case, I was pretty busy with Sheila's wedding."

"It wasn't complicated," McQuaid said. "One of Timms'
neighbors filed an adverse possession claim against about
thirty acres of Timms' family ranch. Timms wanted the
claim thrown out, but he couldn't make it happen. Charlie's
a damn good lawyer, but *he* couldn't make it happen, either.
The neighbor's documentation was too strong: photographs
of the fence he put in ten years ago, a survey, plus the filing
in the county clerk's office. He'd been in possession of the
property for over fifteen years. Really pissed Timms off,

but there was nothing he or Charlie could do about it. Adverse possession is written into the law."

"Ah. So that's what it was," I said. Texas, like many other states, permits land to be claimed by "squatter's rights," on the theory that abandoned land isn't any good to anybody and ought to be put to use—if not by the owner, then by somebody else. As I remembered it from a class in real estate law, somebody could move onto a piece of land and start using it. If he got away with this "adverse possession" claim for at least three years—that is, if the owner failed to notice, or noticed but failed to kick him off—the squatter could begin the process of claiming the property, including whatever mineral rights went with it. I even remembered Section 16.021 of the Texas Civil Practices and Remedies Code, the elements of which generations of law students have reduced to a clever mnemonic device: *Adverse possession is a HELUVA problem.* A successful claim involves *h*ostile, *e*xclusive, *l*asting, and *u*ninterrupted possession, both *v*isible and *a*ctual. H-E-L-U-V-A.

Howard licked McQuaid's hand, yawned hugely, and padded over to his basset basket beside the stove. He climbed in and circled several times, putting himself to bed. Of course, he wouldn't stay there. Howard is a people dog. He'd be on the foot of our bed when we turned out the light.

"Where exactly is Timms' property?" I asked curiously.

McQuaid drew an imaginary map on the table with his finger. "You go west on Limekiln, about two miles past our turnoff. Hang a right at Paint Horse Road, left at a pair of mailboxes a couple of miles later. Down that gravel road another mile or so, you'll see a sign for Paint Horse Ranch. That's it, although it hasn't been used for actual ranching for fifty years or so." He sat back in his chair. "It belonged in the family, all twelve hundred acres of it, going back two or three generations. Timms inherited it from his older brother, minus the disputed chunk, which is a bluff with a spectacular view. That's the piece that the neighbor adversely possessed, during the years when Timms' brother had the property. The brother lived in Houston, Timms said, and never paid any attention to the land."

As I remembered the professor's lecture on this subject, that was the way adverse possession usually happened. Land was passed along in a family, the property wasn't used, perhaps not even visited, and pieces of it were appropriated by other people—usually the neighbors.

"But Timms was making the best of it," McQuaid said. "Last time I was out there, he had just finished building a cabin on Paint Horse Creek, where he could throw parties." He chuckled wryly. "A cabin. That's what he called it. To me, it looked like a fancy bachelor pad, with plenty of parking, a couple of guesthouses for overnighters, and no neighbors to get pissed off when his friends are drinking and the music's too loud. Kind of a secret getaway, where he could hide out from his ex-wives. Not my style, but it fits good old George." He pushed back his chair, stood, and stretched.

"Hmm," I said, frowning. "I wonder if Charlie thought to have a look out there. Maybe Timms—"

McQuaid interrupted. "Did you remember that I'm going to El Paso tomorrow?" He picked up the empty Saint Arnold bottle and dropped it into the recycle bin. "Blackie's already out there. I talked to him on the phone earlier this evening." He went to the back door and checked the lock. "He's got a couple of good leads, although it looks like we'll have to cross over to Ciudad Juárez."

"That's the missing boy?" I asked. I wasn't thrilled at the thought that McQuaid and Blackie might go into Mexico. Juárez is especially dangerous territory. The drug cartels own the city, and scores of young women factory workers have been murdered there. But I had seen the boy's picture on Austin television. The little guy was only seven, with dark hair and flashing brown eyes in a delicate face.

He'd been gone for over a week. The custodial parent, a single father, was desperate. He had come to McQuaid for help in getting his son back. It was a case that tugged at our hearts, McQuaid's and mine. Brian had been taken by his mother once, without permission or notice. He was gone for only a few hours and no harm was done, but the experience had been harrowing. I knew how the little boy's father must feel.

McQuaid nodded. "The mother apparently took him from school. She has family south of Juárez." He came close, dropping his face to nuzzle my throat. "Will you miss me, wife?"

"I miss you already," I said truthfully, and my arms went around his neck. I didn't say so out loud, but I didn't want him to go. Not this time. Not to Juárez.

"Prove it," he whispered against my cheek, after a minute. He took my hand, his voice softly urgent. "Come on, babe. Let's go to bed."

I didn't need to be asked twice. We locked the doors, turned off the downstairs lights, and climbed the stairs. But just as McQuaid was pulling my T-shirt over my head, the phone in our bedroom rang.

"Rats," I said eloquently.

McQuaid dropped my shirt on the floor and began unfastening my bra. "Let it ring, China."

I thought of what had happened that afternoon, and shook my head. "It'll just take a minute," I said, reaching for the phone. "Might be important."

McQuaid growled between his teeth and pulled off my bra, brushing his hands across my breasts.

It was Ruby. "Sorry to bother you, China," she said tersely, "but Ramona and I just thought of something. Larry Kirk did *not* kill himself."

"How do you know?" I sat down on the bed and listened, but McQuaid was beginning to strip, so I have to admit that

I was a little distracted. My husband has a terrific body, lean and muscular, and I enjoy looking at him—especially when he's not wearing clothes.

But what Ruby had to tell me was pretty urgent, persuasive, too. When she finished, I thought I'd better telephone Smart Cookie and pass the information along. But before I could do that, my naked husband dove into bed and pulled me in after him.

Who says married sex is dull?

Chapter Ten

Richie Potts lived in a second-floor apartment in the university's graduate student village, not far from the campus. As Sheila walked up the outside stairs, she saw a bike with a child's seat on the back, chained to the balcony railing. A baby stroller with a blue plastic canopy was folded and propped against the wall beside two pots of dead plants. Sheila could hear rock music and feel the rhythmic *thump-thump* vibrations of the heavy bass, although it was difficult to tell whether the noise was coming from the apartment in front of her or the one on the other side of the double entrance. From somewhere close by, the odor of marijuana wafted into the night, mixed with the sour smell of cooking cabbage. A typical student apartment complex, she thought, remembering her own college days, which seemed like a century ago now. She knocked, then knocked again, louder. The door, on the chain, cracked open an inch.

"Police," Sheila said to the crack, and held up her badge wallet. "Looking for Richie Potts."

Richie Potts was twenty-two, twenty-three at most, red-haired and freckled, with an acne-scarred face and a thin stubble of gingery beard. A red-haired baby—a boy, about eighteen months old—clung to his blue-jeaned leg. A pretty young woman, heavily pregnant, appeared in the kitchen door, then disappeared. The sound of rock music (but not of the bass) was partially shut out when Potts closed the apartment door. When Sheila introduced herself, he pointed to one of a pair of living room chairs, arranged on either side of a sofa and coffee table. She sat down and told him that Larry Kirk was dead.

Watching the young man closely, Sheila thought that the announcement was news to him. Like Palmer, he seemed taken completely by surprise. But his first thoughts were focused more on the future of his employment than on the death of his employer—understandable, since he had a wife, a child, and another on the way.

"Jeez," he said, blinking. "The shop isn't going to close, is it? Will I be out of a job?"

"I don't know," Sheila said, taking out her notebook and pen. "You'll need to keep in touch with Mr. Palmer. He may be able to tell you something." She paused. "When did you see Mr. Kirk last? What can you tell me about him?"

If Potts wondered about the reason for her questions, he didn't say so. He couldn't produce much information, though. He hadn't seen Kirk that day. In fact, he hadn't seen him for several days—they hadn't happened to be in at the same time. He had worked at the shop off and on for only a few months and didn't know Larry Kirk very well—couldn't say much about him, except that he was pretty obsessive about stuff being done according to the book, his book. What else? Well, the guy hated guns, which was kind of ironic, wasn't it? In fact, he had taken a day off to protest the student concealed-carry proposal in Austin, which Potts himself supported.

"You just never know when you're gonna need a gun," he said, shaking his head darkly. "Like, if somebody starts shooting up your history class or something." The baby climbed up on the sofa and crawled into his lap. "We had a big argument about that, me and Larry. I said we oughtta have the right."

"Do you own a gun?" Sheila asked.

Potts shook his head. "Just think we oughtta have the right," he said again.

Sheila nodded. "What about Dennis Martin and Jason Hatch? Do you know them?"

Potts knew Martin, but didn't think he was a very good tech. "Too slow," he said, with another shake of his head. "That's what Larry said, too. I think he was getting ready to tell Martin to take a hike. There's plenty of other guys who can work faster. You know what I'm sayin'? You gotta figure stuff out quick. Martin's slow. Which drives Larry up a wall."

Sheila was taking notes. "Jason Hatch?"

Hatch had been at the shop when Potts himself came on the team. He was older, not a graduate student like Martin and Potts. Richie had the idea that he'd been working there for quite a while, since the place opened, maybe. He was good. "Best I've ever seen," Potts said judiciously. "He could scope out a problem way faster'n me. Faster'n Larry, too, which is sayin' something."

But Hatch had left about three weeks after Potts came on board. Hatch and Kirk had gotten into it, a real knock-down-drag-out, and Hatch was outta there. Fast. No notice, no nothing. Just *gone*.

"Got into it over what?" Sheila asked, looking up from her notebook. "What did they argue about?"

Potts shrugged. "Hatch was talkin' to a customer, was what I heard from Dennis Martin." The baby stood up on his lap and began to pull his hair.

"Talking to a customer?"

"Yeah. The way Kirk has his system set up, it's against the rules for the techs to deal directly with the customers." Potts pulled the baby's hands down and the boy began to cry.

"Why? I mean, why is it against the rules?"

He put the baby on the floor. The little boy plopped down on his bottom and began to scream. Potts raised his voice over the noise, but didn't move to placate him. "Lots of shops operate like that. Keeps the clients out of the techs' hair, is the way Kirk explained it. Clients ask dumb questions—takes the techs too much time to answer them." He grinned crookedly. "If you ask me, it's more like it keeps the techs from lettin' the clients know that they'll work on the side cheaper than the shop can do it. In this shop, the jobs go in and out through Kirk or Henry Palmer, at the counter. Nobody comes around back. The tech's got something to say to the client, he's gotta write it on the job ticket."

The baby was screaming louder. Sheila leaned forward. "But Hatch didn't do that?"

Potts yelled, "Hey, Ruthie, come and get the kid. He's bawlin'."

The woman padded out of the apartment kitchen, picked up the crying child by both arms, and perched him on her hip. She directed a dark look at Sheila, as if the crying were her fault, and went back into the kitchen.

"Hatch didn't do what he was supposed to do?" Sheila repeated.

"I guess not," Potts replied with a shrug. "That's what Henry said, anyway."

Henry? "Mr. Palmer knew why Hatch was fired?" That didn't square with what Palmer himself had said. He'd claimed not to know what it was about.

"Well, he wasn't fired, exactly. I mean, we're not employees, we're just contract. Larry told Henry not to call Hatch in for more work. But sure, Henry knew all about it. He and Hatch were buddies, so if Larry didn't tell Henry what was going down, Hatch would've." He grinned slyly. "It was definitely okay by Martin and me, y'know. Meant more work for us."

Sheila understood that reasoning. "Any idea who the customer was that Hatch was talking to?"

"Nah. But if you really want to know, it wouldn't be hard to find out. Just look at the job tickets from around the middle of August, when it happened. It would be one of Hatch's jobs about that time. Maybe the last one." He frowned. "How come you're asking about all this stuff? It's ancient history."

Sheila nodded and made a note to check the job tickets, wondering why she hadn't thought of that. Or more to the point, why Palmer hadn't suggested it. And why Palmer had lied about knowing the reason for Hatch's firing. That was worth checking out.

"One more thing," she said. "A notebook computer was brought in recently. The customer's name was Timms. Did you work on that?"

"That's the one the cops picked up, right?"

"Correct," Sheila said. "Was it one of your jobs?"

Potts shook his head emphatically. "Nope. Never saw it, never touched it. Dennis and me talked about it afterward—after the cops took it, I mean. He didn't work on it, either."

In the kitchen, Ruthie was banging pots and pans. The baby had begun to bawl again, and the rock music from the neighboring apartment was now so loud that the walls seemed to vibrate. Sheila stood and thanked Potts for his cooperation. When she told him that they needed his prints, he cheerfully agreed to show up at the station the next morning.

"Yeah, okay. I'm cool with that. Anything I can do to help." His shoulders slumped dejectedly. "Sure hope I don't gotta look for a new job," he said. He gestured toward the kitchen. "Ruthie got laid off last week. She's babysitting a couple of neighborhood kids during the day to help out. Things are a little tight around here. I've got two more semesters to go before I can get a full-time job with health benefits."

"I hope everything turns out okay," Sheila said, meaning

it. "I know it's tough to work and have a family and be a student." She grinned. "Good luck, Richie."

"Yeah." The young man's shoulders straightened. "Yeah, thanks, Chief."

Outside in the rain-cooled air, Sheila took a deep breath. At the desk, barricaded behind a pile of paper, she lost the sense of real people, in real trouble, doing real things to try to help themselves out. She hadn't enjoyed interviewing Richie Potts, but she was glad she'd done it. She was even gladder that she could walk away from the vibrating walls, the baby's crying, and the smell of cooking cabbage.

OUT in the car, Sheila radioed for a background check on Jason Hatch, current address and phone, employment, vehicle, and priors. It came back before she'd driven more than a few blocks. She jotted down the address, which matched the one she'd copied from the Rolodex, and the phone number. He was listed as self-employed. Vehicle: Dodge Ram. And he had two priors: a misdemeanor bad check and a third-degree felony possession.

The address for Jason Hatch took her to a single-wide trailer in a trailer park on the east side of the interstate, in a flat, treeless field behind a shopping plaza that featured Walmart, Home Depot, and a five-screen movie theater. The trailers were close together, with motorcycles and pickup trucks parked along the narrow street and dogs chained to makeshift shelters—oil barrels, wooden crates—in the dirt yards. As Sheila pulled up in front of the address in her notes, a couple of neighborhood dogs began barking.

But she knew when she got out of the car that this was a strike-out. The trailer windows were dark and a For Rent sign, red letters on a black background, was stuck into the narrow patch of withered brown grass between the sidewalk and the trailer. But she tried anyway, going up the dirt path—muddy from the evening's rain—and banging on the door. After a few moments, she gave it up and walked back down the path and around the front of the trailer on the adjacent lot.

Her sharp rap on the metal door was answered by a heavyset, blowsy woman who reeked of cigarettes. Behind her, a reality show was playing on the television, the volume cranked up so high that the woman had to yell over it.

"Hatch?" she asked, in answer to Sheila's question and the flash of her badge wallet. She frowned. "Sorry, ma'am, cain't tell you a thing. There was some guy shackin' up over there with his girlfriend, yeah, but I never heard his name. Him and the girl moved out a while back. Good thing, too. Loud music, every night. Rock. Hate it. I'm a country and western fan m'self." She grinned, showing one gold tooth. "Love that Willie."

Sheila wondered whether the rock music from next door had been a defense against the woman's loud television. The battle of the volume controls. "Any idea where Mr. Hatch might be living?"

The woman shook her head. "Manager'd prob'bly know," she offered. "Double-wide at the far end." She gestured with her head, then shut the door in Sheila's face.

The manager's double-wide had a blue metal roof, a blue-painted front porch and shutters, some straggly landscape shrubs, and a nearly leafless willow tree in the front yard. The manager was bald and paunchy, with a red and blue plaid shirt and yellow suspenders holding up baggy pants. The toes of his fleece-lined house slippers had been scissored out and white socks showed through. He had apparently just gotten out of the recliner that faced the television, because a can of beer, a half-finished pizza, and a fat calico cat sat on the table beside it. The room was very warm.

"Hatch," he said, scratching his grizzled, unshaven chin. "Yeah, right. He was here, but him and the girl moved out the end of September. I keep that trailer for month to month, see, which ain't my fav'rite." He frowned. "Fact is, month-to-months are a pain in the patootie. They come, they go, or I wind up bootin' 'em out. Always try to get a six-month lease, if I can. But when I cain't, I do the next best thing, which is month-to-month."

When Sheila asked about a forwarding address, the man went to the gray metal desk, under the big window in the living room. He sat down and opened a drawer, leafed through some papers, then pulled out what looked like a rental record, copied the information onto a scrap of paper, and put the record back. On the chair-side table, the cat got up and stretched.

"Guess this is what you want," he said, handing her the slip of paper. "Address and phone. Anyway, it's what I got. Normally, I don't bother. Them with a lease, I allus get a forward, but not with the month-to-months." He squinted up at her. "Couldn't figger why that one was month-to-month, neither. Or why he was livin' here at all. Bought hisself a brand-new red pick-'em-up truck, right after he moved in. Told Mr. Boggs three doors down he'd paid cash fer it. Anybody could pay cash for a new truck oughtta be on a lease."

"Would that be a Dodge Ram?" Sheila asked. The cat was now eating the pizza.

"You bet. Big baby. Fully loaded. A cool twenty-five grand." He stood and hitched up his pants. "Guess he decided he'd rather drive his money than live in it. Takes all kinds, you know."

The address on the scrap of paper was on Pecos Street, only about six blocks from Larry Kirk's place. Jason Hatch had come up in the world since his month-to-month stay in the trailer park, Sheila thought, as she stopped in front of the house. The residence was attractive and nicely landscaped, on a quiet street lined with well-kept, fairly upscale homes surrounded by green lawns. But the place was completely dark. Sheila flipped her cell open and keyed in the number. The phone rang five times, then an answering machine picked up. When a curt male voice instructed her to leave a number, she cut off the call.

IT was pushing nine thirty when Sheila got home, and the sporadic drizzle had settled into a steadier rain. The doghouse in Rambo's run had kept him warm and dry, but he was delighted to see her. When she opened the kennel gate, the Rotti made a beeline for the back porch, where he turned to wait for her, rear end wagging furiously.

The house that she and Blackie had rented was clean, comfortable, and big enough for the both of them. The fenced backyard and the kennel had been a bonus, as was the large kitchen with an old-fashioned dining nook. Its window overlooked what had once been a vegetable garden, although Sheila knew she'd never have time for gardening. And anyway, she didn't have a green thumb. If a plant had the misfortune to be given to her, it was a sure death sentence for the poor thing.

The house was chilly and the chicken sandwich she'd eaten earlier in the evening was an ancient memory. She loosened her uniform tie and unbuckled her duty belt, hanging it on a hook by the door, next to Blackie's old blue denim jacket. Then she turned up the thermostat, made a cup of hot chocolate in the microwave, and grilled a cheese sandwich, with sides of chips and a dill pickle spear. She turned down the volume on the police band radio, set to the department's frequency. The radio was a habit from her days in Dallas, when every call-out, every crime was fascinating. This time of night, it was generally silent, but it kept her in touch with what was going on in town. In *her* town.

She took her food to the dining nook, sat down at the table, and pulled the Polaroids out of her briefcase, while Rambo fitted his large self under the table and around her feet. She laid the photographs on the table in front of her and began studying them, then took out her notebook.

She was flipping the pages with one hand and holding her sandwich with the other when her cell phone twittered. She saw with a deep pleasure that it was Blackie. He was calling from his motel in El Paso. He sounded tired.

"Just got in," he said. "Talked to some people, picked up a couple of leads on the kid. Looks like his mom has taken him across the border already, probably heading for her parents' village. I'll be going over tomorrow." She heard the sound of a shoe hitting the floor, then another.

Sheila put down her sandwich, feeling a wrench in her gut. The border area had grown increasingly dangerous, with the cartels murdering members of rival cartels—and law enforcement officers as well. The previous week, two Mexican policemen had been murdered in Piedras Negras, across the Rio Grande from Eagle Pass, and an American tourist had been shot on a highway near Juárez. It was war down there.

"McQuaid's going over with you, isn't he?" she asked, trying not to let the worry leak into her voice.

"Yeah. He's getting an early plane out here tomorrow. Don't worry, Sheila—we'll be fine." His voice was strong and sure as it always was, and Sheila pushed her fear down, into some deep place, far away, where it couldn't reach her heart. Blackie and Mike McQuaid were smart, experienced, confident. They could take care of themselves better than any two guys she knew.

And she knew how important it was to find the boy. This was another one of those heartbreaking parental kidnappings, made even more complicated by the fact that the mother had taken her son over the border. The United States and Mexico had a treaty that permitted courts in both countries to enforce the international convention on cross-border child abduction, but that was on paper. In reality and on the ground, and especially in Mexico, it was a much different matter.

"How was your day?" he asked. She could hear his long sigh as he stretched out on the motel bed and the sound of the TV as he clicked it on with the remote. "Anything new going on there?" He muted the TV.

"You wouldn't believe." Sheila gave him a quick summary of the events that had transpired since Clint Hardin had left her office on his way to Rockport. As she spoke, she was surprised by how much had happened in a few hours, and by the rapid pace of developments. But that was normal for investigations into shooting deaths. She and Bartlett had moved from suicide to homicide, and—with Timms' disappearance—to the strong suspicion of a connection between Timms and Kirk.

But she didn't get very far in her story before she was interrupted.

"You skipped over a deputy chief to partner with a detective?" Blackie asked incredulously. "And you gave the lead in the case to the *detective*?"

"Well, yeah," Sheila said, surprised by his reaction and almost immediately defensive. "But I didn't 'skip over' the deputy chief. Hardin was the one who skipped. He's out for vacation—fishing, on the Gulf. Anyway, I've been wanting to get out of the office and do some serious fieldwork." That part wasn't news to Blackie—she had talked about it often enough in the past few months. "I'm sure you know how good it feels to get away from the desk," she added. In Blackie's new career as a private investigator, he didn't have to manage a department, fill out forms, sign papers, write memos. He could do as much fieldwork as he wanted. "Porterfield's ruling is still open, but it's more than likely she'll call it a homicide as soon as the autopsy and forensic reports are in. Left-handers don't shoot themselves in the right temple, and that email to the wife is more than a little suspicious. The date stamp on the email does give us the approximate time of death, though, whoever sent it. I—"

"I'm not talking about the investigation," Blackie interrupted. "Bubba Harris took an investigation every now and then. He'd rather stay in the office and out of the line of fire, but he thought it was good practice to get out in the community, let people see that the chief did something besides push papers around."

"Then what—"

"I'm talking about command structure. I'm talking about you and Bartlett. You didn't stop to think about the political implications of letting that kid take the lead?"

"Political implications?" Sheila rubbed her forehead, her defensiveness beginning to smolder into irritation. "To tell the truth, mostly I thought about finding out how Larry Kirk died and who's responsible. I thought about getting out from behind the desk for a few hours and doing some real-time, serious fieldwork. I thought about backstopping a bright young detective, who is a first-rate investigator, even if Hardin does take most of the credit for—"

"Listen to me, Sheila." Blackie broke in. "I don't want to tell you how to run your shop, but I have worked in Adams County law enforcement for a lot longer than you have. As a matter of fact, I probably know your department even better than you do. Bartlett, I don't know very well, except that I've heard he's quite the young Romeo. It's a departmental joke that he's got girls fighting over him. Teaming up with that guy is a bad idea. And giving him the lead is worse. It's going to look to everybody like you've gone out of your way to pick a favorite. Hardin will be furious."

Sheila's irritation flamed into anger. Her jaw felt tight and her head was beginning to pound. *Let him,* she thought viciously. *Let Hardin be furious.* And what did Bartlett's being a local Romeo have to do with anything?

Aloud, she said, "I really don't think you understand what—"

"I do understand, hon," Blackie said earnestly. "Look. I've been in this business a long time, and I know it's not a good idea for an officer to step outside the command structure and work alongside a subordinate, much less let the subordinate take the lead. It's even more complicated because you're a woman. Believe me. When this gets out, it'll weaken your authority in the department."

Weaken my authority. "Because I'm a woman, you mean?" she asked, feeling the heat rising inside her.

He went on as if she hadn't spoken. "Bartlett will have a hard time dealing with the fallout, too. You won't be in the men's locker room to hear the guys making off-color jokes about being the boss's handpicked favorite, but he will. He'll hear it said to his face, and he'll know that they're saying it behind his back. It'll take him a long time to get past this. And what happens if you and Bartlett don't manage to clear this case—at least, not right away?" He made a gruff noise in his throat. "Jeez, hon, what were you thinking?"

Sheila picked up her mug of chocolate—cold, by now—and took a sip, trying to cool her temper, trying to see things from his point of view. It was true that Blackie understood the politics in the Pecan Springs Police Department. After all, he'd been sheriff for a good many years and he knew many of the guys. They'd shared dozens of investigations, worked out at the same gym, practiced at the same shooting range. And yeah, it was undoubtedly true that the male officers in the department would raise their eyebrows when they heard that the chief had taken what looked like the subordinate role in an investigation. But she didn't feel that it was a threat to her authority. She thought of it as a way to get what she wanted—some field time. A way to give Bartlett a chance to shine, without being eclipsed by a senior officer who'd step in and take the credit for his investigative work. As for not clearing the case, that was ridiculous. Of course they would clear the case! That was their job, wasn't it? Failure was not an option. It hurt to think that her own husband didn't have faith in her ability to do her job.

And what was just as bad: the patronizing tone of Blackie's question. "Jeez, hon, what were you thinking?"—as if she were some airhead bimbo who couldn't figure things out for herself. As for what she was thinking—

She clenched her hand around the phone, making an effort to keep her voice level, conversational. "Actually, I was thinking it would be a good idea to show Bartlett that I had confidence in his ability to handle this investigation. We don't have many cases like this in Pecan Springs, and if Hardin were here, he'd grab it. He—"

Blackie didn't let her finish. "Well, you were wrong," he said flatly. "Tell you what I think you ought to do, babe. First thing tomorrow, you go back to the office. You phone Hardin and brief him on the current status of the investigation. You won't have to tell him what to do—he'll understand that he needs to cancel this fishing trip and get his butt back to work. After all, this case potentially involves George Timms, which makes it highly political and very visible, not the kind of case the chief ought to be working. Hardin can take over with Bartlett, and you can go back to the desk." He didn't say *where you belong,* but Sheila heard the words as clearly as if he had spoken them.

She pulled in her breath, pushing down the anger and resentment that threatened to boil over. "No," she said emphatically.

There was a long silence.

"No?" His voice was wary. "No to which part?"

"Just . . . no," Sheila said. "No to all of it. Bartlett, Hardin, the investigation. This is my job and my department, Blackie. I appreciate your concern." (*Yeah, that was a lie, a big one.*) "But if I'm making a mistake, I'm the one who'll have to live with it."

As she spoke, she was wondering if there was something else going on here. Jealousy, maybe? Was Blackie *jealous* of Bartlett? Or jealous that she had responsibilities—and choices—that he no longer had?

Another silence.

"Okay," he said finally. He sounded resigned. "I don't like it, but I guess you know what you want to do. I think it's a mistake. But I'll support you regardless. You know that." He cleared his throat uncomfortably. "You know that, don't you?"

Did she? Did she know that? She paused for the space of a couple of breaths, thinking that it was a good thing he wasn't sitting across the table, where he could read her face. Where he could see how angry she was, and how disappointed she was in his lack of confidence in her ability to make decisions.

She cleared her throat. "Yeah, sure. I know that." *Another lie.* "Listen, maybe we'd better just say good night and go to bed. Sounds like we're both pretty tired, and tomorrow's going to be a big day."

"Right." He paused, took a breath. "You go get 'em, Sheila." She knew he was making an effort to smooth out the jaggedness of what had just happened between them. There was a moment's silence and his voice warmed. "But be careful in this thing. Sounds like it could get dicey." He paused. "You know I love you."

"Yes, I know," Sheila said, truthfully now. "I love you, too." And suddenly her anger evaporated. She was thinking about where he was going tomorrow, what he was going to do. She wished he wouldn't. She wished it urgently. But it wouldn't do any good to tell him so. She couldn't come any closer to changing his mind than he could come to changing hers.

"Stay safe, Blackie," she added, trying not to sound as urgent as she felt. "Don't take any chances. Please."

She folded the phone and sat there for a moment, struck by the sudden, gut-wrenching thought that it had all been a huge mistake. The coin toss, their decision to marry, the whole thing. It wasn't that she didn't love him. She loved him beyond words. It was just that their life together was so complicated, so damned difficult, so full of nooks and crannies where bad stuff could hide. And the bad stuff could wreck the good stuff that they had together.

What was left of her grilled cheese sandwich was cold, but she ate it and the chips and the pickle anyway, deciding that she didn't have the energy to work with the photographs tonight. She'd have another look in the morning. She got up to fill the automatic coffeemaker and check the timer. Beside her, Rambo whined, and she let him out the back door for his nightly pit stop. She was turning on the porch light when her cell phone rang again. She flipped it open.

Dana Kirk's voice was taut, high-pitched. "Chief Dawson, I just turned on my computer. There's an email from . . . from my husband. It was sent today, at two-oh-four, I guess just before he—" She gulped, on the edge of hysteria. "Before he shot himself." The last words were a drawn-out wail.

"What does the email say, Mrs. Kirk?" Sheila asked quietly and firmly. She knew, of course, but she wanted to steady the woman—and to verify. "Read it to me, please."

"It says . . . it says, 'Dana, I'm sorry. You can stop worrying about me. I'm tired and I just can't go through with the divorce. It's all yours, the house, the business, everything. Have a good life. Love, Larry.'" She was sobbing now. "'Have a good life.' How can I have a good life, after this terrible thing he's done, after—"

"After what who's done?" Sheila broke in, going back to the table in the dining nook to get her notebook.

"Why, Larry, who else? Don't you see, Chief? This email *proves* that Larry killed himself! I didn't think he could do it the way he did, but it was probably just quick and simple. He got a gun somewhere, and he—" She broke off, weeping. "I'm sorry. I can't talk now. He's completely ruined my life." The connection broke abruptly.

"Ruined her life?" Sheila muttered, closing the phone. *What a self-absorbed, self-centered thing to say!* She opened her notebook and jotted down the time of the call and a brief summary of what Dana Kirk had said. On the surface, the call seemed to eliminate the woman as a suspect, but that wasn't necessarily true. She could have killed her husband, or witnessed his killing, then written the email to exonerate herself. Reporting that she had received it could be another means of exoneration—especially reporting it in that half-hysterical tone of voice.

Sheila was still writing when the phone chirped again. She opened it and saw that it was China.

"Hey," she said. She leaned forward, propping both elbows on the table. "What's up?"

"I got a call from Ruby a little while ago," China replied. "She and Ramona have figured out why Larry Kirk didn't shoot himself."

"Oh, yeah? Why is that?"

"Because a left-handed person doesn't shoot himself in the head with his right hand," China said. "Ruby happened to remember that Larry pitched left-handed at the neighborhood baseball game last summer. And Ramona saw the gun in his right hand. Looks like somebody shot him and tried to make it look like a suicide."

"Thanks, China. That's the second confirmation we have on that. The guy who manages the computer shop told us that Kirk was a left-hander."

"Aw, heck." China sounded disgruntled, but there was a smile in her voice. "I guess I should've expected Wonder Cookie to be way out ahead of us."

Wonder Cookie. "Not too far ahead," Sheila said, smiling. In spite of herself, she liked the nicknames China and Ruby came up with for her. "I'm still trying to figure out the stalker angle." She paused, thinking of something. "China, did Kirk ever happen to mention anybody with the initials *JH*? Or maybe the name Jason Hatch?"

"Initials? I'd have to think about that, Sheila. But I know Hatch. He's the guy I worked with first, before Larry took over my projects. Not a very nice person, I have to say. Gruff, brusque. A fault-finder. Larry told me that he fired him, or wasn't going to call him again—something like that."

"Did he say why?"

"It had to do with customer relations, I think. Maybe—" She paused, and her voice tightened. "Wait a minute. Now that I think about it, this might be relevant to your investigation, Sheila. Larry once asked me if Hatch had ever approached me with what he called 'an inappropriate request.' I thought at first he was talking about sex and laughed it off. But that wasn't what he meant."

Sheila frowned. "You're thinking that he might have been talking about blackmail?"

"Could have been. He wasn't specific. It was almost as if he were fishing, trying to find something out without telling me what it was he wanted to know. At the time, I had no idea what he was getting at. But now, knowing about Timms . . ." She began again. "Look, Sheila. I'm guessing that George Timms broke into Larry's shop because he wanted to get his computer back. You don't have to confirm, but if there was any extortion involved, you ought to take a look at Hatch."

"That's already on my to-do list for tomorrow." Sheila was becoming more and more interested in Hatch. One way or another, he was involved with this, either with Timms or with Kirk or both.

"See? What did I tell you? Wonder Cookie is out ahead of the pack."

Sheila chuckled wryly, wishing she were. "If anything occurs to you on the stalker business, you'll let me know. Right?" She heard Rambo give one short, sharp bark, his signal to come in. She got up and opened the door.

"I will," China said. "Have you turned up anything interesting on the case?"

"Hard to say," Sheila said, stepping back to avoid the shower of raindrops as the Rotti shook himself off. "I'm not trying to duck your question," she added, turning off the back porch light. "At this point, there are just a lot of dots on the page, and more to come. Connecting them—well, you know. That happens later."

"All those damn dots," China said, and laughed. "Yeah, I know." She paused. "Have you heard anything more on Timms?"

"Not a word." Rambo put his paw on his water dish and flipped it over, his neat little trick to show her it was empty. Sheila carried it to the sink, where she set it under the faucet and began filling it. "Which is a little weird. Unless—"

"Unless he's vamoosed. Out of town. Way out of town, as in over the border."

"Yeah." Sheila's frown deepened. If they could talk to Timms, they might be able to clear up a lot of things. "Speaking of over the border, Blackie said that Mike is flying to El Paso early tomorrow. Tell him to be careful, will you?" She put the bowl on the floor and Rambo planted his forefeet and began noisily lapping water. "They both need to be careful."

China chuckled wryly. "Oh, right. Listen, if we wanted guys who were careful, we married the wrong ones. This pair takes to danger the way a bullrider handles a bull. There's no stopping them." She sighed. "Gotta say good night now, Sheila. Keep me posted on the investigation, will you?"

"Hmm," Sheila said noncommittally. She picked up her shoes and padded across the kitchen to turn off the overhead light. "Hey, Rambo. Come on." She took down her duty belt from the hook next to Blackie's jacket. "Time for bed, fella."

"You're that hard up for fun?" China asked in a pitying tone. "I could send Howard Cosell."

Sheila laughed and broke the connection.

Chapter Eleven

Cat's claw vine (*Macfadyena unguis-cati*) takes its name from the three-pronged clawlike climbing appendages that grasp and cling to plants or surfaces. A high-climbing member of the trumpet vine family, cat's claw is native to the tropics of South and Central America. In the folk medicines of Brazil, the Yucatan, and Panama, the leaves, roots, and tubers have been widely used to treat inflammation, malaria, and venereal disease. Recent research suggests that the plant may also have antitumor properties.

Cat's claw has beautiful yellow trumpetlike blooms and is offered by some nurseries as the "yellow trumpet vine." Introduced to the U.S. as an ornamental in 1947, it is now classified as a dangerously invasive and ecologically threatening plant across the South, for it can smother and outcompete valuable native plants. Please don't give it growing room in your garden!

China Bayles
"Herbs That Hold Fast"
Pecan Springs Enterprise

It was gray and overcast when I got up early Tuesday morning. The rain had stopped, but the air was damp and chill and tendrils of writhing ground fog clutched the trees. The overnight rain, widespread across the Hill Country, had undoubtedly brightened the hopes of the towns that depend on the April wildflower season for much of their annual tourist revenue. The traditional weather calendar that works in the northeast—April showers bring May flowers—doesn't suit our seasons. For us, it's the rains in November, December, and January that bring up the April wildflowers—bluebonnets and brown-eyed Susans and winecups—and summon wildflower fans by the thousands. You can call me a cynic if you want to, but gardeners and farmers aren't the only ones who get down on their knees and pray for rain. Around here, when the winter is dry, the spring wildflower season is a bust, the bed-and-breakfasts and restaurants in towns like Pecan Springs, Fredericksburg, and Boerne are half-empty, and every small-town shop owner feels a hard pinch in her bottom line. Rain is something to celebrate—although, of course, we don't want a repeat of the flooding that happened when what was left of Hurricane Josephine slammed across Adams County. I caught a glimpse of the TV as I came downstairs and was glad that we weren't experiencing the early-season snowfall that was blanketing the northeast today. I could celebrate the fact that we weren't going to be blitzed by a blizzard. In fact, the temperature was heading for a balmy seventy-plus this afternoon. Not bad for November.

Like every mom with school-age kids, I'm an early riser on weekday mornings, getting the kids dressed and breakfasted and equipped with books and homework and out the door in time to catch the school bus at the corner of Lime-kiln Road and our lane. This morning was more challenging than usual, because McQuaid had an early plane to catch and Austin-Bergstrom International is a good fifty minutes away—longer, when inbound traffic on I-35 is heavy. Once you're at the airport, you have to find a place to park and catch the shuttle to the terminal—and of course, there's security. These days, flying isn't a picnic.

For our breakfasts, I make up a batch of sausage, egg, and bean burritos, wrap them individually, and keep them in the freezer for a quick, nourishing meal-to-go. McQuaid was on his second when I came into the kitchen, dressed in my usual jeans, the shop T-shirt, and a green-and-black plaid flannel shirt, ready for my workday. He got out another burrito, popped it into the microwave, and folded me into a large hug.

I spoke against his shoulder. "When I talked to Sheila on the phone last night, she said to tell you to tell Blackie to be careful. Ditto from me, for you."

"Sure thing," he said, nuzzling my neck. He let me go and turned to fill his thermos mug with coffee. "Don't worry, China," he added, over his shoulder. "We'll watch ourselves."

"I *mean* it," I said urgently. I had awakened early that morning and lay beside him, worrying about the trip he was about to make. "Neither Sheila nor I am very happy about you two gringos going over the border to—"

"I know," he said, seriously now. "We won't go across unless we think the trip is worth making—unless we're sure we can find the boy. Tell Sheila that." He slipped an arm around me, then bent and kissed me, lingering for a moment.

I pulled away, frowning. "If you cross, and if you find him, how are you going to bring him back?"

"We won't," he said. He took out the burrito and wrapped it in a paper towel. "Bring him back, that is. We'll find out where he is, get photos, dig up as much information as we can about the situation, and report to the father."

I was relieved. I didn't like the idea that McQuaid and

Blackie might be arrested by the *Federales* and tossed into a Mexican hoosegow, with a kidnapping charge hanging over them like a Mexican machete.

"After that," he went on, "it's up to the father and his lawyer. These international cases are always difficult. They take longer than you'd think." He glanced up at the clock. "Hell's bells. Look at the time! I'm outta here, China. I'll call you before we go across."

He kissed me good-bye swiftly and was gone. I went to the window and watched him as he went out to the car, overnight bag on his shoulder, mug in one hand, burrito in the other. He was already absent from me, already focused on what he had to do over the next couple of days. As I turned away from the window, I was swept by a keen apprehension, sharper than any I had felt before when I had seen him off on an investigation. I was grateful for Brian's clunky footfalls on the stairs, his almost-man's voice: "Hey, Mom, do I have any clean gym shorts?" and Caitie's higher-pitched, "Mom, I need some lunch money—and I can't find my red shoe!" Their urgent needs (gym shorts, lunch money, two red shoes, burritos, orange juice, and milk) pulled me back into an ordinary morning, in our ordinary family.

The bus arrives at seven twenty, give or take five minutes, and when the weather's clear, the kids walk out to the bus stop on Limekiln Road. When the weather is rainy or very cold, I take them to the stop in the car. This morning, the clouds were beginning to thin, the sun was peeking through, and the day promised to warm up nicely. But since all three of us were ready to go and it was just damp and chilly enough outdoors to be uncomfortable, I gave Brian and Caitie a lift.

We waited in the car until the bus came, listening to the local country and western station and joining Gary P. Nunn in a rowdy chorus of "London Homesick Blues." When I said good-bye to the kids and watched them climb on the bus, I thought that if there was a better way to start the day, I didn't know what it was. A kiss from my husband, hugs from two of the greatest kids in the world, and toe-tapping Texas music on the radio.

On a normal day, I would have driven on to the shop, arrived a little early, and used the time to catch up on chores I hadn't finished the day before. But this morning, after the kids climbed aboard the bus, I hesitated for a moment, thinking of what McQuaid had said the night before about Timms' property. Instead of going straight into town, maybe I should make a quick run out to Timms' place. I flipped open my phone with the idea of calling Sheila to let her know what I was going to do, but decided against it and closed the phone again. She'd either tell me not to go or want to send one of her officers with me. But I was close, just fifteen minutes away, and besides, I didn't think it was dangerous—or maybe I just didn't think.

I put the Toyota in gear, turned left, and drove in the other direction, west, heading away from town on Limekiln Road, across Big Hackberry Creek. This part of the Hill Country is in the Guadalupe watershed. The landscape is cut by streams flowing south and east, carving out deep, wooded canyons. The Guadalupe River rises near Hunt, in the highlands west of Kerrville, and flows all the way to the town of Victoria and then into the Gulf of Mexico. To my mind, mile for mile, it's the prettiest river in Texas. But dangerous. If a storm dumps a lot of water upstream, downstream people can be in danger and not even know it. People are more savvy about flash floods these days, but every year, at least one Pecan Springs driver ignores the Turn Around, Don't Drown signs, and . . . well, drowns.

A couple of miles farther west, on the other side of the bridge over a creek, I spotted the faded sign for Paint Horse Road, a narrow black-top that took off to the right. It slanted diagonally up a steep, wooded rise, then leveled off across the shoulder of a narrow ridge, giving me a beautiful view of folded green hills, limestone bluffs, and steep-banked canyons cut into the limestone of the Edwards Plateau by eons of rushing creeks and rivers. The sky to the west and north—a bright, sharp blue—had already cleared. The low pressure area that had brought last night's rain was giving way to a high pressure system pushing down from the north that would keep us sunny and dry for the next couple of days, until a new storm system was forecast to come in from the north.

This area was far enough away from the road so that there wasn't a house in sight, not even a utility pole or a cell phone tower. When the road slanted down again, I saw a small flock of Angora goats behind a rusty barbed-wire fence that zigzagged up the hill. Angoras produce mohair, a valuable luxury fiber with the sheen of silk and more durable and lightweight than wool. They are more valuable than your everyday, garden-variety goats, which are usually left to fend for themselves while Angoras are sent out to graze with a guard animal. This flock was under the protection of an attentive burro, who was keeping a close eye on his charges. Burros are fast on their feet and can kick like the devil, and they're aggressively territorial when it comes to protecting their flocks. They might not be much good against a mountain lion, like the one I had seen the night before. But they're diligent about keeping coyotes and marauding dogs at bay, and predators have learned to respect them.

That mountain lion. I thought of her—silvery in the rain, in the glint of my headlights—and shivered. She had been so beautiful, so mysterious, so seductively, dangerously powerful. For a fleeting moment, I wished that I could see her again, witness her litheness, her gracefulness, her strength. But only for a moment. I had other things to do. And one glimpse of that kind of danger can go a very long way.

Another hundred yards on the left, I saw the pair of

mailboxes that McQuaid had mentioned. But something caught my attention that he (not being a plant person) probably hadn't noticed. The boxes were half-smothered under a luxuriant blanket of vine. I wasn't in a hurry, so I stopped the car and got out to have a closer look. I knew immediately what it was: cat's claw vine, a long-lived, aggressive plant—a valuable medicinal in its tropical homeland—that can smother trees, structures, and native plants. The vine produces small three-pronged hooks that can cling to almost anything, and showy yellow, trumpet-shaped blossoms in late spring and summer. In fact, you may see the plant sold in nurseries as the yellow trumpet vine and advertised as useful for masking unattractive structures. But in southern states, the cat's claw vine is considered a dangerous nuisance.

I got back in the car and turned onto the narrow caliche-topped road, following it through an open landscape of rangeland and bony mesquite trees, leafless now in the November morning. But there hadn't been a hard freeze yet. The grass was still green, the live oaks still bore their shiny green leaves, and the morning sun was splendid. I saw a Cooper's hawk, a flirtatious mockingbird, a pair of kestrels, and several jaunty red cardinals, as bright as flame.

And then I saw the sign I was looking for, weathered but just legible: PAINT HORSE RANCH. The road, rutted now, dipped steeply downhill, and I guessed that I was headed toward Paint Horse Creek and George Timms' cabin—his bachelor pad, as McQuaid had called it, where he could party as much as he wanted without disturbing the neighbors.

Why was I doing this? Curiosity, was it? Wanting to see what kind of party place a guy like George Timms had built? Or maybe a suspicion that Timms might be using the cabin to escape from the nastiness of his surrender and arrest. Charlie said that he had repeatedly called Timms' cell phone, but Paint Horse Ranch was out in the boonies. It was entirely possible that there wasn't a signal here, so Timms hadn't gotten the calls. It was also possible that Timms wasn't actually hiding—that he had fully intended to come back to town to keep his date with the police but had run into some kind of trouble. That he was sick or maybe injured, with no way to call for help. The closer I got, the more possibilities I could conjure up. Maybe it hadn't been such a good idea to come out here by myself, without letting anyone know where I was. If anything happened—

My cell phone was on the seat beside me. I picked it up and flipped it open. The signal wasn't strong, only two bars, which faded to one as I held it in my hand. Then, as the road flattened out ahead, I glimpsed a log house with a green metal roof, ahead through the trees. I slowed for a curve. A good thing, too, because I nearly ran into the rear end of a low, sleek silver Corvette. It bore the vanity plate GTIMMS 1.

It looked like George Timms was in residence—at least, his Corvette was.

My mouth was suddenly dry, and I was wishing I hadn't done this. But I had, and anyway, I knew George Timms. I conjured up a mental picture of him: blond and boyish, crooked grin, white teeth in a bronzed face. A handsome face. Owner of the local Chevy dealership, golfing friend of the mayor, former business associate of Ben Graves. Not somebody I'd normally be afraid of. I wasn't going to start being afraid now.

I pulled around the Corvette and parked beside it in a largish graveled parking area, in sight of the front of the cabin. Then I turned off the ignition and sat still for a moment, studying the place. I wouldn't call it a "cabin." It was built of logs, yes, and it had a pleasing rustic appearance, with a wooden rocking chair on the front porch and an impressive rack of antlers over the glass-paned front door. But it looked more like an upscale fishing-and-hunting lodge to me, something you'd see in a travel brochure that advertised getaway vacations for world-weary city folk. Off to one side, I could see three cute little octagonal log buildings—guesthouses, no doubt. It was quite a party place.

I hit the horn three times, fast and light—the Texas equivalent of "Howdy—anybody home? You've got company." I kept my eye on the front door. If Timms was awake, he'd come out to see who had just arrived to disturb his peace.

He didn't. Well, okay. I had talked myself out of being afraid. On the other hand, there was an APB out for this man, and it was entirely likely that nobody at PSPD knew about this "secret getaway" place, as McQuaid had called it. I had a responsibility for reporting his whereabouts. I reached for my phone. I'd call 9-1-1 and report that I had found the automobile. The dispatcher would contact the county sheriff and a deputy would come out, take Timms into custody, and notify Sheila. I flipped open my phone.

Uh-oh, no bars. I tried anyway, but all I got was that frustrating message, *No network coverage.* Which left me with a choice. I could drive back up the road to a place where I could make the call—the top of the hill, near the mailboxes and that cat's claw vine, probably. Or I could get out and have a look around, then drive back up the road until I got a signal. I was considering the options when it occurred to me that Timms might be in some kind of trouble here, and that I might need to ask for medical assistance. I opted to have a look first.

A moment later, I was at the front door, ringing the doorbell, which gave a stirring peal of "The Eyes of Texas Are Upon You." I could hear a voice—radio or television, I thought—from somewhere inside. But there was no answer to the doorbell, and after punching the button and calling Timms' name a couple of times, I stepped off the front porch and walked around the side of the house.

It was truly an attractive place, one level in front, two in the back, with a roofed, wooden deck built against the sloping hill and another open deck a little farther down, with the guesthouses off to the left, behind a screen of landscaping shrubs. I stepped up onto the upper-level deck, which was furnished with lacquered bamboo furniture with bright-colored cushions. Two large stereo speakers hung against the walls. On a glass-topped table beside a lounge chair was a half-empty mug of stale-looking beer and a plate holding a partly eaten sandwich and a handful of wilted potato chips. A single-serving cup of yogurt still wore its foil lid, a spoon beside it. I felt the yogurt cup. It had been out of the fridge for a while. A thick white terry towel was draped over the back of the lounge and an open book, its pages damp, lay on the seat, beside a pair of binoculars. In an ashtray, a half-smoked cigarette had burned itself out. It was damp, too. I frowned. Beer, the sandwich and chips, yogurt, a cigarette, a book—they all looked like they had been left out in the overnight drizzle. Yesterday's supper? Yesterday's lunch?

I turned and looked toward the house. A pair of sliding glass doors opened onto the living-dining area. I went closer and called again, louder. No answer, so I stepped inside, noting that the voice I had heard was coming from a radio on the kitchen counter, tuned to KUT in Austin and broadcasting the usual NPR "Morning Edition." I turned it off, called again, and listened. Not a word, not a sound. Where was Timms?

I went quickly through the kitchen, which was equipped with the latest in stainless steel appliances; the vaulted living-dining area with a massive stone fireplace, carpeted in pale beige; a bedroom with a huge unmade bed, the walls hung with framed erotic photographs; a darkroom off the bedroom; a bathroom with shaving equipment laid out on the marble-topped counter. Upstairs, there was another bathroom and two loft bedrooms—both empty—with windows overlooking the tops of the trees in the canyon below. The entire place was beautifully and expensively

furnished and completely deserted. But I spotted a telephone on the table beside the unmade bed in the master
bedroom and another, with an answering machine, in the
kitchen, the message light blinking. I picked up the receiver
and was relieved to hear a dial tone. I could call out from
here, rather than drive all the way back up the road to a
point where my cell could pick up a signal. But first—

But first, I needed to find Timms. I went back outside,
shouting his name, listening for an answer and hearing
none, more and more convinced that the man had met
with—what? An accident? Or something else?

I went down to the lower deck, where I saw a flagstone
path slanting diagonally down and across the steep hill toward a silvery thread of creek forty feet below. I took the
path, noticing that the hillside had been completely cleared
of the usual underbrush, then terraced with native limestone rock and landscaped with yaupon hollies, madrones,
Mexican buckeyes, cat's claw acacia, and clumps of Lind-
heimer's muhly. Agarita, lantana, salvias, and other native
plants were growing in sculpted pockets of lush plantings
along the path. Off to one side, what looked like a miniature concrete-bottomed stream was under construction, and
an unobtrusive network of soaker hoses snaked through the
shredded cedar mulch, ensuring that the plants would get a
drink whenever they were thirsty. A drapery of tiny fairy
lights festooned the trees, and I could picture the hillside
illuminated at night. It would be quite beautiful. Timms
had invested a great deal of effort—and spent some serious
money—in destroying the real wilderness and creating a
"wilderness look" in its place.

The well-groomed imitation wilderness ended abruptly
at the foot of the hill, where the authentic Hill Country
wilderness began, with a thicket of snarled redbud saplings,
elbow bush, and catbrier, under a canopy of live oaks and
cedar elms so thick they almost shut out the early-morning
light. A narrow trail continued on in the direction of the

creek, hacked through the dense underbrush. The sloping ground, covered with loose leaf litter, was soft and moist, and if Timms had come this far, I should be able to see his footprints. I looked down at the path ahead and spotted the track of a running shoe, the sole deeply ridged. Then another and another, long strides, running strides, a man in a hurry. Chasing something?

And then, ten paces farther on, I saw a red Texas Rangers baseball cap beside the trail. It looked as if it had been stepped on and pushed into the soil. It marked a spot where a heavy scuffle of shoeprints roughed up the path's surface. I knelt for a closer look. I was seeing not one shoeprint, but two, very close together and deep, as if the man with the long strides had suddenly stumbled and was trying to regain his balance. Then another short, heavy step, almost a stagger, and the deep, unmistakable print of a hand, palm flat, fingers spread. Just off the trail, a cedar elm sapling was snapped off a foot above the ground, broken branches scattered as if there had been a struggle. On the other side of the trail, I saw a jagged, bloody rock with a scrap of silvery fur on it, and a dark stain, the size of a dinner plate. I bent over to smell it and knew immediately that the ground was soaked with blood. A lot of blood.

My arms broke out in goose bumps, my breath was coming short and sharp, and I had to fight the urge to turn tail and run back up the hill. But I told myself that whatever had happened here had happened some time before—hours, perhaps. The danger was gone and my need to know was urgent. I swallowed my fear and straightened, looking around.

Another ten feet off the trail, in the direction of the creek, I spotted scuff marks in the soil, more broken branches, and patches of disturbed and scattered leaf litter. Something glittered in the leaves and I picked it up: a man's Rolex, solid and heavy, its face studded with small diamonds. There was a smear of blood across the crystal and the gold accordion watchband was twisted and broken. I sucked in my breath. What had happened here? What had *happened*?

And then I looked ahead. Beyond the point where I picked up the watch, I could see the unmistakable furrow created by something heavy—a body—dragged through a thick green patch of river ferns. I followed the trail of torn leaves and broken stems. Twenty yards on, a Nike running shoe, the lace still tied. It was soaked with blood. It had been shredded.

Another twenty yards on, I found the man. He was buried under a pile of twigs and leaves and forest litter meticulously scraped over him, covering all of him but his feet. One foot wore a running shoe, the mate to the Nike I had found. The other foot . . . wasn't there, just a gnawed, bloody stump.

I fought with myself, my heart thumping, my mind racing, my hands sweaty. I didn't want to look but I couldn't leave this place without being sure. On my knees, I frantically scraped the leaves away from the dead man's face— and then fought against the panic that rose inside me like a terrified creature, fighting to get out. I rocked back on my heels and heard my scream echoing through the trees.

His face was gone, too.

Chapter Twelve

Sheila hadn't slept well. She wasn't sure whether it was the investigation into Kirk's death or the almost-quarrel with Blackie, or the absence of his large, warm body in their bed. She missed him. It wasn't the first time they'd been apart since they married, but it was the first time she had *felt* apart from him, as if they were separated by more than just distance. Separated by what they had said to each other. Even worse, what they had not said. Or what she had not said: that their marriage had been a mistake. There had been other times in her life when love (or lust or whatever it was) hadn't been enough to bridge the gap between what she wanted and what she needed, not just in her heart but in her head and in her work life. Would it be enough now, not just for her but for Blackie, too?

So she'd slept badly, in her dreams turning over the events of the previous day as if they were pieces of a puzzle, trying and failing to fit them together into something recognizable. A dead man and a missing man, Larry Kirk and George Timms: two separate puzzles or one larger, interlocking puzzle? She and Bartlett: a good partnership or a bad mistake that she would live to regret? She and Blackie, growing closer or pulling apart, separated by

wants and needs that the other couldn't fulfill? In her
dream, she had only a few hours to find the answers, solve
the puzzles, or—

Or what? That was a puzzle, too.

She woke before the dream brought her any meaningful answers and lay, frustrated and wakeful, in the black-
ness. Rambo slept in his bed on the floor beside her, his
breathing rhythmic and easy. After a while, she fell back
asleep, lulled by the gentle sound as she was often lulled by
Blackie's breathing.

She was up at four thirty and out for a longer-than-usual
run through the dark, cool morning, she and the dog taking the street that led up the hill above her house, tackling
the steep part first, then leveling off across the wooded
ridge, coming downhill as she cooled off, four miles altogether. The asphalt pavement was still wet, although the
drizzle had almost stopped. She loved running while the
houses were still dark, the people asleep, just herself and
Rambo, all alone, moving together through the silent,
empty morning.

Usually, the running silenced her busy thoughts and
filled her with a flowing energy that was all muscle, all
body, no mind. But this morning, she couldn't stop thinking about Blackie, and worrying. He and McQuaid knew
what they were doing, but travel in northern Mexico
right now was dangerous. To locate the missing child,
they'd have to ask questions of people who wouldn't want
the questions answered. They could run into some serious trouble.

By five thirty, she was home again and in the shower. By
six, she was dressed, not in her uniform but in uniformlike
civvies: a dark blue open-collared blouse, burgundy blazer,
dark blue pants, black half-boots, her blond hair snugged
back out of the way. On days when she dressed in street
clothes, she left her duty weapon locked up and wore her
personal gun, a Glock 27, in a paddle holster that fitted into

the back of her pants or skirt. That's where it was now, the solid heft of it smooth and cool in the hollow of her back.

It was still dark when she went down to the kitchen, where she fed Rambo and poured a cup of fresh coffee from the coffeemaker. Then she fixed a bowl of corn flakes and milk, booted up her laptop on the table in the dining nook, and settled down to work, spooning up cereal while she logged into her secure office network and went rapidly through as many emails as possible. Connie Page, her assistant, didn't get in until eight, but Sheila left a message on Connie's answering machine, asking her to clear the morning's calendar. She'd be working away from the office, reachable by cell.

Then she phoned Bartlett, catching him before he had his coffee and his first cigarette. With her notebook in front of her, she reported on her interview with Richie Potts, on her phone conversations with Dana Kirk and China, and the strike-out with Hatch at both the trailer park and the address on Pecos Street that she'd gotten from the trailer park manager.

"Oh, and Hatch has two priors," she added. "Misdemeanor bad check and felony possession. He could be in AFIS." The national Automated Fingerprint Identification System provided automated fingerprint and latent search capabilities, as well as corresponding criminal histories and mug shots. It contained data for more than sixty six million subjects in the criminal master file, much of the information submitted voluntarily by state, local, and federal law enforcement agencies.

"Good," Bartlett said. "We'll pull his prints from AFIS and compare them against whatever prints Butch can lift from Timms' computer. I'll get that done ASAP."

Bartlett hadn't found Dennis Martin at home the previous evening, so that was his first stop this morning. He had worked late setting up the homicide book and was ready to start going through the store files. He would pull Hatch's last batch of job tickets and assign the shop computer to Annetta Blount, to check for anything suspicious. With luck, they'd have the forensic report by noon, the autopsy by tomorrow.

"I checked with Dispatch a couple of minutes ago," he added. "Nothing on the Timms APB yet. We've checked his house—nothing there. He's got a cabin out west of town somewhere, but we don't have a location on it yet. The longer it takes to find him the more I think he's our man." He paused. "When will you be in?"

"An hour, maybe a little longer," Sheila said. "I'm headed over to Kirk's place now. But first I'll check Hatch's residence again. Maybe I'll catch him at home."

There was a moment's silence, then "Give me the address," Bartlett said. "Meet you there in ten."

"Right," Sheila said. Under the circumstances, she was glad for the backup. She clicked off the phone, checked the doors to be sure that the house was locked, and picked up her briefcase, whistling for Rambo. The Rotti trotted eagerly toward the squad car, head up, ears alert, ready for whatever the day was going to bring. But she put him in his kennel with a hug and an apology. She wasn't going to the station just yet, and there was no telling how the day was going to turn out. He gave her a disappointed look, then lay down, nose on paws, watching as she went to the car. Rambo was the most patient creature she had ever met, she thought. Far more patient than she was.

Ten minutes later, Bartlett joined her on the street in front of Hatch's house on Pecos, and they went up to the front door together. But repeated peals of the doorbell brought only silence, and after a few minutes they gave it up.

"I'm headed to Martin's," Bartlett said, back at the cars. "I'll phone the station and get Butch to run Hatch's prints from AFIS and compare them against anything he finds on Timms' computer. If we get a match, I'll put out an alert for Hatch. You're headed for the Kirk place?"

"On my way," Sheila said. "I'll be back for the nine a.m. briefing."

On the way to Kirk's, she tried calling Blackie, feeling the need to connect with him and smooth some of the ragged feelings left from their conversation the night before. But her call went to the voice mail box. Blackie wasn't picking up. Where was he? What was he doing? Would he wait for McQuaid to arrive, so they could go across the border together?

She bit her lip. Too many questions, no answers. "Just me," she said to the phone. "Let me know you're okay." She paused. "Love you," she said, before she clicked off.

When she parked in the driveway at the Kirk house, she radioed her location to Dispatch—Dick Brice was on the desk this morning—and asked for a rundown on the night's police activities. Three routine traffic stops, an injury accident at I-35 and the frontage road, south of the mall. One domestic dispute, a couple of DWIs, a break-in on the east side, a prowler south, a stolen GPS unit, two false alarms. A quiet night in Pecan Springs.

The crime-scene tape was still in place. She ducked under it and unlocked the door. Inside, she set down her briefcase, opened it, and took out a pair of latex gloves. Pulling them on, she went down the hall to the kitchen and flicked on the lights. Everything was just as it had been when she saw it last. The chair on its side, the dark chalk outlining the position of the body on the floor beside the spill of blood and beer, the empty takeout boxes on the counter. She took out her notebook and jotted down the name and address on the side of the box—Wong's, Fourth and Brazoria—then went through the top layer in the trash can, looking for evidence that Kirk might have shared the food with someone. All she found was the cash register receipt, stamped with the date and time of purchase (yesterday, 12:30 p.m.). She stuck it in her notebook.

Then, methodically, she opened all the kitchen drawers

and cupboards, noticing that there were more culinary tools—forks, knives, a blender, a food processor, a pasta maker, even a flour sifter—than she would expect a single guy to have. She guessed that Dana Kirk had not yet claimed the stuff she had wanted to take away from her failed marriage, like the bed linens the woman had asked about the day before. She wondered if Larry Kirk had held on to the things with the hope that the rift might be mended, or if Dana Kirk—feeling the guilt of the affair with Glen Vance—had been reluctant to ask for her share of the property. Somehow, this reminder of their broken relationship saddened her, as if there had been more than one death here.

She righted the chair and put it in its place at the table, then stood for a moment, looking around, letting herself feel the somber presence of ghosts, the ghost of the dead man, the ghost of a dead marriage, the ghost of a couple's hopes and dreams and plans. A deep sadness seemed to fill the room and settle on her shoulders. Alone in the house, without the distractions of the forensics team, of Bartlett in the other room, she could see Kirk sitting at the table with his laptop. He's finished eating, she thought, and he's put the containers on the counter, out of the way. He's online, checking his email, doing other work. He hears a knock at the back door, or maybe there's just a push and the door opens.

Somebody steps into the room and he turns his head to look.

Somebody he knows? Somebody he's expecting? (If so, it's not noted on the wall calendar.) Does he say something? Is he startled? Can he see what his visitor is holding in his—or her—hand? Is he afraid?

Outside, there's the rattle and bang and motor noise of the garbage truck, punctuated by the sharp clang of the empty cans hitting the pavement. That's the assailant's cue. The person steps quickly forward, no hesitation, giving

Kirk no chance to get up from his chair. Lifts the gun, aims, fires directly at Kirk's head, at close range but at a distance too great to leave visible traces of unburned powder. Kirk topples onto the floor with a heavy thud, the chair falls with him. The beer bottle? Is Kirk holding the beer bottle when the shot is fired?

The assailant takes a deep breath, wipes the gun, or is perhaps gloved. Puts the gun into Kirk's right hand—the wrong hand, but the person doesn't know or doesn't remember this—and presses the dead man's fingers over it. Backs away, then pauses, looks at the computer. Considers for an instant, decides. Pops up an email form, types in Dana's name on the "To" line, confident that she's in the address book. Then types the message, fast, and hits the Send button. Then out the door and safely away. The whole thing, the whole terrible thing, could have happened in a matter of minutes. Two minutes, three, four. It doesn't take long to end a life. The space of a breath, and it's done.

She stared for a moment at the empty chalk-lined shape on the floor. Kirk hadn't shot himself, she was confident of that, and the assurance would come with the autopsy report. Not suicide, homicide. So, then. Had the shooter been George Timms, compelled to kill because Kirk had discovered an ugly secret and was blackmailing him? Or an employee or contract worker—Hatch, or even Palmer or Martin or Potts—fearful of being exposed as a blackmailer? Or the wife or her lover—or both of them together? Or the stalker Kirk had mentioned to China, who was or perhaps was not the JH whose initials Kirk had noted on the wall calendar?

Or none of the above. Someone from Kirk's past, someone from the neighborhood (who would know what time the garbage truck always came), someone with a grudge. Right now, there wasn't enough information to know, only enough to speculate.

She turned and went into the small dining room, where

she stood for a moment, surveying the computer parts laid out on the table, the project Kirk was working on. Nothing caught her attention there, and she knew that Bartlett had looked it over carefully. He would have spotted anything unusual.

Kirk's living room contained a large leather sofa, a matching recliner, a wide-screen television and other equipment in an entertainment center. Behind the sofa, in one corner, was a small green-painted wooden desk, a computer tower and a printer on the floor beneath it, and a desktop keyboard and monitor. The message light was blinking on the answering machine that sat beside the monitor.

She sat down at the desk and booted the computer, which was probably only a secondary machine. Kirk likely did most of his work on his laptop. As it came on, she played back the messages on the answering machine, listening as she began going through the drawers. There were four calls, all from the previous afternoon and evening.

Time, two fifteen. *Larry, Henry. Listen, we've got a guy here at the shop who says he's looking for contract work. He's been working at a couple of shops in San Antonio. You interested? Let me know and I'll tell him to come in for an interview when you're going to be here.* It was the message that Palmer had mentioned the evening before.

Time, two forty. A woman's voice, light and cheerful, casual. *Hey, Larry, it's Tina. I was just wondering—like, well, maybe you'd like to take in a movie this weekend—Dutch treat?* A little giggle, half-embarrassed. *You'll probably think I'm pushy, but I figure it won't hurt to ask. You might even say yes. But if you don't want to do a movie, let's just have coffee. I've got a few things to tell you. About Jackie, I mean. I think it's getting serious. I'm worried.* Then, hastily: *But don't call me at work. You know how she feels about . . . well, just don't, please. Okay? I'll be home after six.*

Time, four thirty. Sheila recognized the voice. *Larry,*

*it's Dana. I've got some numbers for you from my lawyer.
I'm sorry that you haven't seen fit to reply to her letters, so
I guess I'll have to bring you these papers and make sure
you've seen them and understand the amount of money
that we're talking about. When I'm there, I want to pick up
a few linens and some kitchen things. Look for me in about
an hour. Okay?*

Time, seven twelve. A man. *Hey, Larry. Just a reminder
that we're climbing at Reimer's Ranch on Saturday. Please
bring that extra rope we talked about—got a couple of
newbies coming along, and we'll need all the rope we can
lay our hands on. See ya then, buddy.*

Sheila sighed. Messages on an answering machine,
ghost voices, sent to a ghost, to a dead man who would
never hear them, who would never again climb the cliffs
along the Pedernales River. She got her briefcase, opened
it, and took out a small tape recorder. She set it to record,
then played the messages back one at a time, jotting down
the callers' names and numbers in her notebook. If the
autopsy determined that Kirk died around two—the time
when the garbage truck usually came down the street—
the messages might be used to eliminate Henry Palmer,
who called from the shop at two fifteen about that potential
employee, and Dana Kirk, who called at four thirty.

Thinking of the garbage truck, Sheila glanced at her
watch, then reached for the telephone directory and looked
up the number of the company that picked up the city's
trash. She made the call on her cell. While she was holding for an answer to her question, she opened the email
program on the desktop computer and began to scan the
messages—which came, apparently, to a different email
address from the one on the laptop. It wasn't unusual, she
thought. Many people maintained multiple email accounts.

The latest email in the inbox folder—a note from a rock
climber asking to borrow some equipment—was dated the
previous Wednesday. She clicked to the sent folder, and

found that Kirk had answered it that same day. She clicked back to the inbox and began scrolling up through the emails, scanning each one. There was plenty of the usual spam, advertisements for Viagra and other enhancements, an email newsletter from Texans Against Gun Violence, a couple of severe weather alerts from KXAN-TV in Austin. And there was an email from someone named Jackie, dated October 17.

Larry: Yes, you did sign the consent form at the same time we set up the health insurance package. It sounds like the matter has slipped your mind. Sorry for any misunderstanding, but I'm afraid it's water under the bridge now. Still friends, I hope. I was sorry to hear about Dana (rocks in her head, if you ask me). I'd really love to get together, for old times' sake. Could we? Soon?—Jackie

Sheila checked the sender's email address and the date, then clicked over to the sent file to see if Kirk had answered the email. If he had, there was no evidence of it. The folder of deleted emails was empty.

She turned on the printer and printed the email, then logged off and began going through the stack of mail on top of the desk. Bills, political mailings, junk mail, a brochure from the Texas Mountaineering Club with an enclosed map to rock-climbing routes at Reimers Ranch in western Travis County, and two unopened letters from Angela Binder, Attorney at Law—Dana's lawyer. She pulled out the shallow top drawer on the right and found pens, pencils, rubber bands, paper clips, all jumbled together. She didn't see the red leather address book that Dana had mentioned, but Bartlett had probably taken that, to do family notifications.

The bottom drawer was deeper, a file drawer. In it, she found several manila folders, fat ones, filled with Kirk's bank statements, credit card bills, and other bills, including paid semi-annual premium notices on the $250,000 life insurance policy that his wife had mentioned. According to his latest bank statement, his checking account had just over $1100 in it. In the previous month, two checks had bounced, costing him a total of fifty dollars in service fees. There were two credit card statements, a Mastercard and a Visa, both cards nearly maxed out. He'd been making minimum payments.

Finally, the garbage company employee was back on the line with the information Sheila had requested. Yes, the truck was supposed to be on that particular street on Monday afternoons. Yes, the pickup time should be about two p.m., although of course this could not be guaranteed. The woman rattled off the names and phone numbers of the two men—a driver and a loader—who had been on the truck yesterday. Sheila hung up and phoned Bartlett, catching him just as he was arriving at Martin's place. She relayed the information about the garbage pickup, and he said he'd get Matheson to try to interview the men right away.

Sheila went back to the bottom drawer, pulling out two more file folders. One was labeled *Taxes* in Kirk's backward slanting hand. In it were paper-clipped copies of his IRS filings for the three previous years. She glanced through them and put the file folder back in the drawer. Probably nothing significant there, but she knew where to look if the information was needed.

The other folder had no label. Sheila opened the file and leafed through it. In it were three photocopied invoices from the American Eagle Life Insurance Company— quarterly notices, it appeared, for premiums on a policy in the amount of one million dollars on the life of Lawrence Kirk. She raised an eyebrow. A million dollars? The invoices were addressed to Harmon Insurance in Pecan Springs and were both stamped PAID. Clipped to them was a handwritten note on lined yellow paper, dated October 15.

Hey, Larry—

Here are the papers I told you about—I found them in your old file, which was way at the back of the cabinet behind all the employee folders. I've looked in all the usual places, like I said I would, but I haven't been able to find the policy or any other invoices on it. I think maybe Ms. Harmon is keeping all that stuff separate and just overlooked these or forgot about them or something. If you want me to try to dig up any more information, just let me know. My home phone (please don't call me at work): 512-2496

Your friend,
Tina Simpson

P.S. I happened to mention this to my sister, who gave me an article she found in a magazine. It says that in Texas, this kind of insurance wasn't legal until 1999, when the legislature put through a bill saying that an employer could do it if the employee signed a form. I guess you did that, huh, maybe? Anyway, I have the article, if you want to read it.

Larry Kirk must not have wanted to read the article, Sheila thought, because it wasn't in the file. Or maybe he had read it and put it somewhere else.

She looked back at the premium notices, then opened her notebook and flipped a couple of pages until she found what she thought she remembered. Yes, Harmon Insurance was the place where Dana Kirk had been working when she and her husband first met. She looked again at the signature on the note. Tina Simpson. The same Tina who had called to make a Dutch treat date for the weekend? None of this seemed related to Kirk's death, but Sheila had learned to be thorough. She liked to tie up the loose ends as she went along.

She opened the telephone directory again. There was a T. Simpson whose phone number matched the number in the message. She copied the address into her notebook, thinking that she wanted to find out more about the insurance policy. While she was at it, she copied the address for Harmon Insurance from the premium notices, and looked up that phone number as well. Then she filled out two evidence cards with the case number, date, and time, attaching one to the unlabeled file and the other to the email from Jackie that she had printed out. She bagged both, separately, and put them into her briefcase.

She glanced at her watch. If she was going to make Bartlett's nine a.m. briefing, she'd need to get moving. She made a careful tour of the living room, noticing nothing out of the ordinary. In the downstairs bedroom, the bed was unmade and there was a litter of dirty jeans, shirts, and briefs on the floor, under a large poster of a rock climber spidered on a cliff.

The adjacent bathroom was even more messy than the bedroom, with damp towels and washcloths on the floor and a clutter of toothpaste and shaving gear on the counter. Amid the general disorder on the floor, she spotted a woman's lipstick tube. Dana Kirk's, left behind in the rubble of her departure? But the lipstick was labeled "Firehouse Red," and through the transparent cap, she could see that the color was fiery—nothing like the softly muted lipstick the wife had been wearing when Sheila interviewed her the day before. "Firehouse Red" didn't seem to fit Dana's personality, either. On a hunch, she bagged and tagged the lipstick and put it into her briefcase.

Upstairs, she found two empty bedrooms and another bath, as well as a linen closet full of stacked sheets and towels and nothing else of interest. She came back downstairs and went out to the detached garage, which housed a five-year-old green Ford with one battered fender, the usual lawnmower and yard equipment, and miscellaneous rock-climbing equipment hanging on the garage walls. There was one large coil of new rope.

She went back through the house, locked the kitchen door, then picked up her briefcase and went out the front. She was inserting the key into the Impala's ignition when her cell phone chirped. She flipped it open. It was China. She glanced at the clock on the dashboard. 8:35.

"I'm here at Timms' place on Paint Horse Creek," China said, in a taut, strained voice. "I've just phoned in a nine-one-one to the sheriff's office, Sheila. It's Timms. He's dead."

Sheila suppressed a gasp. George Timms was *dead*? She said the first thing that came into her mind. "Suicide?"

"Not suicide, no," China replied. "I found his body down by the creek. Looks like a mountain lion kill. There's no weapon anywhere. And no sign that anyone else has been here in the past couple of days."

"Where's *here*?" Sheila demanded irately. She turned the key in the ignition. "And what the hell are you doing there?"

"It's the party place George Timms built last year, a few miles to the west of our house, off Limekiln Road. McQuaid told me about it last night. On my way to town this morning, I decided—on an impulse, I confess—to check it out." China took a deep breath, speaking cautiously now. "I've had a quick look around, Sheila. I think you ought to get a search warrant for this place. There are some items here that might be relevant to your investigation into the computer shop break-in—the blackmail end of things."

"I see," Sheila said, pulling out her notebook. "What, specifically?" The search warrant request required the police to state what evidentiary items they would be looking for.

China paused, then gave a succinct description as Sheila,

only half-believing what she heard, took notes. "I'm guessing that some of this stuff is on Timms' computer as well," China added, "which might be the reason he was so anxious to retrieve it. Now that he's dead, you won't be making a case against him. But there's a distinct possibility that another person or persons might be involved, and if so—"

"I understand," Sheila said. Who could've guessed that the case might go in this direction? "I'll ask Bartlett to get the warrant. We'll have to coordinate with the sheriff's office, but that shouldn't be a problem."

"Great," China replied, sounding relieved. "You headed out here?"

"As quick as I can get there," Sheila said. "Where's here?"

"West on Limekiln about fourteen miles, two miles past the turnoff to our place. Turn right on Paint Horse Road, go approximately two miles, left on gravel at a pair of mailboxes, to the end of the road. You'll see my car and Timms' Corvette—and by that time, the county mounties will no doubt be here."

"Thanks," Sheila said. "Look for me in twenty minutes or less." She clicked off, then reached down and grabbed the light and slapped it on the dash. She swung away from the curb, keying in Bartlett's cell phone as she drove. She caught him as he was heading for the station and relayed the news.

"Jeez." He whistled incredulously. "A *cat*? I can't think of a worse way to go."

Sheila shuddered, agreeing. "I got a tip that there are some items out there that might be relevant to the blackmail case. I need you to draw up a warrant and get Judge Porterfield to sign off on it. Here's what we're looking for." She picked up her notebook and detailed the items on the list China had given her. "Oh, and coordinate with the sheriff's office. They'll be investigating the death, and they'll need to know that we've got a related case."

"Gotcha," Bartlett said briskly. "I'll bring the warrant out myself." He paused. "Guess I need to cancel the morning's briefing."

"Roger that," Sheila said. "It might be a good idea to put the team on standby. It's possible that we'll need them at Timms' place. Oh, and bring your camera when you come, Jack. I want to get on-the-spot photos of whatever we find, and the sheriff's guys will be busy with the body."

She closed her phone, hit the siren, and pushed down hard on the accelerator.

Chapter Thirteen

Sheila stood beside the deputy, looking down at the twig-covered body of George Timms.

"Mountain lion," the deputy said. His face was grim. "Looks like a big one."

The other deputy unhooked his radio from his belt. "We need Parks and Wildlife out here. Ask them to bring a team and get a hunt under way." He looked back at the drag marks in the leaf litter. "Dogs, too."

"You need to talk to the volunteer who coordinates our Search and Rescue Unit," Sheila said. "Martha Meacham. She'll know whose hounds are available for deployment. She could probably have some dogs out here in a couple of hours, with backup, if you need it."

"The sooner the better," the first deputy said, and took out his clipboard and tape measure to sketch the scene. "But this happened nearly twenty-four hours ago. The chances of tracking the animal are slim to none. Still, we can't have a killer on the loose. The ranchers around here will want to see this one dead in a hurry." He looked down at the body again. "A first for Texas, far as I know. Don't think we've ever had a mountain lion kill a human before. They mostly go for deer, goats, sheep."

China Bayles stepped forward. "It might be easier than you think, deputy. Our neighbor shot a mountain lion last night. It was after his sheep. He said that the animal had a four-inch gash on its head. I'm thinking about that rock I showed you, the one with the blood and the fur on it. If Timms was able to pick it up and get in a good blow, he could have made that wound. If that's the case, the cat that killed Timms is already dead."

"That would be one colossal lucky break," the deputy said, sounding relieved. He turned to the second deputy. "Bag that rock with the blood and the fur on it, Mitch." He pulled out his notebook. "Neighbor's name, Ms. Bayles?"

"Tom Banner," China said. "Lives just off Limekiln Road, a couple of miles east of here. He probably hasn't disposed of the carcass yet, Maybe a stomach analysis will show—" She made a retching noise and turned away into the bushes.

Sheila glanced down again at Timms and shuddered. She had seen enough killings to be used to the sight of dead bodies, of accident and—yes—murder victims mutilated in sometimes unimaginable ways. But most of the dead had faces. George Timms didn't. He didn't have a scalp or much of a belly left, either. The animal had ripped him open, satisfied its hunger with the soft parts, and then scraped a neat, tidy mound of sticks over the meal so it could come back for a second helping. No part of the kill was scattered, except for the inedible hat and Rolex and the Nike-clad foot that had been left on the trail. In fact, it seemed to Sheila that there was a kind of ritual fastidiousness about this burial, a scrupulous care, one animal preserving and honoring another in death. And while any taking of human life was terrible, this taking was somehow less ugly and more explicable than many. This wild animal had not killed out of anger or hatred or passion, as so-called civilized humans did. It killed and consumed as part of a natural process, to preserve its physical life.

But Sheila knew that this did not diminish the terror that the victim must have felt in his last few moments of conscious thought. Judging from what she could see on the path, George Timms had died a violent and horrible death. The cougar had been lurking in the brush or lying on a low limb of a live oak, perhaps waiting for a deer to come along the path, up from the creek. Instead, Timms had come down the hill and into the animal's line of sight.

Why? Timms' binoculars were on the table beside his partially eaten meal. Perhaps he had glimpsed the cat and, not quite sure what he had seen, had gone down to investigate, not thinking of the possible risk. Most city people were completely clueless about the predators of the Hill Country, from rattlesnakes and cottonmouths and copperheads to wild cats.

But no one would ever know for certain what had happened, because there was no one left alive to tell the tale. All that could be known was what could be read from the marks along the trail. Timms had been in a hurry, taking long, sure strides toward the creek. The animal had launched itself onto his back, knocking off his red Texas Rangers baseball cap. Timms was fit, but he was only Sheila's height and less than 170 pounds—facts that did not work in his favor. He had staggered, suddenly burdened by an animal that could have weighed as much as he did. Powerful claws sank deep into the flesh of his shoulders, muscular jaws bit his neck, drawing blood. He struggled to keep to his feet, instinctively putting down a hand to brace himself and leaving the imprint of a flat palm and fingers in the soft dirt.

And he hadn't given up without a battle. The bloodied chunk of limestone China had found, with a scrap of fur clinging to it—Timms must have grabbed the rock and hit the animal as hard as he could. And the snapped sapling, the scatter of branches, scuffed soil and leaves, the dark spill of blood. Was it in the fight that the lion had broken

Timms' neck? Or had that come a moment later, when the animal clamped the man's head in his jaws and was dragging his kill through the patch of river ferns?

China came out of the bushes, then left the group and started up the trail. Sheila stayed long enough to be sure that the sheriff's department would be handling the next-of-kin notification, then went after her, joining her on the deck at the top of the landscaped slope.

She put a hand on her friend's shoulder. "You okay, China?"

China wiped her hand across her mouth. "Not the kind of thing you want to see right after breakfast," she muttered.

Sheila nodded sympathetically. "I hate to say this, but it's a good thing you came out here this morning. No telling how long it would have been before somebody else found him—what little would have been left of him." In fact, they might never have known what became of George Timms, until a hiker discovered a litter of loose bones and a DNA test eventually revealed their identity. But after that amount of time, with all the soft tissue gone, it would have been impossible to know for certain how the man had died, or when. His disappearance might have had a major impact on their investigation into Kirk's death.

China's face was grim. "I'm glad he was found," she said bleakly. "I just wish I hadn't been the one to find him." She frowned. "Sheila, I didn't mention this to the deputies, but Banner saw two cats last night. He shot the male—the female got away. I saw her running across Limekiln Road as I was coming home. A beautiful animal, sleek, strong, wild." She shook her head. "I didn't mention her because I hate to think of the sheriff's office sending out a team to . . . to slaughter that lovely creature."

Sheila regarded her friend. "Then let's not say anything about her," she replied. "From your description, it sounds like your neighbor has already shot the killer."

Killer. That was a silly thing to say, wasn't it? Carnivores were killers. They killed to eat. That was their nature. This carnivore hadn't deliberately targeted a human: it was simply a wrong-time, wrong-place situation, for which both man and animal would pay a terrible price.

But China was nodding, and Sheila knew that she understood. "Everybody likes the idea of living at the edge of the wilderness," she said, "until the wilderness tries to kill us. Then it's a different story."

"A different story," Sheila agreed. Parks and Wildlife would pick up the cat Banner had killed, and a necropsy and tests of its stomach contents would show whether that was the animal that had killed Timms. There'd be a brief flurry in the *Enterprise*, and letters to the editor suggesting that a bounty be paid for all dead mountain lions. And then the matter would be forgotten until the next time somebody—man, woman, or child—got in the way of a big cat. With more and more people moving into the animals' habitat, encounters like this one were bound to keep happening.

"Yeah." China straightened her shoulders. "Yeah, well, as I said on the phone, you need to take a look in the house, Chief. Did you get that warrant?"

"Bartlett's bringing it out." Sheila looked at her watch. "He should be here pretty soon. Can you stick around for a few minutes?"

"I called Ruby to tell her I'd be late. Ramona is there— she's opening the shop for me. So yes, I can hang out here for a while."

"Good," Sheila said. "When Bartlett gets here, we'll go through the house. In the meantime, I need to radio the SAR unit and see if Martha Meacham can locate some dogs for Parks and Wildlife. I think when they see the cat that Banner killed, they'll call off the search, but in the meantime, I'll put SAR on standby."

"While you're doing that," China said, "I'd like to use

Timms' phone to call Charlie Lipman. You got a problem if I let him know what's happened with Timms?"

"Nope," Sheila said. "Lipman might as well hear it from you as get the word at Bean's or the diner, wherever he happens to go for lunch." Once the tracking dogs were called out, this death would be big news, in a big hurry, and Hibler would be all over it for the next issue of the *Enterprise*. Sheila knew that this death was worth at least two domestic shootings, in terms of the newspaper's readership. It wasn't just the victim, although that was sensational enough. It was the way he died.

China turned and gestured toward the table, where Sheila saw a partially eaten sandwich, some damp-looking chips, a container of yogurt, a beer, a burned-down cigarette. "I know that you're wondering about the time of death," she said. "Because of Kirk's homicide, I mean. So listen to this. When I used Timms' phone to call nine-one-one a little while ago, the message light was blinking. After I made the call, I played the messages back."

"Damn it, China," Sheila said. "You know better than—"

China raised a hand. "Yes, I know. Not my job. But hear me out. There were four. The first was a girl, at twelve twenty, saying she'd left a gold bracelet here and hoping that George had found it. The second and third were from Charlie Lipman, at two forty-five and three fifteen, wondering where Timms was. The fourth one was from Charlie, too, at three fifty. He was pissed. He told Timms that if he didn't show up for the surrender, he could kiss his lawyer good-bye."

"But by that time," Sheila said thoughtfully, "Timms must have been dead for several hours."

"Exactly," China replied.

"He didn't pick up at twelve twenty," Sheila went on. "So maybe he sat down around noon to eat a sandwich, with chips and beer. Saw something at the bottom of the hill, went to investigate, and died there—well *before* Kirk was killed." That twelve-twenty phone call might eliminate him as a suspect in Kirk's homicide.

China pursed her lips. "Wonder if that girl will ever get her gold bracelet back."

Sheila went out to the Impala, where she radioed Dispatch and was patched through to Meacham. Without going into detail, she asked Martha to telephone the sheriff's office, find out what was going on, and get her assignment. She signed off, knowing that the dogs and their handlers would be on their way as quickly as possible, with a backup team ready to go if they were needed.

While Sheila was down at the creek with the deputies, an EMS van had pulled in and the medics were waiting beside it, talking to another pair of deputies who had just arrived. As she finished with SAR and got out of the car, Jack Bartlett pulled into the parking area. He stopped beside her and got out, patting the pocket of his brown corduroy jacket.

"Got the warrant," he said. "The judge was happy to oblige." He looked over his shoulder. "In fact, she's not far behind me. The sheriff's office notified her of the death while I was there with the warrant. She's on her way out here to officiate."

"Good," Sheila replied. "Did you bring your camera?"

"Yep." Bartlett lifted his briefcase. "Am I photographing the body?"

"No," Sheila said. "We'll let the sheriff's team take care of that." She beckoned. "Come on—we're going inside."

As she spoke, she heard the sound of a chopper and looked up to see a news helicopter from Channel Four in San Antonio circling overhead. The sheriff's office obviously hadn't been able to keep the story contained. Timms' killing by a mountain lion would be the lead story on the network news that night.

As they walked, Bartlett said, "Blount called as I got

about halfway out here, Sheila. She's been working for the past hour on Timms' computer. She's found some photographs that she thinks might have been a motivating factor."

"Lewd?" Sheila asked quickly. "Pornographic?"

"I haven't seen them yet. All she would say was that she thinks she's got something. Plus, she says that the photos are linked to names in Timms' email address book, which may be helpful. Butch dusted before Annetta got started," he added. "He said he picked up several prints. He didn't have any luck with Hatch on AFIS, though. Looks like he's not in the system."

"Disappointing," Sheila said. The AFIS fingerprints and criminal history information were submitted voluntarily by state, local, and federal law enforcement agencies. Smaller jurisdictions didn't always submit.

"Yeah," Barlett said, as they went around the house. "We're calling this a separate investigation?"

"Yeah," Sheila said. "We don't know where it's going or how it's connected to our other two cases. The Kirk homicide, the break-in."

"Agree," Bartlett said. "You're taking the lead?"

"On this one, Jack," Sheila said. She'd already thought about this. It wasn't that she was giving in to Blackie—this just made sense, that's all. But she felt the need to add an explanation. "There's likely to be interface with the sheriff's office."

"No problem as far as I'm concerned," Bartlett said. "Just keeping us straight."

They were on the deck. Sheila pointed out the food on the table and told him about the calls on the answering machine. "Looks like we might be able to eliminate Timms in the Kirk homicide," she said, and Bartlett nodded, agreeing.

"Sounds like he was here when Kirk was killed," he said. "And likely already dead."

In the kitchen, China was still on the phone to Charlie

Lipman. "No, he wasn't a suicide," she was saying, "unless he walked down there, shot himself, disposed of the gun, and was then attacked by a mountain lion. Which doesn't seem at all likely, from the evidence on the ground."

Lipman must have asked her when this had taken place, because she said, "Before he finished his lunch, looks like. Your messages were on the answering machine, un-played, plus a twelve-twenty message from a girl about a bracelet. Since he didn't pick up that call, it's possible that he was already dead by that time."

Sheila tapped China on the shoulder. "I'd like to talk to Lipman when you're finished, China."

China nodded, listened a moment, then said, "Anyway, that's the story. I thought you ought to know. Chief Dawson's here. She'd like a word with you."

Sheila took the phone China held out to her. "Good morning, counselor."

"Not a good one for Timms," Lipman growled.

"No, sir," Sheila said. She cleared her throat. "I hope you're not going to tell me that Timms' secret died with him. The motivation for his break-in at the computer shop, that is."

Lipman was gruff. "Chief Dawson. If that was a question, there's no point to it. I know that you know that attorney-client privilege extends beyond the client's death."

"I understand," Sheila said. "But there's a chance that whatever information you have about the blackmail—the alleged blackmail, that is—might help us to clear the Kirk case. You know about that, I suppose," she added. She gave China an eyebrows-raised glance, and China nodded.

"I thought Kirk shot himself." Lipman's tone was guarded.

"The cause of death has not yet been identified," Sheila said. "We'll have the autopsy report sometime later today."

There was a moment's silence. "Ah," Lipman said. "Yes, I see."

Sheila said. "What about it, counselor? Can you help us out?"

Lipman was silent for a moment, and when he spoke, he was gruff. "I figure you had my client fingered as your chief suspect in Kirk's homicide, Chief—since that's what you obviously think it was. Now that he's out of the running, you'll be moving somebody else into that slot. But I can't tell you any more than I told Detective Bartlett when I set up the surrender. Timms liked to play his cards close to his chest. He never got around to telling me the whole story."

Sheila wasn't sure whether to believe him. "Too bad. Detective Bartlett and I are here with a search warrant this morning. I thought maybe you could see your way clear to giving us some context for what we're looking for. But since that's not the case—"

"Related to Timms' death?" Lipman asked, sounding startled, then puzzled. "I thought he was killed by a mountain lion. You're not telling me that—"

"No," Sheila said firmly. "The warrant is related to possibly illegal activities in which the man was engaged. I don't suppose you know anything about that," she added.

She could hear the lawyer's chair creaking as Lipman sat back. Instead of answering her question, he posed one of his own, warily. "What are you looking for?"

Sheila didn't answer. She didn't have to. The warrant satisfied the requirements of the court. It didn't need anything else.

The silence lengthened. When he spoke, Lipman's voice carried a wry chuckle. "Well, now that we've settled the matter, I'll wish you good hunting." There was a definitive click.

"So much for that," Sheila said, still holding the receiver. "I was hoping he might be at least a little forthcoming."

China looked regretful. "He's a tough nut, Sheila. But he's fair."

"Says you," Sheila said dryly, and put down the phone.

"That's because he's on your side of the fence. You lawyers all hang together." She nodded at Jack. "You and Detective Bartlett have met, I take it?"

"Yesterday afternoon," Bartlett said. "Hello again, Ms. Bayles." If he was curious about China's presence here this morning, he didn't mention it. He glanced around admiringly. "Very nice place Timms had here." He bent to look at a wooden cabinet filled with wine bottles, appropriately slanted necks-down. The adjacent shelves were stacked with sparkling glassware. "Quite the pad, huh? He must've been a real party animal."

"Let's get to work," Sheila said. "China has to get back to town. She has something she thinks we should look at."

China led the way down the hall. "I made a quick tour of the house when I first got here this morning, looking for Timms." She paused beside a door and turned to face them. "I saw the uneaten food on the table outside and thought he might be somewhere here in the house, sick or injured. I called and shouted but couldn't raise anybody. So I came in and looked around. I didn't touch anything but the doorknobs. And this is what I found," she added, and opened the door. "In plain view. Having seen it, I felt I had a responsibility to let you know." China was saying what a lawyer ought to say. Practicing or not, as long as she kept her bar membership current, she was an officer of the court. And Timms was not *her* client.

"Damn," Bartlett said roughly, under his breath.

China had already given Sheila an idea of what they would be seeing, but still, the magnitude of it struck her almost dumb. All four of the room's white walls were lined with erotic photographs, hundreds of them, most framed in either clear plastic frames or in simple black frames. They were artistically presented photographic studies of nudes of both sexes, provocatively posed, voluptuous, beautiful. Most photos featured one figure, some two, in various

positions, at various angles. Most were black-and-white or
sepia, a few were full-color. Some were quite small, others
poster-size.

Timms had obviously been into nude photography for
quite some time, and in a big way, Sheila thought. He must
have been the photographer—at least, he owned a great
deal of photographic equipment, as Sheila saw when she
opened a door to a closet, and he had signed and dated
some of the photographs, perhaps the ones he was most
proud of. But he had apparently taken some pains to preserve the models' anonymity, for of the hundreds of photographs, most were of adult torsos, legs and arms. Rarely
were the faces pictured, so if you wanted to know the identity of the subject, you were out of luck—unless, of course,
the names were on the back of the photographs or Timms
had kept a log of his photographic activities. Either was
possible, Sheila thought. And Blount might have found
something that would help with names.

But while many of the good citizens of Pecan Springs
and all the members of Timms' church would undoubtedly
be horrified if they ever learned about Timms' private passion, they were no more illegal than the XXX-rated films
sold in the truck stops all along Interstate 35. Or so Sheila
thought, until—

She moved closer, pulling in her breath, frowning. On a
section of the wall, beside the bathroom door, a couple of
dozen smaller photographs were displayed—and they were
not adults. They were nude children, mostly girls but a few
boys, around the ages of eight or nine, engaging in some
sort of sexual play. The faces were elfin and smiling or
deeply serious and sad, the eyes large, the mouths tender,
the nude bodies slender or rounded but always supple and
lovely, fragrant with the bloom of youth. Unlike the other
photos, there was no effort made to preserve the children's
anonymity—on the contrary, the faces were an important

element of the photographs. They were documents of a fey and fragile innocence on the cusp of becoming aware of something quite, quite other.

There was another thing different about these photographs, too. Most of them involved a nude adult male, as well, back always to the camera—and not always the same man. At a glance, she thought there might be three, maybe four different men involved. The male presence seemed to fall like an ominous shadow across the children's innocence, a threatening portent, artful and symbolic—and pornographic.

Beside her, Bartlett spoke in a thin, metallic voice. "Like I said, quite the party animal." He set down his briefcase, opened it, and took out a digital camera.

"Make sure the time-date stamp is set," Sheila told him as he got ready to take photographs of the walls. She heard her voice trembling, and there was a sharp, sour taste in her mouth. She wished she could turn away and run from the photographs, wash the images out of her mind. But she couldn't. This was part of the job. Even more, these children deserved her closest attention, her passionate attention to every detail of the activity that was on display in front of her. They demanded that she do her job with as much determination and skill as necessary. She was their advocate now—she and the people who worked with her.

She took a deep breath and straightened her shoulders. "This is the section we're after," she added, "but let's photograph the entire room, including those shelves of photographic equipment. Don't try to capture the details of every image. What we want is a preliminary survey record of everything here, just as it is, so that we have the full context. I don't want there to be any questions after we've taken some of them down for more processing."

"Gotcha," Bartlett said, beginning to take photographs.

China came over to stand beside Sheila in front of the

display of children's photographs. "So what do you think?" she asked bleakly. "Selling photos on the Internet?"

"Maybe," Sheila said. But even if there was no distribution involved, the children's photographs could have brought multiple counts of second-degree felony under Section 43 of the Texas Penal Code, as well as under Title 18 of the United States Code. Because of the federal sentencing guidelines, conviction under the federal law usually resulted in an even harsher sentence. And then there were the child-abuse charges, on top of that. Timms was immune from prosecution now, but not the other men involved. Who were they? What else was going on here?

"I'm guessing that it's not so much an Internet ring as a private club," she added. "Maybe a small group of like-minded guys who took turns with their cameras. This could be just the tip of the iceberg." She shook her head, feeling her stomach turn. "Displaying the photos—that's got to be some kind of special fetish."

"And now he's dead." China turned away with the same expression she had worn when she turned away from Timms' mutilated body. "Is this connected to anything you're finding on Timms' computer? Or to Kirk's death?"

"It's possible," Sheila said. She'd have liked to be able to share the whole story with China, but that would have to wait until the case was wrapped. China would understand.

She took a deep breath and spoke over her shoulder to Bartlett. "We're going to treat this as a separate crime scene, Jack. Timms is dead, yes—but it looks like other people may be involved. There are the men in the photographs. And in addition to those who are obviously children, some of the young women in the other photographs may be underage—or underage at the time their pictures were taken."

"We're going to seal the house?" Bartlett asked.

"Yes. The sheriff's office and Parks and Wildlife can

handle the scene by the creek, but I'll ask Sheriff Chambers to turn this place over to us. It's his territory, but our case, since it's related to our other ongoing investigation. I'd prefer that our people process it, if we can." There was no murder victim and no obvious violence. The forensics ought to be manageable.

"Good deal," Bartlett said from behind his camera. "I'll get Matheson, Blount, and Bedford out here."

"Right. But let's not do it now," Sheila said. "Our plates are pretty full at the moment, with both Kirk's homicide and the blackmail. I'd like to see us make more forward progress with both of those cases—especially the homicide—before we start processing this scene. And in the meantime, let's tape both front and back entrances to this house and post a patrol officer out front, as well. There's going to be a lot of traffic related to Timms' death and Parks and Wildlife's hunt for that cat." She gestured toward the wall. "And once the news hits the wires, some of the people who were involved with Timms may attempt to retrieve their photographs." Which might be a good thing, she thought grimly. She'd tell the officer to bring in for questioning anyone who showed up out here—anyone who wasn't connected with the investigation.

"Understand," Bartlett said, going back to his photography.

"And as soon as you've got a good documentation," she added, "please seal this room. And seal that outer sliding door, too. We don't want anybody coming in that way."

China had taken several steps away, toward the door. "This whole thing makes me absolutely sick," she said thinly. "If somebody like Timms ever got his hands on Caitie, I'd kill him."

"You do that, you'd better get yourself a good lawyer," Sheila said with a small grin. "But we're in your debt, China. If you hadn't walked through the house and seen the photos, they might have disappeared." She shook her head.

"And we may find other incriminating material, when we have the time to get enough people out here to do a thorough search."

"I shudder to think what that could be," China said as they went down the hall. "The stuff in that room is the worst I could imagine." Her voice was gritty.

Yes, what was in that room was awful, unspeakably awful. But Sheila knew she couldn't predict what a full search would turn up here. It looked like Timms was a pedophile. What else was he? Who else was involved?

But she only said, "When this is all over, let's sit down over a cup of tea and some of your fresh-baked cookies and talk about it, China. In the meanwhile—"

"I know," China said with a sympathetic look. "In the meanwhile, you can't tell me what's going on." She shook her head ruefully. "Actually, I'm not sorry, Sheila. I don't envy you your job. After what we saw here today—down by the creek and in that bedroom—I'm glad to be an ordinary citizen. I can go back to my quiet herb shop and let you and your cops deal with the ugly stuff." Her mouth tightened. "And after seeing those girls' photos, I personally believe that cat gave George Timms exactly what he deserved. If Ruby were here, she'd probably tell us that it's natural justice, arranged by the universe in payment for his sins."

"I'd prefer not to trust the universe," Sheila said wryly. "Although I have to admit that the justice system doesn't always do the best job." She had seen far too many cases where the innocent paid the price and the guilty got off scot-free, some of them aided and abetted in their escape by their defense lawyers. But in this instance, she had to agree that if the mountain lion hadn't killed George Timms, it was likely that his cache of secret photographs would never have come to light. Depending, of course, on what they found on Timms' computer, and whether it would have been enough to get a search warrant for both his house in town and this place.

China nodded. "Well, I'll leave you to it. I've got to get to work—and to pleasanter things." She paused, her face darkening. "Except that I'm concerned about our guys. I try to remind myself that Americans are going back and forth across the border every day, thousands of them. But that doesn't help. I still worry."

"I know," Sheila said. "I try not to think about it, but I'm worried, too—which of course doesn't do anybody any good."

Unexpectedly, China leaned forward and put her arms around Sheila. "They'll be okay," she said, with a strong, solid hug. "And so will we."

She lifted a hand in good-bye and was gone.

A half-hour later, Sheila and Bartlett stood in the kitchen, getting ready to head back to town. He had taped the front and back entrances with yellow plastic crime-scene tape. While he was doing that and locating the keys to Timms' house, Sheila had a phone conversation with Sheriff Chambers.

After her brief explanation of what their preliminary search had turned up, the sheriff had agreed that the house wasn't part of his crime scene. But he had also agreed to post an officer out front.

"I've got to have somebody directing traffic, anyway," he said. "When we're done out there and ready to leave, I'll let you know and you can post one of your officers." He had also said an immediate yes to her request to have Timms' body fingerprinted. The prints would be needed for exclusion purposes here at the house and on the laptop Annetta Blount was working on. He also reported that the county forensics team would have a preliminary report later in the day.

"Sounds like you folks have your hands full," he added. "You need any additional assistance, you let me know.

Y'hear?" He paused. "One of our guys told me that Blackie is making a trip to Juárez to try to locate that missing kid."

"Yes," Sheila said. She could hear the concern in Chamber's voice and it reminded her of her own—the worry she had been trying to bury. "He and Mike McQuaid are planning to cross today."

"Tell the truth, it's not something I'd want to do." Chambers cleared his throat. "You talk to Blackie, you tell him luck from me, Sheila. Hope the job goes okay. That's a dangerous place down there, whatever the mission."

"Thanks, Curt," Sheila had said. "I'll do that."

Now, she pushed the worry out of her mind and tried to pay attention to Bartlett, who was filling her in on his activities of the morning. Before she had interrupted him with news of Timm's death, he had completed his interview with Kirk's contract worker, Dennis Martin. He had caught him at his apartment before he left for the shop.

The interview had not produced any new information, but Martin had confirmed what Richie Potts had told Sheila the night before: that Jason Hatch had been let go because of some kind of difficulty with a customer. What it was, exactly, Martin didn't know, but it had made Kirk really angry. "Steaming" was the way Martin had described it. And no, he hadn't worked on Timms' computer, Martin said, although he knew where it was because he saw Henry Palmer putting it into the bottom drawer of the file cabinet. He claimed that he hadn't touched it. Bartlett had sent him to the station to be fingerprinted.

"That should take care of everybody who might have had a shot at that computer," Sheila said thoughtfully. "Except for Hatch, of course. We'll have Timms' prints before we leave here. We've already got Palmer's, Potts', Martin's, and Kirk's."

Bartlett lit a cigarette. "If these people are telling the truth, the only prints we should find on the computer are Timms' and Palmer's. Anybody else's prints show up, he's on our blackmail suspect list." He blew out a stream of smoke. "I've got Matheson working on a summary of Kirk's movements for forty-eight hours before his death."

Sheila took out her notebook and flipped a couple of pages, catching up. "What about the autopsy? Today, is it?"

Bartlett nodded. "I talked to Morse as I was driving out here. She'll phone when she's ready to start the autopsy. One of us needs to be there. You or me?"

"Your call," Sheila said.

Bartlett flicked his cigarette ash. "My case, too. I'll take it." He looked at her. "Next dead body is yours."

"Next dead body," Sheila said wryly, "we'll haul Hardin back here to do his share."

"I'll go for that," Bartlett said, and grinned easily. "On the autopsy, there are two major questions we're interested in, right? Whether there's any stippling around the entry wound and whether there's gunpowder residue on the hands."

"We'll also want the bullet—or the fragments," Sheila reminded him. "There wasn't any exit wound, so it's still in Kirk's skull. The angle of entry would be good if Morse can get it, but she may not be able to." The path of a bullet through hard and soft tissue was often erratic, and it would require careful examination to determine the angle.

"Right." Cigarette in his mouth, Bartlett made a couple of notes. "Did you pick up anything in the Kirk house this morning?"

"Several things," Sheila said. "In fact, there's one that I'd like to follow up on this morning. There's a message on the answering machine from a woman named Tina. Tina Simpson. I'd like to have a talk with her. She sent Kirk copies of a couple of premium notices. Looks like somebody was paying the bill for a million-dollar life insurance policy on him."

Bartlett frowned. "The wife?"

"No. This is in addition to the policy Kirk took out on

himself. Two hundred fifty thousand on that one, with the wife as the beneficiary, according to her. No idea who the beneficiary is on the larger one."

"A million bucks sounds like a pretty fair motive to me," Bartlett said. "Back to the blackmail. I'll check with Butch on the fingerprint situation. If we get a match on Timms' computer with one of the other contract guys, Hatch isn't so urgent. If we don't get a match, I'll put out an APB on him as a person of interest." He dropped his cigarette and ground it out in the gravel. "Guess I'm ready to head back to town."

Sheila glanced around. There was nothing more they could do until the team came in and started its work. Meanwhile, there was plenty of work waiting in Pecan Springs.

"You go on," she said. "I'm going to take a quick walk through the rest of the house. I'll lock up."

The tour produced nothing of interest, although she knew that an intensive search would have to be made. When she locked the place and went out to the Impala, she was met by a deputy with a pair of fingerprint cards—Timms' prints, taken from his body. As she was signing for them, another deputy arrived, with orders to station herself in front of the house. Sheila talked to her for a few minutes, leaving instructions that anyone who attempted to enter should be questioned, logged, and detained for more questioning, if that seemed warranted.

Whatever else was inside Timms' house was going to wait, undisturbed, until they had the opportunity to do a thorough search.

Chapter Fourteen

Another "hold-tight" herb is the devil's claw (*Proboscidea parviflora* ssp. *parviflora*), a pretty pink-flowering annual that grows in deserts and arid uplands. Its sinister common name refers to the seed capsule, which splits open at one end into two curved horns or claws. These claws readily cling to any passing animal or human, so that the seeds may be widely distributed. The fresh green pods and dried black seed capsules were used for food and in basketry by Native American tribes of the southwestern United States.

The plant was also considered medicinal and was used to treat joint pain and rheumatism. Painted and decorated, the dried devil's claws have a striking appearance and are often used for jewelry and other crafts.

China Bayles
"Herbs That Hold Fast"
Pecan Springs Enterprise

I cannot begin to tell you how glad I was to open the door of Thyme and Seasons, take a deep breath of the shop's sweet, earthy fragrances, and feel Khat winding his sinuous self around my ankles, rumbling his velvet-throated glad-to-see-you purr. After what I had encountered that morning, my little shop felt like a dream of paradise, a safe haven against the ugly world outside. There was only one other thing I needed: to wash my hands. A gargle wouldn't be a bad idea, either.

For once, I was glad to see that it was a slow morning at the shop. There were a couple of women outside, walking through the medicinal garden and comparing notes on herbs they wanted to buy. Inside, a mom was browsing through the soaps and lotions while her pigtailed little girl, dressed in white bib overalls and a yellow ruffled blouse, was sitting in the child's rocking chair that I keep in the corner, humming as she turned the pages of a book. It was such a sweetly innocent picture that I could have hugged the little girl. But I didn't. Some affections are appropriate. Others are not—witness what I had seen in Timms' bedroom. I'd save my hugs for Caitie.

Ramona was perched on the stool behind the counter, painting her nails. She looked up as I came in and raised her voice. "Ruby!" she called. "China's here!" She didn't add *finally,* but her tone implied it.

"I'll be here after I've washed my hands," I told her, and headed for the tiny restroom under the stairs. We've painted the floor and walls and decorated it with posters of Texas wildflowers, and there's always a small bowl of fresh green herbs on the commode. But I didn't just wash my hands. I scrubbed them as hard as I could, using plenty of rosemary soap and the hottest water I could bear. As it rushed through my fingers, I bent over to take a deep, full breath of the soap's cleansing scent. And for good measure, I went into the tearoom kitchen and got out the bottle of sage gargle I'd made the week before, a strong sage tea with a couple of spoonfuls of cider vinegar added. Back in the bathroom, I swished out my mouth.

But when I was finished, I felt only a little better. Timms' death had been violent and ugly, but it was a clean kill: a strong, skilled predator obeying an urgent instinct, taking the opportunity that presented itself, killing its prey without anger or malice or greed. But Timms himself had been a predator, and his victims would suffer for much longer than he had. After what I had seen on the wall of that bedroom, it was going to be a while before I felt entirely clean again. I was only glad that I could escape here, to a place that looks pretty and smells good and attracts pleasant people—moms and little children and people who love plants. I was even more glad that I didn't have to do what Sheila was doing right now. For the life of me, I don't know how she does it, how any police officer does it, really. But I reminded myself that they do it for us, and that instead of relief, I ought to be feeling gratitude.

As I came out of the bathroom drying my hands on a paper towel, Ruby bustled through the door that connects her shop to mine. She was wearing her weirdest Queen-of-the-Jungle makeup, complete with amber-tinted contacts and a pair of furry faux eyelashes. She was dressed in a pair of skin-tight black leggings with three half-dollar-sized gold buttons at each ankle, a silky leopard-print top with a boat neck and long, tight sleeves. Around her neck was a curious necklace of devil's claw seedpods, painted in bright colors and decorated with feathers and beads. If you're not used to Ruby, her bizarre style is likely to startle you, but this morning I found it wonderfully comforting. The world beyond our shops had gone completely and totally crazy. Ruby, on the other hand, was completely and totally normal.

"Ruby," I said happily, "you're gorgeous. That necklace is *wild*."

"Oh, thank you!" she exclaimed, fingering the painted pods. "These are magic, you know. When you're wearing devil's claws, you're safe. They frighten away the evil spirits, so nothing bad can harm you." Her long fake fingernails were painted with gold and brown stripes. They didn't quite look like claws, but almost. "When you mentioned the po-

lice, I began to worry, China. Where have you *been*?"
She gave me a closer look. "Are you okay? What happened
to you?"

Over the phone, I had told Ruby only that I would be late
because I was waiting for the sheriff's deputies to arrive at
the scene of what looked like an accident, and asked if
somebody was available to open the shop for me. I thought
I should save the gory details until later, when I could take
the time to answer her questions. Now was later.

"It wasn't me it happened to, Ruby," I said soberly. "It
was George Timms."

"Who's George Timms?" Ramona wanted to know. Her
question took me by surprise. I had forgotten that she hadn't
been around here long enough to recognize his name and
be impressed.

"George Timms is one of Pecan Springs' biggest big
shots," Ruby told her. "He owns the Chevy dealership and
property all over town. And he's friends with everybody—
the mayor, the city council. He gets his picture in the paper
almost every week." She looked at me, frowning, her head
on one side. "What happened to him, China?"

"A mountain lion happened to him," I said.

"A mountain lion!" Ruby and Ramona exclaimed, in
unison.

Keeping my voice low so that I wouldn't alarm the customer and her little girl, I told them the first part of the
story, the part where I found Timms' faceless body down
by the creek, buried under a tidy pile of twigs. The rest of
it—the photographs in Timms' bedroom—was a separate
matter, as was the blackmail situation, which might or
might not be related to Larry Kirk's murder. That was Sheila's territory, and I didn't want to get into it. Not now, anyway. Smart Cookie would tell us about it when she had the
case wrapped and ready to turn over to the DA.

And anyway, the mountain lion was more than enough
for them to handle right now. Both Ruby's and Ramona's

cheeks were pale and their eyes wide and frightened by the time I finished telling them what I had seen—most of it, anyway. I left out a few of the gorier details, like the rip in Timms' belly and the Nike-clad foot.

"That's *grisly,* China!" Ruby cried. She clutched at her necklace, as if it might save her from a similar fate. "Killed by a mountain lion! What a horrible way to die!"

"It's unimaginable," Ramona whispered thinly. "I hope they *shoot* the beast! The idea that in this day and age, a person could be mauled to death by a brutal wild animal—"

"It's the natural order of things," I countered, cutting Ramona off. "The mountain lions were here first." It was my considered opinion that the lion had given Timms pretty much what he deserved, and that the jury was still out as to which of the two was the real "brutal wild animal." But I didn't share that. Instead, I said, "It's pretty likely that the lion is already dead," I said, and told them about the one that Tom Banner had shot.

"So that's it," I said, when I had finished. "Thank you for covering for me here at the shop, Ramona. I really appreciate it. And now that we've all heard the story, I vote that we go back to work. I for one am certainly ready to stop thinking about this stuff." I looked in the direction of the customer and saw that she was still busy with her browsing.

"But we can't go back to work, China," Ruby said, very seriously. "Not just yet, anyway. There are some ladies who are anxious to talk to you about something important." She gestured toward the door to the tearoom. "I gave them a table and a pot of tea and a plate of cookies. Now that you're here, they'll be very glad to see you." To her sister, she added, "Ramona, if you don't mind, you could keep an eye on both shops for us while China and I sit down with a cup of tea and talk to the ladies. I don't think it'll take too long."

"I hope not," Ramona said. "I promised Molly Mc-

Gregor that I'd stop in and see her this morning, so we could continue our talk about the possibility of my going into business with her at the Hobbit House. I had to break our date yesterday, you know."

I was frowning. "What ladies?" I asked. "Really, Ruby, I'm certainly ready to sit down with a cup of tea, but if it's all the same to you, I'd rather skip the powwow with—"

"Sorry," Ruby said regretfully. "You can't skip it. They've been waiting for almost an hour. They don't think Larry Kirk killed himself." She leaned closer and lowered her voice confidentially, glancing over her shoulder to make sure that the customer wasn't listening. "They think they know who did it."

She had my attention. "They think *what*?" I asked, startled. "Who are *they*?"

"The Texas Stars," she replied. "You know, the quilting club."

"Oh," I said, feeling deflated. "You mean neighborhood gossip central." Ruby had taken me to their meetings as a guest, so I spoke from personal observation. The ladies claimed that they got together to make quilts, and their quilts were truly beautiful. But they also got together to trade, barter, and embellish all the local news, about three-quarters of which was garden-variety gossip. I'd be very surprised if they had a single shred of genuine information.

"Well, yes," Ruby conceded. "I suppose they do gossip a fair amount. They don't have much else to do. On the other hand, sometimes neighbors see things they aren't supposed to see. And they tell other neighbors, who have seen other things, and so on."

I had to acknowledge the truth of that. Still— "Who's in there?" I asked, gesturing toward the tearoom.

Ruby began ticking the Stars off on her fingers. "Ethel Wauer from next door—next door to me, that is. I think you know her."

"Oh, I know her, all right," I said. "She's the ringleader. I hope she didn't bring that yappy little dog. Oodles, isn't that his name?"

"Of course she didn't," Ramona said in a snarky tone. "She left him at home to annoy the neighbors."

Ruby continued. "There's also Jane Jessup, who lives on the other side of Ethel—the one with the beautiful vegetable garden. And Mildred Ewell from across the street. And Hazel Schulz. She lives on the far side of the Kirks'."

"Sounds like a quorum," I said, feeling resigned. "But if they have some serious information, they should march right down to the police station and tell the cop at the duty desk. Somebody will be glad to take their information and pass it along to the investigators."

"Well, it's not *that* kind of information," Ruby said, almost apologetically. "I mean, it's not the kind of report that they can walk into the police station with. It's more . . ." She waved her hand. "It's vague. They're not really sure what they *know*, you know. They just know what they think they saw and heard. And it's all kind of mixed up."

I rolled my eyes. *What they think they saw and heard.* It wasn't every day that a neighbor was killed in his kitchen, especially in a small town like Pecan Springs. Larry's death was likely to be the subject of dozens of wild stories flying around the neighborhood. Somebody had seen a mysterious male visitor in the dead of night. Another person had noticed an unfamiliar car parked down the block. The lady on the corner had seen a stranger loitering in the alley. And these sweet little old ladies had compiled all these rumors and bits of gossip into a story they were dying to share.

"Anyway," Ruby went on, "they don't want to tell the police. They're here because they want to tell *you*."

"Me?" I asked, surprised. "Why me?"

"Because you're famous," Ramona replied, with a chuckle that just missed being sarcastic.

"That's ridiculous," I scoffed. "I'm not famous. I—"

"Yes, you are," Ruby said. "Last summer, you helped to locate Jessica Nelson when that guy kidnapped her. And before that, there was the burglar you squirted with pepper spray right here in the shop—remember? And before *that*, it was the drugs that somebody was trying to smuggle in those pots of yucca. If it hadn't been for you, the smugglers would have succeeded."

She paused, and I knew she was thinking of Colin Fowler. He'd been investigating that drug smuggling ring when he was killed. She touched her devil's claw necklace again, swallowed, and went on.

"The Stars have heard all these stories, China, and they've decided that you're a regular Miss Jane Marple."

Ramona smothered a giggle.

"Miss who?" I asked blankly.

"Miss Marple. You know—in Agatha Christie's mysteries. So they want you to listen to what they have to say." She patted my arm. "And anyway, it'll be a chance to sit down and have a nice cup of hot tea and a couple of cookies. You look like you could use a break."

I couldn't argue with that. With a sigh, I followed Ruby into the tearoom.

Thyme for Tea occupies the back half of the building that Ruby and I share. Like our shops, the dining room has limestone walls, well-worn wide-board floors, and an embossed tin ceiling. With its green-painted wainscoting, chintz chair seats and place mats, and pots of ivy and bundles of dried herbs hanging everywhere, it's a friendly and attractive space, appealing to the local clubs and groups that like to meet there for lunch.

But the lunch crowd wasn't here yet. The dining room was empty except for four little old ladies sitting around a table. They were wearing dresses, hats, and gloves, as if they had come for high tea. But one of them had apparently brought a deck of cards, for they were playing bridge while they waited. They were totally engrossed.

"One spade," Ethel Wauer said.

"Pass," said Mildred Ewell.

"One heart," said Jane Jessup.

"Pass," said Hazel Schulz.

They all looked at Ethel, who hesitated. "Four hearts," she said tentatively. "Or maybe—"

"Ladies," Ruby said, "China Bayles is here. Do you still want to talk to her?"

"You bet your boobies we do," Ethel said brightly, folding her cards. Ethel is a spry eighty-something, with very white hair that she wears in a boy's cut, as short as possible. "Girls, put away your cards."

"But Ethel," Mildred said, looking at her hand, "I was about to—"

"Never mind, Mildred," Jane said. "We're here to talk. We can play cards later."

Feeling resigned, I pulled up a chair. "What was it you wanted to talk about?"

"I'll bring another pot of tea," Ruby offered, and went off.

I waited as the ladies handed their cards to Ethel, who put them carefully into their box and the box into her handbag. Then I repeated my question. "What did you want to talk about?"

The ladies looked from one to the other. "You tell her, Jane," Hazel urged. "You're the one who looked out the window."

"No," Jane said, shaking her head. "That was Ethel. Ethel, you tell her."

"All right, I will," Ethel said, and straightened in her chair. "Mr. Kirk was a very nice man and we all liked him. We don't think he killed himself."

"Why?" I asked.

"Because that wasn't the kind of person he was," Jane said indignantly. "He disinfected my grandson's computer. And anyway, we saw—"

"*Ethel* saw her," Mildred corrected her. "Two different times."

"*After* Mr. Kirk had gone to the shop," Hazel said.

"But I also saw—" Jane began huffily.

"Wait," I said, holding up my hand. I turned to Ethel. "Mrs. Wauer, are you going to tell me what you saw, or am I going to have to guess?"

Mrs. Wauer leaned forward, blue eyes sparkling in her lined face. "Well, it's like this, China. I wash my dishes at the kitchen sink, once or twice every day. I was washing dishes, and I looked out the window and saw—"

"You need a dishwasher, is what you need," Hazel said. "My cousin works at Jim's Appliance Store. He'd be glad to install one for you, Ethel."

"Get a KitchenAid," Jane advised. "They're the best. I have never had a minute's trouble with mine, except for the time a fork got into the—"

I broke in. "Mrs. Wauer, just what did you see when you looked out the window?"

"A woman," Mrs. Wauer replied. "Walking down the alley. Two different times—and both of them after Mr. Kirk had gone to work."

"How do you know he'd gone to work?" I asked.

"Because Oodles doesn't like bicycles," Mrs. Wauer said.

I frowned. "What does Oodles not liking bicycles have to do with—"

Mildred Ewell leaned forward. "Oodles barks at bicycles," she said darkly. "He goes totally bananas when he sees a bicycle. Once he knocked down his gate and chased Mr. Kirk down the street. He bit him on the ankle and tore his pants."

"Oodles was very sorry afterward," Mrs. Wauer said repentantly. "He just lost his head for a moment."

"So Oodles barked and you knew that Mr. Kirk had ridden off to work," I said, trying to keep the conversation on track. "And then what?"

"And then I saw the lady in the alley," Ethel said.

"Not just once," Hazel put in excitedly. "Twice! *After* Mr. Kirk had gone to work! Now why, I ask you, would somebody be going to Mr. Kirk's house when he wasn't there?"

"How do you know she was going to Mr. Kirk's house?" I asked reasonably. Ruby appeared at that moment with a pot of hot tea.

"It's mint," she said. "I thought you might need a picker-upper." She pulled up a chair and sat down at the table.

"Thank you," I said gratefully, wishing it were laced with something very strong. I poured myself a cup, sweetening it with honey. "How did you know she was going to Mr. Kirk's house?" I asked again.

"Because she went in his back gate," Mrs. Wauer replied. "She walked down the alley as pert as you please, right past my kitchen window, then opened the Kirks' back gate and went in."

"When was this?" I asked.

Mrs. Wauer frowned. "Well, one time it was Monday, because that's the day Mr. Hamer comes to cut the grass. Monday two weeks ago. The other time . . ." She paused. "I'd have to check, but I'm pretty sure it was the day I took Oodles to the vet to get his shots. That would've been on a Friday. Friday before last." Her voice took on a defensive tone. "And I don't call it snooping, the way some folks do." She gave Mildred Ewell a reproachful look. "When I see people walking down the alley, I notice, especially when they're all dressed up. In fact, I think everybody ought to make it their business to pay attention to strangers in our neighborhoods. There's too much crime everywhere, even in Pecan Springs."

"I agree with that," Hazel said sadly. "Mrs. Howard's mother's watch was stolen at the nursing home. And the police didn't do a blessed thing about it."

"What did she look like?" I asked.

"Mrs. Howard's mother didn't get a look at her," Hazel replied. "She was taking a nap when it happened."

I sighed. "No. The woman in the alley. What did she look like, Mrs. Wauer? Can you describe her?"

"Black hair," Mrs. Wauer said. "Straight, with bangs. Once, she was wearing a red suit, skirt above her knees." She clucked her tongue. "Other time, it was blue. Don't know how women can walk in those short skirts and high heels. Ridiculous."

"Stylish," Jane said, "but too much makeup, in my opinion." She smiled at Ruby. "Although we love *your* makeup, dear, because you're our friend." She turned to me. "I saw her myself, China. Once. But not in the alley. She was getting into a car, out in front of the McNallys'. Fortysomething, trying to look younger. But the red lipstick didn't help, if you ask me."

"Mrs. McNally's daughter Polly knows her name," Mildred Ewell offered. "Polly was there when she parked her car out front. She recognized her."

"Hyundai," Hazel said.

"Her name is Hyundai?" I asked, surprised.

"No, that's her car," Hazel said. "Or something like that. One of those cute little foreign things. That's what Mrs. McNally said."

"Bright red," Jane said disapprovingly. "Like blood."

"The car?" I asked. "Or her suit?"

"Her lipstick," Jane said. She gave me a withering look, as if I hadn't been paying the right kind of attention. "Her suit was blue. Her car was sort of silver colored. I don't know whether it was a Hyundai. It might have been something else."

"A Corvette?" I asked sharply, thinking of Timms' car.

"No, no. Nothing like that." She waved her hand. "If it had been a motorcycle, I could probably tell you what make. My nearest and dearest used to ride Harleys, when he was alive."

"She was just sitting there, according to Mrs. McNally," Hazel said. "Just sitting in her car, like she was waiting." She gave me a meaningful look. "Maybe waiting for him to come home. Mr. Kirk, I mean. So she could kill him."

"Or sleep with him," Mrs. Wauer said tartly. At her friends' frowns, she said, "I have always been one to call a spade a spade."

I took a comforting drink of my tea. "Let me see if I've got this straight," I said. "You're telling me that you have seen a stylishly dressed woman in her forties, with long black hair, straight, with bangs, who drives a silver-colored car that might be a Hyundai. She's been observed in the vicinity of the Kirks' house several times, in the alley and out on the street. And Mrs. McNally's daughter Polly knows her name. Correct?"

The ladies burst into a spontaneous round of applause. "Bravo!" cried Hazel Schulz.

"Didn't I tell you that China is smart?" Ruby asked, beaming at me proudly.

"Sharp as a tack," Mrs. Wauer agreed. "A regular Agatha Marple."

Mildred Ewell leaned over and patted the older lady's hand. "That's Agatha Christie, dear. Or Jane Marple."

"That's what I said," Mrs. Wauer retorted. "Agatha Marple. She lives in England, although I think she must be dead by now. She's been solving mysteries ever since I was a girl."

"If Mrs. McNally's daughter Polly knows this mystery woman's name," I said, "what is it?"

The ladies looked at one another. Finally, Jane said, "We don't know. Mrs. McNally didn't tell us."

"Mrs. McNally herself doesn't know," Hazel put in. "Polly was about to tell her who she was, but the phone rang at that moment and Polly had to go pick up her daughter at school because the girl had a terrible earache, and the conversation never got back to her name."

"Polly's had so much trouble with that girl's ears," Mildred said. "I told her she should take her to a specialist. But Mrs. McNally says that Polly says she'll grow out of it."

"I agree," Mildred said. "People spend too much money on doctors. My grandmother used to put warm olive oil in my ears, with mullein and garlic. Felt real good." She smiled reminiscently. "And then she'd kiss my ears, and that would make it even better."

"St. John's wort, too," Jane put in wisely. "That's the very best herb for ear problems."

"And calendula," Mrs. Wauer added. "My mother swore by calendula oil for ears. She also used it for cradle cap and diaper rash. She said it was good for both ends." The ladies chuckled.

I rapped the table with my knuckles. The ladies stopped chuckling and looked at me.

"Excuse me," I said. "But did any of you see this person yesterday? Around the time that Larry Kirk was killed?"

The ladies interrogated one another with their eyebrows, one after another shaking her head. Mrs. Wauer turned to me. "No," she replied regretfully. "We didn't."

"Well, then," I said, "does anybody happen to have Mrs. McNally's phone number? Would somebody be willing to phone her and get Polly's phone number, then phone Polly and ask for this person's name?"

Hazel raised her hand like a little girl in class. "I can do that."

"Good," I said. "And would you be willing to telephone me with whatever information you can get?"

"Of course," Hazel said. "I'll call you right away."

"Good," I said, and gave her my cell phone number. "If you'll do that, I'll pass the information along to the police and they can add it to their list of things they need to investigate." It was possible that the Little Old Ladies League, as I was beginning to think of them, had just identified the stalker that Larry had emailed me about. I had no way of knowing whether this woman was his killer, of course. But identifying the stalker would be a very good thing.

I finished my tea and looked around the table. "Well, ladies, is that it?"

The ladies traded glances, then all four of them nodded. "That's it," Mrs. Wauer said, with great satisfaction. "I think we can go home now, girls. China can take it from here."

Jane was leaning forward, looking intently at Ruby. "Forgive me, dear. I could be wrong, 'cause I've left my glasses at home. But it looks like something is crawling up your neck."

"It's a devil's claw," Ruby said, leaning forward to give Jane a better look at her necklace. "It's made of the dried seedpods of a Southwestern desert plant. It's for protection against evil. When you're wearing this, nothing bad can touch you."

Mrs. Wauer gave a gusty sigh. "Well, all I can say is, it's a pity that poor Mr. Kirk didn't have some devil's claws. He might have been able to escape from the clutches of that woman."

The ladies nodded soberly as they picked up their handbags and trooped out.

Chapter Fifteen

Sheila was a systematic thinker who habitually made mental lists, constantly fact-checked against her assumptions, and tried to anticipate, rationally, what was likely to come next, since unexpected events could be (and often were) life-threatening. These were habits that she shared with Blackie, a methodical man who thought pretty much the same way. She had often reflected that she would never be able to live with somebody who didn't operate the way she did. A disorganized and impulsive partner would drive her crazy.

She had plenty to think about as she drove back to Pecan Springs, moving fast but without lights and siren. But before she let herself think about any of the casework, she picked up her cell phone and speed-dialed Blackie's number. It rang four times, then went to voice mail. She left a quick "Hope everything's okay. Call when you can" and turned the phone off. Wherever he was, whatever he was doing, she could only trust that Blackie was okay. His image came up in her mind—strong, competent, always careful—and she took a deep breath. He'd be fine. He was on the move, or out of cell phone range, or so focused on what he was doing that he wasn't thinking of anything else. He was fine. Of course he was fine.

She boxed up that thought and put it on the back shelf of her mind, turning to the things that needed immediate attention. Now that Timms was no longer a suspect in the Kirk homicide, she needed to follow up on a couple of things she had found earlier that morning, before she was interrupted with the news of Timms' death. Top of the list: an interview with Tina Simpson, either at home or at work.

It was the business about the insurance policies that puzzled her. She could understand the quarter-million-dollar policy that Dana Kirk had mentioned in her interview. It was prudent to insure a family wage-earner, and a high-value life insurance policy on a young man wasn't very expensive. But who owned the larger policy? It looked as if the premiums were being paid by Harmon Insurance, where Kirk had once worked, which seemed odd. And the total amount of the insurance—a million dollars—was impressive. As Bartlett said, a pretty fair motive. Tina Simpson, who worked at Harmon, had sent the copies of the premium notices to Kirk and seemed to know something about the situation, at least enough to recognize it as an unusual transaction.

Sheila flipped through her notebook and found the home address she had jotted down for Simpson, on the south side of Pecan Springs, in a quiet neighborhood not far from the high school. The small, ranch-style houses dated from the sixties, and the yards, haphazardly landscaped, were cluttered with soccer balls, bikes, and skateboards. By now, it was midmorning, and Sheila thought Simpson might have already gone to work. But when she pulled up in front of the house, she saw an older model red Volkswagen in the driveway. The front door stood half-open behind the screen, and a sleek black cat was sunning itself on the front steps.

Carrying her briefcase, Sheila went to the door and knocked on the screen. Inside, a door slammed and from another room, a woman's hoarse voice called, "Janine, is that you? Come on in. I don't think I'm contagious."

"Police," Sheila replied loudly, through the screen. "I'm looking for Tina Simpson."

There was a silence. Then, "What do you want?" The voice was startled.

"I'd like to talk to you about Lawrence Kirk," Sheila said. She heard the sound of flip-flops, and someone pushed the front door nearly shut.

The woman spoke cautiously, through the opening. "Do you have identification?"

Sheila held up her open badge wallet. "Sheila Dawson."

The woman who opened the door was in her early thirties, a head shorter than Sheila. She wore a flower-print quilted housecoat that zipped up the front and flip-flops. Under other circumstances, she might have been pretty, but her brown hair was uncombed and disheveled, her nose was red, her face splotchy. She pressed the back of her hand to her mouth. "What about . . . about Larry?"

"I'm sorry to be the bearer of bad news," Sheila said sympathetically. "But I'm afraid that Mr. Kirk is—"

"I know," Tina Simpson said miserably. "I know he's dead. I heard it on the radio this morning." She pulled a used tissue out of a pocket and blew her nose. "Excuse me. I've had a very bad cold. Couldn't go to work yesterday. And now this. Larry, I mean. It's a shock. I just don't understand—" She paused and tried again. "The radio said something about a gunshot wound, apparently self-inflicted. Is that true?"

Sheila nodded. "May I come in? I'm hoping you can clear up a few things for me."

The woman looked uncertain and wary. "I don't . . . I really don't think I can—"

"I think you can," Sheila said firmly. "May I come in?"

She stepped back. "Well, I suppose," she said in a grudging tone. She looked past Sheila at the cat. "No, not you, Blackjack." To Sheila, she added, "If I don't make him stay on the porch, he'll be in your lap the minute you sit down."

The door opened directly onto the living room. It was comfortable and homey, with white-painted bookshelves along a wall under a flower-filled window. The furniture—an upholstered love seat, a couple of plump chairs covered with crocheted granny afghans, and a coffee table made from a wooden crate with books stacked underneath—filled the small room.

"Have a seat," Tina said. "I can at least comb my hair."

Sheila took one of the chairs, putting her briefcase on the floor. After a few moments, Tina returned, her brown hair combed back and secured by a stretchy headband, and sat down on the love seat.

"Are you going to tell me how it happened?" she asked.

Sheila took out her notebook and pen. "You and Mr. Kirk were friends?"

Tina crossed her arms and hugged herself. "Well, sort of. I thought he was a very nice guy who got a very raw deal from his sweet little wifey, who had fallen for some sleazy jerk she works with at the library. I felt I could maybe help him get over it. You know, mend that broken heart. But he . . ." She shrugged and tried for a smile. It didn't work. "Once bitten, twice shy, he said. Or maybe it was just me."

Sheila didn't answer. She waited, letting the silence build. After a moment, Tina sighed.

"So no, we weren't friends, if by that you mean that we went out together and had a good time. For a while, I thought he was still hung up on Dana. But then I found out that he and Jackie were—" She looked at Sheila, her eyes defiant. "We weren't close. But I knew him well enough to know that he didn't shoot himself, the way the radio said. That guy *hated* guns. I mean, with a passion."

"We don't have a definitive ruling on the cause of death," Sheila said quietly. She met the other woman's eyes. "But personally, I agree with you."

"You mean, you . . . you think Larry was *murdered*?" Tina took a deep breath and let it out, raggedly. "Well, I guess if he didn't do it himself, it stands to reason that somebody else did it." She narrowed her eyes. "Who? Do you have any leads?"

"That's where I'm hoping you can help me," Sheila replied. "Not long ago, you sent Larry a note about some premium notices you found in the files at Harmon Insurance."

Tina frowned. "How did you know about that? That's confidential, between me and Larry. What right do you—"

Sheila interrupted. "We're investigating a suspicious death that is likely to be ruled a homicide before the day is over. We're looking into everything that might help us learn what happened and why. I hope you'll cooperate." She gave Tina a moment to digest that, then opened her briefcase and took out the plastic evidence bag that held the note written on lined yellow paper. She put it on the coffee table. "This is the note you wrote?"

Tina glanced at it, swallowed once, and said, "Yes. I thought maybe if I helped him a little bit, he would—" Coloring, she stopped, but Sheila knew what she had been about to say. She had hoped that being helpful to Larry might convince him that she was on his side, that she was his friend. He might be grateful. "Yes," she said, in a lower voice. "Yes, I wrote that."

"And you sent him three photocopies of insurance premium notices, along with the note?"

"Yes." Tina hesitated, biting her lip, as if she was trying to decide how much to tell. Obviously, she was weighing the possibility of losing her job against helping the police.

"I'm sure this is difficult for you," Sheila said. "But the

more I know now, the sooner we'll find out what happened to Larry Kirk."

Tina thought another moment, then came to a decision. "I found the premium notices by accident when I was cleaning up some old files," she said. "When I asked Ms. Harmon where I should file them, she got really red in the face and snatched them away, which made me curious. So I—I looked on her desk until I found them. I copied them."

"Why?" Sheila was making notes.

"Well, the notices had Larry's name on them. And the way she acted, it seemed like they were kind of important. Secret, even. Like this was something I wasn't supposed to know anything about."

Sheila kept writing, and after a minute, filling the silence, Tina went on.

"At the time, I just thought it was a little weird. Ms. Harmon is that way sometimes, sort of like a drama queen, even over little things. But when I told Dorrie about what happened—that's my sister, she's really smart—she said she had just that week read an article that might explain things." She fished for the tissue and blew her nose. "Dorrie tore it out of the magazine and gave it to me. When I first read it, I thought it was kind of funny—what it's called, anyway. 'Dead peasant.' That's when I made the copies and wrote that note to Larry. I just thought he ought to know. After all, it was his life that was worth a million dollars."

"I see," Sheila said, noting the term. *Dead peasant* rang a bell and she remembered something she had heard in a radio news broadcast a few months before. She looked up. "Did you give him the article? Do you know whether he read it?"

"Yeah. He called me up as soon as he got my note and said he'd like to have a copy. So we met for coffee at the diner over on Nueces, and I gave it to him. But I ran into him a week or so later, at Wong's, where he sometimes gets takeout." She looked away, half-guiltily, and Sheila wondered if she had gone there, hoping to see him. "When I asked him about it, he said he couldn't do anything. It was water under the bridge. He didn't want to talk about it."

Sheila made another note. "Water under the bridge? What do you think he meant?"

Tina shifted uncomfortably. "He said he asked her about it and she wouldn't let him off the hook. Those are his exact words. 'She won't let me off the hook.'"

Sheila stopped writing. "Who? Who is 'she'? What hook?"

"Jackie Harmon." Tina twisted her hands together in her lap. "She's the one who owns the company I work for. My boss." She laughed mirthlessly. "Dead peasant. Real cute, huh? Well, at least she doesn't have one of those policies on me."

Jackie Harmon. Sheila thought of the email on Kirk's computer, the one she had printed out. *Yes, you did sign the consent form at the same time we set up the health insurance package. It sounds like the matter has slipped your mind. Sorry for any misunderstanding, but I'm afraid it's water under the bridge now.* It had been signed *Jackie.*

"Do you have a copy of that article? The one you gave Larry?"

Tina nodded. "Actually, I've got the original. Want it?"

"Yes, please."

Tina got up and left the room. In a moment, she was back with a piece of paper in her hand. "If you'd like some coffee," she said, "I can make it while you're reading."

"Coffee would be great," Sheila said.

"Black?"

"Perfect," Sheila replied, and settled back in the chair to read.

HOW MUCH ARE YOU WORTH?

by Michael Bailey

Most of us know how much we're worth, on paper, at least. But some of us might be surprised to learn that we are worth more dead than alive—to our employers, that is.

Say, for instance, that you work for one of the big banks—Bank of America, for instance, or Wells Fargo—or a large corporation, like Walmart or Walgreens. You may be insured by your company under a policy known as a COLI policy: corporate-owned life insurance. In traditional life insurance, the insured owns the policy, pays the premiums, and names the beneficiaries. In a COLI policy, the corporation insures your life, pays the premium, and names itself as the sole beneficiary. When you die, your employer pockets the money. Your family doesn't get a nickel.

According to Professor Samuel W. Blake, who teaches at the University of Texas at Austin, corporate-owned life insurance began with companies insuring the lives of their most valuable executives, or "key men." As time went on, Dr. Blake says, the "key man" practice was extended to lower-level employees, many of whom have no idea that they are covered by what has come to be called a "dead peasant" policy. The term "dead peasant" first appeared in a memo written by an insurance brokerage firm to describe the policies on janitors, cashiers, and other rank-and-file employees purchased by the grocery store chain Winn-Dixie. The term caught on when it was popularized by reporters for the *Wall Street Journal* and the Houston *Chronicle*. It also appeared in a documentary by film-maker Michael Moore.

In Texas, such policies were illegal until 1999, when the legislature approved COLIs, with the stipulation that the employee had to consent to the coverage. Dr. Blake points out, however, that employees might be coerced into consent. "If they don't sign off on the life insurance, they don't get the health package either," he says. "Just because somebody signs, it doesn't mean that the person freely consented."

Nationally, it is estimated that between five and six million Americans are covered by COLI policies. What's more, as long as the company continues to pay the policy premiums, these policies remain in force, even after the insured person quits or is fired. The premiums are deducted as business expenses, but the company pays no tax on the death benefits, which can be substantial.

But there's a new twist to this story. Several corporations are being sued by the families of dead employees, who are enraged to learn that a rich corporation has profited from their loved one's death. "Life insurance has traditionally been used to protect the family against the loss of its breadwinner," says the attorney for one of the plaintiffs. "This is an investment scheme, pure and simple. The company is in it for the tax benefits. It's immoral."

To complicate the situation further, some corporations are suing their life insurance companies, claiming that they were not warned of the inherent legal dangers in COLI policies. Walmart, for instance, has filed suit against AIG and Hartford, claiming losses of more than $150 million.

Tina came back in the room, carrying a mug in each hand. "Here you go," she said, and put a mug on the table beside Sheila. She sat down and nodded at the article, which Sheila had laid on the coffee table.

"Guess that tells the whole story, huh? Larry didn't even remember signing the consent form. He said he remembered signing a bunch of papers when Ms. Harmon enrolled him in the company health plan, but he had no idea what they were. I think that must happen a lot. Every

personnel office has a gazillion forms for employees to fill
out. People don't look at them."

Sheila frowned down at the article. "But what did the
company—Harmon Insurance—get out of it? Just the
write-off? That doesn't sound like much." On the other
hand, the million-dollar death benefit sounded like plenty.

"I wondered about that, too." Tina kicked off her flip-
flops and pulled her bare feet up under her. "I looked into it
and found out that it's usually only the bigger companies
that do this. The ones with lots of employees, that is, where
the write-off is big enough to make a difference. And then,
of course, there are the death benefits."

Sheila picked up her coffee mug and sipped. "Harmon
Insurance—isn't it local? It's a small company, right?"

Tina nodded. "Small, yes. There are just five of us in the
office right now, Ms. Harmon, three agents, and me. I'm an
administrative assistant, glorified secretary, really. But
local, no. Actually, we're affiliated with a larger company,
which has its headquarters up in Dallas. I did some digging
and found out that, at the time Larry's policy was written,
the company was putting pressure on all its affiliates to
insure their employees. It was part of some deal they
made with one of the large insurers. The more policies they
wrote, the bigger the commissions." Her mouth twisted.
"I'm willing to bet that somebody got a huge kickback. The
company executives, probably."

Sheila shook her head. Companies betting on their employees' lives, using their premiums to leverage a hefty tax
break in the meantime, then reaping the death benefit. It
was incredibly sordid and sleazy.

Tina was watching her over the rim of her coffee mug,
her eyes narrowed. When she spoke, her voice was taut.
"You're asking these questions because you think Jackie
Harmon might have killed him, aren't you?"

Sheila hadn't walked into the room with that in mind,
but it now seemed to her like a definite possibility. "We're

keeping all options in mind," she said, and paused strategically. "What do you think? Could Ms. Harmon have done it?"

The silence stretched out like a rubber band. "Well, I know she was seeing him," Tina said finally.

"Seeing him?" *Saw JH.* The five yellow sticky notes on the calendar in Larry Kirk's kitchen, the first one dated October 21, the last the day before he died. JH. Jackie Harmon.

"As in sleeping with him." Tina put down her mug so hard that coffee sloshed out. "At least once. Maybe more. But then one day she stormed into the office and said she never wanted to hear his name again. I guess he told her to go fly a kite."

"When was that?"

Tina thought. "A couple of weeks ago. I can't give you the date just off the top of my head, but I might could do it if I looked at my desk calendar." She leaned forward, more intent. "Jackie had a thing for him, you know. From what Dana told me, Jackie and Larry had a relationship going before he and Dana got married. In fact, Dana said that, at one point, Jackie threatened her."

"Threatened her?"

Tina smiled a tight little smile. "Said she'd claw her eyes out, something silly like that. But that's Jackie. She's a manipulator. She's possessive and controlling. Once she gets her hooks into somebody, she just won't let go. I've seen her act like that with other guys." Her face darkened. "Please don't think I'm saying this because I'm . . . well, jealous or anything. I'm not. But yes, I guess she could have done it."

Sheila thought of the email Harmon had written to Larry, the email she'd printed out and had in her briefcase. *Still friends, I hope. I was sorry to hear about Dana (rocks in her head, if you ask me). I'd really* love *to get together, for old times' sake. Could we?*

She thought quickly back through the chronology of

events, as she understood them. Tina's "dead peasant" note
to Larry, with the attached premium notices, was dated
October 15. He could have read the note and the notices,
and then the article, and then—perhaps on October 16 or
17—contacted Jackie Harmon asking for information about
the policy. Harmon had emailed him back on October 17,
inviting him to "get together, for old times' sake." The first
sticky note—*Saw JH*—was dated October 21. There were
four other *JH* notes, the last one dated the day before he
died.

And there was the "stalker" Kirk had mentioned to
China. Had he seen Harmon a couple of times by mutual
consent, then broke off their relationship, only to discover
that she was following him or hanging around his house?

She thought of something else. "I wonder whether you
would recognize this." She reached into her briefcase and
took out the lipstick, in its labeled evidence bag. She put it
on the table.

Tina leaned over it, moving the tube with her finger until
she could read the label on the bottom. "'Firehouse Red,'"
she said. "Yves St. Laurent. That's Jackie's color. It's her
trademark. She wears it with everything—too much of it,
in my opinion. It makes her look hard. Where'd you get it?"
She looked up, eyes widening, comprehension dawning.
"You found this at Larry's house?"

Sheila didn't answer. She returned the evidence bags to
her briefcase and flipped through her notebook again. "I
think that's all for now," she said. "You've already been
very helpful and I very much appreciate it. But I must cau-
tion you against sharing any of this with Ms. Harmon."

Tina gave a bitter chuckle. "That's not going to happen.
I guess you can tell that there's no love lost between the two
of us. In fact, I've already started looking for another job."

Sheila nodded. "And if you can pin down the date that
Ms. Harmon told you she didn't want to hear Mr. Kirk's
name again, please call me." She pulled a card out of her

jacket pocket and put it on the table, on top of a stack of books. Romances, she saw.

Tina glanced down at the card, then up again, quickly, eyes widening. "You're the *chief*," she said. "Wow. This must be a really important case."

Sheila got to her feet. "They're all important," she said, and meant it.

Chapter Sixteen

Sheila was getting into her Impala when her cell phone chirped. It was Bartlett, calling from his desk at the station.

"We've caught a break," he said curtly. "The information is just coming in now. About a half hour ago, there was a traffic incident on Blanco, three blocks from Kirk's computer shop. Henry Palmer was riding his bike in the bicycle lane, on his way to work, I guess. He was sideswiped by Gino's Pizza delivery van. As it happened, Jerry Clarke and her partner—that new officer, Rita Kidder—were in their patrol car, almost on top of the hit. Clarke saw the whole thing. When she called in the report, she said it looked deliberate, like the van swerved into the bike lane. No sign of braking, and the driver didn't stop. Squealed the tires, drove off like a bat out of hell."

"Palmer." Sheila pulled in her breath. "How's Palmer, Jack?"

"On his way to the ER. No word on his condition, although Kidder reports that it looks bad. Touch-and-go is what she said. Broken bones, concussion, internal bleeding." Bartlett paused, said something to someone else on the other end of the line, then came back.

"But here's the kicker, Sheila. When Clarke saw the hit, she dropped Kidder off to deal with the victim and get EMS on the scene. She called in backup, put on her siren and lights, and took out after the pizza delivery van, which was heading east on Blanco. Spahn and Botts happened to be a couple of blocks away. They blocked the intersection of Blanco and Laramie, in front of the Roundup Restaurant. The driver of the pizza van saw the roadblock, veered to avoid it, and smashed into that big brown-painted steer that sits out in front of the restaurant. Wiped out the steer, then ran head-on into a utility pole. He was dead at the scene."

Sheila felt her heart jump, then settle. "Damn," she muttered. She felt sorry for Palmer, who seemed like a nice guy. And sorry, too, for Betty and Steve Baker, who'd bought Gino's Italian Pizza Kitchen a couple of years before. They were good kids, doing their best to compete with national franchises in the local market. To cut costs, Steve often handled the deliveries himself. She hoped he hadn't been driving the van this morning.

She took a breath. "Any idea yet who—"

"Yeah. We got a positive ID—and that's our break." To somebody else, he said, "Hey, cancel that APB. And start drawing up the search warrant for the Pecos Street address." To Sheila, he said, "The driver was Jason Hatch."

"Hatch!" Sheila exclaimed.

"Right. He was wearing a ski mask and gloves. The van was stolen from Gino's parking lot—Steve Baker reported the theft about the time the hit-and-run happened." He chuckled dryly. "Hatch probably didn't want to run the risk of leaving traceable evidence at the scene. Looks like he knew the route that Palmer usually took to work, and maybe even knew what time he'd be riding this morning. So he planned to steal the van, wipe Palmer out, ditch the vehicle, then run for it. And he wasn't going to leave any prints behind."

"Ah," Sheila said. "Sounds to me like a falling-out of thieves."

"That's what I'm thinking, too," Bartlett said slowly. "Like, maybe Palmer knew that Hatch was blackmailing customers and decided to blow the whistle. Hatch found out, and tried to off Palmer."

"More likely, they were in it together," Sheila replied. "It would have been tough for Hatch to have access to the computers without Palmer tipping him off. And Hatch wasn't supposed to be in the shop, so he was probably taking the machines off-site. Or maybe Palmer was taking them to him. However the operation worked, Palmer had to be in on it."

She sat back in the seat, seeing the pieces of this thing suddenly snap together as if they were magnetized. Hatch and Palmer. Palmer and Hatch. Partners in a blackmail scheme. Not big blackmail, probably, just two-bit jobs, a couple of thousand here, another thousand there, enough to buy Hatch a truck and Palmer a Madone bicycle. Back last summer, Kirk had uncovered Hatch's role in the game and given orders that he wasn't to work any more jobs out of the shop. But he hadn't suspected Palmer, who was his cousin, so Palmer and Hatch had slightly shifted their modus operandi and kept their game going. It had been a tidy little low-risk racket—until Timms had come along and refused to pay up. Maybe he didn't trust them to keep the lid on his explosive secret. Or maybe he feared that once he gave in, their demands would escalate and he'd be paying through the nose for the rest of his life. So he had burgled the shop in an attempt to get his machine back, and the break-in had brought the police.

Then what? Had Palmer called Hatch when he went home the previous night, and told him that Kirk was dead and the cops had a search warrant for the shop and were asking more questions about Timms' machine? That they were printing everyone who worked at the shop, that they had his name, that they'd be looking for him?

Or maybe it had gone another way, Sheila thought. Maybe Palmer suspected that Hatch might have killed Kirk. It was a logical assumption, after all—one that she and Bartlett had considered. Maybe he had even accused Hatch of the murder, and threatened to come clean to the cops about their little blackmail racket. At that point, Hatch might have decided that his partner couldn't be trusted to keep his mouth shut. Palmer had to be taken out, and the safest way to do it was to arrange a bicycle accident.

"Prints," Sheila said. "We need to make sure that Clarke gets a set before Hatch's body leaves the scene. Butch may be able to match them up with whatever he finds on Timms' computer. That will tie it up for us—until Palmer can tell us what really happened between him and Hatch." *If* Palmer could tell them, she thought. An important *if.* They needed Palmer. If he didn't make it, there'd be nowhere to go with this.

"Clarke took care of the prints already," Bartlett said with an evident satisfaction. "The cards are on their way to the station now." His voice darkened. "Whether we can tie Hatch to Kirk's murder is a different question, though. Unless we turn up something when we search his Pecos Street address, I don't see that we've got enough to make a case."

"Hatch didn't kill Kirk."

"Hatch didn't—?" He stopped, sounding incredulous. "Hey, you know that for sure?"

"I know that for sure," Sheila said. "Listen."

When she had finished telling what she had learned from her stop at Kirk's house that morning and her just-finished talk with Tina Simpson, there was a long silence. Finally, Bartlett let out his breath with a swoosh.

"Holy cow," he said.

Sheila chuckled. "No kidding. But what we have is

entirely circumstantial. There's motive, yes. We can trace the email she wrote to Kirk back to her machine, but we can't prove that she herself sent it. And while the lipstick seems to put her in Kirk's house—especially if her prints are on it—some smart defense attorney will argue that Kirk was carrying it around in his pocket, and that she was never within a mile of the place." She frowned. "What we need is somebody who actually saw her there around the time of the murder. Did Matheson have any luck with those garbage guys?"

"Dunno," Bartlett replied. "He hasn't reported back in. I'll connect with him—see what he's found. What's your next move?"

"*Our* next move," Sheila said. "I need to talk to Harmon. And I don't want to do it solo." She gave him the address she had jotted in her notebook.

"Got it," he said, then, "Hold on a minute." A moment later, he was back. "Somebody just handed me a message that was called in to the duty desk. Yesterday, you mentioned China Bayles—the woman Kirk emailed about the stalker. B-a-y-l-e-s. That the one? Your friend?"

"Right. What about her?"

"Well, she telephoned the station a couple of minutes ago. Seems that a bunch of the little old ladies who live around Kirk's place have created a neighborhood watch, and they got together and compared notes. They told Bayles that they've been seeing some hotsy hanging around Kirk's place, and they're convinced that she's the killer. Bayles doesn't have a name for the woman yet. Says she's working on it. So far, the description is . . ." He paused. "Not sure I'm reading this right, but here's what it says. 'Tight red/blue suit, high heels, too much red lipstick, black hair, silver foreign car, maybe Hyundai.' Tell you anything?"

Too much red lipstick. "It sure does," Sheila said.

* * *

TEN minutes later, Sheila and Bartlett were standing in a brick-paved parking lot, adjacent to a two-story frame building, painted a classy gray, with blue shutters. The building, which had once been a house, was located just a block off Pecan Springs' business section. The parking lot was empty except for a late-model silvery Hyundai. Bartlett phoned for a make on the car. It was registered to Jacqueline Harmon. No outstanding warrants, no priors. Home address same as the business. She must live upstairs, Sheila thought. And she was here, which was a good thing. Maybe they could get this business wrapped up quickly.

The porch was decorated with Victorian gingerbread, and the small square of front yard was carpeted with green ivy. In the middle of the ivy, a decorative wooden sign was planted. HARMON INSURANCE, it said, in an antique script. *Create a little harmon-y in your life.*

Bartlett regarded the sign quizzically. "You know this part of the story a helluva lot better than I do," he said. "Why don't you take the lead?"

"Works for me," Sheila replied.

The two of them went up the neatly painted stairs to the front door, its oval glass pane a stylish addition to the building's Victorian look. Beside the door, a green Boston fern grew on a white wicker plant stand. COME IN, PLEASE, a small sign invited, with discreet hospitality.

A bell tinkled as Sheila opened the door onto a wood-floored hallway, spread with Oriental-style rugs. The gold-lettered sign near the telephone on the reception desk said that this was Tina Simpson's desk, but the chair was vacant. The walls, painted a silvery gray, were hung with gilt-framed paintings of fields of spring bluebonnets, Hill Country vistas, and nostalgic scenes of abandoned barns surrounded by yellow flowers. On the left, a cordoned-off stairway led up to a second floor. An open door to the right gave a view of what had once been a living room or parlor, now furnished as a small but elegant conference room, also carpeted with an Oriental rug. An open doorway at the end of the hall led to a room with a visible bank of filing cabinets—the files where Tina found the premium notices on Kirk's COLI policy, Sheila thought. Another door appeared to lead to the backyard.

"I'll be with you folks in a minute," a woman called cheerfully from another room on the right. "I'm just finishing something up."

"No hurry," Sheila replied pleasantly. "We'll wait."

A few moments later, the woman came down the hall toward them, striding confidently on three-inch red suede heels. Early forties, Sheila judged, perhaps a little older. She had a competent, in-charge look and wasn't unattractive. But her firmly angled jaw and peaked dark brows gave her a calculating look that was emphasized by jet-black hair, worn straight, with bangs, and blunt-cut just above her shoulders. Her dark eyes and mouth were dramatically made up. She was wearing a bright red suit with a short red skirt so tight that it looked as if it could be sprayed on. The color exactly matched her bright red lipstick.

"Hello," she said, extending a manicured hand, first to Sheila, then to Bartlett. Her long, pointed nails matched her lipstick. "My secretary is out sick today, and my agents are attending a training session in Austin. I'm here all by my lonesome, and the phones just keep ringing." Her self-deprecating smile revealed teeth so dazzlingly white and improbably even that they might have been made of porcelain. "Now then. I'm Jackie Harmon. We offer a full range of insurance services—life, health, casualty, and property—and as I'm sure you know, our uncertain times call for insurance. How may I help you?"

"Police," Sheila said, and held up her badge wallet. "Chief Sheila Dawson, Detective Jack Bartlett. We're investigating the murder of Lawrence Kirk. We'd like to talk to you about it."

Under her pancake makeup, Jackie Harmon's face went

white. "Murder of—" She swallowed, then made a visible effort to pull herself together and tough it out. "Lawrence Kirk," she murmured, frowning. She tapped a red-painted nail against red lips, as if she were trying to think. "I'm so sorry. I'm afraid I can't help you. I don't know anyone by that name."

Standing a few steps behind Sheila, Bartlett took out his notebook and began to write, not making any effort to conceal what he was doing. Harmon's eyes went to him, then back to Sheila.

"Please don't pay any attention to Detective Bartlett," Sheila said smoothly. "We're just trying to pin down a few facts. The Lawrence Kirk we're asking about was employed here several years ago. I understand that you're the owner of an insurance policy on his life."

"Oh, you mean *Larry* Kirk." Harmon tried to smile. "Yes, of course. How silly of me. Yes, Mr. Kirk was employed here, but it was quite some time ago. I haven't seen him for years—since he married, I believe." She pulled her dark brows together. "You're saying that he was . . . murdered?"

"Yes," Sheila said, and offered no details.

Harmon studied her as if she were measuring an adversary. She opted to become dismissive. "I don't think I can help you. Our employee insurance package is a personnel matter. I'm not at liberty to discuss it." She glanced at her watch. "I'm afraid this isn't a convenient time for this discussion. I'm expecting a client at any—"

"I don't think you understand, Ms. Harmon," Sheila interrupted firmly. "We're investigating a homicide, and you are a person of interest. We hope you'll agree to cooperate, so we can get this wrapped up quickly."

Harmon's dismissive facade cracked slightly. "A . . . person of interest?" she faltered.

The term, of course, had no legal meaning, but used wisely, it sometimes encouraged subjects to talk without lawyering up. And suspects who talked were often compelled to lie. Their lies could be used to confront them later, when they were formally detained and questioned. Defense attorneys and civil libertarians might condemn the strategy, but Sheila knew how useful it was.

"That's right," Sheila said conversationally. "We would like you to clarify your relationship to Mr. Kirk and tell us about any recent meetings you've had with him. We can talk here or at the police station, whichever you prefer."

Harmon grasped for control. "But I don't *have* a relationship with him," she replied thinly. She lifted her chin. "I haven't seen Larry—Mr. Kirk—for years."

"I see." Sheila paused, frowning, as if she were slightly puzzled. "Then you haven't corresponded with him, or visited his home?"

Harmon stepped right into the trap. "His home? No, of course not! I haven't written to him, either. So I really can't be of any help to you." She frowned doubtfully. "You said he was *murdered*?"

"Yes," Sheila said. "The killer tried to make it look as if Mr. Kirk had killed himself, but the attempt was unsuccessful."

Harmon was becoming more nervous by the moment. "I still don't understand what you want with *me*. I don't know anything at all about Mr. Kirk." She cleared her throat and looked pointedly at her watch. "As I said, I'm expecting a client any minute now. So if we could—"

"Since that's the case," Sheila interrupted, "it would be better if you came down to the station with us. We'll give you a lift back when we're finished. You can leave a note on the door, postponing your appointment."

"Go down to the station?" Harmon said, barely managing to control the tremor in her voice. She was clearly coming unstrung. "But there's no point. I don't have any information that would—"

"I'm sure we won't take much of your time." Sheila said

reassuringly. "We only want to obtain your fingerprints. Oh, and we'd like you to tell us why we found your lipstick in Mr. Kirk's bathroom."

Harmon's eyes widened. "My . . . lipstick?" she choked.

"Yes. Yves St. Laurent. Firehouse Red." Sheila smiled. "If I'm not mistaken, it's the same lipstick you're wearing now."

Harmon's hand, shaking, went to her mouth. She stood there for a moment, obviously trying to decide what to do. Then blind panic set in and she made a very stupid mistake.

"I'm not going to jail!" she cried, and whirled and darted for the file room.

Harmon was quick. But Bartlett was even quicker, and her tight red skirt and three-inch heels slowed her up. He caught up with her before she managed to escape through the door into the backyard.

Chapter Seventeen

By the time they got to the station, Harmon had gathered her wits, composed herself, and asked to call her lawyer, whose office was in San Antonio. He would get there as soon as he could, but he had a couple of clients and wasn't sure how long that would be. After she was fingerprinted, Sheila escorted her to one of the department's two interrogation rooms, a narrow, windowless space with only a table, several chairs, and a one-way window. The duty officer turned on the tape-recording equipment, read her the Miranda warning, and asked if she wanted a cup of coffee.

"I'm waiting for my attorney," she said, and sat, arms folded, sullenly staring at the wall.

While Bartlett was out with Sheila, Dr. Morse had called to say that she had moved up the time of the autopsy and was ready to begin. When they got back to the station, Bartlett left immediately for the Adams County hospital. Sheila went toward her office. Connie's desk was in the small anteroom, and she stopped there.

"Been wondering where you were," Connie said, reaching for a stack of pink phone messages. "Busy morning, huh?"

Connie Page had been Sheila's assistant for the past

couple of years. A competent, alert woman, not quite middle-aged, she was perfectly capable of handling a lot of the paperwork herself—and she did, with Sheila's signature stamp. She had a good eye for what the boss needed to see and what she didn't, and Sheila was grateful.

"Busy doesn't begin to describe it." Sheila took the sheaf of messages and glanced up at the clock, startled to see that it was just twelve thirty. It felt as if she'd been out of the office for a week.

"We need to get some food down you," Connie said, reaching for a sweater. "How about if I run over to the diner and get a hamburger to go?"

"That would be terrific," Sheila said, suddenly aware of how hungry she was. Breakfast seemed like a century ago. "Fries, too." The diner's fries were crisp and delicious. "Double up on the catsup. Okay?"

She went into her office, sat down at her desk, and reached for the phone. By the time Connie got back with the food, she had finished returning the most crucial calls and had begun to attack the stack of paperwork. She'd been working for a half hour, reading and signing documents while she devoured her hamburger and fries, when Detective Matheson called. Since Bartlett was still at the hospital, Sheila took it.

"Hey, Chief, we got something good from one of those garbage guys," Matheson said enthusiastically. He was a big, burly man with a voice to match, so deep a bass that it rumbled. One of Bubba Harris' team of good old boys, he had been with the department for twenty-some years. "The driver didn't see anything. But the guy who picks up the cans—Carlos Gutierrez—remembers seeing a woman in the neighborhood yesterday, when they were picking up. Some babe in a blue suit, real short skirt." There was a smile in his voice. "Says he whistled at her, but under his breath. Didn't want to get into trouble."

"Description?" Sheila asked, taking notes. "How far

away was she when he saw her? What were the circumstances?"

"She was coming down a driveway between two houses. Gutierrez was at the curb, replacing an empty can. He saw her straight on at about ten, twelve yards, so he got a pretty good look. He said she was plenty startled to see him. Anglo, blue suit, black hair, red lipstick, good legs, nice round little—" Matheson stopped and cleared his throat. "I hear we've got somebody in custody. Want me to bring this guy down for a show-up? Maybe he can give us a positive ID on this chick you're holding."

"We're doing this by the book, Mattie," Sheila said. "Gutierrez could be our case. We don't want to risk tainting his identification."

Driven by too many flawed convictions, the state of Texas was considering legislation to improve police lineups. Too often, the eyewitness was asked to identify the suspect in what was called a "show-up," where the police show a single suspect, often handcuffed or sitting in the back of a police car, to the witness or the victim, and simply ask, "Is this the guy that did it?" Even though the witness might not be sure of the identification, the fact that the cops had the suspect in custody could tip the balance.

The Dallas Police Department hadn't waited for legislation to force a change. They had rewritten their lineup policy a couple of years before, and Sheila had adapted it for PSPD. The new policy put a stop to show-ups altogether. It required eyewitnesses and victims to look at an array of at least six photographs, administered by an officer who had no idea which picture was the suspect's. The lineup procedure was videotaped, so if necessary it could be introduced into evidence when the case went to court.

"No problemo, Chief," Matheson said comfortably, without any indication that he felt he'd been slapped on the wrist. "Let me know when you're ready for Gutierrez, and I'll see that he gets there."

"Good work, Mattie," Sheila said warmly. "We'll need him as quick as we have the autopsy report and a ruling from Judge Porterfield and get some photos set up."

Sheila was putting the phone down when Bartlett returned from the autopsy and came into Sheila's office, grinning broadly and waving a piece of paper.

"Confirmed everything we figured," he said to Sheila. "No powder tattooing around the entrance wound, so the gun was fired from at least two feet, probably or more. Angle of the shot, slightly downward—the killer was standing while Kirk was seated. And no powder residue on Kirk's hands. Morse phoned a preliminary to Judge Porterfield before I left the hospital. The judge just faxed her report to the duty desk. Officially, we've got a homicide."

"Glad that's settled," Sheila said, and added, with a crooked smile, "I'd hate to see it come out the other way."

He nodded. "Oh, and while I was at the hospital, I went upstairs to check on Palmer. He's still out of it, but he's stable. The doc said he'd call us as soon as he can be questioned." He put an evidence envelope on Sheila's desk. It was the bullet, the tip slightly deformed. "And this is the slug Morse took out of Kirk's brain."

Sheila looked down at the spent, misshapen bullet, thinking how small it was, how dangerous, how lethal. She shivered and looked up quickly.

"Things are moving pretty fast, Jack. That was Matheson on the phone. He's got one of the garbage crew, a guy—" She looked down at her notes. "A guy named Carlos Gutierrez. Gutierrez saw a woman in the alley yesterday, when they were picking up on Pecan Street. Sounds like our suspect, down to the good legs. I told Mattie we'd set up a photo lineup here at the station."

Bartlett grinned. "Mattie belongs to the old school. Bet he was rarin' to do a show-up."

Sheila answered his smile. "He's a good man. He'll get the hang of it."

"Yeah. Well, okay." Bartlett sat down in the chair on the other side of the desk. "I'll put Blount on getting some photos together. She can let Mattie know when she's ready, and he can bring Gutierrez in."

"The sooner the better," Sheila said. "Let's try to get the lineup done before that lawyer arrives. Assuming, of course, that Gutierrez can identify her. If he can't . . ." She shook her head. "This thing is too circumstantial. I'd sure like to have a few more pieces. Anything on the gun?"

"Afraid not," Bartlett said regretfully. "There are probably thousands of those old Llamas floating around, with dozens changing hands at every gun show." He was about to say something else when Connie opened the door and came in, a manila envelope in her hand.

"The sheriff's office just sent over these forensic reports on the Kirk case," she said. "I asked the deputy why they just didn't email them." She grinned. "He said their email is down."

Bartlett suppressed a laugh. "High-tech. The county is down more than it's up."

"Could be us," Sheila said, and opened the envelope. She spread the three pages out on the desk and she and Bartlett looked through them.

"Hey!" Bartlett said excitedly, and pushed one of the papers at her. "Look at this, Sheila. It's a partial on that shell casing!"

"No kidding?" Sheila breathed. "Omigod—that's what it is!" She read the text beside the enlarged photograph. It was a print of a right index finger, partial, but very clear. "Let's take this to Butch and see what he can do with it."

Ten minutes later, they were standing beside Butch Bedford, taking turns looking through his microscope at the partial that had been found on the cartridge casing retrieved from Kirk's kitchen. They were comparing the casing print to a print of Jackie Harmon's right index finger.

"Looks like a match to me," Butch said. "If I could put this on a projector, you'd see an island, a bifurcation, and a spur—three pretty strong identification points, especially since this is a partial. Remember, though, it's just a preliminary analysis, on this small microscope, and my confidence level isn't better than about eighty percent. It should go to the county forensic lab, where they've got a comparison microscope. Or Austin, where they've got some pretty sophisticated equipment. Might take a little longer, but—"

"Let's start with the county," Bartlett said. "You've already found three points, they may find a couple more. If the DA wants another lab to look at it, we can send it to Austin." He turned to Sheila. He was grinning broadly, his dark eyes alight. "With everything else we've got, I think we've just about wrapped this one up, Chief."

"Don't get too cocky," Sheila cautioned. But she was grinning, too. "Congratulations, guys." She high-fived him, then Butch.

"Oh, and there's something else, Chief," Butch said. "Before you brought this in, I was about to pick up the phone to tell you that I got a match on that set of prints Clarke brought in earlier this morning. Jason Hatch. The match was left middle finger and right index finger, on the computer belonging to George Timms."

"Hey, Butch, that's great!" Bartlett exclaimed.

"Good work," Sheila said. "What's your confidence level?"

"About ninety percent on that one," Butch said. Sheila smiled at the pride in his voice. He was going to be an asset to the department.

Bartlett's phone gave three digital pings and he flipped it open. "Bartlett," he said shortly, and listened. "Thanks, Doc. Be right there." To Sheila, he said, "Palmer's conscious. He's still in ICU, but the doctor says we can talk to him now. What's more, he's asking to talk to *us*."

"Well, that's a switch," Sheila said. She added, "But before we leave, let's get Annetta to draw up a search warrant for Hatch's house. Specify the computer and other documents. He may have kept records of his victims."

Bartlett was thoughtful. "Yeah. I'll put Matheson on the search with her. No telling where that could go. We might uncover something we don't know about."

THE Adams County Hospital, on the far west side of town, was housed in a two-story red-brick main building, built in the early 1940s and set back from the street on a circle drive lined with large live oaks. Off to the right was the one-story Obermann wing constructed a couple of decades later with a gift from a noted town doctor. To the left was a new two-story wing, which housed the Intensive Care Unit. Today, it was under the careful eye of the charge nurse, Helen Berger, who led them to Palmer's cubicle.

"I know it's important for both of you to talk to him," she said quietly, "but don't stay any longer than ten minutes. And try not to upset him. He's been a little panicky." She frowned a little. "The doctor has told him that he'll recover, but he's convinced that he's going to die. Don't be surprised if he tells you that."

"Thanks," Sheila said, stepping back to let Bartlett go ahead.

Helen smiled. "I don't think I've seen you since you and the sheriff got married, Chief. Just want to say congratulations and best wishes to both of you. You probably don't know this, but I went to high school with Blackie." She blushed. "Actually, I was sweet on him when I was sixteen or so. He's such a great guy."

"He is that," Sheila said, with a little chuckle. She wasn't surprised by what Helen said. She had met other women who, at one time or another, had been sweet on Blackie. He was generally oblivious to the fact, but he had quite a few admirers.

"I was just so sorry when he decided not to run for sheriff again," Helen went on. "Some of the other nurses were saying the same thing. We need guys like him. Not to say that Sheriff Chambers isn't doing a good job," she added hastily. "I'm sure he is—or he will be, once he gets settled. It's just that with Blackie there, well, we all knew things were being done the way they should be. Do you think he'll change his mind and come back?"

Sheila's smile faded. She didn't like to think that people—some people, anyway—felt that Blackie had made a mistake when he left the job, even though she wondered the same thing herself. But that wasn't something she could say to Helen Berger.

"I understand," she said quietly. "But he's doing a different job now—one he wants to do. Today, for instance, he's down in Mexico, trying to locate that little Austin boy who was abducted by his mother."

"Oh, I heard about that child," Helen said. "It's awful. I hope Blackie can find him." She frowned uncertainly. "But—Mexico? That isn't the safest place to be right now, even for somebody who knows what he's doing. I heard on the radio a little while ago that two American guys were shot by drug cartel members just south of Juárez. Right on the main highway, too." Her eyes widened and her hand went to her mouth. "Oh, dear. I suppose I shouldn't have said that. You're probably worried enough already. I'm making it worse."

Two Americans shot? Sheila felt a dark edge of fear slicing through her insides. "Yes," she admitted, suppressing a shiver. "It's true. I am worried. Cross your fingers, Helen." She touched the other woman's arm and turned away. If she stayed an instant longer, Helen would read the fear in her eyes.

Palmer's bed was barricaded with a drip trolley and a monitor panel with assorted dials, displays, and switches. His head was swathed in bandages; his trunk was wrapped in white tape; and his left arm and leg were encased in plaster casts. A clear plastic drip tube was plugged into his right arm. His face bore scratches, almost like claw marks, and one cheek was badly abraded. His eyes were shut.

Before she left the police station, Sheila had picked up her pocket tape recorder. Now, she made herself stop thinking of Blackie—*two Americans shot?*—and took it out and flicked the switch. Then she pulled out her notebook and went to stand near the door, out of the patient's field of vision. Bartlett was leaning over Palmer's still form.

"Hey, Henry," he said easily. "You in there?"

Palmer's eyelids fluttered. "Who—"

"Jack Bartlett, PSPD. Remember? We spoke last night, at the shop. You said you wanted to talk. Still feeling like it?"

"Yeah." Palmer's voice was high-pitched, thin and reedy, with a tremor of hysteria. He didn't open his eyes. "What hit me? Nobody here will tell me."

"Gino's Pizza van," Bartlett said. "Swerved into the bike lane." He paused and glanced at Sheila. She shook her head slightly. It wasn't time to tell Palmer who'd been driving the van. They should save that information. It might be more useful later.

Palmer moaned feebly. "I'm gonna die."

"Naw," Bartlett said, and put his hand on Palmer's shoulder. "The doc says you'll be okay. That van did a number on you, for sure, and you may be laid up for a while. But you'll be back on a bike before long. In the meantime, just concentrate on feeling better."

"No," Palmer whispered. "I'm gonna die, and I know it." He opened his eyes. "That's why I wanted to talk to you. I've got to get something off my chest. It's about Jason Hatch and me and what we . . . we were doing."

"Oh, yeah?" Bartlett asked.

"Yeah. And about Hatch and Larry. Hatch killed Larry. I don't want him to get away with it." His voice became urgent and he tried to raise his hand. "You can't let him get away with it! You've got to see that he pays!"

Bartlett turned toward Sheila. She mouthed the word "Miranda," and he nodded. The courts accepted deathbed confessions without insisting on the need for the Miranda warning. But while Palmer might believe he was on the verge of death, that wasn't the case. What he was about to say might lead to the filing of criminal charges against him or someone else. When that happened, he might argue that his wasn't a deathbed confession because he didn't die. She didn't want his evidence disallowed on that technicality.

"Look, fella," Bartlett said in a sympathetic tone. "I understand why you feel like you're totally wrecked. Been there myself, after a motorcycle accident. But just in case you've got something to say that could incriminate you, I need to give you a Miranda warning. You understand?"

Palmer closed his eyes again. "Yeah. I've seen it on TV. Do it. Do whatever you have to."

Bartlett took a card out of his wallet and read the Miranda warning. Then two questions: "Do you understand these rights as they have been read to you? Having these rights in mind, do you wish to talk to me now?" The second question was required by the state of Texas to comply with the Vienna Convention.

Palmer nodded.

"What did you say?" Bartlett asked, looking over his shoulder to make sure that Sheila was taking notes. "Sorry, Henry. I didn't hear you."

"Yeah," Palmer said. "Yeah, I understand. Yeah, I want to talk. Now. Before I—" He swallowed. "Before I die."

It happened the way they had it figured, although in Palmer's version of the story, he hadn't voluntarily partnered with Hatch. According to Palmer, Hatch had been extorting money from customers for some time, whenever he discovered something he thought the computer owner would feel it necessary to hide. Palmer had found out about his activities by accident and was on the verge of telling Kirk. But Hatch threatened to claim that Palmer had been involved from the beginning, and even though it was a lie, Palmer couldn't defend himself. Then Hatch offered him a cut of the take if he'd keep his mouth shut. All things considered, Palmer said, it seemed like the thing to do. He took the money. And when the next time came along, he took the money again.

"I felt bad as hell about it," he said plaintively. "Believe me, I felt rotten. But I was flat broke. Car needed work. Couldn't pay my rent. I should've told Hatch to go to hell and gone straight to Larry. But about the time I was psyching myself up to do that, Larry found out."

"About Hatch? But not about you?"

"Yeah. He booted Hatch. Gave me orders not to call him for any more jobs, just the way I told you last night." Palmer coughed, then coughed again, with a grimace of pain. Sheila wondered if he had some broken ribs. "I should have drawn the line at that point. I should have told Hatch that it was game over. If I had, Larry would be alive today. It's my fault—" More coughing.

"But instead you and Hatch just reorganized the way you were working," Bartlett said. "It went on the same, only now Hatch was on the outside and you were still on the inside, in the shop. He needed you even more, so you asked him for more money. Right? That's how you got your bike?"

"Yeah." A long sigh. "Listen. What I'm telling you—it's enough to nail Hatch, right? You're going to arrest him?"

"What you're saying implicates Hatch in an ongoing extortion scheme, yes," Bartlett replied soberly.

"Good," Palmer breathed. His face twisted, whether

from pain or penance, Sheila couldn't tell. "But not just for the blackmail—for what he did to Larry. That's the big thing. Larry threatened to tell you guys what Hatch was doing. So Hatch killed him." His voice was shrill. "I hope he gets the death penalty."

For the moment, Bartlett let it slide. "Did you keep a list of the people Hatch extorted?"

"Nuh-uh," Palmer replied. "But Hatch did. He's a nut for that kind of stuff. He's got it all on his computer. Who, when, how much, all that stuff. He said maybe we'd go back for more from somebody, if the need arose. Plus, he was working for at least one other computer shop, in San Antonio. I'm pretty sure he was doing the same thing there, because he always seemed to have more money than we were bringing in. Like, he bought that big Dodge Ram and moved out of that junky trailer. So I figure there was more coming in from somewhere."

"Tell me about Timms' computer," Bartlett prompted.

There was a silence. "Not much to tell," Palmer said. "Timms brought it in to get a virus cleaned off. When he handed it over, he asked me if we messed around with the data files. That's always a dead giveaway that there's something on there that the customer doesn't want looked at. So I told him no, and then I called Hatch and took the machine over to his place."

"That's how you managed it? You'd take the computers to him?"

"After Larry booted him, yeah. Larry was in and out of the shop at all hours, nights, too. So yeah, I took it over there. When Hatch got into it, he found some photos and stuff—kids, he said. That was good, because kid photos are worth more than girlie photos. You know?"

Sheila, listening, felt sick. But she knew that the statement was an accurate one. If Timms had had a thing for women, rather than children, Hatch would probably have asked for less. Child pornography was a different thing altogether.

"Understand," Bartlett said. "How was the extortion demand conveyed? Did Hatch telephone Timms? Did you?"

"Hatch always took care of that end of things." Palmer's lips stretched back in what could have been either a smile or a grimace of pain. "I guess he figured that way, he wouldn't have to tell me how much he asked for. Made it easier for him to cream it off the top."

"I see," Bartlett said. "Did he tell you how much he thought he'd get from Timms?"

"Said he was gonna ask for twenty thousand. It was a lot, but considering who this guy is—his picture's always in the paper, ribbon-cuttings and benefits for the women and kids' shelter, stuff like that—Hatch said we'd get it." He coughed. "I figure he asked for twenty-five, maybe even thirty. I didn't want to know."

"Why not?" Bartlett asked.

Plaintively, Palmer looked up at Bartlett. "Because it was my last job. I was gonna tell Hatch that, and I was gonna tell Larry. I was sick and tired of feeling like something bad was going to happen any minute. But I was scared, because Larry was my cousin and all that. I figured he'd do his best to keep me from being arrested, but I knew he'd tell his mother. And she'd tell my mother. That would be bad, real bad."

Listening, Sheila shook her head. Palmer hadn't been afraid of the police. He was scared of his aunt and his mother.

Bartlett spoke. "So you told Hatch you were quitting?"

"Not then. I didn't get the chance. I put Timms' computer back in the file cabinet and waited. Hatch talked to Timms, who got really hot when he heard how much Hatch was asking. Hatch said he was going to pay, but I guess Timms changed his mind." Palmer coughed, hard, a couple of times. "Anyway, when Larry opened up the next morning, the place was trashed. Didn't take an Einstein to figure out who'd done it."

"When did you tell Hatch you were quitting?"

Palmer closed his eyes, slowly, as if he were very tired. His voice dropped a notch. "Last night. Late. After I talked to you. He came over to my place."

"How did he react?"

"He didn't say much, but his eyes got hard, the way they do when he's really mad. I told him I knew he'd killed Larry."

Eyebrows raised, Bartlett glanced at Sheila. "What did he say to that?"

"He laughed. Like a crazy man. Said he didn't do it, that nobody would believe me."

"Did you have any evidence?"

There was a moment's silence. "No," he said finally. "Not what you'd call evidence. Stuff like fingerprints. But when you told me Larry was dead, I just knew Hatch did it. I figured that Timms went to Larry and told him what was going on, and Larry confronted Hatch about it. That's when Hatch shot him. I know he had a gun. He showed it to me once."

"What kind of gun was it?" Bartlett asked.

"A .357 Magnum. He was really impressed with that gun. Took it out to the range. Said it made him feel like he could handle anything." His voice became bitter. "Big man. Hatch loved the idea of being a big man."

But the murder weapon hadn't been a .357, Sheila thought. It had been a smaller .32. Jackie Harmon's gun. And Harmon had left her fingerprint on the casing of the slug that had killed Kirk.

Palmer swallowed. "So it had to be Hatch, don't you see? Larry must've told him to come over, and he took the gun and—" He began coughing hard, and flecks of blood stained his lips.

Sheila stepped to the door and opened it. Helen Berger was passing through the hallway, and Sheila beckoned. "Coughing up blood," she said in a low voice. "Not much, but some."

"You'd better leave, Chief," Helen said. "I'll have the doctor look at him."

Back in the room, Sheila motioned to Bartlett. He nodded.

"I guess that about wraps it up, Henry," he said. "We may have more questions for you when you're able to talk longer. When you're better."

"I'm not going to get better," Palmer said, almost defiantly. "I'm going to die."

Sheila was walking with Bartlett back to the car when her cell phone chirped. It was China, and she sounded anxious.

"Have you heard anything from the guys?" she asked. "I asked McQuaid to let me know before they crossed the border, but he hasn't called. I've tried to reach him, but I'm not getting any answer. Have you spoken to Blackie?"

Sheila shivered. *Two Americans shot.* She debated whether to tell China what Helen Berger had said but decided quickly against it. There was nothing she could do at the moment, and the report—if it was true—would just make her more anxious.

"I haven't talked to him since last night," Sheila said. "But let's not worry. I'm sure they're both okay. They're just busy." She forced herself to put a smile in her voice. "You know how focused the two of them can be."

"I do," China said with a sigh. "I just wish they'd stop to think about *us.* Don't they realize that we're worrying?" Then she chuckled wryly. "Listen to me. I'm whining. Sorry. I know you've got other things on your plate. Caught any crooks today?"

Sheila laughed—a real laugh this time, completely unforced. "A killer, a hit-and-run driver, a pair of blackmail artists, and a pornographer." She paused. "There's some overlap, but that's the head count."

"You're telling me that you found out who killed Larry?" China sounded incredulous.

"Yep," Sheila said lightly. "Who and why. And we have the killer in custody. Naturally, she's waiting for her lawyer."

"Naturally," China said. "She? She *who*?"

Sheila and Bartlett had reached the car. "I'll tell you the whole gory story later, China. I have to go. If you hear what's going on with the guys, be sure and let me know, will you?" She closed the phone. She wasn't smiling.

Back at the station, Sheila paused at Connie's desk. "Any calls for me?" she asked eagerly.

With a grin, Connie handed her the usual bundle of pink slips. "Plenty. And there's more where those came from."

Disappointed, Sheila took the slips. "No, I mean personal calls. Did Blackie phone?"

Connie shook her head. "Nope, sorry. Are you expecting a call from him?"

"Just hoping, I guess," Sheila said. She went into her office, sat down in the oversize chair, and logged on to the Internet. She brought up a search engine and typed in "two Americans shot in Mexico," with the day's date. The information flashed on the monitor quickly, and she sat back in her chair, feeling a wave of warm relief wash over her, followed by a quick stab of guilt. It was bad news for somebody's family, but not for her. The two Americans who had been killed were a pair of truckers in an eighteen-wheeler, ambushed, their rig stolen. The brief story she had clicked on didn't include names, but the two men were said to be from Oklahoma. Whoever they were, they weren't Blackie and Mike McQuaid.

But the relief she felt was only temporary, and she

picked up her cell phone. Why hadn't Blackie returned her calls? Where was he?

She was flipping the phone open when it pinged in her hand.

"Hey, hon," a strong, deep voice said. "It's me. We've got the boy and plane tickets for early tomorrow. Whatever you've got going tomorrow night, cancel it. I want you all to myself."

Chapter Eighteen

Sheila put the bowl of potato salad on the table and stood back. The kitchen in Blackie's fishing cabin was bright, with white walls, white vinyl floor, and (her contribution) yellow-checked gingham curtains. And while it was small, there was room for four people around the table, as long as they kept their elbows out of their neighbors' plates.

She surveyed the settings, appreciating the colorful Fiestaware plates—genuine antiques, genuinely worn and scratched by decades of forks and knives—and the green pottery bowl of yellow chrysanthemums in the center, a gift from Blackie, delivered with a kiss that made her smile as she remembered it. Behind her, the fridge hummed cheerfully, a pot of Blackie's favorite Creole-style baked beans bubbled in the oven, and an apple pie (China's contribution to their evening meal) waited on the counter. A nicely domestic scene, except that she wasn't wearing an apron. Gingham curtains and Fiestaware, baked beans and potato salad, yes. Aprons, no. Sheila had never seen an apron she liked. They were either ruffled and frilly or totally masculine, with supposed-to-be-funny jokes printed on them. Neither suited.

"Hey, there they are," China called from the deck over-looking Canyon Lake. "I can see the boat, just coming into the cove. Wonder if they caught any fish."

Sheila picked up the binoculars and went outside to look out at the small red-painted fishing boat. Blackie was at the tiller, Rambo beside him, tongue hanging out, looking de-liriously happy. McQuaid sat in the bow, holding up a string of good-size fish for them to see.

"Looks like they've caught enough for supper—and then some," she said, and put the binoculars down on the wooden rail. "We won't have to resort to hot dogs from the freezer."

China picked up the glasses and looked through them. "Yum," she said. "Must be some pretty big fish in that lake."

"Oh, you bet. Blackie caught an eleven-pound large-mouth not long ago. Just missed the record." Sheila smiled. "Me, I don't have the magic touch. I go out there with him and never catch a single fish. But that really doesn't matter. It's lovely out there."

The eighty-two-hundred-acre reservoir had been built on the Guadalupe River west of Pecan Springs in the late 1950s, after decades of serious downstream flooding. The lake supplied water to local communities and a small amount of hydroelectric power to the grid, as well as swim-ming, boating, and fishing to people and habitat to fish and wildlife. But it was still no guarantee of protection from floods. A couple of years before, after a week of heavy rains, the lake had overtopped the spillway and gouged a remarkable mile-long, fifty-feet-deep gorge out of the lime-stone rock below the dam, exposing rock strata a hundred million years old and revealing ancient fossils and dinosaur tracks. Sadly, a number of people had been killed in the flash flood.

But the lake and the river were threatened, both by re-gion-wide drought and upstream pollutants and by increasing demands for water by thirsty communities in the rapidly developing counties north and east of San Antonio. A national conservation group had named the Guadalupe River as one of the ten most endangered rivers in the United States, in part because of plans to divert water from the lake and river for industrial and residential use. Every time Sheila looked across the blue lake cupped serenely in the folds of green hills, she thought about the fierce competition for the life-supporting resource it provided and wondered what lay ahead.

Beside her, China was chuckling. "Please tell me that the guys are going to clean all those fish—and not in the kitchen. Right?"

"They're not allowed to bring a single fish up those stairs unless it's cleaned," Sheila said, pointing down to the wooden steps that led from the cabin to the dock. "That's the rule. *My* rule. It's hard enough to keep things shipshape around here without having to scrub fish guts out of the sink or sweep fish scales off the floor."

China laughed. "Good rule, Smart Cookie. You're a woman after my own heart." She leaned her elbows on the railing, her chin propped in one hand. "It's beautiful out here," she said, musing, "even though it's beginning to feel like winter's on the way. Thanksgiving will be here before we know it."

Sheila knew that the live oaks on the slope below would stay green all winter, until their new crop of leaves appeared in the spring. But there had already been a couple of light frosts and the hackberry and cedar elms had lost most of their leaves. When she looked down, Sheila could see the dock through the leafless branches. In the summer, it was screened by a small forest of green trees. Since the cabin was also set back from the twisting gravel road, out of sight of the neighbors, it still seemed very isolated. Not true, of course. Residential development almost completely encircled the lake.

"I love this place," she replied. "I just wish Blackie and I could get out here more often. Nice that you and Mike can be here with us, too," she added, thinking that now that their husbands were working together, she and China might see more of each other.

But then again, maybe not. China's business kept her busy, and now that she had two children, her life was crowded with family activities. And Sheila often felt that she didn't have a spare minute for herself—or Blackie.

That was her biggest challenge, now that they were married. Making time for the two of them, together. Making time for their marriage. Making the marriage work. She smiled to herself, thinking of what Maude Porterfield had said to her and Blackie before their wedding ceremony. "Gotta grab hard and hold on tight when the going gets rough. Only way to get through the bad times. Grab hard, hold on, and don't let go, no matter what."

"I'm glad we could come, too—by ourselves," China said. "It was nice of Mom to invite the kids to the ranch for the weekend." She glanced back at the kitchen. "Two more around that little table, and we'd be in one another's laps. And to tell the truth, I wanted McQuaid to myself for a day or two. I don't mind telling you that I was pretty spooked about that Mexico trip, especially when I heard that those two truckers were shot south of Juárez."

As things had turned out, of course, Blackie and Mc-Quaid had not gone to Mexico. Blackie had gotten a tip that led them to a small house in the crowded Hispanic neighborhood of Segundo Barrio, where they had found the boy. His mother had heard that agents on both sides of the border were on the lookout for the child, who had been fingerprinted after the mom had made an earlier unsuccessful abduction attempt. If she tried to take him across at the official checkpoints, he would be easily identified and returned to his father.

So the mother had left the child with a family friend and

gone across the border alone. She was trying to make arrangements with a *coyote*—a man who smuggled undocumented immigrants from Mexico into the U.S.—to smuggle her son into Mexico, using a route that would avoid border checkpoints and nosy border agents. She would be taking a terrible risk, for the *coyotes* were notoriously unreliable, often leaving their charges to die alone in the desert.

When Blackie and Mike had gone to the barrio, they had spotted the child playing outdoors. As sheriff of Adams County, Blackie had worked closely with the El Paso police on a couple of cases. Now, he telephoned the El Paso police chief, who sent a team to the house, along with an agent of the Texas Department of Family and Child Protective Services. The child was picked up without incident. The next morning Blackie and Mike and the little boy, in the custody of a female FCPS agent, flew back to Austin. The reunion of father and child at the airport, with Blackie and McQuaid as the boy's "rescuers," had headlined the six o'clock news on all three network channels in Austin that night. When the mother came to the friend's house to pick up her son, she was arrested and charged with abduction.

"I was scared, too, China," Sheila replied soberly. "Actually, I'm glad I had a couple of investigations to work while that was going on. If I hadn't been so busy, I'd have had more time to worry about what the guys might be doing."

On the lake below, Blackie was maneuvering his boat to the dock. McQuaid got out and tied the bow to a piling. China waved to them, then turned to Sheila. "Now that Jackie Harmon has been officially charged with Larry Kirk's murder, are you going to tell me why she killed him? The story in last week's *Enterprise* wasn't terribly informative. Just the who, what, when, and where. Hark skipped the why."

"She had a pretty powerful motive, China. Harmon had a million dollars' worth of insurance on him—one of those corporate-owned life insurance polices. COLIs, they're called."

"A 'dead peasant' policy, you mean?" A look of disgust crossed China's face. "I remember when the Texas legislature approved that practice. Pretty ugly business, seems to me. An open invitation to all kinds of corrupt practices."

"It was certainly ugly in this case. Kirk worked for Harmon before he and Dana were married, and apparently signed a consent form for the insurance without being aware of what he was doing. But he wasn't just an employee there. He and Jackie Harmon were lovers before Dana came on the scene, and Harmon harbored plenty of resentment over being replaced in his affections."

"'Hell hath no fury like a woman scorned,'" China said softly.

"Something like that. When I talked to Dana Kirk about this after Harmon's arrest, she told me that Harmon threatened to 'claw her eyes out' for 'stealing' Kirk. Harmon even wrote a couple of threatening letters to her. Luckily, Dana had saved them. The prosecution can probably make good use of them. And Dana will be a strong witness."

"But their affair must have been several years ago," China said. "You'd think Harmon would have gotten over the jealousy by now."

"You'd think," Sheila agreed. "But some people can carry a torch for a long time, especially if their feelings have been injured. Anyway, after the separation, Harmon seems to have hoped that they could get back together again, and Kirk seems to have encouraged her. Maybe he was hoping to get her to cancel that policy. Or maybe he was just lonely. But then he broke it off, and it drove her over the edge. Being rejected a second time was more than she could take. She started hanging around his place—"

"So she was the stalker Larry emailed me about," China put in. "The same person that the Little Old Ladies' League reported seeing in the alley. Gotta give those ladies credit,

Sheila. It may look like they have their noses in their sewing, but not much gets past them."

Sheila smiled. "She's the one. We found her initials on Kirk's calendar. He was keeping track of the times he saw her, maybe with the idea of using the information in his effort to get a restraining order."

"Ah," China said.

"She was smart enough to figure out that the best time to fire a gun in that quiet neighborhood was when the garbage truck went through. And smart enough to make the murder look like a suicide—and send a phony suicide note to her victim's wife. But one of the garbage pickup crew saw her leaving the house and gave us a positive identification. When we looked at that suicide note in the context of the emails Kirk wrote just before his death, it was clearly a fake. And she forgot—or never knew—that he hated guns, and that he was a southpaw."

"The suicide exclusion on the policy had lapsed, I take it," China said.

"Long ago. If she had managed to pull it off, the insurance company would have paid the full death benefit, no questions asked."

"A million dollars," China mused. "Like a pot of gold at the end of the rainbow. Very tempting."

"That's a good way of putting it, China. And as far as motives go, it's hard to say which was most compelling. Her desire to get even with him for dropping her—twice—or her need to get her hands on that insurance money. We've learned that her business was in trouble. The bank was calling one of her notes. She was strapped for cash." She shook her head. "Those COLI policies are an open invitation to trouble."

China chuckled. "The prosecution is going to have fun with that one. Juries love to be entertained by stories of greed and passion—it's even better when there's a little sex and some corporate scandal thrown in. But juries hate circumstantial cases, and I'm sure her defense attorney will go for reasonable doubt."

"He can try. But the partial print on the cartridge—*her* print—isn't circumstantial. That'll be a pretty tough challenge for the defense. And the garbage crew's identification puts her on the scene at the crucial moment."

"Facts can be difficult," China agreed. "But good defense attorneys love a tough challenge. Don't count her side out. It's not game over until the buzzer sounds."

"Yeah, right," Sheila said wryly. "But Jack Bartlett is continuing to dig. He may turn up even more hard evidence before this thing goes to trial. He's a good guy, China. Strong instincts, logical mind. He handled the blackmail case very well."

She felt a strong sense of relief when she thought about that part of it. There had been some whispering in the department, but there hadn't been the strong political backlash that Blackie had predicted. Bartlett seemed to know how to deal with his fellow cops. They respected him. And Sheila had even gotten wind of some compliments tossed in her direction for giving him the lead on the Kirk case— and the credit for solving it.

"Are you going to press charges against Henry Palmer for his role in Timms' blackmail?" China asked.

Sheila frowned. That hadn't been cleared for public release yet. Palmer was still in the hospital, recovering, and the case was still under investigation. "How'd you hear about that?"

"Charlie Lipman told me. He said he's been retained by Palmer, but he hasn't heard the charges."

"You and Charlie Lipman." Sheila shook her head. "Between the two of you, I doubt that anything happens in this town that you don't know about."

"Between me, Charlie, and Hark Hibler," China amended with a grin. "So where is the investigation?"

"Bartlett's working on it," Sheila said. "There'll probably be a plea deal. Palmer is cooperating. And we were able to find a list of the blackmail victims on Hatch's computer." She grinned. "You'd be surprised at who they were. Several of our town's upstanding citizens."

"Hark will be publishing the list in the paper, I suppose," China said, straight-faced, without a hint of sarcasm. "I'm eager to read it."

Sheila hooted. "Don't you wish—you and Hibler. He likes nothing better than scandal in high places. But that list will never see the light of day. Lipman will use it as leverage to do a deal with the DA. You can bet that Howie Masterson won't want to see it entered into evidence at trial or on the front page of the *Enterprise*. Timms wasn't the only one of Masterson's friends whose name was on it."

"Not to speak ill of those in power, of course." China eyed Sheila. "Now that we're talking about powerful people, what's this I hear about Clint Hardin leaving? My spies tell me he's taken a job down at Rockport."

"Your spies are right," Sheila said with a grin. "And ain't that just too, too bad? Turns out that he wasn't just fishing for redfish on his vacation. He was trolling for a new job. And he got it, too—the chief's job at Rockport. I'm sure he'll love it there, China. When he's not pushing stacks of paper around on his desk or taking credit for the good work of other people, he can get out on the Gulf and go fishing."

Sheila was amazed at how lighthearted she felt about this new development. Maybe her problems with the job had less to do with the paperwork and more to do with Hardin. When she'd heard he was leaving, it was as if a giant weight had rolled off her shoulders. She even felt okay about the paperwork—not good, of course, but okay. And she had decided that she would try to spend more time out in the community, partnering on investigations. Less desk work, more real police work.

"In my experience, it's usually leftovers from the previous regime who cause the biggest problems," China said knowingly. "I've heard it called 'old think.' Some people have a hard time adapting to new ways of doing things." She paused. "How are you going to fill the deputy chief's position?"

"Most likely, we'll do an inside search. Open it up for applications, and take the best. It's a little early to see how that'll turn out." Sheila raised an eyebrow. "Funny you should mention leftovers from the previous regime. You may be interested to know that I've found a new home for my chair."

"Your *chair*?"

"Yeah. You know that big executive chair I inherited from Bubba Harris? It's been a huge pain since the moment I sat down in it. It's designed for a big guy with long legs, not for me, and there's no adjustment that makes it comfortable. I should have gotten rid of it earlier, but I was stymied. I couldn't swap it out with anybody in the department. It was the chief's chair. The *big* chief. If I gave it to somebody else, he'd be the chief."

"The seat of authority, so to speak." China rolled her eyes. "Belongs to he who can fill it."

That made Sheila giggle. "So to speak. I'm trading with the new city comptroller, Steve Seymour. He's as big as a grizzly bear, but the office chair he inherited from Emma Heartwell would just about fit Goldilocks. So we're swapping." She made a wry face. "Of course, there's a three-inch stack of paperwork documenting the trade, which has to be approved by the city council. Ridiculous."

China looked out across the lake. "Speaking of grizzly bears," she said thoughtfully, "what have you heard about that mountain lion?"

"The report came back yesterday," Sheila said. "The animal your neighbor shot is the one that killed George Timms, and there's DNA evidence to prove it. Hark Hibler says there'll be a story about it in the next *Enterprise*." She grinned. "I understand that your friend Jessica Nelson is writing it. She's practicing her human-interest skills from a different angle, I guess. I heard that she was interviewing both of the Banners."

"Not that cat," China said quietly. "The other one. The one that got away."

"It got away," Sheila said. "Totally, I mean. Parks and Wildlife decided not to spend the money to track it. After they looked at that rock you found—the one with the fur and the blood on it—and compared it to the wound on the cat's head, they concluded that the cat that killed Timms was already dead. The DNA confirmed."

"I'm glad to hear it," China said. "I've thought a lot about that cat, the way she looked streaking across the road, all silvery in the rain. She seemed so mysterious, almost ethereal—but incredibly powerful at the same time." She looked a little sheepish. "I talked about it with Ruby, and she said maybe I'd found my animal totem. Wild cats can show us how to understand the natural flow of our environment, she said. How to appreciate the strength and power of the natural world around us and find our place in the order of things. How to observe when observation matters, then act when action is called for." Her laugh was slightly embarrassed. "You know Ruby. She's a genuine mystic. For her, everything is a symbol."

"Don't knock it," Sheila said seriously. "There may be something to that, you know."

China nodded. "Ruby says that maybe the cat had something to do with my going out to Timms' place that morning, and finding him. And it's certainly true that I thought about the cat as I was driving. I wanted to see her again—but I was afraid to. You know?"

"I know," Sheila said. "I also know that if you hadn't found Timms when you did, that part of the story might still be a deep, dark mystery. We wouldn't know anything about Timms' pornographic photographs, for instance, which were the reason for the blackmail and his break-in at the computer shop." She smiled. "Interesting contrast, your methods and mine."

China looked thoughtful. "You know, that's true. I can listen to the neighborhood gossip, and people tell me things they'd never tell a cop. And I don't have to follow as many rules as you do. If I want to find something, I can go look for it, assuming that I stay within the law, more or less. And assuming that the law doesn't discover my illegal activities." Her eyes twinkled. "You have to get a search warrant, or what you find won't be admissible at trial."

"Yes, but when I've got that search warrant and I've followed all the rules, I can arrest the bad guy and put him in jail," Sheila replied. "You can't do that, counselor."

"Good point, Chief. But after you've arrested and jailed him and the prosecutor has brought him to trial, I can convince the jury to let him off." A careless shrug. "Or rather, I used to be able do that. Not in my job description anymore."

"Good thing for me," Sheila said, meaning it. "If you were still in that job, we'd be adversaries. Maybe enemies." She paused, thinking about that. "Not maybe, definitely. We'd definitely be enemies."

"Good thing for me, too," China replied, and her smile lit up her eyes. "I'd rather be friends."

Recipes

China Bayles' Curry and Cardamom Cookies

1 cup butter
2 cups brown sugar
2 eggs, lightly beaten
2 teaspoons vanilla extract
3 cups flour
1 teaspoon baking powder
½ teaspoon baking soda
½ teaspoon salt
2 teaspoons curry powder (sweet or hot)
½ teaspoon ground cardamom
1 cup pecans, chopped

Preheat oven to 350°F.

Cream butter and sugar together. Add eggs and vanilla and beat until incorporated.

Sift dry ingredients together. Add to creamed mixture, a third at a time. Stir in nuts.

Divide dough into four rolls and wrap each in waxed paper. Refrigerate at least 4 hours, or freeze. Slice into ¼-inch-thick slices and place on an ungreased baking sheet. Bake until golden brown, 12 to 14 minutes. Let cookies cool for 2 minutes on baking sheet, then remove to a rack to cool thoroughly. Yields approximately 6 dozen.

Ramona's Corn Chowder with Sausage

- 1 pound bulk pork sausage (mild)
- 1 cup coarsely chopped onion
- 4 cups peeled and cubed potatoes
- 1 teaspoon salt
- ½ teaspoon ground marjoram
- 1/8 teaspoon ground pepper
- 2 cups water
- 1 can cream-style corn
- 1 can whole-kernel corn, drained
- 1 can evaporated milk or 1 ½ cups milk (non-fat okay)
- 6 tablespoons yogurt, for garnish
- Chopped parsley, for garnish

In Dutch oven or kettle, cook sausage and onion till sausage is brown and onion is tender; drain on paper towel. Return sausage to Dutch oven with cubed potatoes, salt, marjoram, pepper, and water. Bring to boil; reduce heat and simmer just until potatoes are tender, about 15 minutes. Add cream-style and whole-kernel corn and milk and mix well. Garnish with yogurt and chopped parsley. Serves 6.

McQuaid's Favorite Breakfast Burritos

- ½ pound bulk pork sausage (mild or hot)
- 1 small sweet red pepper, seeded and chopped
- 1 jalapeño pepper, seeded and chopped (leave the seeds in for extra heat)
- ½ cup chopped onion
- 4 cloves garlic, minced
- 8 eggs, beaten

1 teaspoon cumin
1 can refried beans
10 (8-inch) flour tortillas
1¼ cup taco sauce
2½ cups shredded Cheddar cheese

Cook sausage until browned. Drain and set aside, reserving drippings. Add chopped peppers, onion, and garlic to drippings in skillet and cook until onions are translucent and peppers are soft. Add eggs and cumin; cook, stirring occasionally, until eggs are firm but still moist. Stir in the sausage and refried beans and mix thoroughly.

Warm tortillas in microwave. Spoon one-tenth of the egg-sausage-beans mixture along the center line of each tortilla. Cover with 2 tablespoons of taco sauce and ¼ cup shredded cheese and roll up. Wrap individual burritos in plastic wrap and refrigerate or freeze.

To serve: Heat in microwave until hot. Rewrap in foil for breakfast to-go.

Sheila's Garlic & Herb Potato Salad

2 tablespoons mixed herbs, chopped fine (rosemary, parsley, chervil, chives, thyme)
4 tablespoons olive oil
8–10 small red potatoes, unpeeled, scrubbed
Dash of white wine (optional)
2 tablespoons lemon juice
3 tablespoons minced garlic
Salt and pepper to taste

In a small bowl, mix the herbs and olive oil. Set aside and let the flavors infuse while you prepare the potatoes. Cut into halves or quarters. Cook in boiling water for 10 minutes, or until the potatoes are just tender but still firm. Drain potatoes and return to pot, away from the heat. Cover with a dry towel and let them steam for 10 to 15 minutes. (Potatoes should be tender, yet firm and unbroken.)

To make the dressing, whisk the wine, lemon juice, garlic, salt, and pepper together. Slowly add the oil/herb mixture.

Place the potatoes in a large bowl and splash with dressing. Toss carefully. Cover and refrigerate to allow the flavors to blend. Serve cold, at room temperature, or warm (you may microwave briefly).

Sheila's Creole Baked Beans

An overnight stay in the refrigerator is good for this bean dish—it mellows and enhances the flavors.

   6 slices bacon, diced
   1 cup diced onion
   2 ribs celery, diced
   1 red bell pepper, diced
   4–6 cloves garlic, minced
   1 bay leaf
   1 teaspoon crushed red pepper flakes
   1 tablespoon Creole Spice Blend (see recipe below)
   1 pound small red or white beans, cleaned and
      soaked overnight in cold water
   2 tablespoons brown sugar
   2 tablespoons molasses
   1 tablespoon dry mustard
   1 can tomatoes, crushed, or 1 cup seeded, chopped
      fresh tomatoes
   4 cups chicken stock, or 4 chicken bouillon cubes
      dissolved in 4 cups water
   Salt

Preheat oven to 300°F.

In a large heavy pot, fry bacon over medium heat until bits are crisp. Remove bacon and reserve. Add the onion, celery, and pepper; cook until softened and lightly browned. Add garlic, bay leaf, red pepper flakes, and Creole Spice Blend; cook 2 minutes. Stir in the beans, brown sugar, molasses, mustard, tomatoes, reserved bacon, and chicken stock. Bring to a boil. Remove from heat and cover pot tightly. Alternatively, transfer to a lidded casserole and bake for 1½ to 2 hours; check the stock regularly and add more if necessary. Cook until the beans are tender and most of the stock is absorbed. Remove bay leaf. Add salt to taste. Serves 4 to 6 as a main dish, 6 to 8 as a side dish.

Creole Spice Blend

    1 teaspoon fennel seed
    1 teaspoon coriander seed
    1 tablespoon paprika
    1 tablespoon onion powder
    1 teaspoon cayenne pepper
    1 teaspoon oregano
    1 teaspoon thyme
    1 teaspoon whole black peppercorns
    ½ teaspoon whole white peppercorns

Combine all the ingredients in a coffee grinder or spice mill. Process until smooth and uniform. Store in a tightly lidded jar in a dark place.

SUSAN WITTIG ALBERT

WIDOW'S TEARS

After losing her husband, five children, housekeeper, and beautiful home in the Galveston Hurricane of 1900, Rachel Blackwood rebuilt her home, and later died there, having been driven mad with grief.

In present-day Texas, Claire, the grandniece of Rachel's caretaker, has inherited the house and wants to turn it into a bed-and-breakfast. But she is concerned that it's haunted, so she calls in her friend Ruby—who has the gift of extrasensory perception—to check it out.

While Ruby is ghost hunting, China Bayles walks into a storm of trouble in nearby Pecan Springs. A half hour before she is to make her nightly deposit, the Pecan Springs bank is robbed and a teller is shot and killed.

Before she can discover the identity of the killers, China follows Ruby to the Blackwood house to discuss urgent business. As she is drawn into the mystery of the haunted house, China opens the door on some very real danger . . .

susanalbert.com
penguin.com

M1213T1112

SUSAN WITTIG ALBERT

MOURNING GLORIA

China is relishing in the scents, produce, and even the showers of spring. She's also busy hosting Pecan Springs' Farmers' Market. It brings additional customers to Thyme and Seasons, her herb shop—and residents find rare ingredients they wouldn't otherwise find in the supermarket. Everybody wins.

But as the town bustles back to life in the warmth of the season, one woman's life is tragically brought to an end. China happens upon a burning house trailer and hears a woman screaming for help. The evidence leaves no doubt that it's arson homicide—but who would commit such a ghastly crime?

Jessica Nelson, an intern-reporter at the local paper, is assigned to cover the story. Drawn into the case by its similarity to her own tragic loss—Jessica's family died in a fire—she soon finds herself deeply involved and in danger. And when Jessica disappears, China becomes determined to help find her, before she becomes a headline herself . . .

penguin.com